Bought
bday 2022
- from martin

ONCE IN A LIFETIME
—BECKY

BY
LUANA FERRAZ

*This book has content warnings. Flip to the last page to read about them.

COPYRIGHT

First published in 2020 by Luana Ferraz.

Copyright @ 2020 by Luana Ferraz

Cover design of Once in a Lifetime by Flavia Andrioli.

The moral right of Luana Ferraz to be identified as the author of this work has been asserted by her in accordance with Copyright, Designs and Patents Act, 1988.

This is a work of fiction. All characters, incidents and dialogs are products of the author's imagination and are not to be construed as real. Any resemblance to actual events or persons living or dead is entirely coincidental.

All rights reserved. No part of this publication may be copied, reproduced, transferred, leased, licensed or used in any way except as allowed under the terms and conditions under which it was purchased or loaned or as strictly permitted by applicable copyright law. Any unauthorized distribution or use of this text may be a direct infringement of the author's rights and those responsible may be liable in law accordingly.

Passion (noun)
1. strong and barely controllable emotion;
2. intense, driving, or overmastering feeling or conviction.

… *Once in a Lifetime*

PROLOGUE

I'M SITTING AT MY WINDOW SILL, WATCHING THE RAIN RUN DOWN THE glass. The morning light passing through the gray clouds sucks the color out of everything. For a few minutes, time stands still. I like this time of the day—too early for anyone to be out and about, too late to fall asleep. I feel like I could be the only person alive in the world. To be honest, I feel like the only person in the world most of the time, but it's only in this moment between night and day that I can be at peace with it.

I couldn't sleep after last night's concert. Not even after draining an entire bottle of wine. I've been too worried about the progressive worsening of our gigs. Progressively smaller places, progressively fewer dates. I'm progressively losing my mind. Pete insists it's just a phase, that we had it worse before. As much as I know he's right, there's something different at the pit of my stomach this time. Maybe it's time to go home. Again. Maybe we should have never left home that second time. Or even that first time.

Don't go there, I force my brain to think of something else. I know that following these thoughts will lead me down a rabbit hole that will be hard to crawl out of. I have to stay away from them. But it's exhausting, you know? Especially when they keep resurfacing so often as they have been lately.

I grab my phone from the nightstand and take some pictures of the dead city below me. I edit one of them and upload it to my personal Instagram account—which I only use to post what I believe is called 'conceptual photos'. The caption reads 'morning after'. I don't have to wait long for the fans to start liking it and commenting how much they enjoyed the show the night before, or asking what I'm doing awake at such an early hour, or just shouting their love in all caps. That makes me smile. Ever since I got clean, I've been using these short, instant interactions as my serotonin fix. And it does the trick—I'm not thinking about the past anymore. I think about the future. I think about how, maybe, we do have a shot at this.

We just need a break. We so desperately need a break.

"Becky!" Pete bursts through my bedroom door, making me drop the phone on the floor and jump from my seat.

"What the fuck?!" I yell, resting one hand over my speeding heart.

"You will never believe this!" He holds me by the shoulders, his wild eyes glistening manically.

"What?" I ask, worriedly.

He only shoves his phone screen on my face. I take it from him and sit down on my bed. It's an email.

"Who's Neil?" I ask.

"Just read it!" he demands impatiently.

I scroll down and read what looks like an invitation to... to a...

"A tour?" my voice comes out not louder than a whisper.

"A tour," Pete sits by my side, beaming.

***

"This can't be real," I insist as I watch the tenth video in a row of the American band whose tour we've been allegedly invited to open.

The Hacks. They're brothers, their last name is Hackley. Not very creative, if you ask me, but whatever. It seems they recorded their first album when they were still children and became huge, although I positively have never heard of them. Pete says they're not as popular anymore and have become independent artists, like us. Maybe that's why they invited us to open for them.

"I guess we'll find out soon enough," Pete says as he clicks on an interview video now. It's old. The video quality is awful. They're little, annoying kids.

"What if it's a trap?" I ask, causing Pete to burst into laughter. "I'm serious! What if this is some sick fan's plan to get us alone and... and... murder us!"

Pete stares at me blankly. He pauses the video and opens Google maps. He types in the address given to us in the email and an office building near central London appears. He zooms in so we can look at the facade and adjacent constructions. It looks like a busy street.

"Seems legit to me," he says.

"I don't have a good feeling about this," I insist.

"You don't have a good feeling about anything," Pete replies wisely. I can't argue with that. "Becky, not many unknown artists land this kind of gig."

"More reason for us to be suspicious," I say.

"You're right," he concedes, not without irritation, "but also a reason for us to take it. Maybe this is our chance to get a record deal."

He gets me with that again.

"How do you think they found us?" I ask, failing to pay attention to the videos.

"I don't know. Probably YouTube?"

It makes sense. One of our older videos has recently reached over 1 million views. At last, having someone to professionally record some of our gigs is paying off.

Pete's phone rings and as he wanders off to talk to his parents, I continue Googling the band. It's not hard to find their story. Three brothers from Northwest America, with soulful voices and angel faces. They were barely out of the diapers when their first single, *Wendy*, reached the top of the charts—three long-haired blond kids in pajamas fake-flying to the stars. If I didn't know better, I'd swear the lead singer was a girl.

There are a lot of videos and interviews from that first album era, but anything after that becomes a little harder to find. Recent news are rare and mostly talking about past fame. But their website is decent, and they seem to have a solid fan base. I just hope their fans like punk as much as they like The Hacks' bubbly pop.

I can hear Pete giggling on the phone and I slowly start to share his enthusiasm. It's been almost a decade since we've moved out here to pursue a dream. We have played in every dump this city has, mostly for free. We have banged in every studio door. We have stalked every producer. Still nothing. We did make progress, though, I have to admit that—we have fans, we have some EPs out, we even have merch. Some months we're able to pay for rent solely on the money we make from music, which is already more than a lot of independent artists can manage.

Still, it's not enough. I want more. This feeling is scary sometimes, but it's also what keeps me going. There's nothing else in this world I want as much as this. And, to be honest, it doesn't matter if we're playing on a busy street in Camden or on a stage at a festival—the feeling is the same. I love performing, anywhere, everywhere. And I know I'm good.

Maybe Pete's right. Maybe this is our ticket to the other side. And, if so, The Hacks just got a die-hard fan right here.

***

We reach the label building a full thirty minutes before our meeting, thanks to Pete's anxiousness. I'm anxious, too. But I'm way better at hiding it.

We enter into a modest lobby where an annoyed lady directs us to the third floor. On the wall outside the lifts, a plaque shows the names of all the companies that share the site. Blast Records occupies only the one floor, its name jumping off among such as I.T. Solutions and Data Zoom.

"Boring..." Pete whispers. I'm just relieved to see there are actual companies operating in this place.

The elevator opens at our floor to reveal the tiniest reception hall I've ever seen. We take two steps to reach the smiley lady behind the counter.

"Afternoon," Pete greets her. "Pete and Becky to see Neil Connolly?"

The woman types something in the computer, her absurdly long nails making the only noises in the room.

"You're a little early," she says in a fake cheerful tone. "Please, have a seat."

We huddle together on the small couch and watch the receptionist walk away. It takes all of ten seconds for Pete's leg to start bouncing up and down. I rest my hand on top of his knee.

"Sorry," he whispers and stops tapping his feet. "Isn't she taking too long?"

"Why are you whispering?" I ask, making him jump. "Can you relax?"

"How can *you* relax?" he frowns. After a moment, he adds, "You still think it's a trap, don't you?"

"Can you blame me?" I speak in a normal volume, making him jump once again. "What are the odds that we get such a major opportunity out of the blue? There's certainly a catch."

"I love your pessimism," he says, covering my hand with his.

"Anytime," I wink.

"Hey, guys!" A third voice interrupts our moment, making both of us jump this time. A tall, broad man, with earrings on both ears, reaches out a hand to greet us. "Neil. You must be Becky and Pete."

"Nice to meet you, Mr. Connolly," Pete says as he shakes his hand.

"Please, call me Neil. Follow me," he beckons and leads us through a narrow corridor lined with doors on both sides. "Thank you so much for agreeing with this at such short notice."

It's not like we had a choice, since the tour starts Thursday. This week. Another sign that this might be a trap.

"If you don't mind me asking, what happened?" Pete asks. "I suppose we weren't the first option to be the opening acts."

"To be completely honest with you, you weren't. We had someone else lined up. But the band insisted on getting you on board."

Pete and I exchange a suspicious look. *'The catch'*, I mouth. He smiles.

We enter a rather large conference room at the end of the long corridor, where two other men—in suits, this time—are waiting for us. They introduce themselves as publicist and lawyer. I immediately forget their names.

"Okay, guys," Neil claps his hands together once we're sat around the table, "I would normally start off by giving you a brief history of the label, but we have no time for that. So we're going straight to business—how many people do you have in your crew?"

Pete and I glance at each other again.

"We don't have a crew," Pete answers. His voice is calm, but his leg is bouncing again.

"Oh," Neil can't hide his surprise. "Not even a tech? A roadie? I know you don't have a manager, but..."

"It's just the two of us and we don't usually go on tour. We don't really need a crew," Pete explains.

"Right, right, of course," Neil nods manically. "So, no crew. That's actually good news for us," he laughs, looking at his coworkers.

"What about your brand?" the publicist speaks up. "I've had a look at your website and it's impressive."

"Thank you," Pete smiles.

"Who's responsible for your marketing?" the guy goes on. I glance at Pete, biting my lip to repress a smile.

"I am," he says. The publicist raises his eyebrows. "As I said, it's just the two of us."

As the meeting goes on, I can sense Pete's excitement plummet. It becomes clear that these guys have no idea who or at what level we are. It starts sounding more and more like a favor—the main band requested us and they're going with it because… That's actually the only thing I want to know. I don't have the nerve to ask, though. And since we walk out the building with a booked tour, I think I can find it out for myself.

✖DAY ONE

"Becky!" Pete's high-pitched voice wakes me up. "I knew it! We shouldn't have gone clubbing yesterday!"

I roll over, pushing the covers over my very achy head.

"Rebecca!" Pete's use of my full name indicates he is *very* upset. He pulls the fluffy duvet off my bed. "It's today!"

"What is?" I frown, struggling to make my hungover brain start to work.

"Oh, my fucking God!" Pete grunts. I have my eyes shut, but I can tell Pete is running his hands through his hair. "We have to be in central London in less than an hour! You better get ready!" he yells again, and I hear him stomping out of my room.

I can't remember what it is that we have to do in central London today. Damn, I barely remember my own name.

I sit up on the bed and my head spins. Small dots of light splash my vision. Shit. Am I too old for night outs already?

Before I can muster the strength to stand up, I pick up my phone from the nightstand. Among the notifications of likes on Instagram, replies on Twitter, and junk emails, there is one of the calendar. Thursday. Today. *The first day of the rest of your life.*

"The first day of the rest of your life," I read aloud, squinting. Thursday. Today. "Fuck! The tour!"

I suddenly remember why we went out—to celebrate! Although, in hindsight, getting shit-faced the day before our first day of a long tour might not have been the best of ideas. But Pete was so excited, I couldn't say no. I'm already such a bad friend as it is, I couldn't let him down on such an important occasion—for him, anyway. I still think it's a trap.

I dart out of the room and into the bathroom. As I slam the door shut I can hear Pete rushing me along. I open the shower and get under it, letting out a small cry when the icy water hits my head. But as if by magic, I'm awake. I scrub all that I can in a rush and brush my teeth.

I step out of the bathroom wrapped in a towel and run back to my room—to find a mug of hot coffee beside my bed.

"Thanks!" I shout.

I don't deserve Pete. I think nobody does. Well, maybe Lindsey. She's every bit as caring and compassionate as he is. I still remember the first time we met, because she was the first of all Pete's significant others I got to meet that didn't make a face when meeting the 'girl he lives with'.

I try to dress and do my make-up as fast as I can. Which, honestly, isn't very fast. It might make us late, but at least I'll look like an artist.

I step on the first thighs that I find and pair them with my favorite skirt and lucky t-shirt—the one with a knitted skull on it. I don't have time to lace up my favorite boots, so I just grab a pair that doesn't have laces. I head off as I put on a leather jacket and try to tame my wet blob of hair.

"I'm ready." I announce as I enter the living room.

"Your hair is dripping." Pete frowns, giving me a full-body glance. "And your make-up is banging."

"Thanks," I smile. He never fails to make me feel slightly better. "Ready?"

"You better not get a cold," he says in that big brother voice he likes to use sometimes.

"I won't," I say, interlacing my arm with his. "But if I do, I know you'll take care of me."

"Only because I need your voice to make money," he says. He means it as a joke, so I laugh. But the literal meaning of that sentence lingers in the back of my head all the way to the office.

***

By the time we reach the record label building, my throat is already scratching. I curse myself—and Pete—for being so reckless. Of course I'd get sick on the day of a major concert. I decide to keep my mouth shut and rest my voice until I can get a hold of some lemon and honey.

"Oh, you can go on, they're waiting for you," the bored receptionist says without glancing up from her phone.

Pete and I walk down the corridor, taking the opportunity to snoop. Some of the doors are open today, so we walk slowly to look inside. To my disappointment, they're just offices, although some of them sport plaques that show off their artists' achievements. I recognize some of the names and resist the urge to take my phone out and take pictures. Professional. We're meant to look professional.

The sound of chatter gets louder and louder as we approach the door. There must be a lot of people inside, a lot of people I don't know. I reach out for Pete's hand—a nervous habit. He says nothing but lets me squeeze his fingers. Most of the time, that's all I need, anyway.

The conversation stops as soon as we open the door. And all eyes are on us. Except for Neil and one of the guys from our previous meeting, I don't recognize anyone. That is, until one of the boys sitting around the table stands up and walks towards us with the biggest grin I've ever seen in my life.

"Hello! I'm Tristan. Nice to meet you." He shakes our hands, and then adds, "I like your hair."

Pete gives me a warning look. As if I would engage in a discussion about how lame it is that people compliment the way you look—something you don't really have control of—with our current employers. Yes, I've done that before, but I know better now.

"Thanks," I mumble instead, absentmindedly patting my now almost dry purple mane.

Tristan then proceeds to introduce us to the rest of his team, an attitude that I appreciate. As a band member, that isn't really his job, but he seems to enjoy it. He's loud and talkative, traits I usually despise, but he has a warmth about him that's really engaging. I feel my nerves start to relax a bit.

He informs us that in addition to him and his two brothers, Todd and Tyler, guitarrist and lead singer,—and yes, all Ts—, we'll be joined by Paul and Jake, drum and guitar techs, who are also roadies, and Seth, a sound and light engineer that works for the label. He looks like the oldest of us, and if I had to guess, I think he's not even in his 50s.

I'm pleasantly surprised to see it's a small and multi-tasking group. They suddenly seem a lot more approachable than I thought they would be.

"And I'll be your tour manager," Neil smiles at us.

"We've been working with Neil and Blast since we became independent," Tristan tells us. It isn't lost on me that he's been the only one talking so far.

"Cool, that's cool. How long has that been?" Pete asks, as if he didn't already know even their social security numbers by now. I also notice he's the only one doing the talking on our side, too.

"Six years now, and this is our fourth tour?" Tristan turns to Neil.

"That's right," Neil nods. "A long and winding road."

They laugh. I glance at Pete sideways, but he's still paying attention to the drummer sitting in front of us.

"What about you?" Tristan leans on the table. "How long have you been doing music?"

"Well, uh..." Pete looks at me. I smile, silently encouraging him to go on. I'm not really in the mood for talking to strangers. And my throat hurts! I don't know how much of this he gets by my raised eyebrows, but he continues, "We started writing together when we were fourteen. But we've only been doing it professionally for eight years."

"That's a long enough time," Tristan says.

"Not compared to you," Pete chuckles.

"Yeah, well, not everyone starts at six," Tristan laughs politely.

"Or conveniently has musical siblings," Pete adds, finally bringing the conversation to a halt. It seems the other Hackley boys are not so interested in making conversation. I can't really judge them.

"So, what about we go over the details once more?" Neil suggests.

"That would be great," Tyler snorts. Everyone looks at him. I have the impression he's staring at me, but I can't say for sure, since he's wearing sunglasses.

Yes. Sunglasses indoors. Also, a leather jacket. And ripped skinny jeans. I'm not going to say *cliché*, since I'm self-aware of how I look. Not only that, but I'm pretty sure we're wearing the same jacket? Either way, you know... *cliché*.

"And check this out," Neil interrupts my staring contest pushing a mug in front of me and Pete. It's one of those all-black ones. When he slowly turns it around, I can't hold in the gasp—it has our logo on it.

Pete and I exchange genuinely surprised looks as Neil explains he got our logos printed into t-shirts, mugs and a few other random shit to sell at the venues. He also asks us to authorize him to have more physical copies of our EPs made because he thinks our stock is too low. I snort as Pete gives him the green light. I observe him as he nods and hums at all the appropriate places, knowing he's feeling every bit as overwhelmed as I am. Two days ago, these guys looked like they had no idea what to do with us. Now, we have cool merch, EPs and even interviews scheduled in some cities. I definitely underestimated this Neil guy.

"Any questions?" he asks us when he finally finishes going over the plans for the next two weeks. I look at Pete, who is now biting all his nails, and he shakes his head. "Great! Shall we head to the venue?"

While everyone is standing up and getting ready to leave, I pull a shaking Pete to a corner.

"Are you okay?" I whisper.

"Yeah, sure. It's just…" He looks around the room full of strangers.

I know what he's thinking. We're not only out of our element, but we're also way behind. We don't have a team. We don't have a band. In less than a week, this guy got us more than we've had in almost a decade of our careers. We must look very green to them. Crap, I feel very green.

"Are *you* okay?" he returns the question.

"I'll feel better when we're on stage." I squeeze his hand and he manages to give me a faint smile.

**

It takes us longer than I expected to get to the venue. We drive in two cars—the bands in one, the crew in the other. I resist the urge to put my headphones on, but can't bring myself to engage in conversation. Not that I'd have a chance, since Tristan does most of the talking anyway. He makes sure to let us know that he has seen *all* of our videos and has listened to *all* of our songs. He even has a favorite, which he requests us to play in the show tonight. Pete agrees, even though it's a song we haven't played live in over two years. If I could see his face, I would glare at him.

After a few minutes of trying to keep up, I just give up and turn my attention to the window. I'm sipping water slowly and finally my throat is giving me a break. I'm still going to need hot tea, though.

"So, how long have you been living here?" The question comes from the person sitting by my side, presumably to me. I turn my head to make sure he's really addressing me before I answer. Todd's chocolate eyes are locked on my face, which means that, unfortunately, he is indeed talking to me.

"Eight years this year," I answer.

"Not that long, then," he says.

"No," I agree, although it feels like a lifetime. It feels like I lived a hundred lives in this city.

"Where are you from?" he continues, even though I'm already looking out of the window again.

"Alnwick," I say, predicting what he'll say next.

"Alnwick? Never heard of it," he repeats the same thing everyone always says when I tell them where I'm from.

"No one has," I joke, but he apparently doesn't get it and his frown deepens. "It's a small district up north."

"Right," he nods. "Do you miss it there?"

"No," I say, startling him with my honesty. So, I add, "There's nothing much to miss, really. It's very small."

He nods, still with that deep frown wrinkling his forehead. I don't know what to say next, so I start looking around, hoping to get Pete's attention. He's the one who's good at small talk. Or any human interaction, for that matter. Luckily, he's already paying attention to us. It's his superpower—sensing when I'm about to put myself in awkward situations.

"We're talking about Alnwick," I tell him with a look I hope conveys my predicament.

"It has a population of a little over 8 thousand people, according to the last census," he says. How does he know that? It's truly a gift.

"Wow!" Todd smiles for the first time since the conversation started. I have to suppress a snort. Not amused by my joke, but by a completely boring fact.

"It also has a castle," another voice says from behind us. "According to Wikipedia."

"Yeah. It attracts a lot of tourists," Pete says.

"Cool," is all Tyler replies, and the conversation dies.

Luckily for me, there's no time to start another, since we reach our destination. I get out of the car and follow Neil as he guides us through the backstage. It's a venue I've never been to. It's no O2, yet still bigger than any venue we've ever played at.

We'll play two shows here before really kicking off the tour, both of which are sold out, according to him. He sounds far more surprised by this fact than I suppose he should have, but no one seems to be bothered. After showing us our dressing rooms—the first proper dressing room I'll ever have—he takes us to the front. The stage. The part that really matters.

To my surprise, instruments and sound system are already in place. I can see my bright pink guitar sitting next to some classic Gibsons. It looks as out of place as I must. I wonder if anyone else notices the deep abyss that exists between me and Pete and the rest of them, or if it's all in my head.

I also notice a keyboard, acoustic guitars, basses and a piano on stage, which reminds me that I haven't heard a single current song from The Hacks. Pete made me watch their old music videos and read some of their interviews, but I totally forgot to listen to recent material. Well, I'll experience it live in just a minute.

As we walk on stage and people begin to discuss how each set is going to work, I wander off towards the piano. I can't believe there is an actual piano here. I try to imagine the logistics of transporting it from city to city. I try to imagine how much it costs. Is it theirs? Did they rent it? Can I use it?

"What are you doing?" a voice startles me just as I'm about to sit on the leather stool.

I turn around to meet Tyler's glare. He's not wearing his sunglasses anymore, which weirdly makes him look even less friendly.

"I couldn't resist. It's a beautiful piano," I say.

"And expensive, too," he adds, never breaking eye contact. I'm taken aback. Even though I'm not really sure what he means, I feel offended.

"I know," I snort. "I have one of these back home."

"Do you play?" Tristan walks towards us.

"A little," I lie. My twelve years of classical training aren't something I like to mention. Especially because they turned out to be useless.

"Cool! You never play piano in your concerts," he remarks.

"Well, there's not a lot of piano in punk songs." I also don't have access to a piano in the city. I also stopped playing piano a long time ago.

"That's true," he chuckles. "What do you usually play on piano, then?"

"Well, I don't usually play piano," I admit.

"That's sad. Don't you miss it?" Tristan asks.

"Sometimes," I shrug. Although I do miss it, I don't miss the memories it brings along.

"Do you want to try?" he asks, and Tyler and I both shoot him wide-eyed looks. "Go ahead!"

I'm inclined to say I don't think it's a very good idea, but the thought of antagonizing Tyler and his shocked face gets the best of me. So, I sit on the leather stool and raise the fallboard... just to find out I have no idea what I'm doing.

I can feel the weight of everyone's eyes on my shoulders as I stare at the keys.

"Play *Getaway*," Pete suggests from somewhere behind me. He knows I'm in trouble.

I take his advice and start to play one of our oldest and easiest songs. It's one of the many that we wrote together before leaving our hometown and one of the few that survived in our setlist.

"You sound fantastic!" Tristan claps when I finish.

"You sound rusty," Tyler remarks.

"Tyler!" Tristan gives him an appalled look.

"You were very slow on the leaps and the transitions were blunt, not to mention the heavy pedal markings," Tyler says.

He's right. He has a good ear. Well, given that he plays it every fucking night, he *should* notice these things. Just maybe don't point them out?

"As I said, I haven't played in a while," I shrug.

"Clearly," Tyler says and Tristan sighs.

"Don't listen to him." He shakes his head. "Feel free to use it in your set if you want. Or just for fun."

"Thanks," I smile.

Neil calls for lunch and as a herd of cattle, we all start to make our way backstage again. Tristan taps Tyler's shoulder as he walks past, earning a glare. My smile broadens. He turns his contracted face to me, and I just can't bite my tongue.

"Don't worry, I won't break your little toy," I say.

I brace myself for a comeback, but his glare just becomes a blank stare. And then he walks away.

I immediately regret this little exchange. Something tells me I shouldn't be bickering with one of the people who is meant to be opening doors for us.

***

My hands are shaking. I notice it when I'm trying to apply my eyeliner. I know that in punk fashion straight makeup lines are not a thing, but I sigh anyway. I pause, taking a sip of the tea Neil managed to get me, as I watch Pete pace back and forth behind me. His anxiousness is not helping mine.

It's not the first time we're going to play for people that know nothing about us and can potentially hate us. We've 'put ourselves out there' a lot—and I despise that saying. I shouldn't be so nervous, I can't be so nervous. Before I can pinpoint where this sudden fear is coming from, Pete stands behind me and squeezes my shoulders.

"It's not make or break, you know," he says in his usual big brother tone, the one he uses when I'm unreasonably preoccupied. "It's just one opportunity."

"It's just one big, fat, life-changing opportunity," I correct him, gazing suspiciously at his fake-calm expression through the mirror.

"One of many," Pete smiles at my exasperated look.

"In eight years—"

"We've got this," he interrupts me, turning me around to face him. "In eight years, in twenty years, as a supporting act, at our own concert, in a crowded pub or Wembley—I don't care."

His smile broadens and he squeezes my shoulders again, relieving them of the weight I'd put there.

"How come you always know the right thing to say?" I ask him, always astounded by his way with words.

"One of us has to, eh?" he chuckles, pulling me into a hug.

"We've got this," I repeat into his chest.

He lets me go and I finish getting ready—still trembling, but with new-found confidence. We walk out the cupboard that is our dressing room to find the venue's stage manager waiting for us. He leads the way and the rumble of the crowd intensifies. My heart jumps in my chest at the sight of my pink guitar on stage.

He gives us some directions, tests our mics and we're ready to go. Pete and I do our pre-show handshake and we're suddenly on stage. The crowd cheers, to my surprise. I take it as a good sign.

I walk up to grab my guitar while Pete sits at Tristan's drums. I walk back to the mic and look out to the sea of young faces looking at us expectantly. Probably praying for us to be brief so they can feast their eyes and ears on the main attraction.

"Good night, everyone! I'm Becky, this is Pete, and we're gonna warm you up for The Hacks!" At the sound of their idols' band name, they roar.

I glance at Pete, he counts, and we start playing. We had agreed to start on one of our slower tunes, easing our pop crowd into our usual bangers. As I start to sing, I hear a few cheers here and there, and some heads start to bob. Someone starts clapping at the chorus, and by the end of the song we have half of the place dancing around.

The second song is more successful, winning over those who were doubtful at first. When we're about to move to the third, someone shouts, "Play *She's Not Mine!*"

I turn to the crowd, confused and amazed at the same time. Someone here knows our songs! Someone is our fan!

"Wow, that's an oldie," I comment, trying to locate the source of the voice.

"It's my favorite!" The girl raises her hand and I see her—third or fourth row, to the right. She's wearing a The Hacks' shirt, which only leaves me more confused and amazed.

"We haven't rehearsed that one," I say, glancing at Pete, unsure of what to do—I don't like this song. He winks, silently encouraging me to indulge this one fan. "Sorry if we sound awful."

The girl grins and shouts as I start playing the intro.

Playing the guitar oftentimes is like riding a bike—you can't forget it. It may take a few tries to find your balance but, eventually, you're speeding down the street as if no time has passed. Unfortunately, the memories attached to the songs have exactly the same effect.

It must have been six years ago. Maybe longer. Maybe not. I have fuzzy memories from that time. I wrote the song after one of my break-ups with my then on-and-off boyfriend. It was a complicated relationship, if I can even call it a relationship. It was more like a shipwreck, where we slowly sank and inevitably drowned in the freezing waters of our metaphorical ocean.

It's a weird song, because it's from his perspective. He sings—well, I sing—about all of these things I love—well, he loved—about this girl. Me. It's a mix of all the nice and terrible things he used to say about me, and to me. I never knew where I stood with him, probably because he never got to actually know me. He never really wanted to.

'I could tell you a million things about her, you'd never know if they're all lies, because in the end, in the end she's not mine,' I sing in the chorus as I see his face in my head and remember how much I wanted that to be true. How much I wanted to not be his. And how hard it was when I was finally free.

I open my eyes and spot a handful of people singing along. I can't say if they knew the song before or if they just learned it, but I can tell they like it. I look back at Pete again, he sticks his tongue out to me. We're definitely adding this one to our short set.

***

We bow in front of a rambunctious audience and, for a few seconds, I pretend they're here to see us. Only us. It feels good.

We're greeted off stage by Neil—who kindly has a cup of steaming hot tea for me. I like him already. Which is rare.

"That was fantastic!" he says, as he hands us towels.

"Thank you," Pete grins.

Neil says something else, but it's hard to hear since The Hacks are finally hopping onstage. Tyler mumbles something into the mic that I can't understand as he points to where we're standing and the crowd cheers louder. Then, they start to play and the arena comes alive.

"Can we hang out at the merch table?" Pete asks, getting my attention again.

"Oh," Neil widens his eyes in surprise. "Are you sure?"

"Yes, we usually do at our concerts. Since we have fans in here, I think they'd be expecting it," Pete explains.

"Okay, well, go ahead, then!" Neil agrees, not hiding his worry.

We head out anyway, dissecting our performance as we walk. This is one of my favorite parts—when we get to look objectively at what we did and point out what we can improve.

"About *She's Not Mine*..." Pete trails off, testing the waters.

"I think we can add it to the set," I say, faking indifference.

"You sure?" he asks suspiciously.

"No," I admit. I can't lie to him. "But we can try."

"It's just a song," he tells me, still watching me closely. I sip from my tea, deciding to go on vocal rest again, since my throat is burning.

We reach the merch table and, as Pete predicted, there are a handful of our fans already there waiting to catch up with us. We chat, sign stuff, take pictures. Some of the other fans that are watching The Hacks concert notice our presence and whisper to each other. I notice most of their audience is female, which is not surprising—women are usually not afraid to admit they like shitty bands and songs.

After our fans walk out, Pete engages in conversation with Seth—who in addition to the light and sound stuff, is also in charge of the merch. I sit on the only stool behind the table, dividing my attention between his tour stories and the band on stage.

I watch closely the way they interact. The way bands communicate with no words during a concert always fascinates me. Something as simple as glance at the right time can tell you how long people have been playing together, if they enjoy what they do, if they get along. In The Hacks' case, after just a couple of songs, I can tell it's Tristan that commands the band, even though they make it look like it's Tyler. He looks back at his younger brother on the drums every few minutes, making it look like he's giving instructions, when in reality he's taking them. It's weird yet satisfying to see him do that.

My eyes fall on him for a moment. I slowly start to put his attitude into place. No wonder he feels like a rock star—his fans treat him like one. He's clearly the most popular of them, not unusually, though, lead singers often are. And he enjoys it. He takes advantage of it. Although he's not a very sexy figure on stage—more like a clumsy rag doll—, he has the crowd on the palm of his hands.

He owns the stage, he owns his instruments, he has that nice out-of-tune-yet-still-pleasant voice, he demands attention. He makes sense in this context. And he definitely knows what he's doing—every wink, every hair whip, every thrust is so clearly calculated. And the effect they have on the crowd is ridiculous.

When they're halfway through the set and my eyes are still glued on Tyler, I have to admit it—he has it. Whatever 'it' is.

He walks from his piano to the crowd and puts one leg up on the speaker, slightly pushing his hips forward. I laugh.

"What's funny?" Pete asks, startling me. I'm embarrassed to notice I spent so long watching their set, especially when they didn't watch ours.

"Your teenage crush," I say, pointing my head to the stage. Pete made the mistake of telling me he used to have a poster of Tyler on his wall when he was young. I'm never gonna let him forget it. "He's ridiculous."

Yet, I'm still watching him.

"Still hot, though," Pete shouts over the music and the crowd. I roll my eyes, knowing it's a trap.

I take my phone out of my pocket and start to scroll through social media. I've had enough of The Hacks already.

✳DAY TWO

I have trouble sleeping. Firstly, because the flat reeks of vomit—apparently Pete got sick in the morning and decided it was a good idea to leave it untouched until we came back. Even after lightning all my scented candles and leaving the windows wide open, I still can smell it from my bed. Sometimes I hate him so much.

Secondly, because I'm already anxious about our interview in the morning. Although we're no strangers to interviews, we've never done anything this professional. We've mostly spoken to blogs and indie podcasts, and the casual music critique—the worst kind of interviewer. But never 'the press'. Never in a room prepared for it. Never unrequested.

I can't help but feel this is a test. Neil will be observing how we deal with the situation, how prepared we are, how reliable we can be. And, sadly, this only makes me more nervous.

I sit up on the bed, sipping from my magic sore throat potion, and decide to check my social media. I usually avoid doing it right after concerts since fans can be vicious, but I might as well just get the complete nervous breakdown experience. So, I open Twitter.

To my surprise, we've already gained a few dozen followers. First, I go through my mentions, liking concert pictures and nice fan messages. I have a handful of them who I like to stalk because they have the best snarky comments. Tonight, they don't disappoint—I laugh out loud as I scroll through their feeds and read comments about The Hacks. It looks like we have similar opinions.

Speaking of them, I decide to have a look at their Twitter account. I find only the promo picture for the show tonight and no related likes. It seems they don't use much of the platform.

I search for their tag and click on some of their fan accounts, but find nothing interesting or current. So weird. What band doesn't rely on social media nowadays?

I change platforms, then—Instagram. First, I post a picture Pete took of us with the fans at the merch table on our band's account. Our handle is @wecurrentlydonthaveaname. Self-explanatory. We've had a few different ones for every different formation we tried. But since we decided to remain as a duo, we've been struggling to find the perfect name. Mainly because Pete doesn't want to agree with my current idea—Unnamed Duo. Cool, right? Could you tell him, please?

The Hacks' Instagram page is a mess. Black and white pictures mixed with colorful ones of concerts, travels, selfies and even walls? I swear to God... They clearly don't have a theme, which is distressing for someone who likes so much to curate her own page like myself. They have considerably more followers here, though. It kind of makes sense—I too would rather look at their handsome faces than read their words.

There's a photo from the show tonight, already. It was posted less than thirty minutes ago. One of them is also still up at three in the morning. I wonder who it is. The caption is just an England flag. Lame.

I go over the comments and some of them startle me. I had no idea *these* were the type of fans they had. Or, actually, Tyler has. Every single inappropriate comment is about him. Interesting.

I search their tag and now I find a lot of content. There are a million pictures and videos of the concert, including of mine. I open some of them to see what The Hacks fans have to comment about Pete and I and I'm pleasantly surprised. Many of those who bothered to post about us enjoyed our duo, some are absolutely confused as to why they chose a punk band to open their concerts, and a few are complaining we were too loud. That makes me laugh. But if the worst they have to say is that we're loud, I'll take it!

I go back to their official page, scrolling down to read the photo captions. I have a theory that you can tell whether different people are taking care of an 'official account' by the way they write their captions. It doesn't take long to find a pattern—there are at least two different people who post often. One always uses emojis and almost never hashtags. There's a pattern to the pictures, too—one person is in charge of the business-related stuff, the other person posts everything else, which doesn't make much sense. Some of the pictures are clearly selfies, taken by different members, but none of them share the same dry captions. There's always a little information or joke under those. And I have to say, they photograph *very* well. Although, if it wasn't a widely known fact, I'd never tell they're brothers.

I come across one of the very few pictures where Tyler isn't wearing sunglasses and you can actually see his eyes are blue. All three of them are in the pic, all three of them look gorgeous. Like, illegally gorgeous. I send the pic to Pete along with the text *'who would you rather?'*

He's online but he doesn't answer me. He must be angry that I didn't let him sleep in my room tonight. I can't afford to have both of us sick, though.

***

You know when, sometimes, the autopilot takes over in your brain and you suddenly 'wake up' with no memory of how you got to the place you are?

Pete hands me a water bottle and it's only then I notice we're already inside one of the meeting rooms at the hotel waiting for our round of interviews. I know I have taken a shower, I know I am properly dressed and my makeup is in place, and I know we had a quick breakfast before this. I just don't remember any of it.

I sit nervously on the red cushioned armchair. My throat is recovered but I still dread the prospect of talking to people. I'm not very good with words—that's Pete's department. I pray to Gods old and new that these people will let him take over and not ask me anything. He takes the twin chair beside me, observing me closely. He takes my hand and squeezes it. He always knows.

"Are you guys comfortable?" Neil asks. He adjusts the black leather chairs in front of us, where the journalists are supposed to sit. "There'll be only a handful of the local press, each will be given fifteen minutes. Do you have any restrictions?" He pauses, looking at us.

Pete and I exchange a confused look.

"Any subject we should ask them not to touch?" he explains and I stiffen a laugh. He clearly forgets who he's talking to.

"I don't think so," Pete answers, looking at me and raising his eyebrows. It will be a surprise if these people even know our names, let alone our dirty secrets. Right?

Neil smiles, nods and then leaves.

"We'll be here for over an hour," I quickly do the math.

"Relax." Pete squeezes my hand once again.

"I wish I could."

Neil re-enters the room with the first couple of people—two guys in baggy, ripped clothes and long beards. I recognize one of them immediately since we've tried to book an interview with him several times. Pete even followed him on the street once. We exchange wide-eyed glances.

"Pete, Becky, this is Graham and Otto," Neil introduces us. We shake hands and they sit down.

"We're from *Peroxide*, it's an online magazine," Graham, Pete's stalking subject, says.

"Oh, we know," Pete chuckles, unable to repress his fanboy nature. "It's our favorite nowadays."

Graham seems genuinely surprised with that.

Peroxide is one of the last and coolest outlets still exclusively dedicated to punk culture. Pete says Graham is the sole reason this isn't a dead genre, which is obviously an overstatement. However, having a piece written by him is the dream of any up-and-coming band in the scene. I make a mental note to thank Neil for this later.

The interview runs smoothly. He asks pretty basic questions—where we're from, how we've started, why we don't have a name, how we feel by opening the tour for a major band like The Hacks. Pete and I resort to our usual strategy: I begin the answer and he takes over after a couple of sentences. He's funny, he's charismatic, he's eloquent—everything I'm not.

Their fifteen minutes are over in the blink of an eye, and Graham seems genuinely pleased with what he's got.

"This has been fun," Pete says as we get up to shake their hands again.

"Indeed! Let me know when your next solo gig will be, I can't wait to watch your full set. For what I remember, you can bring down a room," Graham says. Pete and I freeze. What does he mean? Has he seen us perform before?

"Wait, wait... what?" Pete asks.

"Oh, I've seen you before, at The Ditch," he continues, mentioning a show we played in another life. I instantly start feeling dizzy. If he saw us then, he saw *him*. "What was it, five years ago? Six? You were a three-piece back then, right?" he asks, confirming my theory.

"Yeah, yes, that's right," Pete nods, stuttering a little bit.

"It was a great gig. But you fell out of my radar after that," he says.

"Yeah, we..." Pete pauses, looking at me. I'm staring at the floor, trying not to faint. "We took a break."

"Right, right," Graham says. I can sense his eyes are on me, too. "Well, I'm sorry for your loss. And I'm glad you've kept going."

"Thank you," Pete answers politely.

When I see their shoes passing through the door, I collapse on the armchair again. My heart stampedes in my chest. My eyes burn. I'm angry. It's been such a long time. Why do I still have this type of reaction? Why does he still have such power over me? I hate him. And I hate myself.

"You played at The Ditch?" Neil asks as soon as we're alone again.

"A thousand years ago," Pete says, causing a new wave of memories to wash over me.

Or, rather, flashes of memories. To this day I still haven't decided if my lack of clear recollections from that time is a blessing or a curse. I just know I hate knowing such a time existed.

"Are you okay?" Pete squeezes the back of my neck.

"What did you lose?" Neil asks.

Pete remains quiet. He's not going to say anything if I don't want to. And I never want to. Maybe that's the problem.

"Not what, who," I say quietly.

"The third guy?" Neil pulls one of the chairs closer and sits down in front of us. I only nod. "What happened?"

"He od'd," I blurt out and watch as his eyes widen, his mouth gapes open, his eyes dart to Pete. Everyone reacts like that.

He stays quiet for a long time, probably waiting for me to steady my breathing. Which I manage to do. The silence in the room is warm and melts away the lump in my chest. I'm still angry, but the threatening tears are contained behind my eyes now.

"So..." Neil says when I finally look up. "You *do* have something you don't want to talk about."

"What are the odds he would know about that?" I snap.

"You shouldn't underestimate the scope of knowledge of a member of the press," he says calmly. I snort. "Is there anything else?"

At the same time I shake my head, Pete says, "Her parents." I shoot him a hurt look. He doesn't see it and goes on, "And relationships. You know, personal stuff."

"Got it," Neil says, getting up.

"Won't that only make people more curious, though?" I ask as he rearranges the chairs.

"Yes," he says. When he stops, he looks at me, "Would you rather take the chance of dealing with one of those questions during the interview?"

I shake my head. I can't deal with those things inside my own head as it is. I'd rather not have to hear any questions about anything.

"I'll give you a few minutes, okay?" he says as he heads to the door.

"Are *you* curious?" I ask before he leaves.

"Oh, yes. Yes, I am," he smiles. And goes away.

I let out a heavy breath. I'm still thinking about him. I'm always thinking about him—another thing that I hate. But I can't help it, I was the one stupid enough to let him shape and define a big part of my life. *Our* lives. Unfortunately, Pete had to go through it with me, and I think that's what hurts the most. Sometimes I wish I was the dead one.

"I can't believe Graham was there," Pete says after a while.

"We were close, weren't we?" I ask, my mind swimming with fractured memories. "We were so close."

"We're still close. I mean..." he says, motioning around the room.

He's right. I let that sink in for a moment.

"So... who would you rather?" he speaks again. I frown, not knowing what he means, so he continues, "You know I know who you would choose, right?"

I smile. It's about last night's text.

"I know who *you* would choose," I answer, happy to lighten the air.

"I don't think you do," he challenges me.

"Oh, please," I snort, "Blond hair? Blue eyes? That sounds familiar to me," I joke since those are exactly his girlfriend's characteristics.

"Good point," he frowns in a fake-thoughtful expression. "But he's also got that leather jacket and bad-boy attitude. That's more of your type."

I roll my eyes and laugh. Because it's true.

"I guess we'll have to share," I joke again. He doesn't take it as a joke, though, as he turns to me with a suspicious expression. So, I add, "I'm joking."

"Right," he says, narrowing his eyes.

I don't have time to argue since Neil re-enters the room with the next interviewer. But I know Pete will want to continue this productive discussion later.

***

The hour and a half we spend talking to four of the coolest specialized local press end up not being as excruciating as I thought it would be. Even though we had to answer the same questions to all of them, each approached something different about our craft—our influences, our ambitions, our skills on instruments. And none mentioned past dead band members or made personal questions. Another mental 'thank you' to Neil.

We leave the conference room and Neil leads the way to the restaurant, where we're supposed to have lunch all together before heading to the venue a second time. As we walk across the hotel lobby, we spot Tristan and Todd chatting to a group of excited girls—fans. They're taking pictures and signing stuff.

"Becky!" a female voice shouts. I jump around to see the fan from the night before waving and jogging towards us.

"Hello, love!" Pete smiles, pulling her to a hug. I can hear her squealing in his arms.

"Oh my God, I'm such a huge fan!" she says, turning to me for a hug, as well. I don't like hugs. I do hug her, though.

"Thank you," I say as she starts listing all the gigs she's been to, as if to prove she's not lying.

While we're taking a picture, two more girls from the group that was chatting with The Hacks approach us. One of them hands us the first EP we ever sold, and Pete almost faints.

We sign stuff, we take pictures, we chat. It's not because they're ours, but our fans are so cool. I wonder if every artist thinks like that. I'll have to ask one of the Hackley boys some time.

Pete is in the middle of discussing our setlist with them when a scream startles us. Everyone looks around in search of the source. I notice a concerning number of people running towards the lifts. Tyler is walking out of it, running a hand through his damp hair and adjusting his sunglasses. He waves to the approaching group of people, doesn't even bother smiling, and rushes to the restaurant, whose entrance is blocked by security guards. A few of the girls still try to reach him, calling out his name, but he disappears as suddenly as he appeared.

The three girls in front of us exchange knowing glances and roll their eyes.

"Can I ask you," one of them turns to me, "is he a douche bag?"

I glance at Pete, and he gives me one of his warning looks.

"I probably shouldn't answer that," I say and they laugh.

Neil declares the meet and greet over, so we say our goodbyes and they walk away.

Pete gives me the same suspicious look he did earlier after the interview. I try to shake it off and start walking towards the restaurant. I really don't want to talk about it.

"It's only our second day," he says in a low voice so only I can hear it. "Please, behave."

"I'll try," I say, the same promise I always make when he asks me that. He knows there's not much I can do, I'm not usually good at controlling my tongue. I do try. But I tend to fail too often.

We walk around filling our plates with sandwiches and fruits and join the big table where the crew is seated at the back. Tristan moves his chair closer to us and he and Pete start a never-ending conversation about nothing. It always baffles me how some people can waste their breath for little-to-no information exchange.

I eat in silence, pretending I'm listening to whatever they're saying, until I feel it—someone is watching me. I glance to the other side of the table and, sure enough, Tyler is facing our direction. Again, I can't say if he is indeed staring because he's still wearing those hideous sunglasses of his, and he doesn't turn away when I catch him.

I look to the people sitting next to him—they're in the middle of an exciting conversation. My gaze falls back on Tyler and I realize that, like me, he's only pretending to listen. I wonder if that's why he wears those glasses so often. Is it easier to ignore people with them? Should I try it?

"Becky." Pete's hand on my shoulder startles me. I turn around to find him and Tristan staring at my face.

"Sorry, what?" I ask, deciding I'll definitely need to give sunglasses indoors a go.

"I was saying I really liked your set last night," Tristan smiles broadly. "You have quite the voice."

"Oh," I'm taken aback, first because I can't handle compliments, second because I thought they didn't watch us.

"You guys have a rich sound for a duo," he continues.

"Well, drums and guitar are really the spine of any song," Pete says.

"For sure," Tristan agrees, as he obviously would. "But have you ever considered adding some members? I think a bass line would take you guys to another level."

"Well, we tried..." Pete trails off. And, once again, *he* is on my mind.

"I feel you," Tristan nods. "Finding the right fit can be an arduous task."

"Yeah, plus the fact that we've been together for so long. It's hard to find a new band member that gets our dynamic," Pete adds, giving me a silly smile. What he means is: it's hard to find someone to put up with Becky's shit.

"It doesn't need to be a band member, though," someone says from behind us. Pete and I turn around to find Tyler standing there, eating a banana and eavesdropping our conversation. "You could try supporting musicians. Hire different people just for the gigs. I'm sure you can handle more than one instrument in the studio, right?"

"Sure," Pete nods.

"You just can't play all of them at a concert," he says. Then, in a quieter tone, he adds, "Unfortunately."

"It's an idea." Pete shrugs, glancing at me.

"We don't have money to pay for supporting musicians," I bring the conversation down to earth.

"Yet," Tyler adds. We look back at him. He finishes his snack and walks away.

"He's so weird," I say out loud before remembering his brother is sitting right in front of me. Pete gives me a murderous look, but Tristan laughs.

"Tell me about it," he comments.

I give Pete an apologetic smile and he shakes his head slowly.

***

Our soundcheck is short. After talking to Neil, and at his request, Pete and I add three more songs to the set. We're still done pretty quickly, since there's nothing much to change from the day before.

We decide to sit at the balcony to watch The Hacks run through their set. Pete is curious to see the view and sound from there. Meaning, he's curious to see what they saw last night when they watched us from here.

I notice he's distracted, though. He has his phone on his hand and turns on the screen every few seconds. I also notice his girlfriend wasn't at the concert last night. She hasn't been around for a while, actually.

"Lindsey?" I ask.

"Yep," he says, shoving the phone into his pocket now. "She can't make it."

"Bummer. Maybe next weekend?" I watch as he tries to hide a sigh.

"Maybe," he smiles. I'm about to ask if everything is okay when we're interrupted.

"Hey, guys!" Tristan sits in front of us. Is their soundcheck over already? "Do you have plans for this afternoon?"

"Not really," Pete answers, glancing at me. I shrug.

"Some of the guys want to go sightseeing," he comments. *Good riddance*, I answer, but only in my head.

"Not really our thing," is what I say out loud. Not that I don't like sightseeing, I just don't want to spend the rest of the day socializing with them. And if Pete agrees to it, I'll have to go.

"Okay, well, you're welcome to stop by my dressing room," he offers as if he's talking about the Buckingham Palace. "I usually hold videogame championships before the gigs, you know, to pass the time. Do you play videogames?"

"No," I answer. Probably too quickly, judging by the way they both look at me.

"I do," Pete smiles, trying to balance my bluntness.

"Cool," Tristan smiles back. It almost makes me change my mind. "Well, you're invited."

As he walks away, I glance at Pete, who's actually checking him out. I frown, ready to make fun of him when he notices I was looking. But when he turns to me, he only shrugs.

"He has a great ass," he remarks, no shame in his voice.

"You're disgusting." I shake my head in fake disapproval. I can't say I didn't notice his ass. Or his arms. "Not Tyler, then?"

"Shut up," he says and promptly gets up.

"Are you accepting his invite?" I mock him.

"Yes," he answers sharply. "And can you at least try?"

"To play videogame?" I frown.

"To be nice!" he clarifies. "We're going to spend two weeks with these guys. Please, behave."

"I *am* trying," I argue. I swear I wasn't intentionally rude. Not this time.

"Try harder." He raises his eyebrows.

I roll my eyes but follow him to The Hacks dressing room. I manage to sit with them for an entire hour before deciding I better get away if I'm not to punch someone.

I sit alone in my cupboard for a while, do some warm-ups and wait for showtime. When they start to open the gates, I decide to sneak to the side of the stage and observe people coming in. I like doing that, I like to feel the excitement that emanates from each one. It's such a fantastic concept that such different, unique people, who perhaps have nothing else in common, choose to share one night of innocent bliss together. For just a couple of hours, nothing else matters—not their jobs, not their beliefs, not their fears. Just the music. Just the moment.

So I watch them as they get ready for that weird communion, filling the room, making everything warmer and noisier. There are people in groups, there are people alone, dressed up for the occasion or comfortable as if they were at home, of all colors, sizes and shapes. Not one is the same as the other. But their eyes all glisten alike.

"Someone you know?" a voice too close to my ear startles me. I jump and kick one of the guitar cases, making it fall down with a loud thump. Luckily, there are enough people in the crowd to drown out the commotion. "Are you okay?"

"Yes," I grunt, rearranging the cases and cursing the bruise I'm sure will appear later on my shin.

"So?" Tyler raises his eyebrows when I finally look at him.

"So what?" I bark. Then I remember Pete asking me to behave.

"Do you have friends in the crowd tonight?" he asks, apparently ignoring my manners.

"No," I shake my head. Not tonight, not ever. I turn my face back to the crowd only to realize their numbers have already doubled. "It's filling up fast," I comment, trying to make small talk.

But Tyler doesn't reply. He just stands there, behind me, silently watching the crowd with me. Or silently watching *me* watch the crowd, as I catch him staring at the back of my head when I turn around again. I frown, but he doesn't even flinch. Which makes me think about all the times he seems to be staring through his sunglasses—maybe he is.

"What are you doing down here?" I ask, trying to keep my tone casual and not accusatory.

"Hiding," he says. I chuckle, thinking it's a joke. But, actually, I don't think it is. "What about you?"

"Watching," I look back out. The rumble is loud enough now that we have to talk out loud to hear each other.

"We seem to have some fans in common," he comments. "Some of them were singing your songs last night. And at the hotel this morning."

"Yeah," I nod, looking back at him. I remember his swift escape from said fans. I decide not to mention it. Instead, I try to think of something nice to say about it, but all that comes out is "who would have thought?"

His mouth slowly curls up into a smile. I'm relieved he doesn't seem offended. This counts as behaving, right?

"We should play something together," he suggests after a minute. "They would go crazy."

"We should," I nod slowly, actually liking the idea. "I have to learn one of your songs first, though."

"Or we could learn one of yours," he says and I can't help the disbelief in my eyes. "I liked the one that girl requested yesterday, what is it called?"

"She's Not Mine," I say. Of course that's the one he would like.

"*I could tell you a million things about her, you'd never know if they're all lies, because in the end, in the end she's not mine,*" he sings softly and my eyes widen.

"You already know the lyrics," I can't shake the surprise off of my voice.

"It's a repetitive chorus," he shrugs.

"It is," I agree.

"Almost like..." he pauses, widening his eyes. "A pop song."

"Don't push it," I frown again, fighting back a smile.

"I bet we can rearrange it as a pop song," he continues, purposefully to annoy me.

"You mean *murder* it," I stress my disapproval and he smiles again. Second time in the same conversation? Pete would be proud of me.

"Who wrote it, you or Pete?" he asks.

"Me," I answer, bracing myself for having to talk about the subject matter of the song.

"Does she know you wrote a song about her?" he continues.

"Who?" I frown.

"The girl in the song," he explains. Of course. The song is about a girl.

"Oh, no," I shake my head and wonder how self-absorbed I will seem when I explain it. "The girl in the song is me."

"Oh?" It's his turn to frown.

"I wrote from the point of view of my boyfriend," I say. It sounds weird to call him boyfriend. Should I mention he's dead now? How do you gently introduce this information into a conversation?

"I see," he nods slowly, still with a confused look on his face.

"It makes it all a little confusing, I know. But I think it's what I like about it," I admit. I like that people don't get it at first. I like having it as a little secret. Well, not so secret anymore.

"Yeah," he nods again, pensive. I have a feeling he's reciting the lyrics in his head and taking in the new meaning. "Yeah, I like it, too," he says, finally, and I smile in return.

The conversation ends there—he doesn't ask any more questions about the song or my relationship. It's a relief. We remain in silence, getting acquainted with the noise and the heat until the time for my set comes. Pete joins me hesitantly as the stage manager hands us our mics. I can see the question in his eyes: '*What the devil is going on here?*' I smile softly while our mics are tested and he seems to take it as a good sign.

"Break a leg," Tyler says as we step on stage, and I don't have a chance to say thank you.

The crowd cheers, louder than the night before. I quickly spot the requesting fan from the other night, as she's closer to the stage and waving frantically. I wave to her, give my introductions and we start.

After the first song, as I'm turning around to look at Pete, I see that Tyler is still there. He's still standing at the side of the stage, watching, a red plastic cup in his hand. My heart suddenly jumps. I get nervous. Why is he there?

I have no time to mull over this, as Pete starts counting for the second song. I focus on the crowd, on the people who are singing along and those who are not, but are enjoying nonetheless. I try to get back into the mood and have a good time, but now Tyler's figure is imprinted on the left side of my peripheral vision. I can see him, it doesn't matter where I'm looking at.

We finish the second song and I decide not to pause. Now I'm eager to get this over with. I feel judged, and I don't like it.

We run through the third and the fourth songs and, before we start the next one, Pete motions with his hands: '*slow down*'. I take a deep breath. I'm ruining it. We have only a handful of songs in our set, and I'm ruining it.

I look back at the crowd and try to ignore the ghost watching me. I lock eyes with the fan I recognized and start the riff of *She's Not Mine*. Her smile broadens and a few people scream—they know what's coming. I smile and keep looking at the small group of girls I know are our fans as I sing. They dig it.

After the first chorus, I risk a glance at the side of the stage again. I can see the whole band there now, but my eyes focus on Tyler—and his moving lips. He's singing along. He knows the lyrics, not only the chorus. And he seems to like the song.

I try to make eye contact with Pete, to warn him somehow because I know he'll die if he sees it. But he's not paying any attention to me, he's busy being a star. I smile with the joy that seeing his messy hair whip around brings me. Then I get back to the crowd for the last chorus.

I can't help but look at Tyler again. He's bobbing his head, dancing in place, and when he notices I'm looking, he starts singing louder. And the idea of playing together gets more and more appealing.

✴DAY THREE

WE'RE ALL UP AND PACKED QUITE EARLY IN THE MORNING. NEIL changed our traveling schedule at the last minute, I suppose to miss the fans. Apparently, there was a group of them waiting at The Hacks hotel last night after the concert, and there are still some of them there when we arrive to meet the band and crew in the morning. It's early. I admire their... dedication.

The lobby door is now decorated with a security guard and we have to show our credentials to be let in. Serious business. Pete and I exchange funny glances as we walk past him, but we have no time to make fun of the situation since everyone is already around and waiting for us.

"Morning," Pete says as we approach Neil, who's talking with the hotel concierge.

"Hey, you!" he smiles, taking a look at his clock. "On time! I'm afraid you'll have to wait a while."

"No problem," Pete says while I snicker beside him. Not on time, then. Early. I hate being early.

"Can you please drop your bags over there?" Neil asks, pointing to a corner full of bags and backpacks.

I follow Pete as he does what we're asked. Then I follow him back as he greets the band and crew, pretending to do the same. Then I follow him to the restaurant where we go grab a coffee. Then I stand with him awkwardly at the door, observing the rest of the sleepy people lounging around.

I start to notice how silent Pete is—it's strange because he's never silent. Silence makes him nervous, so he's always quick to fill it with his voice. He's not doing that right now, which makes *me* nervous.

"Are you okay?" I ask.

"What?" He seems to come back down from wherever his mind was.

"You're too quiet. I'm worried," I say, and he rolls his eyes.

"I'm just tired," he says. "I've been sleeping on the couch for days now."

Now, I roll my eyes. It's not my fault that he ruined his bedroom floor.

"We should go mingle," he continues. I frown.

"If you want to get rid of me, just say so," I complain.

"Okay," he says in a serious tone. "Get lost."

I laugh and don't move.

"Or come with me talk to people."

Then I walk away to sit alone on a chair. From there, I watch as he walks back to the lobby and actually goes talk to people. I'm a little offended that he wants to talk to someone other than me. When I see him walking towards Tristan, who is leaning against a wall all by himself, the feeling intensifies. He's been spending a lot of time with Tristan. And it's only been two days.

I sigh and take my phone out of my jacket pocket, deciding to distract myself with social media. Just because I can't make new friends it doesn't mean Pete shouldn't. I can't resent him for that.

I open Instagram and go through my feed, mindlessly liking all the photos. A few minutes later, someone sits on the chair in front of me. I look up to see Tyler—in my twin leather jacket and those hideous sunglasses. I'm not sure if he's looking at me and I don't want to make small talk, so I only smile and nod. He smiles and nods back. Then, he also gets his phone out and starts fumbling with it.

I get back to my mindless scrolling, but I can't concentrate now. Much like last night, I'm too aware of his presence. I keep moving my thumb, though, because I don't want him to notice he's disrupting my peace. Why didn't he go sit somewhere else? All the couches and armchairs are empty.

"Ty!" a female voice gets both of our attention. "I'm on my way, babes."

Tyler gets up and lets the woman hug him—a very tight, personal hug. When she lets go, I recognize her. It's Anna Kusek, the model. I think she is the only British person in the top 10 celebrities with the most followers on Instagram? I follow her. She's gorgeous. Even in person.

"Let me know when you're back around these parts, will you?" she asks in a flirty tone, poking his chin with a finger.

"Will do," Tyler answers with a smile.

Then, her eyes fall on me. *Oh, no. She's gonna speak to me.*

"Hey," she points one long, manicured finger my way, "you're the girl who opened the concert last night, aren't you?"

"Yes," I say dryly. I think I'm expected to say something else because both of them just stare at me in silence for a while, but since I don't know what, I say nothing.

"Great concert," she says, finally. "And I like your style."

"Thanks," I say and, again, it's all that I say.

"Okay," she says slowly, in that way people use to close an interaction with a weirdo. I can't blame her. "Bye, then."

She turns once more to Tyler, winking, and walks away. Then he turns to me. I feel judged again.

"Didn't you meet her yesterday?" he asks. "She was backstage last night."

"And now she's here," I reply. He pauses in the middle of sitting back down and his head jerks up. *Smooth, Becky, very smooth.* In an attempt to remedy my indiscretion, I add, "I didn't stay for long."

Backstage was crammed last night, full of celebrities and fans alike. Since they were all there to see the Hackley boys, I kept pestering Pete to leave until he gave in and we went home.

"I noticed," he replies. I don't believe him. I doubt he even remembered I existed after the concert. "I didn't, either."

Of course not. Well, to be fair, if I had Anna Kusek willing to spend the night with me, I wouldn't want to waste time hanging out. Except, I normally don't want to waste time hanging out, anyway—hot model or not.

I keep staring, expecting him to go back to his phone, but he doesn't. He keeps staring back. Is he waiting for me to do it first? Or to continue the conversation? Which one should I choose?

"I didn't know you had so many friends on this side of the pond." I opt for conversation since I know I won't be able to concentrate on my phone.

"Oh, I wouldn't call them friends," he says.

"How would you call them, then?"

He remains silent for a while, thinking. I wish he'd take off the glasses so I could read him better.

"Occasional supporters," he says, at last, making me snort.

"Is that an American term?" I joke.

"I don't know. How would you call them here?" he asks and I swear he's fighting a smirk.

I take my time thinking, as he did. Then, I say, "Friends."

Now he smiles, wide and bright. It's satisfying. And I hate to notice that.

"Alright, guys," Neil starts calling from the reception desk. "Let's get going?"

***

It's the biggest and widest bus I've ever seen in my entire life. It has a shiny golden exterior, blackened out windows, air-con and there's a part in the back that expands, making an actual *room* inside of it.

The interior is every bit as glamorous as the exterior. Shiny wood and black leather everywhere. There are three different ambients, in addition to a corridor with 12 bunks. It's hard to hide my astonishment and I let out a 'bloody hell' every time I turn around.

After everyone chooses their beds—I end up with the top one closest to the back room—, some of the boys get right to sleep. I don't want to sleep, so I amble to the back room, where Tristan is already setting up the videogame. I don't want to play videogame, either, so I go to the *kitchen*—which is possibly bigger than my flat's kitchen—where I find a pot of coffee brewing. Neil is there, talking on the phone to someone about our next show. He motions to the pot, asking with his free hand if I'd like some. I accept it and sit down on one of the booths. Yes, there are booths and tables—as in more than one.

"Everything seems to be in order," he says when he hangs up. Then I regret accepting the coffee because now I'll have to make small talk with him. "How do you like your coffee?"

"With plenty of sugar, please," I say and he raises his eyebrows, as if surprised by my request.

"Sometimes I feel I'm the last person on Earth who still consumes sugar," he chuckles, putting a mug in front of me and sitting on the opposite booth.

"Well, you've just found a fellow rebel," I say and he chuckles again.

"So, are you comfortable?" he asks.

"Sure! This bus is bigger than my flat," I say, and it's no exaggeration.

"No, I mean, being the only girl around," he clarifies, but it only gets me confused. When he sees my frown, he continues, "I only thought of asking you if it was okay to get one single bus after I had done it."

"It's fine. I'm used to being the only girl around," I admit. Sad, but true.

"I can imagine. You know, they're implementing this new program in the label now to have more women working in leadership positions," he informs me.

I nod, not sure why he's telling me this.

"And also to find more female talent," he continues and then it starts making sense.

"Good for you. Women are awesome," is all I can think of replying. I kick myself internally, but he laughs.

"Indeed, they are. You're a fine example of it," he says and my blood freezes. In my vast experience of being the only girl in the room, I know this kind of remark usually stirs the conversation away from the music.

I struggle to keep quiet and wait for his next move. I can't just start a fight with the man we're hoping to sign us—unless I have good reason to.

"I mean it," he searches my eyes. "The way you shred that guitar, mate..." He starts playing an air guitar and I release the breath I was holding in.

"Thanks," I mumble, suddenly aware of every beat of my heart.

"How long have you been playing?" he asks.

"Guitar? I don't know, ten years, maybe?" I can't remember when I first picked up a guitar. I just remember I did so because I couldn't stand playing piano anymore, and I missed the music.

"That's a long enough time for someone so young. And I have to tell you, a woman playing guitar the way that you do will definitely stand out for a label."

A label? *Your label?* I really, really want to ask. Yet, I don't. I'm not sure he'll have an answer for me right now. And even if he does, I'm not sure I'm ready to hear it.

It looks like he wants to tell, though, since he keeps staring at me with the clear intention of saying something but unsure whether to do it or not. *I'm not ready*, I think. *Please, don't say it.* Where's Pete when I need him?

I just wait, staring back. I'm good at staring at people in silence.

"I knew about Alex," he blurts out. I temporarily lose the ability to breathe. I sure wasn't ready for *this*.

"H-how?" I manage to ask.

"Well, he had a bit of a reputation in the industry," he explains.

I remember some instances where he'd talk trash about someone or some place, only to later find out he wasn't allowed to get even near said person or place.

"I never met him, though," he continues when I don't. I really have nothing to say about this subject. "Were you guys... you know..."

It takes me a moment to reply. I nod.

"I'm sorry. I didn't know about that part." He gives me a sympathetic smile. I don't smile back. "I'm also sorry to bring this up again, I can see how hard it is on you. But I felt like I owed you the truth. And an apology because I could have done a better job yesterday."

That actually makes me feel better. Still, it's weird to have someone else know about him. It kind of makes him... real. I don't know, sometimes I think it was all a figment of my imagination. Like I made him up. I wish I had made him up.

Then it occurs to me that if he knows about this, maybe he knows about...

"Do you..." I struggle to find my voice. "Do you know about my parents?"

"No," he shakes his head. I watch him for a while, deciding whether to believe him. I do. "Do you want to tell me?"

Tyler walks over just then, looking through the cabinets for a mug. He finds one and pours coffee in it. He turns around, leaning against the little counter. His eyes jump from Neil to me a few times.

"Did I interrupt something?" he asks.

I shake my head. Then I turn to Neil and shake my head again, answering a different question. He nods once. *Got it.*

Tyler sits beside Neil, in front of me. The silence lingers, hot and heavy. I can feel dark memories creeping in from the edges of my mind. I need a distraction.

"So, we had an idea," I say suddenly. They both look at me. "We want to play a few songs together during the show."

"Oh?" Neil's eyebrows shoot up. He looks at Tyler, who almost choked on his coffee.

"Yeah, we kind of talked about it last night," he says, to my relief. "Since we have mutual fans."

"I thought of swapping songs—ending our set with one of yours and starting yours with one of mine. Of course, playing them together," I make it up as I go. It's a half-ass idea but I kind of like it.

Tyler nods slowly. For a moment I think he's going to argue or decline or just give me one of those 'yeah, we'll see' and then never do it. Instead, he smiles—the one from the lobby again. It looks different now that I can see his eyes. It looks *better*.

"I like the sound of that," he says.

"Me, too!" Neil says excitedly. "It's a great idea!"

"What song would you like to do?" Tyler asks.

"Oh, I don't know," I say, biting my lip. "Maybe—"

"I want *She's Not Mine*," he cuts me off. It takes me by surprise. Yet, somehow, I knew he'd want to sing that one.

"I was thinking more about *Overdrive*," I say.

"Nope," he shakes his head, "it's *She's Not Mine* or nothing."

Bossy. It suddenly makes me want to tell him 'well, it's nothing, then'. But I also want to hear what that one will sound like in his voice.

"Deal," I say. "But then I get to choose any one of yours."

"Knock yourself out," he grins.

"What do you have in mind?" Neil asks.

Nothing. I have nothing in mind.

***

"So?" Tyler turns around, a look of triumph on his face. I want to punch him.

"I hate it," I'm blunt, for Pete's dismay.

"What?" Tyler and Pete ask in unison.

"It sounds awful! This piano line completely decharacterizes the song. It's all wrong." I rest my hands on my hips for dramatic effect.

"Isn't that the point, though? Make it sound like their song?" Pete argues, trying to knock some sense into me.

"No," I resist stubbornly. "The point was to make it sound pop, not bad."

"I give up," Tyler groans and walks off stage.

We'd been jamming for two hours trying to realize our idea. When I explained my plan to everyone else, they got excited. Neil said it was going to be a good showcase of our versatility. Pete was dying to rearrange one of their songs and put his producer abilities to test. Everybody was eager to work together.

Only they ignored the fact that Tyler is a self-centered diva and I'm a proud brat.

"I can't believe you," Pete complains, putting down the bass he's holding.

"Just give him a few minutes, he'll come back," Tristan says from where he's sitting behind the drums, completely overlooking the fact I'm the one throwing a fit. Even Todd gives him a dirty look.

"I knew this wasn't going to work out," I lightly strum my pink guitar.

"Then why did y'all insist on trying this out?" Todd complains and I can't even reply. He's right to complain. It has been two hours of soundcheck down the drain.

"Because it's a great idea!" Tristan bites back.

"In theory," I add, being the adorable pessimist I am.

"It will be in practice, too," Tristan insists. "Tyler has been trying to learn this song for weeks, he won't give up now."

"What?" Pete and I gasp. Did he just say *weeks*?

"I thought he'd suggest that we do a cover, though," Tristan continues, ignoring our shock. "This idea is definitely better."

"But we only played this song two days ago," Pete argues.

"But he's been listening to your music nonstop since he found you online," he informs and I can't help but gasp again.

That's what happened, then? Tyler was the one to 'find' us and bump whoever the label had lined up in our favor?

"I can't fathom Tyler enjoying our style," I admit, trying to get more out of him.

"Me neither. But I was mistaken," Tristan chuckles. "He studied you for days and then insisted for the label to get in touch," he continues and his choice of words doesn't escape me. "He's very meticulous."

"You mean critical," Todd corrects him, speaking my mind for me.

It takes me a while to process this. It explains why he was singing along the other day. It also explains why he's been observing us from afar. And this idea. Why didn't he tell me, though? God, what a psycho.

I glance at Pete and he's looking at me with an 'are you happy now?' expression. I roll my eyes, because even though I am surprised, I don't regret what I said. He *was* murdering our song.

I put my guitar down and walk to the piano. I sit on the stool with a sigh—I'm about to make a fool of myself. I struggle to find the chords I'm looking for, and then someone interrupts my efforts.

"It's B minor," Tyler's voice echoes in the empty theater.

We all look up to see him perched at the balcony, eating what seems to be peanuts, and smirking. He's been there the whole time. I glare, and the desire of punching his smug face returns full force.

I get back to the piano, purposefully avoiding the B minor. I struggle a little more, but I find the notes I wanted him to play. I don't want the piano to lead the song, it has to just accompany the original track on the acoustic guitar.

When I'm satisfied with what I've done, I ask Pete to play the song on the acoustic guitar, slower than we usually do. I play along what I managed to arrange in the piano. And there it is, the pop version of our punk banger.

"It sounds nice," Tristan nods, trying out some light beats to give the song rhythm.

Pete and Todd both play acoustic guitars, with Todd trying to find a harmony for him. And I repeat the notes on the piano. It's only four chords, but my fingers are so rusty I keep getting them wrong.

After six or seven runs, we appear to find the song. I look up to the balcony with what I hope is the exact triumphant expression Tyler had on his face before he stormed out of stage. I think I manage because he stops chewing and narrows his small eyes.

"I'm not playing that," he declares, standing up and disappearing again.

I'm livid. I start to count to ten before I turn around, otherwise I know I'm going to say things that will be impossible to take back. But before I even finish, Tyler is back onstage.

"I'll sing, you play," he orders in that bossy tone of his, grabbing the microphone as he walks past me.

Before I have any chance to protest, Tristan starts a countdown and everyone starts to play. I get back to the keys, running my fingers more smoothly through them now, and brace myself for hearing Tyler singing my words.

Part of me is ready, even wishing to hate it. But Tyler doesn't give me a reason to. He sings. And, oh boy, how he sings. I hate to admit it, but it sounds like the song was made for his voice—the gravelly in the low notes, the crying falsetto in the chorus, the pain. He knows what he's doing, and I can't hate him for that.

"So?" he asks again when we finish. I'm aware of all eyes on me.

"Let's do one of yours now." I get up from the piano, walking back to my guitar and refusing to say I liked it. Even though I did. I think I might have liked his vocals better than mine.

He says nothing, only walks back to his piano, and we start the process all over again. Except, now, no one storms out.

***

It takes us much less time to rearrange one of The Hacks' songs into punk. Mostly because, unlike me, they don't seem too precious about their music. That makes me feel a little ashamed. I also have a pretty hard time learning their lyrics, which, in comparison with Tyler 'studying us for weeks', is pretty shameful, too.

After only a few runs, even though I don't feel at all prepared, everyone decides they're happy with what we've got. We're putting the plan into action during the show tonight. I freak out. I can't play the piano. I can't sing their song. I'm a disaster. But no one hears me out.

So, after a late lunch, and before the doors open for the show, I decide to practice a little more. Alone this time, mostly because not even Pete wants to spend one more minute playing with me. Whatever.

I decide to start with the piano, which will probably be the easiest. It's only four chords, for Christ's sake, I've had over a decade of lessons. I can do this.

Except I can't. I keep getting it wrong, I keep rushing it along, I can't play and sing at the same time. *Ugh*! Whose idea was it again?

"You take it too seriously," Tyler's voice causes me to hit both hands on the keys and the empty venue reverberates the 'bang' it makes for a long time.

I take a deep breath and don't turn around to look at him. When the echo dissipates, I start again.

"Correct your posture," he commands.

I do notice I'm all hunched over the piano when he says that, but for some reason, I refuse to sit up straight.

"Just relax," he says in a softer tone and suddenly his hands are on my shoulders, which have the opposite effect of what he's asking me to do—I jump again, squirming under his touch. "Sorry," he mumbles, retrieving his hands. "I'm just trying to help."

"I don't need your help." I finally turn around to glare at him, but it only makes me regret my words. He looks hurt. Like, actually hurt. *Fuck.* He sighs and turns around to walk away, but then I speak again, "You make me nervous."

He stops on his tracks, but doesn't turn around. I regret it again. But I also couldn't stand his puppy eyes. Not that he deserves any pity, just hours ago he was criticizing my piano skills.

When he finally turns around, instead of the cocky expression I was expecting to see, he's wearing a serious one.

"Then don't let me," he says simply. I don't know what he means.

"How?" I find myself asking. He shrugs.

"Let's find out." He walks back towards me and around the piano. He leans over it and stares at me. "Play."

I already hate his bossy tone. Part of me wants to resist just for the sake of antagonizing him, but I decide to do as he says. Mainly because I really need to practice.

He just stands there for several minutes, staring at my contracted face, judging. And making me nervous.

"I can't," I sigh after the third try.

"You play in front of hundreds of people every night," he argues.

"Not the piano!" *And not to you*, I add mentally.

"Forget the piano," he waves a hand in the air and I frown. Play, forget, can he make up his mind? "Let's try talking while you play."

"About what?" I ask suspiciously.

"Play!" He demands again and I roll my eyes. But start to play. "Why do you think I wouldn't like your music?"

"I don't know," I shrug. "You don't look like the type of person who's into punk."

"You don't look like the type of person who'd believe in stereotypes," he retorts.

"Really? Have you looked at me?" I look up again, raising my eyebrows, and he smiles. "Why didn't you tell me you're a fan?"

"I didn't want to inflate your ego," he replies and it's my turn to smile. What an asshole.

"I can't believe Tyler Hackley has been stalking me online," I joke.

"Not stalking, researching," he doesn't miss a beat. I look at him again. He doesn't seem even a little embarrassed about being outed. I envy his confidence.

"I *researched* you, too," I mock him.

"Yeah? What did you find out?" he rests his chin on one hand.

"That I don't like your songs," I glance at him again and his smile widens. I think I like making him smile.

"What happened to the third guy?" he says and my hands hit the wrong keys again. I curse under my breath and try my hardest to not stop playing now. "Alex, right?"

"How do you know about him?" I ask in what I hope is a casual tone.

"There are some videos of you together online," I can see him shrug from the corner of my eye.

"He died," I say and feel his entire body react. I risk looking up again. By the surprise on his fine features, I can tell he didn't know about this particular detail.

"I-I... I'm..." he stutters. Turns out I like him embarrassed, too. "I'm sorry."

I look back at my hands, indicating the end of this particular conversation. I play the entire song twice more while he just watches in silence. My fingers hurt, so I stretch my hands.

"The song is about him," he says. It's not a question. I shouldn't be surprised that he'd put 2 and 2 together. When I don't answer, he continues, "I can pick a different one. I like *Overdrive*."

Now I'm the one smiling. I look back at him and his concerned expression. How can he be the same person that was dragging me in front of everyone just a few hours ago?

"No need," I say.

"You sure?" his frown deepens.

"Yep. I like how it sounds in your voice," I say and, guess what? Regret it. Even though his frown turns into a smile. *Especially* when his frown turns into a smile. I feel my face getting warm, so I stand up and turn away from him. "Now I just need to learn your lyrics."

I open the lyrics to *Hey* on my phone and rest it against Tristan's drum. Then I strap on my guitar and sit on the floor. Then I glance at Tyler. He's sitting at the piano, where I was just a minute ago, but facing me. His arms are crossed over his chest and his eyes are locked on mine.

He holds my gaze for a few seconds and then smirks.

"Do I still make you nervous?" he asks.

I roll my eyes and don't reply. Because he does.

***

As much as I hate to admit it, Tyler was right—the fans go absolutely bonkers when they see us all together on stage.

When The Hacks joined us after Pete and I announced we were finishing off with *She's Not Mine*, they cheered so loud I couldn't hear my own thoughts. To my surprise and amusement, they sang the whole song with us. It was surreal. I also nailed the piano. Well, maybe not nailed, but nobody seemed to notice the mistakes. I do take it too seriously.

When it was my turn to sing their song, things didn't go as seamlessly. After the first chorus, I forgot the entire second part of the song. Tyler refused to take over, but thankfully his fans were a lot kinder. They sang the bridge back to me and even when Tyler ironically asked "how good of a job was that?", they cheered and clapped and chanted my name.

This time, Neil doesn't let us hang out at the merch table, so we watch The Hacks' set from the side of the stage. Although I can't repay Tyler's gesture and sing any of their songs, I try my best to enjoy and find one that I like. It's no easy task, I have to admit. Most of their songs are so sugary I fear I'll get a cavity by the end of the night. But they do have the odd-one-out, a few ones talking about life and loss, heartbreak and growing up—these are the ones I identify with. As I pay attention to their lyrics, it becomes clear they have more than one writer, the same way they have more than one person taking care of their social media. It's impossible that the same person that writes about how their soulmate is a perfect inhuman being is the same one that describes the pain of being misunderstood. I make a mental note to ask them about it later.

We're all in a high when the concert ends, so we decide to go out to celebrate. In a club. Dancing and drinking. I'm never one to pass on a night out, but even I know this sort of activity can't end up well. We all go, anyway, directly from the venue, because I suspect everyone knows we're going to change our minds if we have a chance to wind down.

We end up in a pretty popular club. It's so crowded that we have to jump off the cabs two blocks away, and walk through a corridor of paparazzi before entering. I know they're not there for The Hacks, but they recognize and take photos of them anyway. This seems to make Todd and Tristan a little uneasy, but Tyler is as unfazed as ever.

We are greeted inside by the loudest of music and the brightest of lights. The heat of the bodies crammed together hits us in a big wave, and I'm instantly transported to a parallel universe. This is what I like about these places—nothing feels real. You get to be whoever and do whatever, nobody notices, nobody will remember. I can stand in the middle of the dance floor and scream at the top of my lungs and no one will even flinch. I know it because I have done it. More than once.

After taking a few steps towards the bar, I notice I'm already lost. I turn around to try to locate someone of our crew when I feel a warm hand rest on the back of my neck.

"What is your poison?" Tyler asks, making me turn around again. He's so close I almost head-butt him.

"How old are you, 60?" I joke, but he apparently doesn't find it funny. "Anything mixed with vodka."

He says something that I don't hear and walks to the bar. His tall and skinny frame seems to make way easier than I would, so I don't follow him. I turn around again, trying to locate Pete, or anyone, but still can't. I start to retrace my steps and get to the back of the room, but I move very slowly.

"Here," someone screams and grabs my hand. It's Tyler again.

He pushes me through the crowd to one side until we have enough room to stand two inches apart. He hands me a glass—one of two that he was holding with just one hand. He has big hands. And long fingers.

"Cheers?" He raises his glass to me, a question in his eyes. "That's how you say it here, right?"

"Right." I nod once. "Cheers!"

I take a sip of my drink, which is too sweet for my taste, and watch as Tyler downs his in three long gulps. For all I know, it could be water.

"How do you say it in America?" I ask when he's finished.

"Cheers." He raises his eyebrows and smirks. I feel my lips curl up and start to look around again. I need to find Pete.

"Do you dance?" he asks again to my ear. He's close enough that I can smell the alcohol in his warm breath.

"Not really," I shake my head, not turning around this time. "Do you see Pete?"

"The alcohol is supposed to help," he says, making me turn back around. His smirk is still firm in place, and he adds, "With the nerves, you know."

Oh, boy.

I look down at my glass, tapping a nervous finger against it. I *do* know what he means. But I can't. Maybe if we were in a different situation, a different place, a different moment, I wouldn't be thinking twice. We're not, though. And I am thinking twice. I can't.

"It's not gonna happen," I blurt out, looking back at him.

His crooked smile disappears with this. He frowns, kind of confused at first, but then in understanding. I have a feeling I misinterpreted his intentions, but now it's too late. Why is he so hard to read? He's cocky and aggressive one minute, and sweet and attentive the next. And then we have this whole weird situation we're in—what kind of relationship are we supposed to have? Is he my boss in a way? Can we be friends? Is it okay for me to flirt with him in a night club?

He opens his mouth to say something but gives up before any sound escapes it. He looks away, seemingly frustrated, and when he looks back, it's not nice Tyler anymore.

"I'm gonna go get another," he says, raising his empty glass and walking away.

I watch as he slowly disappears through the crowd. I debate whether I should stay around and see if he'll come back, or if I should go after him. I decide to follow my original plan and walk towards the back of the club. If we're not talking, we're not fighting—or doing other things—and I'm positive this counts as behaving. Right?

It's with much effort that I reach the back wall. I lean beside a couple making out and finish my drink. There's a little platform to the side where people are dancing on. I decide to get up there and see if I can find Pete.

I look directly at the dance floor since I know he likes to dance. I don't see him, but I locate someone else, his blond head standing out under the stroboscope light. He's dancing. It's different than the way he moves on stage. Some girl gets close. He lets her run her hands through his silky hair. She pushes him closer, her hands disappearing down south. I can't see what she's doing, but I can have a pretty good idea by how Tyler's eyes react. She smiles. He suddenly grabs her neck and ferociously devours her face. It's kind of gross. Even at a distance, I can see their tongues move in an unsynchronized motion.

A second girl approaches them from behind, embracing him by the waist. One of his hands moves to her hair, while she kisses his neck. I'm revolted, but I can't stop looking. And then I wonder if he knows I'd see it. And then I sigh at my arrogance. Really? Do I really think he's doing that to get to me? I don't even think he meant what I thought he meant. And judging by the girls he's making out with now, I'm definitely not his type.

I step down and decide to make my way to the exit. I'll text Pete and ask him to meet me outside when he's ready to go.

Somehow, the place seems to be even more crowded now. I make my way slowly, trying not to step on anyone's toes.

"Becky!" I hear Pete's voice to my left, but the only thing I can see is his tattoed hand waving in the air.

I try to turn towards him but the crowd is too thick. It's like everyone is pulling in the opposite direction I want to go.

"Becky!" Pete calls again, his hand closer.

He's the one to get to me. His eyes are wild, which makes me preoccupied. He seizes my hand and starts pulling me. Hard. I want to shout for him to calm down, but then I look to the dance floor again.

It's mayhem. There are security guards rudely shoving people aside, trying to get to someone. Is someone ill? Is someone *hurt*? What happened?

I cling to Pete's arm as if my life depends on it—which it probably does—and he steadily guides me to the exit. When we're almost out, I turn around again. Now I can see Tyler being dragged out by three of the security guards. I can't locate the other boys and can't help the overwhelming feeling of concern.

Once outside, Neil comes up from nowhere and shoves us both inside a cab, where Paul and Todd are already waiting. We immediately drive off and I turn around to try and see something.

"That was... crazy!" Pete exclaims.

"Could be worse," Todd says in a seemingly calm tone that makes me turn around again.

"How often does this happen?" Pete asks, voicing my curiosity.

"At least once per tour," Paul chuckles. "We still have five shows, right? I trust this will happen at least once more."

"Once?" Todd frowns. "I'll bet on three."

"That's really pessimistic," Paul remarks.

"Yeah, but you know Tyler," Todd continues.

"Okay, I'll raise mine to twice," Paul says after giving the matter some thought. "Do you wanna bet?" he then addresses

Pete and I, who had been watching the interaction with our mouths gaping open.

"I don't feel I have the necessary knowledge to do that," Pete says nonchalantly, and they both laugh.

They then start telling some of the horrific situations Tyler has put them in, some of which remind me of a lot of things I've done, and I stop listening. I feel uncomfortable. I feel I'm intruding. I feel he wouldn't like them to share these things, as much as I wouldn't like Pete talking about my past mistakes with so little regard. Like I wouldn't care. Or not caring if I would care. And then I start panicking. Would he ever do that? Has he ever done that?

We arrive back at the venue, where our bus is parked waiting for us. I let Paul and Todd hop on first, holding Pete back.

"Would you ever do that?" I ask bluntly.

"Do what?" he frowns.

"Bet. On me being an asshole."

"Of course not, are you even serious?" His eyes widen and the genuine shock of his expression makes me relax. "Mostly because I'd have no one to bet against me," he adds and I punch his shoulder.

"Idiot."

"I'd never do that to you, Becks." He squeezes my hand, which is still holding his in a death grip. "That's just plain cruel."

"I know, right?" I agree and can't help but wonder if that's part of the reason why Tyler is an asshole sometimes. I can't help but wonder who might be his Pete, or whether he even has a friend like that. I hope he does.

"Stop thinking about him," Pete interrupts my thoughts.

"Who?" I widen my eyes, trying to sound surprised. In vain, of course.

"I know you, Rebecca. Too well."

But I can't stop thinking about him.

✳DAY FOUR✳

I'M BACK AT THE CLUB. THE MUSIC IS LOUD AND PEOPLE AROUND ME are dancing, their bodies whacking and pushing me. I try to walk away, but I can't move. Every time I try to take a step, someone gets in the way. I'm getting frustrated, shouting for people to make way, but nobody listens. I turn to the other side, and see him—Tyler. He's really close, but he doesn't see me. Suddenly, two faceless girls approach him and they start to make out like I witnessed earlier. Only, this time, they take it further and start undressing. To my surprise, nobody seems bothered by it.

I turn around again, trying to escape the disturbing scene in front of me, but he's there again. He's dancing with a different girl, running his hands down her body. She does the same, glancing at me sideways while she does so. I want to shout that I don't care, but no voice comes out.

I turn my back to them, but there he is again. Twerking. Humping. Sticking his tongue down someone's throat.

I shut my eyes tight, cursing him. When I open them again, I'm sitting at the piano. I look around—I'm on stage, in front of a whole crowd. Everyone is looking at me. And I don't know what to do. I can't play. I forgot how. Someone puts their hands on my shoulder and I startle awake.

I almost hit my head on the bunk ceiling, a little disoriented by the strange dreams. *For fuck's sake*, I grumble in thought. Pete was right, I have to stop thinking about him.

I hear the bus door open and close. We're parked. My phone tells me it's almost 9 in the morning. I'm not sure if we've arrived in Cardiff or are still halfway there. I debate getting up as my body aches from all the twisting and turning of the night, but then I hear someone say my name in the backroom.

"Keep it down!" someone hushes the voice. I can't tell who it is.

"Relax, she's asleep," the voice that said my name argues.

"She won't be if you keep saying her name." Now I recognize Todd's mocking tone.

"Becky, Becky, Becky!" the first voice repeats, in *moaning*. My heart races. I'm nauseous. I turn around and move closer to the edge of the bunk, trying to hear them more clearly.

"You're disgusting," a third person says, and I'm almost sure it's Tristan.

"Come on! Don't tell me you wouldn't tap that?" *Tap that?* I dig my fingers into the mattress, resisting the urge to get down and fly to his throat.

"Shut up, Paul!" Tristan's voice rises up a notch. Paul. The drum tech. *Ugh*. He's a dead man.

"Oh, right, I forgot. *Pete* is more of your type," he says and starts to laugh. My heart starts beating in reverse.

"Shut the fuck up!" Tristan talks again and I hear some hustling.

"Hey, now," Todd interrupts again.

"Relax, I'm just joking with you," the dead man says.

"You know I don't like it," Tristan hisses.

The next words are said too low for me to listen. I'm utterly disgusted. Though I should have known something like this would happen, sooner or later. What would be the odds that all these males would be decent humans?

I take a deep breath, trying to decide what to do. There's no way I'll be able to keep it inside. I *shouldn't* be able to keep it inside. But *what* should I do? Do this qualify as harassment? Dammit. I need to talk to Pete.

I'm in the process of texting him when I hear a laugh and Paul's voice, loud and clear again.

"Whatever, that leaves more Becky for me," he says. I can hear him moaning again. My rage peaks.

I can't take it. *Sorry, Pete.*

I jump down my bunk, not even caring I'm only wearing knickers and a t-shirt. It'll add for dramatic effect at the very least.

The laughter stops as soon as they have a glimpse of my disheveled hair and livid face. I take two steps towards them, locking eyes with Paul. I can tell he's already shitting himself before I even open my mouth, which only makes me angrier. Coward.

"If I ever hear your voice again," I pause, taking a deep breath and raising one finger. "I will fucking *kill you*."

I keep my voice as low as I can manage. Menacing is one of very few things I'm good at.

I can't see the other two, but I can tell their mouths are gaping open in shock. I can feel Paul debating whether I'm serious or not—looking like a psychopath has its advantages.

I hold his gaze until he decides it's better to believe me and nods. Then I glare at Todd.

"I'm sorry," he's quick to say. "This will never happen again."

"It better not," I add.

"What is going on?" I hear Pete's voice behind me and my strength immediately starts to crumble. Not because it makes me weak, but because it makes me safe. His voice reminds me I can be vulnerable, which is not what I want right now.

So I turn around, a familiar burn stinging my eyes. I fish for my pants in my bunk. I put them on in front of them. Then I grab my phone and finally turn around, trying to not look directly at Pete. And only then I see everyone else is up and watching what is going on.

My eyes fall on Neil, who takes two steps forward. His jaw is set and his expression is dark.

"I meant it," I manage to tell him.

He just nods. And then I run, already feeling hot tears streaming down my face.

***

I step outside to find we're still parked in the middle of nowhere. I decide this is good, it means there'll be no one around to recognize me or anyone else.

We're at a rest stop. I walk into the mall-sized convenience store with the purpose of a murderer. The bell chimes, but the guy behind the counter doesn't even look up. Good.

The store is otherwise empty, which is also good. I grab hold of a cart and start walking up and down the aisles, shoving everything I can into it with the maximum strength my arms allow. I avoid the bottles, even though I'm in the mood of breaking something, because I know myself—if I start, nothing will be able to stop me. And it will only make things worse.

I'm in the third row when I hear the entrance bell ring again. I turn around, looking for Pete's jet-black hair behind the shelves, but finding light brown curls—it's not Pete. I turn back around as fast as I can when I see Tristan walking into the aisle. I'm still crying, and I hate myself. I hate Pete. Why is it not him? Why would he let someone else come after me?

"Pete asked me to tell you he'll be joining us in five minutes," he says, pausing behind me. He's seen I'm crying, that's why he won't walk around to face me.

"Don't worry, I won't tell him," I decide to give him what he wants at once.

"What?" he sounds confused, but I don't turn around to check.

"What I heard," I explain. "I won't tell him."

"Oh," he says, and then silence. He only talks again when I restart walking and shoving things into the cart. "Actually, I was wondering..." He sounds hopeful and it kind of breaks my heart. I stop again, drying my face and turning around.

"He has a girlfriend," I inform and watch as he deflates.

"Of course he does," he smiles shyly and starts to examine something on the shelf. "A serious girlfriend?"

"I'm afraid so," I take whatever he's looking at and throw it in the cart.

"Do you think he'll change when he finds out?" He turns back to me. "Will he stop hanging out with me?"

"I doubt it," I smile at his juvenile concern. "Although maybe he will be more careful not to break your heart."

"That'll only make things harder for me." He blushes a little and chuckles.

"I know. He's too adorable." I offer some sympathy.

"How did you manage?" he asks, and when I give him a confused look, he adds, "Not falling for him?"

"Well, we were raised as siblings, so that would be weird." I can't even count how many times I've repeated this sentence. But this time, for some reason, I add, "And I don't deserve him. I'd ruin him. I ruin everyone. I'd never do that to him."

I don't know why I say that. I turn around before I can gauge Tristan's reaction and start to walk again. But I don't want to throw things into the cart anymore. The rage is gone. The tears are gone. I'm empty.

Tristan walks by my side, staring at the pile of garbage I gathered.

"You remind me of Tyler, sometimes," he says casually, quickly adding, "Please, don't take offense on that."

"I can't make any promises," I joke as images of him twerking flash in my mind.

"I wish I was as close with him as you are with Pete," he sighs, looking away as we take a turn to enter another aisle.

"Well, maybe Pete could give you some tips." I wink when he looks at me and he smiles again. "I'm pretty sure he has a very detailed manual of how to deal with me."

We walk in silence along the remaining aisles. Tristan adds some things to the cart, and I wonder if he's planning to actually buy them, since I wasn't.

"I'm sorry, by the way," he says after a while. "For all... that."

I don't know what to say. I mean, I know what I *want* to say: your brother is trash and where the fuck did you find this Paul character? I don't, though. I'm just relieved that at least one of them isn't a complete lost cause.

More than five minutes go by until we finally hear the entrance bell again. Pete finds us and points at the cart with a curious look.

"Anger management," I say, and he nods slowly.

"Come on, breakfast is on me," Tristan offers, pushing the cart towards the cashier.

"I'm not going to buy those!" I try to stop him.

"I am," he gives me that wide, full-of-teeth grin and doesn't accept my protests.

"We'll wait outside," Pete announces, pulling me by the hand.

As soon as we step out, I blurt, "I'm fine."

"Okay," he nods, not entirely believing me. "But, you know, if you want to—"

"I'm not going to give up," I interrupt him. "Not now, when I finally started having fun."

"Okay," he nods again, still frowning. "But I was going to say that if you really want to murder him, I'll help you get rid of the body."

His delivery is so intense that I have to look around to make sure no one is within listening range. Then I laugh.

"I wouldn't expect anything different from you," I say, and he pulls me into a hug. "How much of it did you hear?"

"Not much," I feel him shrug. "But Todd kind of told us what happened."

"Everything?" I ask, pulling away to see his face. "Including..." I glance at the shop door.

"What about him?" he asks, the frown back on his face.

Shit. I just told Tristan I wouldn't tell Pete. And here I am, on the verge of telling Pete. I bite my lower lip, unsure of how to proceed. It's already too late to make something up. Not that he would believe me, anyway.

"I can't tell you," I say at last.

"What?" he gasps in fake shock. "You tell me everything!"

"Yes, but this isn't about me," I explain.

His joking expression changes as he glances at the shop door again. The curiosity and doubt give way to certainty. He even nods a little, almost imperceptible.

"You know," I accuse him.

"Know what?" he asks bewildered, confirming my suspicions.

"Pete!"

"I have no idea what you're talking about!" he argues. "I can't read your mind, so unless you tell me with words what you're implying, I can neither confirm or deny knowing about anything."

"Tristan has a crush on you," I spell it out. I can tell he didn't expect me to do it. But his prolonged silence tells me I was right—he knew. "Pete!"

"Okay, okay, I kind of suspected," he confesses.

"And when were you planning to tell me?" I cross my arms.

"Never?" He scrunches up his nose.

"Pete!" I try to punch him, but he's faster than me and dodges my fist.

"What? I just didn't want you..." he pauses, clearly choosing his words. "... assuming things."

"Why would I assume things?" I narrow my eyes.

"Because we're hanging out a lot."

"I wouldn't assume anything," I say offended. He must know me better than that. Unless... "Unless there's reason to assume."

"There's none," he says loudly. A little *too* loudly.

"Pete..." I take one step towards him.

"Seriously, now." He regains his composure. "I have a girlfriend."

"A girlfriend that's been quite absent," I think out loud. The hurt look he gives me makes everything click together—his unusual silences, his jittery nerves, his avoidance of me. "You're fighting."

"I don't want to talk about it," he mutters, annoyed.

"Clearly," I say bitterly. "Not with me, anyway."

"What do you mean?"

"Well, you've been spending an awful lot of time with Tristan."

"Yeah, playing videogames!" he argues.

"Right," I snort.

"He distracts me," he sighs. "I don't really think about Linds and how stupid I was when I'm around him."

I study him, not quite sure I believe this reasoning. But I know that if there's any more to it, he'll just blurt it out if I hold my tongue. That's his way of dealing with uncomfortable silences—sharing all his thoughts, unfiltered.

"He also has a killer smile," he adds after a minute, as I knew he would.

"Oh my God..."

"It's a fact," he argues, blushing a little. "He does. Not even you can deny it."

"Yeah, well... I can't," I admit. It *is* a killer smile, what can I say?

We stand there, just staring at each other for a while. Then I walk over and hug him by the waist. He hugs me back, resting his head on top of mine. I hate it when he tries to keep me out. He thinks he's protecting me when, in reality, he's just hurting me. And himself.

On the other hand, though, there's nothing I could really do to help. I'm not the most suitable person to be giving out relationship advice.

"Are you really okay?" he asks softly. I hate this, too. I hate how he's always worried about me.

"I will be," I answer because no, I'm *not* okay. I don't think I'm ever okay. But I also can't lie to him.

"I love you, Becks."

"I know."

Our moment is interrupted by Tristan stepping out of the store with a dozen of bags. Pete rushes to help him out and... he smiles. Pete shoots me *a look*. I roll my eyes, but laugh. Maybe I need someone to distract me, too. God knows I'd love a few moments outside my own head.

***

When we're finally back in the bus, Neil asks to talk to me alone. I can see some of the guys in the back room. Some are nowhere to be seen.

He demands to know what happened—apparently Todd and Paul didn't give him details. Obviously, they wouldn't. So I tell him, but only the part that involves me.

"What would you like me to do?" he asks.

I don't know. I don't know what he means. What *can* he do?

"Do you want him gone?" he asks after a while, which surprises me a little bit.

I actually would love him gone, but then I start to think of the *implications*. What would it mean for me and Pete? How would this impact the rest of our tour? What good having the drum tech gone would actually make?

I chew on my thumb nail as I think. I replay the whole thing in my mind and slowly start to convince myself it wasn't *that* serious. He didn't touch me. He didn't even talk to me. I wasn't supposed to hear what he said. Of course, none of it invalidates my right to be mad. But let's be real for a second—if I have him punished, I'll quickly become the villain. I'm still the only girl around trying to make it in a male-dominated industry. Maybe showing a little mercy now will demonstrate I have enough of a thick skin to deal with this type of situation.

"No," I say, then. "But on one condition—he can't talk to me."

"Consider it done," Neil nods once, and then leaves the bus.

I sit there alone for a while, debating whether it was the right decision. Christ, how I miss having someone to just tell me what to do. How I miss having someone to point me in the right direction. How I miss my dad.

I really need to find something to distract me, fast.

Neil comes back with the missing boys and Paul walks past me without a second glance. *Good*, I think. But as I hear them preparing to play videogame in the back of the bus, I decide that's not enough. I'm not gonna make things easy for him. So, I get up and join them, making a point of sitting across the asshole and glaring. After a few minutes, he and Todd leave for the kitchen to play cards.

"Chicken shit," I snort. I feel better, although I'm surprisingly deeply disappointed in Todd. Who knew that he would turn out to be the jerk brother?

"He can't talk to you," Pete says, not knowing it was my idea.

"Lucky me! This tour is about to get 200% better," I say full of sarcasm.

"I wouldn't count on that," Tyler says, smirking as he gets up and heads towards the corridor. "*I* can still talk to you."

I follow him with my eyes until he disappears, trying my best not to smile. Maybe I can think of something to forbid him to talk to me, too. Although... I'm not really sure I want that.

I can see Pete staring at me from the corner of my eye, so I decide to head back to my bunk. We still have a couple of hours before we get to the venue and all I can think about is sleeping.

***

I don't, though. Twerking Tyler keeps threatening to make a comeback into my dreams, so I just spend my time on the Internet. I update the band's Instagram, like some comments on Twitter, and try to find any articles about last night. There are none. I'm quite surprised since the whole commotion caused quite a scene and there was a lot of paparazzi outside.

Someone is clearly doing a good job of keeping the incident under wraps.

We arrive at the venue a few hours after we had planned. Our instruments are all set up already, but everyone decides to have lunch before jumping into rehearsal. I decide to skip it. My stomach is uneasy due to, well, everything, plus I really need some time alone. I need to regroup, to think, to put my feelings in order. I can't do that when I'm surrounded by people. I'm not used to being surrounded by so many people at all times. I'm not used to people.

I wander off the dressing room and into the arena. This one has the best acoustics yet. There's no one around, so I take the opportunity to scream at the top of my lungs. The sound bounces off the walls like rubber. I walk to another corner and scream again. The same magical reflection occurs. I always wonder how they do that. How is it possible to have such great clarity in every corner of a room?

I walk up to the stage and scream from there. It's therapeutic. I wait for a few minutes to see if anyone has heard it and is coming to see what has possessed me. When nobody shows up, I decide to take my chances on the piano again. I've been dying to have a chance at it without Harvard-expert-Tyler watching and judging me.

I sit on the leather stool and let my fingers run up and down the scale. I play the pop version of *She's Not Mine*. I'm still very much rusty. My hands are stiff, like I'm banging a plank of wood on the delicate keys of the Yamaha. If I was Tyler, I'd be concerned to let me use it, too.

I try to play some of my other songs, but can't seem to find the right notes. I try to play some of the songs I like, but they also don't sound right. I stop and take a deep breath. I know what I have to play. I know how to make my joints warm up. But there's still a part of me resisting.

I hold my hands up, above the keys. I can hear the first note before I hit them. Then I just give up. *Fine. I'll play it.*

Clair de Lune was the first song I ever wanted to learn because it was my father's favorite. It was the song I played the most because of the same reason. I will never forget the way he looked at me when I did. Which is exactly why I didn't want to play it now. Or ever again.

"Interesting choice," Tyler's voice startles me and I stop. My heart races and I notice, embarrassed, that I'm on the verge of tears. Again.

"Good God, why do you keep doing this?"

"Doing what?" he asks, and I hear his footsteps approaching.

"Just... never mind." I shake my head and concentrate on the keys. I don't want to leave. But I don't want to continue.

"You've had lessons." It's not a question. Of course he would know, he's probably studied piano, too.

"Yeah," I nod, turning to look at him. He looks amused.

"I've never had the hands for Debussy," he says and, suddenly, he's seated on the stool with me.

He starts playing the same song and, indeed, it doesn't sound nearly as elegant as it should be. The thought that he might be doing that on purpose occurs to me, but I think again. It's Tyler. He wouldn't do that.

"You sound like an elephant playing piano," I joke when he stops.

"You sound like my piano teacher," he smiles. "Beethoven is my guy."

He starts playing *Für Elise*.

"Ugh, such an obvious choice." I roll my eyes.

"Oof. Tough crowd tonight."

He then changes to the *Moonlight Sonata*. It's as soft as *Clair de Lune*, but he's way better at this one.

I watch his bare long fingers slowly move over the keys. It's hard to believe these are the same hands that bang pop music every night. Well, at least he's still doing it. At least he can still do it. I wonder what my father would think if he could see me now. What would he say about my purple hair, my loud guitar, my tight clothes. What would he say about what happened on the bus. Or on every other occasion I felt so small I could barely breathe.

"Hey." Tyler bumps his shoulder into mine. He has stopped playing. I'm still staring at the keys. "Are you okay?"

"Yep. Yes." I stutter, embarrassed. As if I needed one more reason for him to think I'm crazy. "Just lost in the song."

I can feel him nodding. I can feel him staring. I can feel he has something to say.

I want to leave. I want to hide. I want to cry. But I don't move. He doesn't, too.

"What else have you got?" he asks after some time.

I feel like the weight of the world is lifted from my shoulders. I feel like... he gets it. Even though he didn't say anything. Even though he didn't ask anything. I look at him again. He's still studying my face.

"Maybe some Vivaldi?" He wiggles his eyebrows and I smile.

And we spend the next hour showing each other our knowledge of classical piano. Maybe those twelve years weren't so useless, after all.

***

We have quite a successful concert, all things considered. Our joint set runs more smoothly tonight—we play better, and the crowd enjoys it more. I'm still surprised to see them singing my song. It's quite a rush.

Today, Pete and I have a green card to work at the merch booth with Seth. I think it's Neil's way of keeping us away from Paul. I can't complain.

"We're almost out of EPs!" Seth informs us cheerfully. "Thank God we'll have some days off, it'll give Neil time to order more."

"Our EPs?" I ask in disbelief.

"Yep, lass. Look!"

I walk to our side of the table, surveying the boxes beneath it. Sure enough, there are only a handful of EPs left. The stock of mugs and t-shirts is not too different. I still can barely believe we have merch to sell and it's all already almost gone.

"Let's see if we can sell them all by the end of the night," Pete winks.

And from then on, he shouts at everyone who's close enough to hear him, chatting them up until they buy a damn EP. I'm always stunned by how charming he is, how people warm up to him almost immediately, how he can get them to do what he wants. It's almost like magic. Sometimes I think the universe brought us together to balance itself out.

A group of girls—clearly our fans—come over when they see we're at the table. They buy stuff, we sign it for them and take pictures. They hang out for a bit, asking questions and making fun of The Hacks. I laugh at their accurate remarks while Pete tries to defend them.

Then, suddenly, out of nowhere, one of them asks, "Is it true that you and Tyler are having a fling?"

"A what?" My eyes almost pop out of their sockets.

"Come on," the girls says, a little embarrassed now. "He's a pop princess, but no one will judge you."

"From where did you get that idea?" I snap.

She laughs nervously, apologizes and then leaves with her friends.

"Smooth," Pete shoots me a dirty look.

"What?" I snap at him now. "Am I supposed to humor this nonsense?"

"You could just laugh it off," he says. I snort. "I think I know where this came from."

He gets his phone, tapping here and there with his thumb, and then hands it to me. It's a page filled with text.

Becky watched closely as his arm muscles flexed and contracted while he ran his long, calloused fingers over the piano keys, his shiny, smooth hair falling over his face. She couldn't help but imagine what would it feel like to have him run those same fingers over her body—

"What *is* this?" I turn the phone back to him, appalled and disgusted.

"I believe it's called fanfiction," he says, struggling to keep a straight face.

"Why the *fuck* are you reading fanfiction?" I demand.

"I wasn't reading it," he argues. "I just stumbled upon it."

"How?"

"I... it's just..." he stutters, making me very suspicious. Was he *looking* for fanfiction? What the hell? "It's everywhere!"

"It's not—"

"And some of it is actually good," he cuts me off.

"*What?!*"

"Listen," he takes the phone back from me and starts to read. "*The wind blew softly on her purple hair, making it fall over her big, almond eyes. The sight made Tyler chuckle. He reached over, trying to tuck her short strands behind her ear. She yelped, taken by surprised but Tyler didn't remove his hand from her smooth hair. Their eyes locked together for a second and—*"

"Stop!" I yell. I don't want to know what comes next. "That's disturbing!"

"It's cute!" He pouts.

"And what's up with all this smooth hair falling over eyes? Eek!" I fake a shudder, ignoring him.

"Your hair is pretty smooth," he says, now only to annoy me. "I bet Tyler's is, too."

"Shut up," I hiss.

"Oh, please, don't tell me you wouldn't let Tyler tuck your hair behind your ear," he raises his eyebrows.

"I wouldn't let Tyler anywhere *near* my hair," I answer. If those fans knew me at all, they'd know I hate when people touch my hair.

"Hmmm..." Pete narrows his eyes. "Do you think he'd let you near his hair?"

"Pete!" I try to make him stop before Seth thinks we're on drugs or something.

"They have really good hair." But he doesn't stop.

"Pete!" I try to cast a furtive glance at Seth and maybe make him understand.

"They do, look at them," he insists, pointing to the stage.

I don't want to look, but it's stronger than me. I look over. They *do* have good hair. I'm actually quite envious of Tyler's golden, smooth locks. Smooth! Goddammit. I'm already infected by that horrid text.

"Do you think *Tristan* would let you touch his hair?" I turn back to Pete, attempting to throw him off for a change.

"Honey, I *know* he would," he answers confidently.

I observe him as he bobs his head to their annoying song. I know it's true, Tristan would more than likely let Pete touch more than just his hair. Does Pete *want* to, though?

When The Hacks end their set, Neil gathers us backstage to say he's booked a hotel for the night, changing our plans once again. We were originally supposed to continue the trip to Manchester tonight and spend our three days off there. I wonder if this has anything to do with me and what happened earlier in the day. Either way, I'm not going to complain—the prospect of sleeping on a real bed is more than enough to lift my spirits.

We hang out for a while, waiting for the crowd to thin out. Tristan invites everyone over to his room to, guess what? Play videogames. He keeps nagging me to show up and I end up saying I will. But I won't. I know this is part of the job—meeting people, talking to people, being agreeable to people. It's just not in my DNA. My thing is to perform—being on stage gives me a high nothing else does. It's something I know in my bones I'll never get tired of doing. Dealing with the rest of it is Pete's thing.

Plus, without me around, Tristan will probably have a better chance of flirting with my friend.

***

I take the longest shower I've taken in days and put on my comfies. I lie on the bed and turn my phone off to avoid possible calls and my social media. Now I'm actually afraid of this whole theory of me and Tyler having a fling. I doubt anyone can have an affair with him, anyway. He strikes me more like the one-night-stand type of guy. I recall the bizarre scene of him groping those girls in the club—and then twerking in my dreams—and can't help but wonder if he even makes it worth it for them.

'*Stop thinking about him,*' Pete's voice plays in my head.

I'm really not looking forward to having him visit me in my dreams again, so I try to follow this command. I close my eyes, taking a few deep breaths, enjoying the silence and the dark.

My ears are ringing. My muscles are tense. I still have too much energy from the concert running through me.

I sit up again and briefly consider going to the little gathering in Tristan's room. I walk to the window to open it up and shiver a little with the rush of cold air that comes in. The sky is clear and there is no moon, so I can see a few stars here and there. And then I decide that's what I need—star gazing and alcohol.

I grab a few of the bottles from the minibar and walk out of the room. I round the building and climb the fire escape ladder to the roof. The floor is filthy, but I don't mind. I walk to the edge and sit with my legs dangling out. I feel like a child again. I can't even begin to count how many times I did this back home. Sitting on the roof and telling my dreams to the stars was my favorite thing. There were a lot more back then, though. Stars and dreams. Over time, they just faded away. One by one, they were slowly quenched. I can't remember which ones were lost. I can't tell if I care. Which is probably the worst part of it all.

"Are you gonna jump?" a hoarse voice startles me and I almost do fall.

"Fucking hell!" I shout.

"I'll take that as a no," Tyler adds and sits beside me on the edge of the roof. Uninvited. He points to my mini bottles forming a line of liquid happiness and asks, "May I?"

"No," I say. He frowns, but a small smile plays on his lips. "What are you doing here?"

"What are *you* doing here?" he returns the question, shamelessly taking notice of what I'm wearing.

"I asked first," I argue childishly.

"I saw you. I thought you were going to jump," he says.

"You didn't think I was going to jump," I roll my eyes.

"But I did see you," he says as his smile brightens. I notice this is happening more often. I don't smile back. "What are you doing here?"

"Looking at the stars," I say, looking back up.

"What stars?" he snorts and follows my gaze up to the sky.

I open one of the bottles, taking a sip and trying to remember the names of the constellations. When I was a kid, my dad would quiz me about them. I could point them out even in clouded nights. Now they escape me. Like everything else.

"I count a total of three," Tyler speaks again.

"When your eyes adjust to the dark you'll see more," I say, taking another sip from my bottle. It's all it takes to finish its contents.

Neither of us speaks for a long time, sitting in silence and dangling our feet in the air. It is surprisingly comfortable. Of all the people to be in silence with, who knew Tyler would make it so enjoyable. Granted, he's far more enjoyable with his mouth shut anyway.

"I can see more now," he breaks the silence. I look at him—he is really looking at the sky. I don't know why, but that makes me smile. He looks back at me and catches me staring. "What?"

Despite my best judgment, I motion towards the bottles. He narrows his eyes suspiciously, but takes one. After opening, he hands it to me and then opens another. We clink it together before drinking.

"Why are you not at the party?" I ask.

"I don't really like parties," he answers, holding my stare.

"Really? It didn't look like it the other night in the club," I continue, already feeling the alcohol work in my blood.

"That's not really a party. Parties, originally, involve social engagement. In clubs there's rarely any interaction. I can barely hear my own thoughts," he explains.

"That's what I like about clubs," I confess. He turns to me with a confused look, so I clarify, "That I can't hear my own thoughts."

"Why are you not at the party?" he asks.

"I don't really like parties," I repeat his words and grin. He grins back, slow and wide. And then stares at my lips.

Fuck. What am I doing? I look away, trying to think of a way to get out of the roof.

"Or any social interaction," Tyler adds.

"You're observant," I comment.

"I told you, I see you," he says and my stomach flutters, even though it's a lousy pick-up line.

I decide to ignore him. If I keep my mouth shut and my eyes on the sky, I'll be fine. So that's what I do.

To my surprise—or disappointment, I can't tell—he doesn't say another word. We stay in the roof until we finish drinking all the bottles and then he helps me down the stairs so I don't fall on my face. We walk together down the corridor to our rooms and when we part ways, he just mumbles a weak 'good night'.

I lie back on my bed, full of confusion. Maybe I'm reading him all wrong. Maybe he's not interested at all. Am I, though? Should I?

Stop thinking about him.
No can do, now. I think I found my distraction.

*DAY FIVE

I START MY FIRST DAY OFF WITH A BATH. YES, THERE'S A BATHTUB IN the room and I take full advantage of it. I wish I had had the spirit to have bought a bath bomb, but as soon as I lower my aching body down into the steaming hot water, I decide it doesn't matter—it's going to be relaxing either way.

I rest my phone on the floor beside me, ignoring all the notifications I have, and watch baking contest videos until the water gets cold. I take a shower and for the first time in days think about the clothes I'm going to wear. The cold is picking up, so I put on thick woolen tights beneath my black jeans shorts and my favorite gray hoodie. I ditch my usual boots for sneakers today, since I'm planning to go out and explore the city.

I spend twenty minutes blow-drying my hair to shape my curls, and then maybe the same amount of time doing my make-up. Again, for the first time in days, I'm satisfied with the result.

I like having time to get ready. Not that I care that much about how I look, it's just that the time I spend layering stuff on my face and customizing my outfits relaxes me. Whenever I'm too concentrated trying to make my eyeliner even or knitting the perfect skull on a t-shirt I don't have time to think of anything else. I don't have time to be nervous. And I like not being nervous. I like the sense of being in control, that whatever the day throws my way, I'll be able to deal with it. It's not true most of the time. I still like the feeling, though.

Before getting out, I finally pick up my phone from the bathroom floor where I left it. Among the notifications, there are several texts from Pete.

'BECKY! I need to talk to you'

'Sorry, good morning, sunshine. How are you feeling this fine morning?'

'PICK UP YOUR PHONE!'

'I'm banging at your door, how can you still be asleep?'

'Going for breakie, meet me there'

'They have cinnamon rolls, wake up!'

'Ran into Tris, we're heading out, DO NOT DARE TO JUDGE ME'

'Update: ran into everyone else, we're all going out. Hope you're happy YOU WITCH'

'We're already lost. It was nice knowing you, we had a good run, goodbye'

I chuckle with his drama and text back.

'Leaving in my white horse right now, don't fret!'

I chuck the phone into my black leather backpack and step out of the room. It's only after I lock my door that I notice Tyler standing in front of the elevator. Apparently, Pete's 'everyone else' didn't include him. I freeze, debating what to do, as I'm not really sure how to act after last night. Should I keep my distance? Should I be friendly? Is he thinking of me as much as I'm thinking of him?

Before I can decide whether to run back to my room, the lift doors open and he steps inside, finally seeing me when he turns around. He's surprisingly not wearing sunglasses, so I have a clear vision of his blue eyes locking on me.

"Are you coming?" he asks as he holds the doors open.

"Yep." I throttle towards him, deciding there's no point in avoiding him.

The trip down the three floors is rather silent. I keep glancing at him, debating whether to say something, even just a 'good morning', but nothing comes out. When we reach the ground floor, he turns to head to the restaurant and I decide to go towards the exit.

"Where are you going?" he asks when I'm about five steps away from freedom.

"I'm going to meet Pete." I turn around to find an inquisitive expression on his face.

"Don't you want to eat first?" he asks, taking a look at his watch. "We have about twenty minutes."

"Uh, sure, I could eat," I say. Even though I don't want to, I can't say no.

"Do you know where they are?" he asks as we walk to the restaurant.

"Pete said they're lost," I inform and he snorts.

"Great."

We fill our plates quickly—unfortunately there are no cinnamon rolls left—and sit together. I observe him while he eats and scrolls through his phone. The restaurant is in an open area and even though it's a really cold day, the sun is out, which makes Tyler squint because of the brightness. Every now and then he runs a hand through his hair to push it away from his face, which is useless, since it is so silky—so *smooth*—that it doesn't sit in place not even for a second.

Do you think he'd let you near his hair? Damn you Pete. It's totally his fault that now I want to.

"Do you have something on your mind?" he asks suddenly, still not taking his eyes off his phone. Crap. I've been staring for way too long.

"Where are your sunglasses?" I manage to ask and earn a surprised look.

"That's a good question." He rests his phone on the table, giving me his full attention. Again, crap. "I don't know where I left them."

"I thought you never took them off your face," I say, hurrying to finish my eggs.

"You noticed," he smirks.

"Just because it's ridiculous," I blurt. Crap. Crap, crap, crap.

His eyes widen in surprise. I can't hold his gaze, so I avert my eyes towards my half-empty plate.

"So, you think I'm ridiculous," he says after a while.

"Not you, just..." I risk looking at him again. He's naturally not pleased with this conversation. "Just the whole sunglasses indoors is a bit too..."

"Too rock'n'roll?"

"Too diva."

He snorts, looking around the same way he did in the club. I'm sure he has a good comeback but, unlike me, he does a better job of holding his tongue.

"Ridiculous and a diva," he nods, looking back at me. "Anything else?"

"No, I think that's about it," I say, trying to make it sound like a joke. By the look on his face, I'm not successful. So, I resort to eating in silence under his glaring blue gaze.

After a minute or two, he speaks again. "Do you ever regret the things you say?"

First, I'm a bit offended by the question. But, on second thought, what right do I have to be offended when I just offended him for no reason at all? I swallow my pride and decide to take my guard down a bit.

"Just 99% of the time," I confess.

"Really?" he sounds skeptical. "You never apologize."

"Because there's no point," I explain.

"How so?" he asks, frowning, more curious than angry now.

"Apologizing won't change the fact that I said shit. It won't make people forget it. It's done."

"But it makes them aware that you didn't really mean it," he argues.

"But... I really do mean it. I just regret that I say it out loud."

His mouth gapes open for a few seconds, and then he starts to laugh, which takes me aback. I'm not sure if he thinks I'm joking or if he thinks I'm not. It doesn't matter. It makes me smile anyway.

My phone buzzes interrupting the weird moment. It's Pete.

'Did your horse break a leg or something?'

I reply asking where they are and me and Tyler leave to meet them—silent again, but a bit more comfortable now.

***

We end up finding them at a souvenir store in Morgan Quarter, browsing like true tourists—including Pete. He's holding a basket already full of crap, observing intently a shelf of steel cups in the medieval style.

"You're aware these are not antiques, right?" I approach him.

"How would you know? This might have been the cup from where King Arthur had his last sip of wine!" He grabs one at random.

I take it from him and turn it upside down, exposing the 'made in China' tag.

"These are to fool the tourists." He takes the cup from me and throws it in the basket.

"Don't you think you're going a little overboard here?" I point to the pile he's already made.

"It's your fault," he says as he moves to another shelf—mugs. "If I was to depend on you to rescue me, I'd be dead by now."

"I doubt that prince charming over there would let that happen," I tease and he blushes violently.

He pushes my shoulder lightly and stands on the tip of his toes, looking around, probably to make sure our subject matter didn't hear us. When he finds him, he stops and gives me an odd look.

"Speaking of prince charming..." He raises an eyebrow and it's my turn to blush.

"Don't start." I turn to the shelf, picking up a mug at random.

"That's what took you so long?" he asks.

"I didn't take long," I argue.

"Exactly 21 minutes from the time you said you were leaving to the time you actually left," he informs me, making me turn to him again.

"You know, sometimes our relationship worries me," I joke, trying to make him drop it.

"What were you two doing?" he asks and I get angry. I'm both offended and amazed by how well he knows what to expect from me.

"Having breakfast," I say in an outraged tone. That seems to make him back off. I can see he has something else on his mind, but he decides to keep it to himself.

We both look through the colorful mugs together and in silence, and Pete throws a matching 'king & queer' pair in the basket. I laugh.

"What did you want to talk to me about?" I ask. He stiffens. But before he can tell me what it is, his phone rings.

It's his mom. I zone out for a few moments, until I hear him saying, "Yes, she's here."

"Send her my love," I say, as I always do whenever she calls. I watch as his expression drops again with something his mother is telling him. He stops dead in the middle of the aisle, his eyes slowly meeting mine. Color drains from his face.

"Grandma?" I whisper, already feeling my knees giving in.

"She's fine," Pete is quick to say, putting his basket down to grab one of my arms. "She's at the hospital."

"What happened?" I grip his shirt. I only half listen as he repeats his mother's words—something about her falling in the street, her heart and an unknown diagnosis.

"They're going to hold her up until they know more," Pete says, pulling me closer to a half embrace.

Guilt consumes me. My relationship with my grandmother is... complicated. She wasn't prepared to take on the responsibility of raising me, especially not the way it happened. I think it made her a little paranoid. When life became just the two of us, she used to track me down at all times. She would call me at three in the morning to make sure I was okay, even when she knew I was soundly asleep on Pete's floor. I complained a lot, we fought a lot, for this and for several other reasons. But when things got serious, she got my back.

She let me be an angry teenager, she let me drink until I passed out, she let me invest in this music thing. She got me out of trouble. She let me leave—more than once. Sometimes I wonder if I ever would if she had asked me not to. Sometimes I wonder if she wanted me gone.

We don't talk enough, we don't see each other enough, we don't participate in each other's lives anymore. But when things get serious, I got her back.

"Eileen is strong," Pete runs a hand up and down my back.

"I need to see her," I say, pulling away.

"Becky..." Pete shakes his head, ready to give me an extensive list of reasons why I shouldn't make the trip.

"What if this is my last chance?" I don't want to think about it, but I do. People leave me. That's the only constant in my life.

"It's not," Pete sighs, probably already aware it's a lost battle.

"I need to go. If I leave now, I'll probably arrive by tonight. I can meet you up in our next city, we have three days off, I won't even miss any concert," I speak fast, a plan already forming in my mind. I take my phone out of my pocket to start researching bus tickets. The fact that I don't have any missed calls doesn't go unnoticed.

"I'm not worried about the concerts." Pete takes the phone out of my hands.

"I need to go," I say slowly, more and more convinced of it.

"When was the last time you were ever there?" he asks, knowing very well when it had been.

"That's why I need to go!" I argue childishly.

"Go where?" Neil approaches us with a few bags in hand.

"Home," I say and the word sounds so foreign that it feels like it comes out of another person's mouth.

"Oh, Seth is driving back to London—"

"Alnwick," I interrupt him. "My grandmother is hospitalized and I need to see her."

"Wow, wait, what happened?" he asks with genuine concern.

"We don't know yet," Pete answers calmly. "It just happened, they're going to run some tests to find out what's wrong."

"Okay," Neil nods, observing me for a little too long. "Let's get back to the hotel, shall we? Then we can discuss."

He squeezes one of my shoulders and I already know he's not liking the idea of me going anywhere.

I shoot a desperate look at Pete, but he has the same resolution on his face. Fuck it. Fuck them. I'm going and no one will stop me.

***

Back at the hotel, Neil got into a meeting that conveniently lasted the rest of the morning. Tristan was the one that convinced me to wait and talk to him, promising he would help my case. Apparently, I'll need his permission, since he's technically responsible for all of us throughout the duration of the tour—including the days off. It all sounds like bullshit to me, but I decide to try it the 'right' way before flipping everyone off. Neil has been a good boss up until now, besides he's willing to help us, I can't just throw it all in the bin.

So I wait. Impatiently. I sit quietly during lunch while Pete tries to talk me out of my decision. I call his mother twice in hopes she'll have some news, which she doesn't. I'm about to call her again when Neil finally appears.

"So, any news?" he asks sitting down at our table.

"Not yet," I say, reluctantly putting my phone down. "Grandma is still sedated and the doctors haven't come back with test results."

"Maybe we should wait—" he starts, but I don't let him finish.

"I can't. I have to go."

"Look..." he sighs and pauses, clearly choosing his words. I promise myself I'll try to not freak out with whatever he's about to say. "I can't authorize this, not without having the full picture."

"Oh, you mean I can only go after she's dead," I say, unable to keep the sarcasm out of my voice.

"Rebecca," Pete whispers, reaching for my hand. "She's not dying."

"You don't know that," I snap, angry that he's not taking my side.

"Come on," Tristan speaks, in an attempt to keep his promise. Only then I realize everyone is listening to this conversation. "It's her grandmother, and she's in the hospital. We have three days off."

"I know it's a delicate situation," Neil agrees, and then looks at me again, "but if anything happens to you, I'll have to answer for it."

"Nothing will happen," I say. He gives me a look of disbelief. "What do you think can happen?"

"I don't know, and that's the problem. You're too upset now, rightly so, but I just can't let you go," he says with finality.

"Okay…" I nod slowly, taking that in. "Hypothetically, what are the implications if I decide to go anyway?"

"Rebecca!" Pete exclaims. "Just listen…"

"I'll be in Manchester in time for the next concert," I ignore him.

"It's a ten-hour trip," Pete continues.

"I can make it in six with a car," I argue.

"You can make it in two if you wait until Edinburgh," he insists.

"We won't have a day off in Edinburgh," I remind him. Plus, we're four days away from our Edinburgh concert, and, for all I know, Eileen might be dead by then.

"Rebecca…" Pete sighs, closing his eyes for a moment—a sign that I'm getting under his skin.

"The last thing I said to her was that I was never setting foot in Alnwick again," I say and my voice falters.

I know he remembers it, he was there, he heard me. I'm sure this is part of the reason why he doesn't want me to go.

But it's why I need to. I don't know how often my grandmother thinks about it, but I know this can't be the last thing I said to her in life.

"Hypothetically..." Neil breaks the awkward silence that falls upon us. "If anyone notices you're gone, you could get fired. There might even be a fine involved."

"Will anyone notice?" I ask, my hopes building up.

"If something happens..." he trails off.

"Nothing will happen," I insist.

Neil sighs again, biting his bottom lip, thinking.

"You can't go on your own," Pete says before Neil makes up his mind.

"Then come with me!" I suggest, even though I'm absolutely pissed off with him.

"Lindsey is coming to visit me," he informs.

"Is she?" Tristan and I ask at the same time. I glance at him and he drops his eyes to his hands. So *this* is what he wanted to talk about earlier.

"I can ask her—"

"No, don't," I interrupt him before he suggests it. He has his own problems to deal with at the moment. Also, I have a good relationship with Lindsey, it's better not to push it, especially when I know they're not in a good place.

"I could go."

There is a moment of silence before the unison '*what?*' that follows this suggestion.

"I could go with you. We could take turns driving, keep each other awake," Tyler explains.

"What about no one goes?" Pete gives me an exasperated look.

"Yeah, I don't think this is a good idea," Tristan says.

"Good thing we're not asking your opinion," Tyler retorts.

"I'd be less worried if you didn't go alone," Neil chips in.

I stare at him and then at Tyler. His expression is unreadable, as usual, but genuine. I'm not gonna lie, the idea of spending time alone and in close proximity with him stirs something in my stomach, something I know shouldn't be there, something that screams trouble. But I don't want to be fired. Even hating Pete at the moment, I can't ruin our biggest opportunity to date. I also shouldn't drive six hours to a place I swore never to go back to again before having concrete information. But I know I won't be able to rest if I don't see her. And if I don't go now, maybe I really won't ever go.

"Okay, then," I agree, for Pete's dismay.

"Rebecca—"

"Stop calling me that!" I hiss and get up. "I'm going to get my stuff."

"I'll take care of arranging a car," Neil says, getting up too.

"Thanks," I mumble as I walk away. While I'm waiting for the lift, Tyler catches up with me.

"So... Alnwick," he says.

"Yep." I bite my lip. The elevator arrives and we get inside.

"Just so you know, you can kick me out at the side of the road after we leave, if you want to," he says out of nowhere.

"Do you want out?" I ask, confused. Wasn't he the one to suggest this?

"No," he says firmly, but I sense his nervousness. As we get out on our floor, he turns to me. "Do you want me in?"

I take a deep breath, trying to see past his blue eyes. I recall Tristan telling me I reminded him of Tyler sometimes. I remember that he was the one to find us online and request us as opening act. I think of us playing piano together. I think of us drinking on the rooftop.

"Yes."

***

"Can't you just wait until we at least know what happened?" Pete asks for the millionth time.

"Peter," I stop trying to fit clean underwear into my small backpack to look at him, "I'm really close to saying things I don't want to say. Please, drop it."

"Okay, fine," he sighs, defeated. "It's a free country, you're a free woman."

"Exactly," I say, rolling my eyes. He only says that when we disagree.

"Just tell me if you want me to go with you." He grabs my hands, making me look into his eyes. "Just say the word and I'll drop everything."

How can someone be so supportive even when they think you're making a mistake? I sigh. I really don't deserve him. And I really want him to go. But if it causes him any more trouble than he's already in, I'll never be able to forgive myself. Chances are he's right, grandma is strong and will be fine, and this trip will only serve to hurt me.

"I *don't* want you to go," I say, then. He knows I'm lying, so I sit beside him, avoiding his eyes. "It's not your problem. It's time that I start dealing with my own shit. Besides... you can't babysit me forever."

"Becks!" He turns to face me, an appalled look on his face. "It's not like that! It's not like that at all!"

"You know what I mean," I say, although it's *exactly* like that. He's just always around, always picking me up, always ready to drop everything for me. It's not fair. It's not healthy. For neither of us.

"I love you," he says, making me roll my eyes.

"I *know* that. And it's enough for now." I rest my head on his shoulder, squeezing his hand. If me being deprived of a traditional family has any bright side, it's that it pulled me closer to him.

"Hey," Neil appears at the open door, rattling his knuckles on the frame, "the car is here."

"I'm ready," I say, getting up and closing my backpack.

"Please, keep me updated. Please," Pete pleads, knowing I'm not the best at maintaining contact.

"Will do," I say, kissing his forehead and turning to leave.

"Drive safe!" I hear him yelling when I step outside.

Then I retreat my steps and glance at him again, sitting dejected on my unmade bed. I smile. As much as I hate how much I make him worry, it still makes me feel special. It's good to know I can count on him no matter what.

"I love you," I say, making him look up.

"I know."

As I skip down the stairs, my heart speeds up on my chest. I round the building to the parking lot, already questioning my resolve. And then I spot Tyler leaning against the car trunk, chatting to Neil. He's found his glasses. I walk towards them slowly. Am I doing this for the right reasons?

They stop talking when they see me. I stare at my feet until I get to them.

"Call me as soon as possible," Neil says, handing me the car keys. "And be careful."

"I will," I say, taking the keys.

"You, too," he says to Tyler.

"I'm always careful," he frowns. I can't see it, but I can hear it.

Neil sighs, looking back and forth between us. "If anything, *anything*, happens that makes me regret this decision..." he trails off.

"Yes?" Tyler asks after a few seconds of silence.

"I didn't think of a good threat yet," Neil admits, making me laugh a little. "But rest assured I'll have a lot of time to come up with something."

"Can't wait to hear it," Tyler says, patting his shoulder. Then, he turns to me, motioning to the car, "Shall we?"

"Yeah," I nod, watching as he makes his way to the passenger's seat. I wait until he gets inside to turn to Neil. "Thank you."

"No problem," he gives me a sympathetic smile. "If you need anything, just let me know."

I nod, not knowing what to say next. So I say nothing.

I enter the car, throwing my backpack on the backseat. I pause for a second, staring at Tyler. He stares back. Or, at least, I think he does.

"You found your glasses," I say dumbly.

"Yep," he smiles, "back to my ridiculous self."

I snort, rolling my eyes and biting my lip not to smile back.

***

"Can I change the playlist?" Tyler asks after nearly two hours of silence. I almost forgot he's here.

"Sure," I shrug.

He unplugs my phone and plugs his. After a few seconds, a Beatles song comes on and I make a face.

"Don't tell me you don't like The Beatles," he says.

"I don't like The Beatles," I admit. If I could sum them up in one word, it would be *overrated*.

"Everyone likes The Beatles!" he argues.

"Apparently not."

"But they're your fellow countrymen."

"I don't see how their nationality affects my ears."

He chuckles. And then turns the volume up. Idiot.

"Why don't you like your name?" he speaks again over the music.

"What?" I frown.

"When Pete called you Rebecca... you didn't seem very happy about it," he continues.

"What?" I ask again. He stares at me blankly. "I can't hear you over this noise." I point to the radio.

He turns to where I'm pointing and then back to me. I swear I see a shadow of a smile from the corner of my eye. Then he turns the volume down.

"Better?" he asks.

"Much," I say. And then silence.

I glance at him again. He's looking out of the window. He doesn't repeat his question, although I know he knows I heard it, and the fact that he's not insisting on it makes me glad. Yet, I find myself willing to answer. At least in part.

"Pete only calls me that when he's angry with me." I feel his head turn around again.

"He seemed more concerned than angry, though," Tyler says.

"Yeah. He does that, too," I sigh.

"He reminds me of Tristan," he says.

"How so?" I frown, struck by the familiarity of his remark.

"The way he treats you like a child," he says and I immediately get defensive. "Tristan does that to me, too."

"He doesn't treat me like a child!" I argue, offended as if he had said that about me.

"Oh, no? Doesn't he think he can tell you what to do? Doesn't he get frustrated when you don't do things his way? Isn't he constantly afraid of what you're going to say next?" he lists and gets angrier with each question. I know he's talking more about his relationship with his brother than mine with Pete, but it doesn't prevent me to get annoyed.

Why does everyone assume they know what goes on in other people's lives?

"It's not like that." I shake my head and he snorts. "He may do all those things, but because I gave him a reason to. Because he cares about me, not because he wants to control me."

"Are you really convinced of that?" I see him turn to me from the corner of my eyes.

"Mate..." I sigh. "You have no idea what he has gone through because of me. You have no idea how much pain I have already caused him. And, yet, he didn't leave. I think I can deal with a little overprotective attitude if it means he'll stick around."

I can feel my skin burn. I can feel his eyes on me. I'm not really sure why I said that, but when it comes to Pete, I'm equally overprotective. He's a saint in so many ways I can't even begin to explain. He's the best friend I ever had. He's the only friend I still have. Yes, he acts like a big brother. Because, in a lot of senses, he is.

"What's the deal between you two?" he stirs the conversation in another direction.

"The deal?" I snort.

"Yeah... you know." He shuffles on his seat.

"No, I don't," I bite back. But I do know. It's what everybody asks when they ask me about Pete.

"Yes, you do," he insists. I glance at him again and he doesn't seem angry anymore. He's just curious. So I answer him.

"We're friends," I say with a heavy sigh.

"With benefits?" he asks next and I can't help but laugh. "I'll take that as a no," he adds in a boring tone.

I get it, it's hard to understand our friendship. We grew up together, we formed a band together, we left our hometown together, we live together. We spend every waking hour—and sometimes sleeping hours—together. Sometimes we do resemble a married couple. But, no, ew! Regardless of what most of his exes thought, we do not have benefits. Only the friendship. The only one I managed not to screw up. Not thanks to me, though. Anyone else would have jetted years ago. But it's Pete.

"Correct. He only has eyes for his girlfriend," I say, even though he's been having eyes for Tristan, too.

"Oh," he interjects, making me glance at him. "So he *does* have a girlfriend."

"Yep," I say, and he nods. My curiosity is stronger than me, so I ask, "Why?"

"Nothing. It's just... I thought..." he struggles, not really wanting to say what's on his mind. But, then, he does, "I thought he'd be the type to have a boyfriend."

"He's had some of those, too," I say, trying to watch his reaction at the same time I pay attention to the road.

"I see," he nods again, apparently unsurprised. Which earns him points with me—anyone who doesn't react like Pete is a zoo animal upon knowing he likes both girls and boys ranks a little higher on my list. "Do you have a boyfriend?"

"No," I frown at the unexpected change in the subject.

"A girlfriend?"

"What is this now?" I chuckle.

"Nothing. Just trying to make small talk." He throws his hands up defensively.

"Feels more like an interview," I complain.

"Use it as practice, then. For when you're famous," I can hear his smile. I'm not sure if he's mocking me, but it makes me smile, too. "So, girlfriend?" he repeats.

"I don't talk about my personal life," I joke and he chuckles.

"You learn too fast," he says. And, once again, doesn't insist on it. I find I like this trait on him. Prying, but never pushy. I also realize he got answers to all his questions. I decide not to break the streak.

"No girlfriend," I say. "Nor boyfriend."

"Me neither," he shares spontaneously. Not that I wouldn't know—the way he made out with those girls the other night would suggest exactly that.

"Not ever?" I take the opportunity to put him on the spot for a change. I feel his head turning to watch me again. I wonder if he's trying to read my mind like I try to read his.

"Once," he finally says.

"Were you in love?" I half-sing the last word, making the question sound less deep than it actually is.

"What is this now?" he chuckles.

"Just small talk!" I glance at him. "According to experts."

"Such a smart-ass," he remarks.

"I'm learning from the best," I retort and he laughs. But doesn't answer. Which, for me, is answer enough.

***

It's eleven p.m. when I finally drive through Alnwick's city sign. I slow down and navigate around the streets I still know like the back of my hands, no matter how hard I try to forget them. It's absolutely empty. Quiet. Like a zombie apocalypse.

In no time, I'm turning left on my old street and parking in front of the house I grew up in. The sight of the big white building with its dark windows always overwhelms me. Every time I come back, it looks more sumptuous. And less welcoming.

I finally turn the engine off and glance at Tyler. I debate for a moment whether to wake him up—he's been asleep for the past three hours. I don't know how he managed to find a comfortable position, but he even talked a little. Something about pasta and drumsticks.

I turn the car light on and before I poke his ribs, I pause for a second to really look at him. He looks almost completely like someone else—every trace of sarcasm and grumpiness erased by unconsciousness. He looks like a boy.

A pretty boy.

It's clear that it's not just the blue eyes that make his fans swoon, he has every handsome trace in the book. Strong jaw? Check. Immaculate skin? Check. Soft lips? Check. Long neck? Check. Even his hair is perfect, no matter how hard he tries to make it look disheveled. I chuckle when I remember he used to look like a girl. I can definitely see why, with his refined features and fair complexion.

He grunts in his sleep, saying something I can't understand, and turns his head to my side. His long blond locks cascade down, covering his face. I suddenly feel an irrational desire to run my fingers through those golden strands and uncover his flushed face. I startle myself with this thought and decide it's time to stop delaying the moment I'm dreading. So I get out of the car, take a deep breath, and walk up to the house.

I reach under the garden gnome for the spare key, and am not surprised to find it still there. I unlock the front door and walk in. The smell of wood and old furniture immediately brings me back. It's the smell of my childhood.

I turn the porch light on and walk slowly through the hallway over to the kitchen. The walls are still covered in old pictures of us. First, grandma and my dad. Then my dad with some friends. My dad with my mom. My mom with me inside of her. My mom holding me in her arms. My dad with me on his shoulders. Me and my dad lying on the grass under the night sky. And then me and grandma. I don't look at the last ones and hurry into the kitchen.

There are still unwashed plates and pans in the sink, which are a painful reminder grandma is not here. There's also a freshly made apple pie on the counter. I open the cutlery drawer and pick up a fork. I can't remember the last time I ate grandma's pie.

"What are you doing?" Tyler's hoarse voice almost makes my soul leave my body. I forgot about him. Again.

"Fucking Christ, why do you keep doing that?" I yell in a whisper.

"Doing what?" He approaches me with a frown.

"Appearing out of nowhere."

"First of all, I do not appear out of nowhere. I'm always somewhere before I appear. In this particular case, in the car, which brings us to second: if you had woken me up and not left me alone in the dark to figure out on my own where the hell I am and what the hell happened, I wouldn't have to make an entrance and wouldn't have startled you." He pauses for a second, studying my surprised face. "To sum it up, it's all your fault."

"Are you always this talkative when you wake up?" I ask, noticing how his just-woken-up voice cracks at the end of the words.

"Only when I'm annoyed." He raises his eyebrows.

"Then, yes, always," I add and he smiles. An image of him sleeping in the car flashes in my mind. And the sudden craving to touch his hair. I look away. To the apple pie. Yes, the apple pie.

I uncover it and take a bite. And, again, it takes me right back. When I was a kid, I could tell grandma was arriving just by the smell of her baked goods. She always brought something over when she visited. And then, after... when she moved in, I'd always come home from school to find her in the kitchen baking something. The entire house permanently smelled of vanilla. I loved it. And hated it.

"Apple pie?" Tyler interrupts my trip down memory lane.

"Yeah. Want some?" I offer.

"Sure," he shrugs.

I open the cupboard and grab two plates and two glasses. I cut two generous pieces of pie for us and put the plates on the kitchen island. I walk to the fridge and grab the milk, filling our cups. I sit down in one of the stools and Tyler follows me in silence. He takes his first bite and shoots me a wide-eyed look. I smile.

"This is better than my mom's," he says through a mouthful. "Don't ever tell her that."

"I won't," I chuckle.

"So, are those your parents?" he asks suddenly. "In the pictures in the hall?"

"Yes," I nod and my stomach sinks. I haven't thought about this part. I haven't thought about him seeing the pictures. I haven't thought about having to tell him what happened.

"You look a lot like your mom," he points out.

"Yeah," I sigh. "Unfortunately," I add and, as usual, regret it immediately. I concentrate on my pie and on eating it. When I hear Tyler resting his fork on the plate, I brace myself for his next question.

But it doesn't come. He says nothing. I can feel his eyes are on my face—for some reason, I can always sense when he's looking at me, but he remains silent. When I finish my pie and have nothing else to distract me, I look up.

He is indeed looking at me, with that curious expression he had while he was interrogating me in the car—except now I can fully see it, without those hideous glasses. I want to ask him what he's thinking. I want to ask him what he's doing here with me. But I can't. So I just stare back. He shifts on his seat, getting uncomfortable. Then he reaches for his glass and drinks the milk all at once. When he finishes, he puts it down, wipes his mouth with the back of his hand, and glances up at the clock on the wall.

"It's late," he remarks, still looking at the clock.

I follow his gaze to see it's past midnight. Upon this knowledge, my body seems to remember I spent seven hours driving and I get instantly tired. I yawn and rub my eyes.

"You should sleep," he says.

"Yeah," I agree, taking my phone from my pocket to check for news. There are none. The last time I spoke to Pete's mom, she was going home, grandma was still sedated.

"Any news?" he asks.

"No," I sigh, grabbing our dishes and walking to the sink. "We'll know more in the morning."

"Right," he nods.

We stare at each other awkwardly for a moment, as I don't know what to do next.

"Can I crash on the couch?" he asks, pointing a finger to the hall.

"Sure, yes," I say, leading the way. I turn the lights on to find everything exactly like it was when I was last here, unsurprisingly.

"Vintage," he comments as he observes our decor choices.

"Old, you mean," I chuckle. I still remember the day we bought that couch—I was ten. "Do you need anything? Should I show you around?" I suddenly remember he's a stranger. And a guest. And I don't know how to deal with either.

"No. I think I've seen the inside of houses before," he jokes. "I'll just try to sleep."

"Okay. But if you need anything—"

"I won't," he assures me.

"Right," I nod. "Good night, then."

"Night," he says.

I feel weird leaving him alone in my living room. I feel weird climbing the steps to my old room. I feel weird lying on the bed where I spent the first 16 years of my life. Gosh, what am I doing here?

✳DAY $IX

I WAKE UP TO THE SMELL OF COFFEE. I ROLL AROUND MY EXTREMELY comfortable bed fishing for my phone. I slept with it under my pillow, just in case. I try to find out what time it is, but can't. I sit up with difficulty. When I can finally focus, I see it's only seven in the morning and there's only one message—from Pete, around the time he must have estimated I would arrive. Unsurprisingly, I forgot to text him.

'I'm here. I'm alive.'

I text back and stretch. I can't remember the last time I slept so well. I think there's something about the bed you spent your childhood on.

The smell makes my stomach rumble, and the thought of Tyler perusing my house alone makes me jump out of bed. I run to the bathroom, as I really need to pee, and my own reflection on the mirror startles me. I have those big dark circles under my eyes due to sleeping in my make-up, and my curls are one big tangle. I do my business, wash my face, wet my hair, trying to comb through it with my fingers. But no matter what I do, I still pretty much look like an upside broom, so I give up.

Then, I walk to my old wardrobe. I open it and cringe at my colorful teenage fashion choices. It's hard to believe there was a time I actually wore pastel pink. Or trousers. I fish around for something that will not hurt my punk pride. I settle for a grey pair of skinny jeans and a navy, over-sized sweatshirt. I loved this sweatshirt! I don't remember why I left it here, but I'm certainly taking it back with me this time.

As I climb down the stairs, I can hear Tyler's voice. For a moment, I panic about someone else being in the house, but as I approach the kitchen I realize he's singing. I don't recognize the song, but his voice is nice on the ears and his runs are pretty. I stop right outside the door, just to listen to him a little bit longer. When he turns the sink on and his voice gets muffled, I decide to go in.

"Morning," I say, startling him for a change.

"Morning," he half turns to me, a pan in hand. And then he does a double-take, frowning as he checks my outfit.

"What are you doing?" I ask, eying the pan in his hand.

"Uh..." He tears his gaze from me to the pan. "Just washing."

He stares for a moment before continuing what he was doing. I watch as he rinses the last of the dirty dishes that were in the sink the night before.

"Tyler..." I gasp as I walk over to him. I don't know what to say. Actually, I do, I should say 'thank you', but the words don't come out.

"I made coffee," he says as he dries his hands on a dishcloth.

I just look at him, suddenly taken aback by his presence. By his attitude. By how good he looks under the morning light in my childhood kitchen. By how calm I am about all of it.

"Are you angry?" he asks carefully, cocking his head to one side.

"Wha-no! No, of course not," I stutter, looking away.

"Right. I thought you might get angry because I went through your stuff without you to make coffee. That's why I decided to wash the dishes, I thought it would make you less angry," he babbles, making it evident he really gets talkative after waking up.

"I'm not angry," I repeat, unable to suppress a smile.

"So it worked," he says it like a question, narrowing his eyes. My smile broadens. "Good."

I shake my head and proceed to get a mug, fill it with coffee, and help myself with another slice of apple pie. I sit at the island again and as I eat and drink I decide this is the best breakfast I've had in a long time.

"How did you sleep?" I ask as Tyler sits opposite me again, with his own coffee mug and pie.

"Fine. Your couch is surprisingly comfortable."

"Is it? Why did you wake up so early, then?"

"The sun." He points his thumb back to the big kitchen window. "I can't sleep if it's not completely dark."

"Yeah, the living room curtain is a sham," I complain, remembering the days I used to wake up with the sun on my eyes there.

"I got a good six hours, though."

"Plus the three in the car, you should be able to go 24 hours awake now," I joke.

"Is this a dare?" He narrows his eyes.

"No," I chuckle.

"We can make it a dare," he suggests.

"Why?" He sounds like an eight-year-old.

"No sleeping until tomorrow morning." He points one finger to me.

"You'll regret this." I shake my head, amused. "Sleeping is probably the most interesting thing to do around here."

"We'll see." He finishes his breakfast and leans over on the island. "Dare?"

"Fine," I roll my eyes, but the smile never leaves my face. "You weirdo."

Before he can protest, my phone interrupts us—it's Johanna, Pete's mom. My heart races.

We chat briefly about the visiting hours. She says she won't be able to make it today, trying to apologize for something that isn't even her responsibility. Pete has *a lot* of her in him. I say that there is no problem, she shouldn't even have to worry about this, and we only hang up after I promise I'll stop by to see her and Dan at the store.

"News?" Tyler asks.

"No," I sigh. "But I'll find out soon enough. Visiting starts at nine."

I look up to the clock. We still have an hour to go. I immediately start to panic—how am I going to fill an entire hour of waiting alone with Tyler? I look at him then and, sure enough, he's staring at me, that curious look on his face.

"What?" I ask.

"What what?" he asks back, his curiosity frown deepening.

"What do you want to ask?" I say. His eyes widen a little.

"How do you know I want to ask something?"

"You're making your inquire face," I say.

"My what?" he chuckles.

"You have an inquire face. Every time you want to ask something, you look like this," I say and then I try to mock his expression.

He laughs, the lines on his forehead smoothing out. I like this expression better.

We remain silent for a while after he calms down. He sips his coffee, and then he looks back at me, with an expression I can't read this time.

"You're observant," he remarks.

I told you, I see you.

I feel a tug in my stomach. I know he wants me to say it. And although I *do* see him, more than I'd like to admit, I can't say it. Mostly because it really is a lousy pick-up line. So, instead, I say, "What's the question?"

His smirk fades a little—at least I think it does—as he speaks what's on his mind. "*What* are you wearing?"

I frown, looking down at myself. "Clothes?"

He rolls his eyes.

"What?" I frown, not willing to talk about it.

"They're normal clothes," he says, gesticulating with one hand.

"Oh, my other clothes are abnormal clothes?"

"That's not..." he sighs. "That's not what I meant."

I know it isn't. I still enjoy irritating him, though. I stare, raising my eyebrows, silently asking him to explain himself.

"I'm not... you look... different," he stutters.

"That's the whole purpose," I say.

"Why?"

"Maybe I just want to look like a regular person for once."

"That would be hard," he scoffs. I give him an offended look. He smiles and points to my head, "You still have purple hair."

"Right," I say, reaching up to the tangled mess on top of my head. "Can't hide that."

"Hide?" he repeats, the curious look back on his face. Before I have time to think of a smart-ass comeback, though, he understands what I'm doing. "Oooh, grandma."

"Yep," I say, standing up and collecting our dishes.

"You shouldn't have to pretend to be someone else just to please people," he says, making me turn back to him in anger even though I agree with him.

"It isn't *people*, it's my grandmother," I argue, as if I cared about it before. "And she's at the hospital. The least I can do is try to not upset her even more."

"Right," he says, clearly embarrassed. "Right, you're right, I'm sorry."

I stare at his sheepish face for a while, wondering if I was too harsh. I never know when I do it. Maybe because I do it all the time.

I sigh, once again frustrated with my lack of social abilities. I look down at my outfit, trying to see it through his eyes. It *is* a stark contrast to what he's been used to see me in.

"I do miss the skirt, I'm not gonna lie," I joke.

"Me too," he says, almost giving me a heart attack.

I look up with wide eyes. He seems to notice what he's said and starts to *blush*. Like, get properly red on the face.

"I mean, I mean, i-it suits you," he stutters. Oh, God. I can't let it slide, can I?

"And this doesn't," I snort, looking back down.

"I didn't say that," he argues, still nervous.

"I look like a sack of potatoes," I pull the sweatshirt, feigning irritation.

"Hardly," he says softly.

"I'm not even wearing make-up," I cover my face with my hands, this time actually self-aware.

"You still look beautiful."

I freeze, my own face heating up now. I can't believe he said that. I can't believe he's gonna throw me off because he said that.

I risk a glance at him from behind my fingers. He meets my eyes and smiles. Not that idiotic smirk of when he's being arrogant. Not the sarcastic grin of when he's making fun of me. No, it's an honest smile. One that makes me smile back.

Shit.

I turn around, suddenly very worried about the dirty dishes from our simple breakfast. I roll up my sleeves and start to wash them, all the while thinking of something to say. And very aware of his eyes on me. But the only thing I can think about is that he thinks I'm pretty. *Ugh.* I don't even like it when people comment on my looks. Why now, with him, my brain thinks it's a good time to get all mushy over it?

Then, I spot the car keys near the sink, reminding me of what I have to do. *Grandma. Hospital. Stop lusting over the pop star.*

I finish the dishes and grab the keys, finally turning around to look at him—to find that he is, again, looking at me.

"I think I'll get going," I say awkwardly.

"Do you want me to come with you?" he asks, his face unreadable. When I take too long just staring into his small blue eyes, he speaks again. "Can I come with you?"

"Don't you rather stay?" I suggest. I don't think I can handle sitting with him in the car right now.

"No," he says, standing up and walking to the hall.

"Actually, you should stay," I follow him.

"I'll go," he insists, putting on his jacket and opening the door.

"What will you do at the hospital?" I follow him outside, mildly desperate now. "I'm certain you'd be more entertained here, going through my stuff unsupervised."

"Good point." He actually pauses with this and turns around to face me, making me regret the suggestion. But then he smirks—the sarcastic one. His eyes light up in amusement at my surprise. I roll mine. "Come on."

So I lock the door of the house and unlock the car. And drive Tyler Hackley to see my grandmother at the hospital.

***

The short drive is excruciating. Neither of us says a single word, and I know he knows I'm thinking about what he said. Which means he's thinking about it, too. And I don't know why I'm making such a big deal out of it, since I have actual problems to deal with at the moment, but the more I think about it, the more uneasy I get. Some psycho theory about the reason he's come with me to Alnwick starts to form at the edges of my mind, but I don't have time to let it develop, as we reach the hospital and I park near the entrance.

Tyler follows me out of the car and into the building in silence. I identify myself at the desk and a nurse directs me to the right floor. My heartbeat picks up as flashes of the last conversation—or the last fight—I had with my grandmother start to torment me.

I talk to yet another nurse at the main station of the fourth floor and she points me out to grandma's room, even though I'm 30 minutes early for visitation. I choose to not mention that to her.

"I'll wait here," Tyler says, sitting down at one of the benches in the waiting area.

Then I freeze. I can't turn around. I can't take another step. Pete was right, I'm not ready for this. I shouldn't be here.

"Unless you want me to come," he adds softly, deepening my mortification. But I still can't move, so he stands up again and takes one of my hands on his, leading the way.

We reach her door and I can see she's awake through the strap of glass.

"If we leave now..." I whisper, suddenly wanting to be anywhere else but here.

"We're not leaving," Tyler says firmly.

"I wish Pete was here," I blurt out.

"Me too." This makes me look at him. He's looking at me, his brow furrowed, his eyes concerned. Crap. It shouldn't be him. It shouldn't be here. What am I doing?

"You don't have to—"

"I know," he interrupts me, like we're long-time friends and this is a common exchange. "Go on."

He squeezes my hand, the one that's still holding his, and I finally let go.

I take a deep breath and one step forward. And another. And another. Until I reach the door. Then I open it.

Grandma's eyes meet mine. Her face darkens with a mix of surprise, regret, and disappointment. At least that's what she *should* be feeling. I remember the last time I saw that look.

"If you step out of that door, don't even think about coming back!"

"Don't worry, granny, I have no intentions to set foot in this hell-hole ever again!"

That was our last interaction. That was four years, three months, and twenty-one days ago. I wish I could say I wasn't counting, I wish I could say I don't wake up every morning and mentally add a day to that invisible calendar. *One more day alive. One more day after him.*

Four years, seven months, and thirteen days ago, Pete dragged me to Alnwick for the holidays. I only came because he was too close to taking matters in his own hands. He was paying too much attention. My lies and justifications weren't working anymore. He was worried sick and I was a mess, so I came.

Two days after Christmas, we received a call—our landlord, saying someone had broken into our flat. Someone had *died* inside our flat. Someone who happened to be my boyfriend at the time. I wish I didn't remember that call, that day, the feeling of relief that washed over me when Pete came back from London with the confirmation it was really him. Externally, I didn't react. Internally, I was so... happy. I wouldn't have to see him anymore. He wouldn't be able to put his hands on me anymore. I wouldn't have to deal with the situation. I could just move on. Of course, it wasn't as simple as it initially seemed it would be.

The first time he hit me, it was across the face—one of those open-hand slaps, that leaves your skin stinging and your vision blurry. I think I might have even fainted for a while, because the next thing I remember is him kneeling beside me, burying his head in my stomach, crying and apologizing, promising he would never do that again. I believed him. At least, that first time, I did. The next morning, when I looked in the mirror, the first thing that occurred to me was: *you're lucky you like wearing make-up.*

I didn't know it would be so easy to let it happen. I didn't know it would be so easy to convince myself that the good parts were worth the bad ones. To lie to the people that cared the most about me. To give up control. Pete says it was because of the drugs, of the alcohol, of his rhetoric. I'm not so sure. Sometimes I wish it was worse—maybe if I was below rock bottom, I wouldn't remember. If I had used harder stuff. If I had stayed with him that Christmas.

I never told anyone what happened. No one even knew I was dating him, so there was no point in explaining he was dead. Or why he was dead. Pete, on the other hand, spilled every detail to his parents as soon as it happened. I don't blame or resent him, that's just how he is. Actually, I think I envy him a little bit. I wish I had such a close relationship with my parents. I wish I had parents to have a close relationship with.

He said he asked them not to tell anyone, and for a while I believed they didn't. But when we decided to go back to London and try this music thing again, it became clear everyone knew about what had happened. They all flipped. We spent days in family reunions, explaining ourselves, recounting our steps, reliving our horrible mistakes. In the end, Pete managed to convince his family we deserved their trust. I didn't convince Eileen.

At the same time that I was deeply hurt by her lack of faith in me, I could understand her reasons. She was abandoned, too. Her son left her, too. And now I was leaving her, telling her I was going to make sure it was for good. Part of me hoped it was. It seems I was wrong, though. It seems she didn't expect me to be wrong.

"Rebecca?" she says hoarsely, her eyes open wide. "I thought you were on tour."

"I am," I say, already feeling hot tears fill my eyes. "But I had to see you."

For an endless second, I think she's going to tell me to leave. I think she's going to yell, call the nurses, kick me out. She doesn't, though. She smiles and opens her arms and the next thing I know I'm sobbing all over her hospital gown.

"It's okay, petal, I'm okay, everything is okay," she whispers in my hair as she holds me, running a soothing hand up and down my back. Honestly, I think this is why it's so hard to come back. Because she makes it too hard to leave again.

"You scared me," I mumble into her chest.

"I know, I know," she sighs, "but it was only a scare."

I pull myself together enough to pull away and look at her. Her face is gaunt and colorless, her eyes are deep into dark circles, her hair is thinning out. She looks so much older than I remember. She looks so fragile.

"I'm sorry, granny," I whisper as more tears threaten to spill out of my eyes.

"I know, I know," she holds my face with her hands, "me too."

"How are you?" I ask, drying my face on my sleeve.

"I'm fine, dearie," she gives me a weak smile.

"You are in the hospital," I argue.

"Really? I hadn't noticed," she looks around, chuckling.

"What happened?" I ask, never letting go of her hands.

"I don't know," she shakes her head. "One minute I was walking back home, the other I was waking up here."

"What did the doctors say?"

"Nothing yet," she says, averting her eyes. I don't believe her. "They still want me to do some tests."

"Right," I nod, deciding not to push her. I can interrogate Pete's parents later, when I fulfill my promise.

"How are you, my darling?" she asks, patting my face. "You look so thin, are you eating well?"

I smile. Leave it to her to worry and reassure me while lying on a hospital bed. We chat for a while—about the tour, and Pete, and her busy life out here. She has friends and meetings and church obligations. She's as active as she ever was, which eases my guilt. At least she's not lonely, right?

Despite the fact we haven't talked properly in a while, and that I was a bitch to her the last time we did, it seems no time has passed at all. I wonder why we take so long to appreciate these moments. Why does it take a tragedy to make us cut the crap and value what really matters? Why don't I ever learn?

"Good morning," a nurse enters the room rolling a cart. He smiles broadly when he sees me. "Oh, hey! You have a different visitor today!"

"Yes, this is my granddaughter," she says, casually rolling her eyes to me. "Rebecca."

"You didn't tell me you had a granddaughter!" he says excitedly, but it hurts a little. He walks over to me and reaches out a hand. "Hi, Rebecca, I'm Patrick. I've been keeping an eye on grandma for you."

"Just Becky, please," I say as I take his hand. It's really soft.

"Okay, just Becky," he beams and I feel my face flush, "I'm going to ask you to wait here a moment while I take grandma to take some tests."

"You don't need to wait, hun," she rushes to say. "You should go."

"We will be a while, actually," Patrick tells me.

"And I'll probably just sleep for the rest of the day," grandma says. Then, closer to her normal mood, she adds, "They've been mixing some heavy stuff into my saline, I tell you."

Patrick chuckles with that. It makes me chuckle, too.

"I can stay. It's not like I have anything else to do around here," I say.

"No, petal, you go, you have your work—"

"I have a few days off," I cut her off.

"You're not planning to spend them here, are you?" She widens her eyes. "Darling, I'm fine!"

"I'm not gonna leave before I know what happened," I tell her.

"We should have a concrete diagnosis tomorrow," Patrick informs me.

"What's the not concrete diagnosis so far?"

"There isn't one," he gives me that professional sympathetic smile.

"Can I talk to you outside?" I ask.

"Sure," he says and turns around to leave.

"I'll be back later," I tell grandma. She opens a cheeky smile. "What?"

"It's good to hear that."

My heart catches in my throat and I just nod because, if I speak, I'm certain I'll cry again.

I step outside and interrogate Patrick, but all he tells me is that it's definitely something to do with her heart, although it wasn't a heart attack. I thank him, give him my phone number and make him promise he'll call me if anything changes. He agrees, although I'm not sure I can trust him, and then I walk away.

I almost run past Tyler in the waiting room, as I forgot he was here.

"How is she?" He jumps up when he sees me. It makes me smile.

"Seems fine," I say.

"That's good," he nods, stuffing his hands into his jacket.

"Yeah, come on, let's go," I restart my sprint to the parking lot.

"Where are we going now?" he asks as he follows me.

"To see Pete's parents."

***

We enter the car and drive off in silence. I can sense Tyler's restlessness and wonder what is on his mind. I get restless, too.

"Thank you," I blurt out, not looking at him. I hope he knows how hard this is for me, because I'm not elaborating any further.

Through my peripheral vision, I see his head whip around from the window to look at me. He stays like that, in silence, for the longest time, which doesn't help the feeling in my stomach.

I risk looking at him when we stop at a red light and he doesn't seem bothered that I caught him staring.

"You're making me nervous," I confess, just to see his reaction. He looks away.

"Sorry," he mumbles, to my surprise. "How are you doing?"

"I'm fine," I say mechanically, tapping my fingers on the steering wheel.

"I really want to know," he says, which makes me turn back to him. "I know that when people ask that question they usually don't expect an honest answer. But I want an honest answer. Don't say you're fine if you're not."

I just stare at him until the car behind us honks. The light has turned green. I have a hard time stepping on the pedal and getting the car moving.

My heart beats in my ears all the way to Pete's parents' store. The short journey is otherwise silent, since none of us speaks another word.

"Do they sell food here?" Tyler asks, as I park somewhere in the back. "I'm starving."

"Yeah. They have sandwiches, I guess."

"Nice," he says, unbuckling his seatbelt. He's about to hop off when I interrupt him.

"I'm not," I say. He takes his hand off the door handle. "The thing is... the thing is I'm not *ever* fine."

He frowns, sitting back against his seat. He bites his bottom lip, thinking. I regret saying that, feeling extremely uncomfortable and awkward, but I really want to know what he's going to say. That is, if he's going to say anything at all.

"You don't need to have an answer to that," I say after a while.

"I do, though," he says, finally looking at me again. I can tell he's also uncomfortable, but he decides to go through with it, anyway. "This morning, when we were talking... weren't you feeling okay?"

I feel my face heat up. "Yeah..." I confess, looking away. "Yeah, but it was just a moment."

"But that's all we have," he argues. "Just... moments. One after another. Until the end of time."

His cheesiness makes me smile. "Is that one of your lyrics?"

"No," he chuckles, "but I might turn it into one now."

"*Moments* would be a good song title," I continue, making him look away and shake his head. I wait until he looks back at me to smile. He smiles back—the genuine one. I kind of feel better. But I don't tell him that.

We exit the car and enter the store, and Tyler immediately wanders off in search of his snacks. I appreciate his discretion, but kinda wish he was with me when Pete's parents find me looking for them.

"Oh my God, look at you!" Johanna holds me by the shoulders after giving me a tight hug. "I can't believe Pete didn't come with you."

"He couldn't. Actually, even I couldn't—I had to fight for them to let me come," I explain.

"As usual," Dan, his dad, chuckles. "Have you seen Eileen yet?"

"Yes, I'm coming from the hospital," I say. They visibly tense up, bracing themselves for my next words. Gosh, I'm really a horrible person, aren't I? "She seems fine, but I was hoping you guys could give me some details? Maybe Evie has some inside information."

Evie is their eldest daughter, and works at the hospital. She's not in the health department, but you know how small towns work—if she asks, she can find things out.

"In fact, she does," Johanna says, clearly relieved with the topic. "It was her heart. Evie said Eileen was lucky to have been in a public place where she got help right away."

"The nurse said it wasn't a heart attack," I continue, shamelessly taking advantage of their good heart.

"It wasn't, it was a... What was it, Dan?"

"Fibrillation," Dan chimes in.

"That! They're holding her up until they know what caused it and the best line of treatment," Johanna resumes her report.

"How serious is that?" I ask, with a sudden urge to Google it.

"I don't know, hen," Johanna says with a sad sigh. "I could call Evie—"

"No, please!" I stop her as she takes her phone from her pocket. "I'll go back and try to talk to her doctor."

"Don't worry dearie, everything will be fine."

I just nod and let her hug me again. I miss it, as much as I hate to admit it. Johanna has treated me like one of her daughters since... well, since forever. I probably spent more time in her house with Pete, Evie and Avie than I did in my own. We were really like family. I just wish I could feel like family.

"Thank you," I mumble when she lets me go, again hoping she knows what I mean.

"She loves you, you know?" she says out of nowhere. I feel my face burn slightly. "You have a lot of her in you."

I know that's true. I'm every bit as stubborn, headstrong, and determined as Eileen is, if not more. Maybe that's what ultimately irritates me about her—seeing myself.

"Excuse me," Tyler's voice startles me. I turn around to find his smiley face. "Where is the cashier?"

"Just follow me, I'll help you." Dan walks to the other side of the counter and Tyler follows him.

"I guess I'll be going," I say, suddenly not wanting to explain Tyler to them. "Talk to you later?"

"Sure, sure! It was so good to see you." Johanna hugs me again. "Come by the house, I'll make you dinner!"

"Maybe tomorrow?" I scrunch up my nose. I love her food, I just don't think I have it in me to hang out with them today.

"Are you staying, then?" Dan shouts from behind the counter, surprised. "You must be really worried."

"Dan!" Johanna gives him a reprehending look. But I know he didn't mean anything by that, it's just an observation. An accurate one. "I'll cook that casserole that you like!" She claps her hands together.

"Thanks, Jo," I smile, turning away and heading to the exit. "Bye, Dan!"

"Bye, hen! Help yourself with any snacks you want." He winks.

I grab a few chocolate bars before leaving and walk to the car. I see Tyler walking back as soon as I close the door.

"It's kind of unfair that you don't have to pay for your stuff," he complains as he enters.

"What?" I chuckle.

"Especially since I bought snacks for us both," he continues.

"You did?" I reach for his bag to find a beer case, mints and two vegetarian sandwiches. I look at him again, intrigued.

"You're welcome," he says.

"How did you know I'm a vegetarian?" I ask, that strange feeling creeping up again.

"You must have mentioned it," he shrugs. It doesn't convince me. "What?"

"I feel like you know too much about me," I say and he laughs.

"Knowing you're a vegetarian is knowing too much?"

"You know what I mean," I roll my eyes.

"Well..." he sighs, sitting sideways on his seat to face me. "Besides Tris and Todd, I have a fourth brother. Timothy."

"What?" I gasp, mainly because I wasn't expecting this spontaneous sharing, not because of the actual information.

"He's fourteen and a nightmare. My zodiac sign is Scorpio. My favorite color is red. I'm a natural blond, despite what it may look like."

"That's hard to believe," I joke, glancing at his incredibly light hair.

"I know. But it's true, look at my roots." He lowers his head, pushing his hair in different directions, and I laugh. "I drink too much, but rarely get drunk. I hate our first single.

My favorite song I've ever written is one no one has ever heard."

"Really? The one you were singing this morning?" I ask and his eyes widen. He didn't expect me to have heard it, apparently.

"Yes," he nods. "Well, one person, now."

"I liked it," I say and he smiles, embarrassed.

"Are we even now?"

I just look at him for a moment, taking it all in. It is a lot of information, but nothing really special. Nothing personal. Just facts that I could probably find out about online. I still feel uneasy. I still feel like he knows more. I still feel like he can see through me.

"Do you know what my favorite color is?" I ask.

"Purple," he answers with certainty, glancing at my hair.

"Nope. It's green," I correct him and he smiles.

"Do I have to tell you one more thing now?" he jokes.

"There's something specific I want to know," I say and watch as his smile disappears. "Why me? Why us, why Pete and I?"

"What do you mean?" he frowns.

"I mean, we're not in the same genre. We're not at the same level. We don't even have a name."

"So?" he asks, seemingly still confused.

"So why? What made you choose us?" I finally ask, something that has been consuming me more than it probably should.

"Your talent," he shrugs.

"Right," I snort, rolling my eyes.

"It's true!"

"We're not the only talented group out there. And I'm sure your label had a long list of suggestions for you."

"They did."

"So?" I insist. I know we're talented, and I know we're good enough to be openers of a relatively big band like The Hacks. What I want to know is what made someone like Tyler pick us. What did he see in us? In me?

"You're passionate," he sighs, running a hand through his hair. "You feel what you do so much that it made me feel, too, through a low-quality video on the Internet. Do you know how hard it is to find nowadays? Someone that cares about the craft and not about the by-product of it?"

"Fame?" I ask tentatively.

"Exactly," he nods. "You don't seem to care about it."

"I don't," I admit. When I think about 'making it', I think of me and Pete on stage of a sold-out concert at the O2. I don't picture the money, or the magazine covers, or the paparazzi pictures. I picture the crowd singing along to something I wrote. It's that connection I crave, that makes everything worthwhile for me.

"There you go."

"It's all about the music," I nod slowly.

"Well," he gives me a curious look. He bites his lip, looking away, thinking. "It starts with the music."

"And where does it end?" I frown.

"I don't know," he chuckles, looking back at me. "Yet."

"Okay," I take a deep breath, nodding again. "We're even."

"Thank God," he laughs. "Can we eat now?"

"Yeah, we can eat now."

***

We go back to the hospital and, sure enough, Eileen is sound asleep. Patrick tells me he's certain she'll be out for the rest of the afternoon and that I should come back the next day to catch the doctor who's taking care of her case. I leave a little note by her bed, informing I'll be there in the morning and giving her my phone number. I'm not sure she still has it.

After that, I end up driving around town and showing Tyler random tourist points. I also show him the school I went to, and the music store where I got my first job—making things uneven again. We don't talk much, but it isn't a problem. I don't feel the weight of the awkward silence, on the contrary, it's quite pleasant. When we're not quiet, Tyler is the one that does most of the talking. He drinks all of the beer since I'm the one driving and that seems to loosen his tongue a little bit.

He tells me about his siblings, about the start of his band, about why he hates *Wendy* so much. He tells funny stories of past tours and asks to hear mine. We bicker over 'real music' and he surprises me with his knowledge of punk classics.

We stay on the surface for a change, and it's nice. It's easy. It makes me forget about time and place. It makes me almost feel like a person. I don't know if Tyler knew that, but I was really needing to chill. I'm not sure I knew that myself until I realized we'd spent hours doing nothing and talking nonsense.

"Jesus, I'm freezing," I complain when we arrive back at the house.

"Me too." Tyler is hugging himself.

"Do you want to take a shower?" I offer, as it's what I'm about to do. His eyebrows shoot up and I realize what the question sounds like. At least to him, the prick.

"Sure," he answers simply, even though the dirty joke is palpable in the air.

He gets his stuff from the car and I show him grandma's bathroom upstairs. I hand him a towel and turn around to go back to my room when he stops me.

"Wait, are you not joining me?" he asks with a serious face. I knew he wouldn't be able to keep it to himself. Smartass.

"You wish." I roll my eyes and he smirks.

I go into my room with a smile on my face, not thinking much of it. I undress and get into the shower. And then it hits me. We're not friends. We're not even acquaintances. We're strangers, he's technically my boss, and here we are, making sex jokes at each other.

Was it even a joke? I remember the way he looked at me on the roof the other night and that weird feeling I had about him being here reappears. Why is he here? How does he know so much? Is he a stalker? Is getting into my pants his ultimate goal? Maybe this is what it is all about—the band, the trip, everything. Maybe that's all he wants.

Then I snort and shake my head.

"Who's being ridiculous now?" I ask myself as I look in the mirror. Why do I keep reducing him to that? Maybe that's what *I* want. Is it?

I put on my flannel pajamas and step out of the bathroom, letting out a small squeal—Tyler is there, standing at the door, looking around. He's wearing gray sweatpants and a blue hoodie. His hair is damp from the shower. And then he meets my eyes. I feel my face burn, as if he can tell I was just thinking about him and sex.

"I half expected it to be entirely pink," he jokes. "Or to find Justin Timberlake posters on the wall."

"As if," I snort, looking away, uncomfortable and hot. *This is not happening. This is not happening. This is not happening.*

I fuss around a little bit, folding my clothes, trying to hide my dirty underwear in the middle of them, painfully aware of his eyes following me. When I have nothing else to occupy my hands with, I look at him again.

"So?" he asks, putting his hands inside his hoodie pockets.

"So what?" I frown, trying to keep my eyes on his face.

"What do we do now?" he asks. It's a simple question, with no sarcasm or hints behind it. It doesn't stop my mind from coming up with a naughty suggestion, though. "Remember we can't sleep."

Fuck. We could...

"Eat!" I say loudly, trying to stop my thoughts. *This is not happening.* "Pizza?"

"Sounds great," he nods, smiling. Why is he smiling? What happened to him being rude? Grumpy? Closed off?

I sigh, closing my eyes for a moment, cursing my social inability. Why do I have to be such a weirdo?

"Rebecca?" he calls and I open my eyes. He's stepped inside, looking concerned. And I think it's the first time he ever said my name.

"Yes, pizza," I repeat, and he only nods.

I walk past him, smelling grandma's shampoo, and my stomach churns in a dozen different emotions.

***

I order the goddamn pizza and we wait for it in silence. Not the same light, easy silence of before, but silence filled with the weight of my confusion. I try to use it to put my thoughts in order, but I have always struggled to segregate my feelings. I think it's because it takes me too long to allow anything in—when I finally do, it overwhelms me.

The pizza arrives and I decide to move our little dinner to the backyard. It's freezing outside, but at least I can breath better. We sit on my old swing and for a while the only sound is the creaking of its chains.

"How did you and Pete meet?" Tyler breaks the silence.

Pete. I wish he was here. I also remember I haven't talked to him all day, he must be pissed. I sigh.

"We went to school together."

"When did you start the band?"

"I think we were 13, or so."

"Was it always punk?"

"Yes," I chuckle, remembering our early haircuts. "Can you picture me doing anything else?"

"Hell no. If even seeing you in pants was weird…" he shakes his head and I laugh. "How did you decide to leave?"

"It was never a decision," I shake my head. "It was the only option."

"Was Alex from here, too?" he asks and I turn to look at him.

"No," I frown. "We met him in London, right after we arrived."

He lets the silence take over again as we munch on our pizza slices.

"Do you still have feelings for him?" he asks out of nowhere.

"What?" I gasp.

"You kind of flinch every time I say his name," he explains, watching me closely. Then, he says, "Alex. See? You flinched."

"Can't you think of any reason for that, Tyler?" I ask him angrily.

"Because you still have feelings for him," he says. My blood boils.

"I don't," I almost yell.

"Hate is a feeling," he insists.

What the fuck? Who does he think he is to talk to me like this? To talk *about* this with such ease? Fuck him.

"Do you still have feelings for her?" I return the question.

"Who?" he frowns, like he doesn't know who I'm talking about.

"Your *girlfriend*," I spit out the word.

"I don't have a girlfriend," he argues.

"Not now, but you had once," I recall what he told me in the car journey here. He frowns, confused and uncomfortable.

"A long time ago," he mumbles.

"So, what happened? Did she break your heart?" I ask. Now, he flinches, the same way he claims I do when he talks about... him. "She did! Shocker, I didn't think you had a heart."

The hurt look he gives me is enough to make me instantly regret lashing out. He doesn't know half of the story, it's not his fault that I didn't get over it. That I can't get over it. *Congratulations, Rebecca.*

"Fuck you!" he yells, getting up and storming to the house.

"I'm sorry!" I get up, too, calling after him.

"Are you?" He turns around angrily. "Or are you just sorry you said it out loud?"

Ouch.

"I'm sorry, Tyler," I repeat. I mean it. It's useless. Because saying sorry doesn't change the fact I said shit.

"Right," he snorts. "You know what, I'm going to bed. You were right, sleeping is the best thing to do around here."

"What about the dare?" I remind him vainly.

"Fuck it."

***

I spend another hour outside in the cold, kind of punishing myself. I want to call Pete, but I left my phone in the house, and I don't want to go get it. I don't want to risk running into Tyler. I don't want to see his glare.

I blame the house for my outburst. I hate coming here. There's too much history, too much hurt, I always end up saying things I don't mean.

I blame grandma. For being stubborn and not taking care of herself properly. Was it really that hard to keep healthy?

I blame Pete for being so reasonable and not being here with me. He should be here, or he should have convinced me not to come. None of this would have happened if he'd been an actual friend.

I blame Tyler himself. What is he even thinking anyway? What does he want? Why is he here? If he had kept to himself, if he stopped making questions, trying to get to know me...

I bury my cold face in my cold hands. How do people do this? How do they overcome? How do they move on? How do they connect? Why basic human function is so fucking hard for me?

I blame my parents. I blame them for leaving me and not teaching me how to be a person. I blame them for having me. I blame the universe for making them even meet.

My tears sting my eyes, tracing warm paths down my frozen skin. I get angrier. I'm so tired of crying. I'm so tired of being angry. I'm so tired of being myself. Why can't we have days off of ourselves? I just wanted one day, just one day outside my head. Just one day away. One day of nothing.

I take deep breaths, recognizing this thought pattern, knowing I can't let myself spiral down. The air is so cold my lungs hurt. I decide I've had enough of a pity party, so I grab the pizza box and head inside, before I too end up in the hospital.

I stop in the kitchen, letting my limbs warm up and eating another slice of cold pizza, as I'm still hungry. I put the rest into the refrigerator and turn off the lights. I walk over to the living room trying to make no noise, but Tyler is awake. He's scrolling down on his phone, still wearing his pissed-off expression. I pause at the door, debating whether I should say anything.

"What?" He lifts his eyes from his phone, glaring.

"You're not sleeping," I remark. He doesn't answer and goes back to his phone. I sigh. "I *am* sorry. I'm sorry I hurt you and I'm sorry I'm being so ungrateful. I'm not used to... this is all..." I stutter, unable to voice my feelings. I shake my head. I'm helpless. "You were right... about me... having feelings... it's a sensitive subject."

He looks at me, his face lit by his phone screen.

"Why didn't you say just that?" he asks.

"I don't know..." I sigh, leaning against the door frame. "It's still... I can't... I can't even say his name."

"I'm sorry," he says, then, and I look back at him. He's still frowning. "I won't mention it again."

"Thanks," I say, smiling faintly. He doesn't smile back. And it hurts.

✱DAY $EVEN

I FEEL A HAND ON MY SHOULDER. I GRUNT, COMPLAINING, BECAUSE I don't want to wake up. I'm still tired and my bed is so warm. The hand touches me again, shaking slightly this time. I open one eye. There's someone beside my bed. I close it again, turning to the other side.

"You lost," he says. It takes me too long to process that.

"What?" I ask, rubbing my eyes.

"You lost," he repeats. "You fell asleep."

I sit up on my bed, frowning. Tyler is standing there, in the same gray pants and blue hoodie from the night before and with a smug smile on his face.

"What?" I ask again. He lets out a rough laugh.

"I made coffee. It's almost eight." He turns around and leaves.

I take my phone from the nightstand, squinting to read the time. It is indeed almost eight. Visiting starts at nine. I can't fucking believe his consideration. I was expecting to wake up with him gone. But not only he's still here, he prevented me from missing visiting grandma and made coffee again. I feel worse than I did last night, if that's even possible.

I get out of bed and into the bathroom and grunt again. I look terrible. My hair is flat on one side, my eyes are puffy, my skin is greasy. *Ugh.* I can't believe he saw me like this. As if I needed one more humiliation. I wonder if he still thinks I'm pretty.

I wash the thought away in the sink and brush my teeth. I push my hair up, tying it into a small knot, and put on the same clothes as yesterday.

When I enter the kitchen, he's already dressed—his usual tight jeans and tight tee-shirt, topped with a black jacket. He's going through his phone and doesn't even glance at me as I pour myself coffee and eat yet another slice of apple pie. I open my phone to read the countless texts I'm sure Pete has sent me, but find only one. From yesterday. It makes me uneasy.

'How's it going?'

'So far, so good. What about you?' I text him back, but set up an alarm to call him later.

"The boys are going to Manchester this afternoon," Tyler says, without glancing up.

My stomach sinks further—Pete should have told me that. Then another thought occurs to me: we have to leave soon. I stare at my half-finished mug, torn about what to do. How can I leave grandma in this state? How can I stay and throw this chance out of the window?

I take a deep breath, closing my eyes and pressing them with my palms. *One thing at a time, Rebecca. One thing at a time.*

When I open them again, Tyler is staring at me, a mix of confusion and concern on his face. Did I say it out loud? Geez, as if I didn't have enough reason to be mortified right now. One pro of staying—at least I wouldn't make a fool of myself in front of him anymore.

I sigh, taking both of our plates to the sink and washing them. I pick up the car keys from the counter and Tyler follows me. I wait until we're at the door to be sure he's meaning to come with me again. He is. I pause, turning to him.

"Do you want to wait here today?" I ask, before stepping outside.

"No."

I stare. He stares. I open my mouth, trying to start a sentence a dozen times, but nothing comes out. I roll my eyes, defeated. I shouldn't be speaking, anyway. I should just stay silent for the rest of the trip. Or the tour. Or my life. Surely I'd lead a more fulfilling life if I never spoke again.

"Come on, then." I finally open the door.

We head to the car, enter, and I drive off. I turn the radio on to make the silence less unbearable.

"You think too much," he says after several minutes. My hands tighten around the steering wheel. *Don't speak. Do not speak.*

"Some would say I don't think enough," I snort. It's stronger than me. I need practice.

"'Some' as in yourself?" he asks and I just shrug. "Well, I say you think too much."

I don't reply. I keep driving, looking straight ahead. I manage a side glance at him as I enter a curve.

"See? You're thinking," he says and I shake my head.

"What am I supposed to do, then?" I frown, getting irritated even if I don't have any right to.

"Talk," he says simply. I snort.

"Apparently I don't have much success doing that."

"That's because you only talk at the wrong times," he explains, sounding like a kindergarten teacher. "At the right times, you just think."

Oh, I didn't know I was sitting with the queen of conversation here! Because you talk a lot, right? At the right time, as well. See? Practice.

"Does it work for you?" I ask after I finish my internal monologue. "Talking?"

"No."

I can't help but smile. And then laugh. He ends up laughing, too. God, what a pair of weirdos we make.

***

This time, thankfully, I don't need Tyler to hold my hand and push me towards grandma's room. I leave him in the waiting area and walk alone the few steps to her. She's awake and lively, even though her face is still drained of color and those dark circles are still very much present under her eyes. Patrick is adjusting some wires on her arm and she's complaining about his heavy hands when I enter.

"Oy, lad, you don't really have the hand for it, you know?" she's saying. "The night nurse didn't even wake me up."

"Sorry, Eileen, I'll be done in a second," Patrick answers absentmindedly.

"You keep saying that but keep pinching my skin," she continues.

"Morning," I decide to interrupt her.

"Petal! You came!" Grandma gives me a once-over, checking what I'm wearing, which already tells me she's feeling better.

"Hey, just Becky!" Patrick turns to me with a grin. He might not have good hands, but he certainly has a good face.

"Is grandma giving you a hard time?" I ask, walking over to sit at the edge of her bed.

"Not at all," he replies, winking, before resuming what he was doing.

Grandma shoots me a raised-eyebrow look and we wait in silence until he's done. He tells me the doctor will be with us in a few minutes and then leaves.

"Frisky lad," grandma mutters.

"Grandma!" I reprehend her but smile. "How are you feeling today?"

"As good as new," she says, tapping my hand. "I can't wait to go home."

"Let's see what the doctor will say," I tell her.

"Doctor," she scoffs, "she's a *child*."

"Grandma!" I scold her again.

"How long are you staying, dearie?" she asks, suddenly.

"I... I don't know yet," I answer. She narrows her eyes, knowing I'm hiding something.

"I don't want to disturb your life," she continues.

"You're not," I argue.

"You should go, if you have to."

"I don't, not yet."

"You should go if you want to."

"Grandma!" I gasp. I know she's thinking of the last time we saw each other.

"It's okay." She observes me with calm eyes.

"It's not!" I snap. "It's not okay and you're not doing anyone any favors by pretending it is!"

"I'm not pretending," she says with an annoying smile.

"Right," I snort. "So you're absolutely completely fine with how we left things?"

"I don't know what you want me to say, Rebecca," she sighs.

"The truth!"

"I'm telling you the truth," she insists. "I appreciate you coming all the way here, and I'm sorry I scared you like this. But I'm fine, I'll be fine. I don't need you here."

"You don't need me or you don't want me?" I blurt out, feeling her words in my gut. My hands start to shake and I have a *deja vu* of the last time I was here.

"Um, excuse me," a tiny voice says behind me. I turn around to find a short, plump woman in a white coat behind me. "Hi, I'm doctor Haddish. You must me Rebecca."

She reaches out a hand and I take a little too long to snap out of it.

"Hi, sorry. Just Becky, please," I say mechanically.

"How are we feeling this morning, Eileen?" She asks grandma in a much kinder tone. *Great,* I think. Now she thinks I'm a bitch.

"Better," grandma answers curtly.

"Good," doctor Haddish says, patting her hand. "Well, I finally have a diagnosis for you. And a treatment."

I stand there while I listen to her explain about atrial fibrillation, what might have caused it, and how it must be treated. Apparently, it's a common condition at her age, not serious, but like any other heart disease, it needs attention. I bite down my thumb nail as she explains grandma's new diet and medications.

"Good Lord..." grandma whispers as the doctor hands her the prescriptions.

"Don't worry, I'll be following you up very closely. I already scheduled an appointment to check if the meds are having the desired effect. It's important that you take all of them at the correct times, though," she says.

"I will, I will," grandma says, folding the sheet and putting it on the side table. "Can I go home now?"

"Not yet," the doctor answers, making grandma grunt. "I'm sorry, Eileen, but you still need to rest and I want to monitor your heart for a little longer. But if everything is fine, I'll let you go tomorrow morning."

"Everything *is* fine," grandma argues.

"Yes, and I want to make sure it stays fine, okay?" Doctor Haddish smiles sweetly, patting her hand again. Grandma sighs, defeated, making the doctor chuckle. "Okay, I'll leave you now, but if you need anything, Patrick is right out front."

"Thanks, doctor," grandma manages to say, even if frustrated.

"No problem," the doctor smiles, then turns to me. "Can I talk to you outside for a minute?"

My heart sinks in my chest. In the two seconds it takes me to follow her outside, my mind already comes up with the worst possible scenarios. It's not so simple as she said it is. Grandma is not leaving the hospital. She's dying.

"Is she going to be okay?" I ask in a low voice as soon as we step out.

"Rebecca, right?" she asks.

"Becky," I correct her, but she seems to ignore me.

"She's going to be just fine. It's really a common condition, but I really need her to take her meds, okay? The treatment will have no effect if she doesn't," she says in a serious tone.

"Okay," I nod.

"And she really needs to rest," she adds. She glances over at her door, and then back at me. When she speaks again, her voice is soft but her expression is hard. "I don't mean to sound rude, but Eileen shouldn't go through any stress right now."

"Okay, right," I nod again.

"At least for these first few days, it's important that she's not subject to any kind of intense emotions," she continues and I can feel myself blush with embarrassment.

"She won't, I assure you," I say, mortified.

"Good," she smiles and pats my arm the same way she did with grandma. "I'm gonna leave a copy of all the information I gave her at the nurse station. You can request it before you leave."

"Thank you, doctor," I say. She only nods and then walks away, leaving me alone with my shame.

I lean against the cold wall, bracing myself and closing my eyes. I take several deep breaths. How hard can it be to be a decent human? This is not about me. This is not the time to make it about me. I'm not going to mend the last four years in a day. I might not ever mend the last four years. But I'll have to live with that. I have to be there for her, the same way she was there for me when I needed it. That's all I have to do right now.

Someone touches my arm and I jump away, opening my eyes. It's Tyler. He's standing in front of me, that curious and concerned expression on his face.

"Sorry," he sighs, retrieving his hand. His eyes never leave mine. "Are you okay?"

I open my mouth to say that I am but stop myself. Does he want the honest answer now, too? Or is he just asking? I can't tell. But I know what option I want to take.

So I shake my head, biting my lip to hold in the tears that are threatening me again. His frown softens into a small, sympathetic smile, and he reaches out his hand again, slowly, until he touches my arm. He runs his thumb carefully against my sleeve. Without thinking, I take a few steps forward and bury my face in his chest. He stiffens, clearly not expecting this reaction. But then he lets out a long sigh and his arms snake around me. I hug his waist, pulling him closer, and, for a blissful moment, just enjoy how good it feels. And, in that moment, I don't wish those arms were Pete's.

"She's going to be discharged tomorrow," I say to his shirt.

"We can stay," he says back, and the closeness of his mouth to my ear sends shivers down my back.

I reluctantly let go from the embrace, taking a few steps back. I look him in the eyes, debating how to tell him I'm thinking about staying longer. But I can't. I can't say it. And I'm not sure I can do it.

"I'm... going..." I stutter, pointing to the door.

"Do you need anything?" he asks softly.

I really want to ask for another hug. Like, *really*. But I shake my head and smile, going back to grandma.

***

I reenter the room in silence, my head down, my arms crossed over my chest. I feel like a child again. I can't face her.

"Come here," she says.

I walk over and when I'm close enough, she sits up and holds my chin, so our eyes are leveled.

"I will always want you," she whispers. "Always."

That's all it takes for the dam to break. I throw myself at her, washing her gown with my tears once again. She pulls me closer until I'm almost sitting on her lap, running that soothing hand up and down my back. She doesn't say anything for a while, waiting for me to calm down.

"I'm sorry," I say in between sniffs.

"No, honey, *I'm* sorry," she answers.

"It's not your fault I'm so messed up."

"Don't say that!" she tuts, slapping my arm softly. "You're perfect, dearie. Just perfect."

I snort. If there's anyone as far from perfect as possible, that someone is me. I decide to drop this line of conversation, and, instead, I say, "I'll stay if you ask me to."

"I know, dearie. That's why I'm not asking," she sighs. Then, she pushes me until I'm sitting up and looking at her. "You know what my greatest fear is? That you're not happy. And I know that this place doesn't make you happy. You're right, maybe I haven't been entirely honest with you, maybe this fact bothers me, but I have no right to hold you down."

"You don't hold me down, granny," I argue, guilty welling up my eyes again.

"Well, I've certainly tried," she chuckles. And another sigh. "Yes, I wish you had made better choices. I wish you were healthier. I wish you had a more stable job and that you didn't ruin your hair..."

"Grandma..." I roll my eyes. She always complains about my hair.

"But above all, I wish you were happy. I wish I had done a better job of making you happy." She holds my face, smiling sadly.

I wish I had done a better job of being grateful.

"You did the best job," I tell her.

She just pulls me closer and we stay like that for a long time. She holds me firmly, and the tightness is familiar—she's held me like this for days after my parents left me. Left us. It was the only thing that kept me from breaking apart. I can't believe how much I missed it. I can't believe I once swore to never let her hold me again.

We're interrupted when Patrick comes in with her lunch and I'm startled by how long I've stayed in here.

"Do you want me to bring something for you, too?" he asks with that bright grin I'm becoming used to.

"No, thanks," I smile back. Then I remember poor Tyler waiting outside all this time.

As I tell grandma I'm going out to eat, she asks me to come by the house and bring her some stuff—mainly clean clothes for her to wear tomorrow. I agree and step out. I find Tyler spread across one of the benches in the waiting area, going through his phone.

"I should have told you to leave," I say as I notice how tired he looks.

"Oh, I wouldn't have," he says nonchalantly. Something tugs in my stomach, and it's not by the lack of food. "How is she?"

"Better," I nod. "She asked me to bring her some stuff, so I'm going back to the house."

"Okay," he says, standing up and stretching his arms above his head. His t-shirt rises up, revealing a strip of skin that involuntarily captures my gaze. He notices, quickly pulling it down. For some reason, it makes me smile.

"Are you hungry?" I ask.

"I could eat," he answers.

"Okay, come on," I turn around, leading the way back to the car.

***

I make a few stops along the way—the grocery store and the pharmacy. I want to make sure grandma has everything she needs when she comes home.

I decide to cook, a half-assed attempt to make it up to Tyler. He frowns when I announce my plans, but says nothing. He helps me out, washing some stuff, opening some cans, setting the table. We don't talk but it doesn't bother me. After last night, I think it's better if we keep it to ourselves, anyway.

"Did you really stay up all night?" I ask as we eat. He's yawning and rubbing his face a lot. It could just be regret, though.

"Yes, I did," he answers through a mouthful.

"Why?" I frown.

"It was a dare," he says as if it explains it.

"Yeah, but you were the one who said 'fuck it'. I asked 'what about the dare', and you said 'fuck it'," I remind him, despite it not being a good idea.

He looks up, squinting his eyes. For a moment, I feel like he's about to ask 'are you crazy, woman?' To which I would have to reply 'unfortunately, yes'. But then he chuckles.

"I clearly didn't *mean* it," he says, raising his eyebrows slightly. He's still pissed, I can tell. But being able to joke about it must be a good sign.

"You should sleep," I say, deciding to drop the subject. He sighs heavily, nodding, and then something else occurs to me. "Or go."

He whips his head back up, frowning again. "Go where?"

"To Manchester," I explain. Then I try to think of a way to say he doesn't need to stay without sounding ungrateful. "Well, things are calmer now. I think. I'm just going to be at the hospital until I can bring grandma home. You don't need to wait around."

He nods, still frowning, and I'm not sure I was successful in my attempt. Then, when I break our gaze to continue eating, he says, "I'm not leaving here without you."

Now it's my head that whips up in surprise. There's resolve on his features, and I'm strangely glad he said that.

"Sleep, then," I say and he nods.

We finish our meal in companionable, warm silence. I let him wash the dishes again as I run around gathering the things grandma requested to bring to her. I meet him back in the living room, already splayed out on the couch. I feel like I owe him. For putting up with me. And for staying.

"Do you want to sleep on my bed?" I offer, then.

He looks at me, his eyebrows rising slightly. He chews on his bottom lip as he thinks.

"Yes." His face is unreadable, as usual. I should stop trying.

I lead the way up the stairs and into my room. I don't know why I do that, he knows where my room is, he's been there before. I stop at the door and he enters, standing beside the bed.

"So..." I say, unsure of what to do. "Do you want me to leave the car?"

"Nope," he says, putting his hands in his pockets and just staring. Awkwardly.

"Okay," I nod. Awkwardly. "If you need anything..."

"I won't, but I'll text you," he says. Then, he pulls his phone out of his pocket. "I don't have your number, though."

As I type it in his phone, I can only think that this is such a smooth way of getting my number. I'd probably not give it to him in a different situation.

"Here you go." I hand him the phone back. "I'll be back around eight, it's when visiting ends."

"Okay."

"I'll bring something for dinner."

"Okay."

I don't know what else to say, so I leave. I leave Tyler Hackley standing alone in the middle of my childhood bedroom. What is wrong with me?

I stop myself from thinking about it. I climb down the stairs, grab the car keys and grandma's stuff, and leave again. Before I can even start the car, though, my phone buzzes. It's an unknown number.

'If you need anything...'

***

Midway to the hospital, my phone alarm goes off. It's the reminder to call Pete I recorded earlier. So, as soon as I park outside, I grab my phone and call him. He picks up after the second ring.

"Finally!" is the first thing he yells.

"I know, I know," I sigh.

"Okay, give me one second to settle down and then lay it on me," he says, making me smile. God, I miss him already. "Okay. Shoot. Spare no detail."

That's what I do. I try to recount the last 48 hours in as much detail as possible. I tell him about my reunion with Eileen, seeing his parents, getting called off by the doctor, and even the cute nurse. I also tell him about my constant want to cry. I leave out Tyler's parts. He doesn't need to know about those.

"So, that's what you missed on Glee," I joke when I finish.

"Not so much glee, it seems," he sighs, gloomy.

"No," I sigh, too.

"I'm sorry, Becks," his heavy breath indicates he means it. "I should be there with you."

"No, you shouldn't. But I wish you were," I admit.

"I'm sorry," he repeats.

"Don't be. I'm fine. Everything will be fine."

"Right." He pauses. I know what he's going to ask next, so I start preparing an answer. "And how is our favorite pop star?"

"Currently asleep," I inform mechanically.

"That's not what I asked."

"But it's the only answer I have."

"Right," he sighs again, knowing he'll have a better chance to interrogate me when we're face to face.

"How is Tristan?" I return the question and he chuckles.

"Ask Lindsey," he replies, making me sit up straight.

"What?"

"Ah, it's quite a long story, but they're getting along *too* well." I can practically hear his eye roll.

"No way!"

"Yes way."

"How do you feel about it?" I ask because he sounds annoyed. "Did Lindsey notice the chemistry between you two?"

"First of all, there's no chemistry," he says offended. "Second, yes, of course she noticed."

"Oh my God, Pete!" I can hardly conceal my amusement.

"I'll tell you all about it when you get back," he says. "By the way, when are you coming back?"

"I don't know yet," I feel the heaviness of the reality install its weight back on my shoulders. "I can't leave grandma alone."

"Call my mom," he says it like an order.

"Pete..."

"Call her."

"I can't ask—"

"Just call her," he interrupts me and I sigh. "You know you won't have to ask her, right? She'll probably just offer as soon as you mention Eileen will be discharged tomorrow. But it will mean the world to her if you call her."

"I'll call her," I end up agreeing, because Pete's right.

"Okay. You have about an hour."

"Pete!" I complain.

"Call her!"

"I will."

"And come back soon. We're on our way to Manchester, by the way," he tells me, as if I didn't already know.

"I know, *Tyler* told me," I say, hoping he notices the accusation in my tone.

"Good," he replies simply. It bothers me. I don't think this whole situation with Lindsey and Tristan is as simples as he's implying. But before I can ask anything, he adds "We're arriving within the hour." He says it as Todd does, and we laugh.

"Okay, I'll let you know when we leave."

"Okay," he pauses again, and I know a joke is coming up. "Enjoy your last hours alone with *Tyger*."

I can't even answer. I can't even come up with an answer. I howl, laughing so hard, I start to cry. After a full minute, my stomach hurts. I thank the heavens that I made this call while still in the car, otherwise I'd earn another scolding from the hospital staff.

"I hate you!" I manage to say, drying my face. "You've ruined his name forever."

"Good luck not thinking about it whenever you look at him," he says, still laughing.

"You're the worst!" I yell. Then we say goodbye and hang up.

And I'm back to the silence, alone. Except now I feel a little less desperate. I still hate the idea of asking for help, of throwing responsibility onto someone else. Johanna has done more than enough for me over the years.

I hate that grandma is unhealthy, and old, and is probably going to die. Yes, everybody dies. I still hate it.

I'm still debating whether to follow Pete's advice when I enter grandma's room—and find Johanna already there.

"Pete just texted me saying that if you didn't call me in the next hour, I should call you," she says as she hugs me fiercely. "What do you need, sweetie?"

Damn you, Pete.

I can't ask her to take care of my grandmother in front of my grandmother. We just barely got back to being on good terms. Then, I remember something.

"Oh, I was just going to ask if the dinner invitation is still up," I say and she beams.

"Of course, my love!" She pulls me into her arms again. "You didn't need to ask!"

***

We end up leaving a couple of hours before visiting ends as grandma gets tired. I suspect she only said she was tired to get rid of Jo—they don't get along all that well. I mean, grandma doesn't get along with her all that well. She's always been annoyed by the way Jo basically adopted both of us as part of her family. I think she's always been a little jealous because I spent so much time in her house. I was mostly with Pete, but there's no reasoning with Eileen sometimes. I guess I do have a lot of her in me.

I end up going to Pete's parents' house and helping Jo with dinner. I mostly listen as she talks about Dan, Evie and Avie, and even Pete. She's always been like this—talkative, open, not a fan of silences. The more I don't participate in the conversation, the more she talks. Pete really has a lot of her in him.

After the casserole is in the oven and the table is set, we sit down on the couch with a glass of wine while we wait for everyone to get home. I grab my phone to check the time and notice Tyler didn't reply to my text. I tried calling him on the way over, but he didn't pick up. I'm kind of relieved he won't be here and that I won't have to deal with explaining his presence.

"So, Pete said he's already in Manchester," Jo says when I put the phone back into my pocket. "For the next concert."

"Yeah, it's tomorrow night," I answer, wondering how much Pete told her in that message.

"What time are you planning to leave?" she asks casually. "Just so I know to bring enough for lunch tomorrow."

"What do you mean?" I frown.

"Oh, I'm coming over tomorrow after Eileen is discharged. Didn't we talk about this?" she asks, sipping her wine and failing to fool me.

"No, we didn't," I say, sighing. Once again, damn you, Pete.

"We must have chatted about it before you arrived, then," she continues. "Eileen and I agreed that I'll bring her lunch every day for a few days, until she feels she can handle it herself."

"What?" I gasp. Eileen agreed?

"Yeah, and then Dan is going to repair a few things around the house, as well. You know, so we can keep an eye on her," she winks.

"Wait, Jo—"

"I thought she would give me a harder time, to be honest. I had at least three speeches prepared to convince her, but she didn't fight me back as much as I was expecting. I think this accident might have really scared her, poor thing." She shakes her head, taking another sip of wine.

"Was it... was it your idea, then?" I ask.

"What?"

"The lunch thing."

"Of course! Did you think I'd leave Eileen unsupervised after this?" she chuckles.

You thought I would, I think. And it hurts. Especially because it's not such an absurd assumption.

"I was thinking about staying," I say and she can barely hide her surprise.

"Oh," she nods slowly, putting her glass down. "That explains why Eileen didn't resist."

"She must really not want me here," I sigh, frustrated.

"Oh, Rebecca!" she exclaims, scooting closer to me. "No, dearie, it's not like that."

I don't want to argue. I don't want to talk about this anymore. But, of course, since I stop talking, Jo continues.

"She just doesn't want to be a burden, you know?" she says, pausing for a while, kind of unsure if she should be saying these things. "You know she blames herself. About... about your parents. You see, your mom wanted to leave Alnwick. But your dad didn't want to leave Eileen alone. And Eileen would never leave Alnwick. And then... well... you know... I think she doesn't want the same to happen with you."

"I would never..." I shake my head, feeling my eyes burning again.

"I know, dearie, I know." She pats my knee, caressing my face with her free hand. She's so good at this mother thing. "It's not that she doesn't want you here, it's that she wants you to live your life, you know? As I want Peter to live his. As painful as it is to have you both so far, it's better than have you close and..."

She trails off and I look away. I'm not sure I agree with her. I'm not sure staying away is better. I don't think the place has anything to do with the weight I carry around. Because it's not here, grounded in Alnwick or in my childhood home. It's inside me.

"You were meant for great things, sweetie, both of you," she speaks again, resting her hand against my cheek. "I really believe that."

"Thanks, Jo. For... you know... for everything," I stutter.

"No need to thank me, hen. We're family!"

She pulls me for yet another hug. I let her. I missed this, too.

A few minutes after that, Dan and Avery walk through the door, and there's more hugging and squealing. We sit around, chatting—or, rather, listening, as Jo and Avie do most of the talking, until Evie arrives and we finally get to the dinner part. I learn none of the girls live in the house anymore, but they came when they heard I would be around. At the same time it makes me feel good in a way, it makes me feel bad, as well. They all have way more consideration for me than I think I have for them. That's why I try not to get irritated when they start to shower me with questions.

"Oh, speaking of which," Avie turns to me suddenly, "Becky, who's the guy you brought with you to town?"

"What guy?" Evie widens her eyes.

"Um..." I don't know what to say, but I don't have time to.

"A blond bloke, really handsome," Avie answers, nodding. "Or so I've been told."

"Where is he?" Evie asks.

"Oh, was it that young fellow that was in the store yesterday?" Dan barges in.

"You met him?" Avie turns to her father with wide eyes.

"Kind of, yeah," he shrugs.

"He was very handsome, indeed," Jo confirms.

"What's his name?" Evie asks at the same time Avie says, "Who is he?"

"Tyler. He is... um... he's..." I don't know what to say to the sudden silence that follows that. "Back home."

"Rebecca!" Jo gasps. "You should have brought him over! Where are your manners?"

"He didn't—" I try to argue, but I am interrupted.

"I'm making him a plate and you're getting it back to him," Jo says matter-of-factly.

"Or you should invite him over right now," Avie winks.

"Avery, don't be sassy," Jo points a fork to her.

"Is he your boyfriend?" Evie asks.

"Pete didn't mention anything about a boyfriend," Jo says, shaking her head. But then she opens a smile and looks at me. "Oh, but I'm so glad you found someone, dearie!"

"Is he a good lad?" Dan asks. He's also good at this dad stuff.

"Yeah, but—" I say, only to be cut off again.

"Do you have any pictures of him?" Avie asks.

"Avery!" Jo reprehends her.

"What, I'm just curious," she shrugs.

"Don't listen to her, sweetie," Jo pats my hand. "Eat, eat before it gets cold!"

***

By the time I leave—with a packed dinner for my very handsome boyfriend Tyler—I'm exhausted. I drive home in silence and notice my ears are ringing almost as much as they do after a concert.

I creep inside the house slowly, meaning to surprise Tyler as he goes through my stuff. Because I'm certain he's going through my stuff. I leave his dinner on the kitchen island and climb up the stairs, skipping the creaky ones. But my bedroom light is out and Tyler is still asleep—as I make sure by entering and listening to his calm, rhythmic breathing for a while. I debate whether to wake him up, mainly because I'm really tired and want my bed back, but decide against it. The stupid boy stayed up for over 24 hours straight. Let him recover.

So I climb back down and head outside, turning off the kitchen lights. The night is clear and if it's dark enough, I'll be able to see some stars. I walk to the side of the garden, where that picture in the hall with my dad was taken and lie down. The grass is moist and cold, but I'm not bothered enough to get a blanket or a towel.

I just lie there, breathing in the cold air, letting my eyes adjust to the dark, and emptying my mind. One by one, the small spots of light start to appear. I hold out a hand, connecting the dots with imaginary lines.

"What are you doing?" Tyler's head appears in my line of sight, his hair falling over his face as he looks down at me.

"Looking at the stars," I say.

He then looks up, standing near my head. He's already in his comfies and barefoot. I silently hope neither of us gets sick tonight.

"This makes my neck hurt," he complains after a while, but doesn't look down.

"It's better if you lie down," I say, more of a suggestion than a fact.

Without even thinking, he throws himself down next to me, so close that our arms touch. He puts one hand under his head and I briefly wonder what would it feel like to lie on his chest.

"It *is* better," he says after a while. Then he turns to me and catches me staring. I'm glad it's dark and he won't be able to tell I'm blushing. "How is she?"

"Better, thankfully," I say. We stare at each other for a moment, and then I look back up. I can feel him doing the same.

"Why are you so obsessed with the stars?" he asks.

"My dad," I blurt out and a lump instantly forms in my throat. Even so, I manage to continue, "It was our thing."

He stays silent for a few more moments. When he speaks again, I notice his voice cracking the way it did the night we arrived, "So this is how you spent your childhood?"

"Most of it, yes," I answer, smiling in the dark.

"Do you miss it?"

"Sometimes," I shrug in the dark. Then, for reasons I can't explain, I add, "I miss my dad."

"I miss my dad, too," he says, startling me. I look over, trying to assess his expression. "Music was our thing."

There are a million questions I want to ask. Why does he miss his dad? What happened? When did it happen? But I know that if I do, it'll give him the opportunity to ask, too. And I don't want to answer. And maybe he doesn't want to answer. So I ask something else.

"Did he teach you how to play?"

"Guitar, yes. Piano was by my own choice."

I can't help but snort. He looks to me then, frowning a little.

"I learned piano because of my dad. Guitar was my own choice," I explain.

"I guess that's why you suck at piano," he says, without missing a beat.

"Shut up!" I elbow his side lightly. "I bet you suck at guitar."

"I don't," he says cockily.

"I'll need proof of that."

"You won't get any," he says, then he grins. "But you have my word."

"Pfff!"

"What? Isn't my word good enough?"

"Not on this matter," I argue.

"That really hurts my feelings," he says, trying to hide a smile.

"You can get over it," I blurt. *Crap.*

His small eyes widen to a point I can almost see the blue. I don't know what to do, I don't know if I should apologize—again—, I don't know if he's offended. So I just wait while *he* decides what to do.

After a while, his expression softens, slowly, and he smiles. Then, he says, "I think I can."

He rolls over, so he's lying sideways, facing me. His knees touch my thighs and his eyes never leave mine. I don't know if I imagine it, but I can feel myself being pulled by his gravity.

"I'm not gonna kiss you," I blurt out before I can think straight.

He looks surprised once again and this time I brace myself for a fight. He laughs, though. He laughs and moves away and I think I would have preferred a fight.

"What makes you think I'd want to kiss you?" he snorts. "As it happens, darling, you're not my type."

As it happens, Hackley, you're exactly mine.

I bite down my tongue, hard. This is not me talking, it's this place. The place, and the last 48 hours, and how his eyes glisten in the dark, and that stupid fanfiction Pete showed me the other day. It's not me. It's not happening. It *will not* happen.

"Don't call me darling," I say suddenly, maybe still trying to pick up a fight.

But he bites his lip, clearly trying not to laugh again, with little success.

"Jesus, Rebecca, you're impossible," he says, his face a mix of amusement and annoyance.

"I don't like Rebecca, too."

He finally looks back at me. Not angry at all. Which is not helpful at all.

"What should I call you, then?" he asks.

Gosh, what a stupid question. What exactly does he expect me to say? He knows what to call me.

"Queen of England," I say, and now he bursts into laughter.

He rolls away, holding his sides with his hands. I laugh, too. It wasn't even that funny, honestly, but his reaction is contagious.

"Elizabeth it is," he says when he recovers.

He rolls back to his original position. And stares. *Ugh.* I can't take it.

"I brought you dinner," I say as I sit up, preparing to run away. "It's on the counter."

"Okay," he sighs, not moving from the ground. "Thanks."

I get up, shaking the grass off my slightly damp clothes, while he watches me—still lying down, a hand still under his head, his eyes still glistening.

"We're leaving tomorrow, by the way," I say before I turn away to enter the house.

"Okay," he repeats.

"After I bring Eileen home," I continue.

"Okay."

Then I stand there, staring, again not sure of what to say. Again wanting so bad to know what's going on under that blond hair of his, but too chicken to ask.

"If I said I wasn't leaving," I say, curiosity getting the best of me, "what would you say?"

"If you said *we* weren't leaving..." he says, stressing the word, "I would say 'okay'."

"Would you really miss a concert because of me?"

"It's just work," he chuckles. "We could cancel, reschedule. We still can."

"No, there's no need," I shake my head, too overwhelmed to make sense of his words.

"Okay," he smiles. I hate that I can still see it in the dark.

"Goodnight, Tyler," I say, turning my back to him and finally walking away.

"Night, Elizabeth," he calls after me.

*DAY EIGHT

I WAKE UP BEFORE HIM, FOR ONCE. IT'S WEIRD TO CLIMB DOWN THE stairs to utter silence. It's also weird to have him sleeping on my couch. Tyler Hackley in my childhood home, in my small town, on my couch. Now *that* is fanfiction material.

I run into the kitchen to make coffee. I open the fridge, gathering some eggs and bread to make a proper breakfast, when I spot some apples. Grandma's pie is long gone, so I think about making her another one. It will certainly not be anything like hers, but I feel like I owe her. So, as silently as I can manage, I start to work.

I search for some basic recipe online as I sip my coffee and, soon enough, I'm kneading the dough. It brings back old memories. I used to help grandma with her pies. I used to help mum...

While grandma has always been great with desserts, mum's thing was pasta. She knew how to make every single type, and she'd let me choose which one we'd eat whenever she decided to make it. I remember once I went to the school library to 'research', and wrote down every pasta type I could find. Then, when mum asked me which kind I wanted next, I raced up to my bedroom and picked up my list. I tried to choose the most difficult ones, or the ones I thought she wouldn't know how to make. But she always knew. She knew all of them. She made all of them, with my help. The kitchen was a nightmare by the time we'd finish, and dad would always complain about the flour stains we'd leave on his clothes when we hugged him after work.

But then I grew up. She stopped making pasta. She stopped wanting my help. She just stopped.

Some days I wonder if these memories are even real or if it's just a trick my mind plays on me because those are literally the only nice memories I have of her. I don't even know how old I was. And I never mentioned them to anybody. Because, if they're not real, then I'll have nothing.

"What is this smell?" Tyler walks into the kitchen, yawning and running his hands through his hair.

"You have one guess," I joke as I put things away.

"Apple pie?" he asks surprised as he walks to a stool and sits down.

"We have a winner!" I smile brightly. He frowns.

"You're awfully cheery this bright morning," he says in a terrible British accent. I start to feel self-conscious about my mood.

"Don't worry," I sigh as I move to make us breakfast, "it won't last. Eggs?"

"You're making me breakfast?" he asks in such a surprised tone that it actually offends me. I just raise my eyebrows until he answers, "Yes, please. I'll have them boiled, but not too long that it hardens the yolk. I like it soft."

I stare for a moment before I say, "Scrambled it is."

He chuckles. He was joking, apparently. Well, with him, I can never tell.

As I crack the eggs on the pan and put the bread in the toaster, he walks to the sink, meaning to wash the dirty dishes I used to make the pie.

"Leave it," I say, in vain. "Please, I'll do it later."

"I'll do it now," he answers, already scrubbing things with soap.

He has his back turned to me, so I just watch him for a moment. I watch Tyler Hackley barefoot in my kitchen washing my dishes—another good fanfic moment right there.

He looks so at home. I can tell his hair is a bit greasy already. He starts whistling, the same song I heard him singing the other day. The one he apparently never showed anyone.

I'm startled by the toasts jumping out of the toaster. And then the eggs almost burning in the pan. I curse under my breath and start to stir.

I make our plates, then I fill two mugs with coffee, and we settle down to eat in silence. He scrolls through his phone as he eats, squinting and trying to keep his hair away from his eyes. I'm surprised to realize this is already familiar to me. I'm surprised to realize I already have memories with Tyler.

It's so crazy. This is all so... easy. Which is another surprising discovery.

***

"Oy, lad, I can do it myself, thank you very much!" I can hear grandma's voice from down the corridor. "Now, hand it to me."

"Eileen, I can't let you exert yourself," Patrick retorts, in that calm tone of his.

"Since when putting on clothes is exertion?" grandma argues.

"Good morning," I say, entering the room and interrupting their bickering.

"Ah, see? Now I'm not alone, you can go. Go, go!" Grandma waves her arms as if shooing away a dog. Patrick just chuckles.

"What's going on?" I ask. The nurse opens his mouth to tell me, but grandma doesn't let him.

"The lad doesn't want to let me dress," she complains.

"Well, just Becky," he turns to me, "as I was explaining to grandma, she has to restart her daily activities slowly. And," he turns back to her, "dressing *is* exertion after spending 72 hours on a bed."

"My granddaughter will help me," she says, staring at him blankly.

"Okay," he sighs, handing me her clothes. "I'll be just outside."

Grandma waits until he's gone to sit up on the bed. When she tries to stand up, of course, she loses her balance. I catch her before another accident occurs and decide to make no remarks. She does let me help her, silently and grumpily.

"So, you've been discharged?" I ask her.

"Not yet," she answers in a steady voice. "They were waiting on someone to come pick me up and sign the papers. As if I'm a baby who doesn't know how to take care of herself."

"Grandma!" I exclaim but smile. "It's just protocol, I'm sure."

"Protocol, protocol," she mutters.

After we're done, I help her on the bed again and decide to go look for Patrick to ask what's the procedure. I don't have to look, though—I open the door to find him waiting with a wheelchair.

"Ready to go home, Eileen?" he asks excitedly as he walks back in.

"I can walk," she says bitterly, eying the chair.

"I know you can, I'm just spoiling you," he says and winks.

Grandma doesn't say anything and accepts the ride. I watch as Patrick helps her on the chair and retrieves her stuff, always smiling. He must really love what he does.

"We're gonna stop at the reception desk to sign you off, okay?" he says as he pushes her out and I follow.

She complains about that, muttering unintelligible things. I chat briefly with the nurse at the main hall, sign some papers and while grandma goes through the same process, I look around for Tyler. I frown when I find him talking to Dr. Haddish. She's grinning, a look of pure adoration on her face. I can't believe it. I watch as she asks him a question, takes her phone and snaps a selfie. That's when Tyler spots me. He points to me, says something else, and the young doctor's smile fades slightly. *Great.*

They start to make their way towards us, which makes me a little nervous as I remember I haven't told grandma about Tyler. My brain starts to work extra fast to come up with an explanation.

"Morning, Rebecca," she says when they're close enough, immediately approaching grandma to talk to her about her next appointment.

"Just Becky," Patrick whispers beside me. It makes me smile. "So, will I see you around?"

"Uhm..." I hesitate, taken by surprise with this. "Not really. I don't live here."

"Oh," he nods, a bit disappointed. Or, at least, I think he is. "Where do you live?"

"London," I say.

"Cool!" He fully turns to me now. *Oh, no.* We're gonna have 'a conversation'. I'm not good at it. "What do you do there?"

"Uhm... I'm a musician," I start fidgeting with the hem of my sweater.

"Cool! Anything I've heard?" he goes on, either unaware of or indifferent to my discomfort.

"I don't think so," I smile politely. He doesn't look like someone who listens to punk.

"Too bad," his smile broadens. Gosh, it's a beautiful smile. "Where can I hear it?"

"Well, I'm currently on tour," I find myself saying. Tyler snorts somewhere behind me. I ignore it.

"Nice! Are you coming anywhere near?"

"We're playing Edinburgh and Glasgow this weekend," I continue, not really sure why.

"Nice! Maybe I'll come around to see you." I feel the warmth of his tone climb its way to my face. "What's the band's name?"

"Actually, I'm opening for the main act." I turn to Tyler now. "The Hacks."

Patrick's expression transforms. He looks at Tyler, eyes wide, a finger loosely pointing to him.

"Right. You're that guy from that band." He gives him a once-over, realization washing over his features. "The one who looked like a girl."

I snort, chocking with laughter that I try to disguise as a coughing fit.

"In person," Tyler says unamused, giving me a side-eye.

"Brilliant! My older sister had posters of you all over her walls," Patrick continues, which doesn't help my mood. "Can I take a selfie? She's gonna lose it."

"Sure," Tyler agrees, immediately putting on his professional heartthrob smile.

That's when grandma finally finishes with the receptionist and the doctor. Dr. Haddish gives a few last instructions and we say our goodbyes. Patrick motions to start pulling grandma's chair, but Tyler stops him.

"I'll get it from here. Thank you," he smiles coldly to him.

"Okay, then. Bye, Eileen! I hope you don't miss me!" He squeezes her shoulder and she mumbles something under her breath.

"Thank you, Patrick," I feel compelled to say.

"No problem," he smiles again. "See you soon."

I don't answer him. I turn around and start walking, followed by Tyler and grandma.

"What a cheeky young man," she remarks when we're far enough. "I couldn't take any more of his bright mood. Thank you for rescuing me, dearie." She looks up, tapping Tyler's hand.

"You're welcome," he says politely.

"And who are you again?"

That guy from that band who looked like a girl. I manage to not say it aloud, but I laugh anyway. I can't help it. Tyler glares.

I then explain to her who he is and why he's here—or, at least, some version of it. I tell her they wouldn't let me come on my own.

"Why, are you a prisoner now?" she asks, making me laugh again.

Tyler helps her into the car, and I'm still grinning wildly when he closes the door and turns to me. He rolls his eyes, giving me an annoyed look as he pulls me to the side so he can get to the passenger seat. I take several deep breaths as I round the front of the car to get to my seat, and finally drive home.

***

The first thing grandma does when she steps into the house is walk into the kitchen. She opens the fridge, inspecting its contents, glances at the empty sink, smells the freshly-made pie I left on the counter. Tyler and I watch in silence as she does that.

"Did you bake it?" she asks, poking the pie.

"Yes, this morning," I confirm. "Do you want some?"

"That would be great, I'm starving," she says, moving slowly to sit on the kitchen counter.

I take three plates from the cupboard and cut three slices of pie. Tyler sits down beside grandma, awkwardly staring from her to me. I can only imagine how he must be feeling. This must be so much more than what he bargained for. Well, he's here now, and this is what he gets.

"This tastes good, sweetie," grandma says with a mouthful.

"Yours was better," Tyler argues, making me glare.

Grandma turns to him with a suspicious expression, at first, but then she smiles. "Thank you, my boy."

Silence falls upon us once again as we finish eating. Tyler takes our plates to the sink and washes them as I try to ignore grandma's amused stare.

"Are you tired?" I ask her. "Do you want to go lie down for a while?"

"Gosh, no, the last thing I wanna do is lie down," she chuckles. "Let's sit in the living room and have a chat."

My stomach sinks at the suggestion. I don't want to talk. I don't want her talking to Tyler. I don't want her telling him about my life here, about my parents, about what happened last time I came home. I decide to text Jo and see if she can come over already so we can leave. I don't want to be here anymore.

"So, tell me about yourself," grandma asks Tyler as soon as we sit down. He looks at her with wide eyes and as much as I would love to hear his answer, I interrupt.

"Tyler plays piano," I say. "A lot better than I do. Do you want to hear it?"

"And will you let him play *your* piano?" She gives me a surprised look. I can feel myself start to blush. Then, she turns back to Tyler, "She's very possessive of it, you know."

"I know," Tyler answers, smiling. A stark contrast to the image of him glaring the first time I played *his* piano.

"Go ahead," I tell him.

"How did you learn?" Grandma interrupts.

"I took lessons as a child," he says simply.

"Oh, just like Rebecca," grandma smiles, patting my knee. "But she doesn't play anymore, such a shame."

"She's been playing it on tour," Tyler says. I curse him mentally.

"Indeed?" She turns to me again, eyebrows high on her forehead.

"Yeah, just... a little," I mumble.

"That's wonderful, dearie!" She squeezes my leg. It feels awful. Because she knows the reason why I stopped playing. And, now, the fact that I am playing on tour has a different meaning to her, a meaning that's not at all true. Because I'm not at all over it. "What song, though? I don't imagine you playing piano with the noise you and Peter make together."

"Grandma..." I sigh. I knew she'd find a way to criticize my music.

"It is one of their songs, actually," Tyler continues. I make a face when grandma turns to him, in hopes he'll stop talking about it. He doesn't. "We rearranged it together."

"Wonderful," she repeats, and then suddenly changes the subject. "What do you play, dearie?"

"Ah, noise, I suppose," Tyler says, smiling brightly.

"Well, at my age, everything that's not a classic is noise," grandma answers with an actual grin. Christ. I can't believe it. He's seducing her and she's falling for it.

"I do play classics, though," he continues.

"I'd imagine you did, you have the hands for it," she says and my eyes automatically focus on them. I have to agree. He has elegant, fair hands, with long, skinny fingers... "What do you play?"

"Some Beethoven, some Vivaldi..." he shrugs, as if he's talking about items in a grocery shop list.

"Chopin, by any chance?" grandma asks, making my heart start to race.

"Absolutely!" he confirms, excitedly.

"Oh, dearie," she leans over, putting a hand over his, "could I bother you to play just a little bit?"

"Sure, of course!" he agrees, to my dismay. As he gets up and installs himself in front of the piano, *my* piano, he says, "I'm a little rusty, though, be warned."

It's a lie. He doesn't sound rusty at all. He sounds like he's played Chopin every day of his life. He sounds like someone who's had classical training. He sounds like... my dad. Actually, I think he sounds better, which makes me angry, at first. How dare he show off like this, with *that* song? How dare Eileen request someone else to play it? How dare I... like it? I can't. I can't like it. And yet...

It's so weird. There are so many emotions competing inside of me to see which will win. I can't decide what I should be feeling. It's like I'm somewhere else watching me watch this moment. And then, for a second, I imagine dad watching it, too. What would he think? What would he say? I can't even begin to count how many times a day I ask myself these questions.

What would he think? What would he say? Why can't I ask?

"Dear boy," Eileen gasps when Tyler finishes. I look at her elated expression. And then I'm angry again. "You have such a talent!"

"Thank you, ma'am," Tyler smiles, turning around on the bench to face us.

"I'm not just saying that, believe me," grandma continues. "I'd never heard anyone play Chopin as well as my son. Until now."

What? That's such an exaggeration! What is she thinking? Why is she doing this?

I have to look away and bite my lip to hold back the tears. But my eyes fall on him, and his expression, and his small blue eyes glued on mine. He can tell. We look at each other for only a second, but I know he can tell. Or, maybe, I just wish he could.

"That's the best compliment I've ever received," he says, at last, turning back to Eileen. "Thank you."

I want to punch him. I want to punch him so hard that he falls to the floor and stays there. I also want to kiss him. Goddammit. I want to kiss him so bad. *This can't be happening.*

"You are most welcome," grandma answers.

"Do you wanna try?" he asks me now. It takes me several seconds to find my voice.

"I can't follow that," I say, shaking my head.

"Play me your song," grandma asks.

"What?" I gasp.

"The one you said you rearranged. Maybe I'll like it on the piano," she says, smiling and patting my knee again.

"Come on." Tyler scoots over on the bench, making room for me. "I'll sing."

"You sing, too?" grandma asks him, surprised. He chuckles.

I don't know what possesses me, but I actually join Tyler on the bench. His back is to the piano now, but his eyes are on me. I can feel them.

I stare at the keys, a strange, familiar feeling bubbling up inside. I don't even remember the last time I sat here. I don't even remember the last time I played *my* piano. I always remember why I stopped, though.

"Whenever you're ready," he says, his voice so close to my ear. If I turn my head now...

I don't give myself time to think and just start to play. And it doesn't feel nearly as painful as I was bracing myself to be. It's nice. It's familiar. It's... easy.

Tyler nails the song. I envy his falsetto so much. I envy the way he can make the song his own. I envy grandma who's able to just sit there and watch this, while I have to watch my hands, otherwise I don't know what I'm doing.

"Your voice is not as good as your fingers, I must say," she blurts out when he finishes.

"Grandma!" I turn around, taking the opportunity to take some distance from him.

"It's a nice song. Sad, but nice," grandma continues.

"Thanks," I mumble.

I walk back to the couch and sit in silence while grandma keeps requesting songs and Tyler keeps obliging. This is so surreal. I suddenly have the urge to register what's happening, just so I know I'm not dreaming. So I take my phone out and snap a picture of him. And then send it to Pete.

***

Johanna and Dan arrive for lunch with lunch—she's cooked her famous shepherds' pie, and the smell immediately fills the house. I introduce them to Tyler but, thankfully, he doesn't have time to answer none of Jo's questions. I help her in the kitchen while she interrogates grandma and they go through their arrangements for the next days. Jo and Dan will be in the house some time or another every day of the week. I can see grandma is not super thrilled with this, but she does her best to not complain and accept the help. It makes me equal parts relieved and guilty.

"Are you both staying for lunch, hen?" she asks me.

I glance at the clock and I'm surprised to find it's almost 1 p.m. I glance at Tyler then, but his blank expression is extremely unhelpful.

"We have to hurry," I end up saying.

"We have time to eat," Tyler argues. I look back at him. "It's a short trip to Manchester, we only have to be there at night."

"Great!" Jo squeals before I can say anything.

I try to not make a big deal of his willingness to stay longer.

As we sit down at the dinner table with our plates, my phone buzzes. I take it out to find Pete's reply to the photo I sent.

'WHAT IS THIS? IS THIS YOUR LIVING ROOM? IS THIS YOUR PIANO? IS THIS YOUR BOYFRIEND?'

I snort. Everyone looks at me.

"Pete," I say, hoping it explains everything.

"Oh, I talked to him this morning," Jo says. *Of course you did.*

'Yes, yes, and ABSOLUTELY NOT,' I text back.

'I've received reports saying otherwise,' he replies immediately.

'Your source is misinformed,' I say.

'Or just able to foresee the future,' his text says. I ignore it and keep eating. A few seconds later, he texts again, 'Is his hair soft?'

I choke on my food, which makes everyone look at me again. I stand up, walking to the sink and filling a glass with water. I leave my phone there when I come back to the table.

We finish eating and then grandma asks me to serve the apple pie. I do. We eat again, talk again, stay some more. When I start to get restless, glancing at the clock every few minutes, grandma puts her hand over mine.

"I'll pack the rest of the pie for your trip," she says, getting up and taking the pie to the counter. I follow her, wanting to have a moment alone.

"Are you sure—"

"I am," she interrupts me. "I'm feeling much better now."

"Granny," I stop her for a second.

"I'm telling the truth, dearie," she says, resting her palm against my cheek. "And I'm so, so happy that you came."

I can't answer because if I talk, I'll cry. Christ, how much water can a person shed through her eyes? I feel like I should be out of tears for a lifetime by now.

I nod, give her a little smile, and hug her. She pats the back of my head, the way she did when I was a little girl.

"I'll be back when the tour is over," I promise, even though that's not what she expects. It's not what she wants. I'll come back anyway.

"Alright, petal," she doesn't argue, giving me a sweet smile.

She finishes packing up the pie, Tyler and I gather our stuff, and I let Jo and Dan hug me goodbye. I tell them to send the girls my love and that I'll let them know when I come back. They all walk us outside, making everything a lot more dramatic. I don't think they believe I'll come back. I don't think *I* believe I will. I still want to try, though.

"Do you want me to drive?" Tyler offers as we step outside.

"Do you know how to drive on the right side of the road?" I ask suspiciously.

"You mean the wrong side?" He raises his eyebrows and I roll my eyes. "Yes, I do."

"Fine." I hand him the key while I throw my backpack on the backseat.

Tyler follows my lead and enters the car. I buckle my seatbelt while he adjusts his seat and the rearview mirror. I look up to the house I once called home one more time. As much as I don't want to feel tied to it, I know I am. Places have such a mysterious way of blending into our essence, and this place will always be part of who I am. It will always be responsible for who I became. And I hate it. But I also love it.

Tyler drives off and I watch grandma's silhouette slowly disappear in the side mirror. He turns right into the main avenue and she's gone. I blink hard, taken aback by the burning feeling behind my eyes.

"Are you okay?" Tyler asks after a few seconds.

"Yes," I say. Then I look at him, waiting for him to glance at me, and say it again, "Yes."

He smiles. Then he glances down my legs. I follow his eyes to find I'm still wearing my 'normal' clothes.

"We might have to stop on the way," I say and he chuckles, but doesn't argue. And, then, I have an idea. "Are you up for a tourist trip?"

"Now?" he frowns.

"Yeah, it won't take long," I say.

He fully turns his head to me, trying to read my expression. I try to remain as blasé as possible. He sighs, which means I succeeded.

"Fine," he says. "Where to?"

***

I buy our tickets on my phone, so we head straight to the entrance once we arrive. There's no line, since it's not a very popular destination this time of the year. Sure enough, Dean is working the gate. It's like everyone here is trapped in an endless time-space loop—they do the same things over and over again until they die.

"My, my, my, are my eyes deceiving me?" He adjusts his cap and rests his hands on his hips. "Or is this really Rebecca Olamina that I see?"

"Hey, Dean," I nod as we approach.

"What happened to the blue?" He points to my head.

"I'm into purple now," I reply.

"Right," he nods and his eyes fall on Tyler.

"This is my friend, Tyler. We're visiting," I say and he and Tyler shake hands.

"I thought you were on tour," he comments. That's the worst thing about small towns—everyone knows about everything.

"I am. Just passing by," I say while opening the tickets on my phone.

"Eileen, right?" See?

"Yep," I sigh.

"Ah, don't worry. She's strong, that one." He squeezes my shoulder and I give him an awkward smile. I turn the phone screen to him and he chuckles. "You didn't need to buy tickets, you know."

"I know," I say while Tyler snorts.

"Go on ahead. Be careful going up, there are new security guards," he instructs.

"Got it," I say and we walk in.

"Do you ever pay for anything in this city?" Tyler asks as soon as we're alone. I pretend I didn't listen. It's amazing the treatment you get in a small town when you're struck by tragedy.

"So, do you want the tourist tour? Or the VIP one?" I ask Tyler.

"Do you really need to ask?" He raises one eyebrow and we start our way to my secret spot.

The Alnwick castle still serves as residence to the royal family, so not all of it is open to the public. Which doesn't mean it's not accessible to the public. After years of coming here and visiting, I know my way around these cold corridors better than I know my own house, and getting into the restricted area is easier than one might think. Especially because no one watches or uses most of it.

In all of my years of living here and sneaking around, I not once had an encounter with the Duke or any of his family members or servants. If they do use the castle, it's a corner I was never able to find.

We walk around in silence, and I open some doors here and there to show Tyler inside. He looks a lot more interested than I thought he would be. I almost regret taking him to this side, he would probably enjoy the tourist stuff a lot more.

We reach the tower in no time—my favorite place in the whole town. I listen closely for any sound at the top of the stairs, and since there's none, we climb up. It's not the tallest one, but it's the one with the best view—we can see the sun reflecting off the lake and the endless hills beyond it, in a mix of greens and yellows you only see in storybooks.

"Wow," Tyler gasps. He squints his already small eyes until they almost disappear. Only now I realize he hasn't worn his glasses the entire time we've been here.

"Welcome to Alnwick," I say. I don't know why, it sounds lame and unnecessary. Luckily, Tyler smiles at that.

He takes a few photos on his phone and I fight the urge to do the same. It doesn't matter how many times I've been here, it always stuns me. I only have happy memories here.

"How do you know your way around this place?" Tyler asks.

"I used to come here a lot," I explain.

"To the side visitors are not supposed to come?" He gives me a suspicious look. I shrug. "You never got caught?"

"All the time," I chuckle.

"God, you get away with everything," he jokes.

"The perks of living in a small town," I point out.

"You have a lot of friends," he remarks.

"They're not my friends," I argue. Which is true. "Pity is different than friendship," I say aloud. I regret it. He whips his head around to look at me. But his curious expression turns into one of understanding within seconds.

"Your parents." It's not even a question.

"Yep," I nod and look away.

"Did you come here with them?" he asks. He's still looking at me.

"With my dad. I used to do a lot of things with my dad. My mom didn't like me very much," I blurt out again. Now that it's on the surface, it will be hard to hold back.

"Why?" he frowns.

"Don't know. Don't care. I didn't like her very much, either." I have flashes of her yelling for the silliest things—lying on the grass with a white dress, jumping into mud puddles, tying my hair with elastic bands. And always blaming my dad for it.

"What happened?" he asks.

I look at him. It's too personal. I never told anyone about my parents. In Alnwick, I never had to, everyone knows. Outside Alnwick, I chose not to tell, to start over, to pretend it didn't happen. But it did, didn't it? It happened and it changed me and it drove me away.

Tyler waits patiently while I make up my mind. I don't want to tell him. But I also kind of do. He's already too close, he's already seen too much, he already knows too much. And, for some reason, it doesn't bother me. Not anymore.

"One day... one day they drove off. They were supposed to go to Glasgow for something, but they never made it."

"Car accident?" he asks, never looking away.

"No. Well, I don't know. They just... disappeared." I break eye contact. They say time heals everything—whoever came up with this shit, they were lying. "I kinda wish it had been an accident, at least I'd know what happened, you know? Grandma thinks they just ran away, that my mom just finally turned my dad's head around. But I don't believe it. I can't. My dad... he wouldn't do that to me. He just... he wouldn't." I shake my head, childishly.

"Do you think they're dead, then?" he asks. It's a heavy question. It's a question no one else has ever asked me. A question that is on repeat on my mind for over a decade now.

"They must be. They have to be," I say, although a small part of me still wonders if it's possible they're living their best life somewhere else. Without me.

"And everybody knows." Again with the non-question. I just nod. "Is that why you left?"

"Yes... and no," I sigh. "There never was much for me here."

"I see." He finally looks away. "It's a beautiful place, though."

"It is." I follow his gaze towards the silver lake.

"I still live in my hometown," he says out of nowhere, making me smile.

"How is it like?" I ask.

"It's alright," he shrugs. "Quiet, small. But we don't have these views." He points to the hills.

"Do you think about moving out someday?" I ask. I can't picture him living in a small town.

"No," he says firmly.

"Not even for a while? Not even somewhere like LA?" I continue.

"No." He looks back at me, smiling knowingly. He must be asked this a lot.

"Why?" I frown getting more curious.

"I like it there. It's... it's the only place where I feel..." he hesitates before whispering the last word, "... real."

He looks away into the distance and when he speaks again, it's like he's not even speaking to me anymore.

"Sometimes, all of this is overwhelming. I feel like I'm this character in everyone else's narrative. I'm an actor in other people's stories. Clivesdale is the only place I don't feel like that. It's the only place I can go out and walk to the grocery store unconcerned. Where I can drive to my mom's house and talk about something other than myself. I can sit alone in my kitchen and just... exist."

I don't know what to say to that, so I don't say anything. I just stare, trying to reconcile this person standing in front of me and the guy who told me off just because I wanted to play his piano. It's impossible. I wonder if he feels the same. I wonder if he sees me differently now. I wonder if he thinks it's easy to talk to me like I'm beginning to think it's easy to talk to him.

"You're making me nervous," he says, glancing at me from the side of his eye. I laugh.

"What happened to your dad?" I ask. He stiffens, so I add, "You don't have to tell me if you don't want to."

For a moment, I think he's going to tell me anyway. But, then, he sighs in defeat, shaking his head.

"I don't want to," he says. Then, he looks at me with an apologetic yet mischievous expression. "It's a sensitive subject."

"Got it," I smile. And then he smiles. And then I get nervous. "Okay, turn around now."

"What?" he frowns.

"I'm going to change," I say.

"What?" His eyes widen.

"Turn around!" I demand.

He does and I take my usual clothes out of my backpack, changing as fast and as secretively as I can.

"Okay, I'm done," I say as I stuff my jeans and sweatshirt in the backpack and smooth the front of my skirt. He waits until I'm looking at him to give me a once over. *Bastard.* "Better?"

He cocks his head to the side, biting his lip. He's gonna come up with a smart-ass remark.

"Not really," he says. "I think I like you better as a regular person."

"Excuse me, sir," I joke, "would you like me to change back, then?"

"No," he says. "I can picture it in my mind."

Heat. Heat creeps up my legs and arms and chest. I'm sure he can see it. Shit, I'm sure he can *feel* it. I narrow my eyes, trying to hide it.

"Come on," I say, failing to give him a proper answer. But I'll have three hours alone with him to think of one. *Crap.*

***

I'm in the lake. Naked. I'm swimming naked in the lake. I don't know how I know I'm naked—I don't actually feel it and the water is too dark to see much further than the surface. But I know. I'm naked. In the lake.

The sun is setting on the horizon, making the body of water shimmer with that silvery glow I like so much. I can smell the grass in the soft wind that blows my wet hair. I turn towards the castle, afraid someone will appear and find me here. But there is no one in sight, no sound to be heard. I scan the shore looking for my clothes, but can't find them. I try to swim, but I can't move. I mean, I can, my arms and legs push and kick the water in the right way, but it doesn't matter how much I try, I'm still in the middle of the lake.

I stop, prepared for the fear. But my heartbeat is steady. My breathing is relaxed. The warmth of the sun on my face feels good. What is going on?

In my head, I know I shouldn't be so calm. I shouldn't be in the lake. I shouldn't be naked in the lake. Not only it is a public space, but it's also disgusting. God only knows what kind of things visitors and tourists throw in here. Or what kind of animals lurk in the dark.

As if on cue, I feel something moving near my feet. I'm about to scream when the creature breaks the water surface—a blond creature.

Unlike me, Tyler is able to swim around easily. He's smiling, punching water at me, teasing.

"Stop!" I grunt. He swims closer and I try to grab his wrist, but he pulls away.

"Help me!" I cry again. He laughs. But then he turns to me and starts to approach. Slowly.

"Are you naked?"

"What?" he asks, although his mouth is not moving.

"Are you naked?" I repeat my silly question. And then he laughs.

I feel a tug on my shoulder, which is so unexpected that startles me awake. I sit up, trying to cover my body with my hands. Only I'm not naked. I'm not in the lake. I'm fully dressed and dry inside the car. With Tyler. Who is now bending over in laughter.

"Please, tell me I didn't ask it out loud," I groan, knowing very well I did.

"You so did!" He punches his leg. "What the hell were you dreaming about?"

"I was swimming naked in a lake," I confess, and then quickly change the subject. "Have we arrived?"

"Yes," he says, drying tears from his eyes. "Wait, *a* lake or *the* lake?"

I don't answer and hop off the car. We're parked in front of the venue. I grab my backpack from the backseat and rush to the side door.

"Who were you talking to?" he asks as he runs to catch up with me. "You were asking someone else if they were naked."

I speed up, holding the backpack's shoulder straps harder.

"Wait," he says, and then lowers his voice as I stalk the corridors in search of Pete, or anyone, "Was it me?"

"You wish," I scoff.

And then, in the most nonchalant tone I've ever heard, he says, "Oh, yes, I do."

I stop on my tracks, whipping around to look at him. He almost collides with me, but stops himself just in time. And really close. I look up at his face, at his shameless face, as he smiles and raises his eyebrows and... *argh!* He didn't... he can't... I don't...

"Becks!" someone shouts behind us. The next thing I know, Pete is trying to break my ribs with his arms tight around me. "Oh my God, finally! What took you so long? Why didn't you text me? My mum said you left the house like five hours ago!"

"I fell asleep," I say with the little breath that remains in me.

He lets me go and holds me at arm's length, studying my face. I hold his gaze, unsure of what he is seeing, but very aware of my heart stampeding inside my chest. His eyes then travel to somewhere behind me.

"Hey, Pete," Tyler says. "Good to see you."

"You, too," Pete says.

"Where's everyone?" Tyler asks.

"On stage, we were about to start soundcheck," Pete says.

"Cool," Tyler answers and then walks past us to go to the stage. We stare at his back as he slowly disappears down the corridor.

"So," Pete turns back to me. "How was the trip?"

Christ. How can I describe it?

"Crazy."

"Okay," Pete nods, his eyes wide. "Tell me everything."

"We don't have time now," I argue, glad for soundcheck and the opportunity to gather my thoughts. "Show me our dressing room."

***

Except I can't gather my thoughts at all. I keep seeing Tyler's face when he said that, and when we were lying on the grass, and when he told me I was pretty. Which means I keep hitting all the wrong notes and singing the wrong words at the wrong times. It's all a mess. I'm a mess. And I literally have no time to pull myself together, as we're already late as it is. We leave the stage 30 minutes before the doors open and I still can't remember the lyrics to that Hacks stupid song.

"Did you actually forget it?" Pete asks as he follows me to our dressing room. "Or are you trying to be funny?"

I shoot him a murderous look. He only shrugs.

"Becky!" someone squeals as I open the door and then hugs me. Again. "Finally, you're here!"

"Hi, Linds," I hug her back. She smells like cupcakes. "It's good to see you."

"You, too! How is your grandma? How was the trip? How are you doing?" she asks all at once, with a serious face, looking me in the eye. It makes me smile.

"I'm fine. Tired, but fine. Grandma is fine. The trip was fine," I say.

"I thought you said it was crazy," Pete argues behind me. I fight the urge to shoot him yet another psychopathic look.

"Good crazy or bad crazy?" Lindsey squints her eyes.

"I... I don't know yet," I answer, not sure if I want to go over it right now.

"Well, tell us everything in detail and then we can decide together," Pete says, putting one arm over his girlfriend's shoulders.

I stare at them, noticing how cute they look. How happy they look. I don't think they're fighting anymore. I think they made up. What does it mean for Tris, then? I can't tell if he looked upset during soundcheck, I was too distracted to notice anything else. *Anyone* else.

"I need to relearn that damn song," I say, taking my phone out and looking it up online. "We can talk later."

Pete doesn't complain or insist, which already raises a red flag for me. I don't mention anything, either. He helps me with the song while Lindsey watches and in no time we're called to be onstage.

The show ends up being our worst on the tour. In my opinion, anyway. The venue is too big for the crowd that turns up, and the people that do come seem to be having a mediocre time. Possibly because we're being mediocre musicians. Much like it happened during soundcheck, our sets are full of mistakes and forgetting lyrics, which stresses everyone out and messes up the experience for the crowd.

Things get worse when we leave right after the show without talking to the fans, since The Hacks have an early morning show appearance in Edinburgh tomorrow. It takes no time for them to start complaining online. Todd and Tyler have a bit of a fight in the back room of the bus, which the rest of us thankfully don't witness. We still hear a raised voice every now and then, but keep pretty much out of it.

I also don't get a moment alone with Pete. Or Tyler. Or anyone else. It's really weird. It's like all the previous concerts and all the hours I spent crammed with all of these people inside a bus didn't exist. Everything feels so strange, different, new. I feel so out of place. I can't think straight. Just a few hours ago I was sitting in my living room, enjoying a private concert by Tyler Hackley, and now I can't even catch a glance of him.

We reach a rest stop after a few hours, where we're parking for the night, and I'm really thankful I'm not the only girl around anymore. Lindsey and I band together for dinner, and for a shower—something I'd probably wouldn't have the courage to do if I was alone, sadly. We keep watch for each other, and she asks about Paul since Pete obviously filled her in about what happened. She's appalled and we spend a few moments talking trash about him.

Then, I ask her if she's staying until the end of the tour.

"Hopefully," she answers. Damn. I feel so out of the loop. I really need to talk to Pete.

But when we get back to the bus, he's nowhere to be seen. I spend some time talking to Neil, who politely asks about grandma and how I'm holding up.

"Fine," I say, and, for once, it isn't a lie.

He tells me about the plans for the next day, to which I only half listen. I'm only half present. I think a part of me stayed behind.

I decide to try to get some sleep, so I head to my bunker. I check social media, just to realize the fans are really angry, so I update the band's account and close the app. I watch some random episodes of British Bake Off—my favorite—until the bus is completely silent. Everyone is asleep.

And, just like that, it's over. Everything is back to normal. Everyone is where they're supposed to be.

DAY NINE

I TOSS AND TURN IN THE CUBICLE, TOO COLD ONE MINUTE, TOO HOT THE next. Everything is too still, too silent, too closed off. I wish the bus was moving, then it would probably lull me to unconsciousness. Since that's not gonna happen anytime soon, I get up. I'll just spend the rest of the night watching videos online. It's the safest bet.

I wrap myself in my blanket and head to the kitchen area. I pause when I see someone sitting on the farthest booth, his back turned to me. It's all dark, except for the light coming out of the window, to where his face is pointing. His profile, lit up by the yellow glow, looks almost supernatural. And ravishing. Which is irritating. For all I know, he could be posing for a magazine. It should be illegal to look this good, especially in the middle of the night, at such a distance, and in the dark.

I take my phone out as quietly as I can manage, giving in to the urge to capture the moment. And then I walk towards him with the same caution.

"Can't sleep?" I ask, and he jumps. "See?" I point to him, grinning.

"Well, you came out of nowhere." Tyler rolls his eyes.

"I was somewhere," I argue.

"Somewhere very quiet," he narrows his eyes. "Can't sleep?"

"I asked first," I say, sitting opposite him on the booth.

"No," he says.

"Yes, I did!" I insist.

"'No' is the answer," he gives me a pointed look.

"Oh, right," I nod. "Same."

"Not in the mood to dream of me naked again?" he asks unflinchingly.

My heart beats in my ears as I am reminded of the last thing he said to me. I decide to play his game.

"I didn't know whether you were naked or not, hence why I was asking," I say, trying to keep the quiver out of my voice.

"I probably was," he smirks.

"Oh, I see, you're the skinny dipping type of guy," I squint my eyes in what I hope is a judgmental look. He shrugs.

"And you're the skinny dipping type of girl," he says.

"No, I'm not," I argue.

"Then why were you dreaming about being naked in the lake?"

"Probably because it's one of my greatest fears." I mean, honestly, how many diseases would I contract if I did that? I shudder only to imagine. Then, I add, "Which makes it a nightmare, not a dream."

"You should try it," he says with a serious face. "Face your fears, you know."

"Right," I snort. "Not in the lake, though."

"I recommend the ocean," he continues.

"Another public place, great," I joke. Then I narrow my eyes, studying his shameless face. "How often do you do it?"

"Not often," he chuckles. He looks away, towards the light, and for a moment his whole face is lit by that yellow glint. "We have this studio place in Malibu, it's near the beach. I know a spot nobody ever goes to because you have to climb down a steep hill. So, not exactly public."

"You have a studio in Malibu?" I raise my eyebrows.

"It sounds fancier than it actually is. It's a rented place, an old house. It only has one bedroom. But you can sleep to the sound of the waves at night."

"You like the beach," I remark.

"Who doesn't?" he asks, then he gives me a baffled look. "Don't tell me you don't. First The Beatles, now the beach, you're making it hard for us to be friends, Lizzie."

Lizzie. That makes me smile. Damn him.

"I like the beach," I confess. "We don't have many options around here, though."

"Well, if you're ever in California…" he trails off. Then, he smirks and adds, "Then maybe we can make that little dream of yours come true," he smirks again, looking at me.

"Nightmare," I correct him.

"Nightmare," he repeats in a whisper. And keeps staring. I keep staring back. I'm trying really hard not to picture that scenario in my head. "What?" he asks after a while.

"Nothing," I shake my head, trying to get rid of the images. Then I decide to change the subject a little, "I was just wondering how many girls you took skinny dipping in Malibu."

"None. You'd be the first," he says with no hesitation. Then the smirk comes back and he adds, "Don't you wanna be my first?"

"Tyler!" I gasp.

"Sorry, sorry, I'll stop," he laughs, looking away, actually embarrassed.

"You're making it hard for us to be friends, Hackley," I tell him.

"Well, in my case, it's on purpose," he answers, making me shake my head.

"Are you always this forward?"

"Hmmm... yes?"

"And it works?"

"Well..." he shrugs, thinking for a while. "Most of the time, I don't even have to talk, so..."

"Right," I snort. Flashes of that night in the club come back to me. "It shows."

"Jesus..." he sighs, widening his eyes. "Should I change my strategy, then?"

"You have more than one?" I ask, leaning on the table and resting my chin on one hand. He laughs again.

"What's *your* strategy?" he asks.

"Ignore them until they go away," I say, which is actually true.

"And it works?"

"Usually, yes."

He chuckles, and then insists in a different tone, "No, I'm serious."

"Me, too!" I say. "I don't flirt with people, Tyler. You shouldn't be so surprised."

"But... you do... like... you..." he stutters and I can see his cheeks turn slightly pink.

"Hook up with strangers?" I help him, even though I'd love to just wait and see what he'd come up with. He nods. "Yeah, sometimes. Usually with those who don't talk."

He smiles with that. Not the smirk. The smile. I start to like this interaction.

"But nothing serious?"

"No. Not since... not in a while," I sigh. "You?"

"Not in a while," he repeats. Then, he takes a deep breath, and adds, "In five years and two months, to be more specific. I wish I wasn't counting."

"It's hard not to," I blurt out. I look away when I see his surprised face.

"How long?" he asks softly.

"Four years," I say. Then, I take a deep breath and add, "Seven months, and sixteen days."

"I'm sorry," he says, making me look back to him. I hate to see the pity in his eyes.

"I'm not," I say firmly. He doesn't react. "At least it's over, you know?"

"I know," he nods. I don't want to talk about this anymore. How do we go back to flirting? "Her name was Brittany," he offers voluntarily.

I try not to scoff at that.

"How long were you two together?" I ask, since he seems to be wanting to talk about this.

"Three years," he says.

"That's a lot."

"Yeah."

"What happened?"

"She... she..." he stutters again, looking for the words. After a while he sighs and looks back at me. "She *did* break my heart."

Ouch. That still hurts. I shouldn't have mocked him. This is not the direction I wanted this to go.

"And made you swear off the female species," I try to joke.

"Not really," he chuckles. "Did A—" he stops himself before he says his name. I appreciate the consideration. "Did he make you swear off the male species?"

"Something like that," I shrug.

"That's bad news for me," he says. I look back at him, unable to hide the smile. How is it so easy for some people?

"Shouldn't be, since I'm not your type," I remind him.

"You're not," he says.

Then he leans over the table, a bit farther than the middle. I retreat in reflex. But he just stops there, staring. Staring into my eyes. And, then, staring at my lips. *Dammit.*

When his eyes are back on mine, I lean forward. I can see him stop breathing. I don't think he actually expects me to do it. His eyes widen the closer I get, but he doesn't move. That is, until I touch my lips against his.

It's light and soft. He motions to move his hands, but I hold them in place. He doesn't fight. So, I press a little harder against his mouth. He releases the air he was holding and cocks his head to the side, so we can fit better. His tongue snakes out and he licks my bottom lip. Slowly. Now I'm the one holding my breath.

I bite the corner of his mouth and smile at the way he tries to turn it into a real kiss. I resist until he stops, letting out a small sigh, but not pulling away. He rests his lips against mine again and just stays there. That's when I open my mouth and let him show me what he's got.

He's *such* a good kisser. It's slow, and soft, and sultry. Nothing like I'd imagined. Well, given that the image I had was him eating off that girl's face in the club...

Shit. What am I doing? My mind flies away, to the corners where I kept my worst assumptions hidden. I break the kiss suddenly, looking at him in despair.

"Is this what you wanted all along?" I ask.

"What?" he frowns.

"Is this why you insisted on the label to hire us? Was this your plan all along?"

"What are you talking about?" he asks, confused.

"Getting into my pants! Was this—"

"What?!" he gasps. "Of *course* not! What kind of person do you think I am?"

He stares at me in disbelief. It's enough to make me believe him, really. But now I ruined it.

I let go of his arms and sit back on the booth, unsure of what to say. I mean, I could say sorry, but now he knows what I think about apologies. There's a chance he'll get even more offended if I say sorry.

"I told you, you're passionate," he breaks the awkward silence. He doesn't sound angry but I still can't look at him. "You're talented. You're... honest."

"And paranoid," I add.

"I kinda like that," he says.

I look back at him, at his smiling face. Why is he smiling?

He leans over the table again, pausing and waiting for me. Gosh. What is he doing to me?

I kiss him again and this time I let his hands free. He only uses one of them, to cup my face, while the other is supporting his weight over the table. I run a hand through his hair as well, his *smooth* hair. Damn, those fanfiction writers have *no* idea. Or maybe they do. I wonder how many other girls got to run their hands through his hair in those texts. How many other ships there are. How many other supporting bands. *Shit.*

"What now?" he asks when I pull away.

"I'm just..." I shake my head. I'm helpless. "How many times did you do this? How many opening acts did you... kiss?"

"None. You're the first," he says quickly. Then he cocks his head to the side, thinking. "You're the first female opening act, though. So, maybe the first of many."

"You wish," I snort, rolling my eyes. Such a Tyler thing to say.

"I don't, actually," he smiles. "Not many, anyway. Just the one."

Crap. Crap, crap, crap, crap, crap. When did he get so good with words?

I'm about to give him his reward for being so poetic when Neil walks in on us.

"Good morning, night owls," he says, observing us with sleepy and suspicious eyes.

"Is it already morning?" I take my phone to check the time.

"Not quite, but we have an early start today," he says as he gathers the things to make coffee. "Not you, actually, you should be asleep."

"I couldn't sleep," I say.

"I see," he turns to me, and then to Tyler. "What are you doing?"

"Talking," Tyler answers. I just nod. Vigorously.

Neil glances back and forth from me to him, but says nothing. He turns around to start on his coffee and I see my opportunity to slip away.

"I think I'm gonna go to bed," I say, faking a yawn.

Tyler glares as I walk past him. I make sure Neil is not looking to blow him a kiss and wink. He only shakes his head, but bites his lip to hold back a smile.

Of course, I'm not physically able to sleep. I can only think about his lips and his eyes and his hair. *Crap.* What will we do now? I have to talk to Pete.

***

I lie still as if my life depends on it. The hours drag on. I fall asleep for a second when the bus takes off, but wake up again with the chatter going on around. Apparently, everyone is up already. I grab my phone to see what time it is and find a message from an unknown number.

'Hey just Becky! Sorry to bother you, but grandma forgot a few clothes at the hospital.'

Beneath it, there's another message, sent fifteen minutes later.

'It's Patrick. The nurse.'

I frown. Why is he texting me about forgotten clothes? I'm about to tell him to call grandma's house as I'm sure the hospital has her number, but stop myself. She might want to get there herself to collect them. Maybe Patrick sensed that, too.

'Thanks,' I reply. *'Will have someone come by to pick them up.'*

As I'm typing, I receive another message, this time from Lindsey.

'Are you awake? I'm really hungry but Pete is still sleeping.'

Pete. I'm worried. We haven't had a proper conversation since I left. I need to get him alone. I'll have to tell him what happened.

Ugh. What happened? I can't decide if it was right or if it was a mistake. As much as I really wanted it to happen—and that it was *really* good—it doesn't change the fact that my relationship with Tyler is mainly professional. That I barely know him. This tour was supposed to be about our careers. These past few days were definitely not about anyone's careers. I don't want last night to get in the way of what really matters here. That's why I need to talk to Pete—he'll have the answers.

'Yes,' I text Lindsey back. *'Really need a wee, getting up now.'*

I open the curtain of my bunk at the same time Lindsey opens hers. She hugs me as I walk by her to the bathroom. I grimace as I see my reflection—the wild hair, the dark circles under my eyes, the spots that are starting to appear on my skin due to all the junk food we've been eating on tour. I sigh, cursing myself for not bringing my make-up bag in here with me. But then I think *fuck it*. We're all way past appearances by now.

"... we're gonna have like half an hour for you guys to get ready," Neil is saying as I enter the kitchen. The Hackley boys are seated in a row, listening to his instructions, resembling small children.

"Morning," I mumble as I move to get a mug and fill it with coffee. They answer in unison and Neil goes right back into detailing how their morning is going to go.

I avoid looking over as I move to sit with Lindsey, my back turned to them.

"Morning," she smiles.

"So, how did you sleep?" I ask.

"Not so great, to be honest," she makes a face. "You?"

"Same," I say, looking down at my cup.

"Do you ever get used to sleeping in a bus?" she asks.

"I wouldn't know," I shrug. This is my first time having to do this.

"You better," she says, "soon this will be your life."

I look back at her, smiling. She's always so supportive.

"You'll have to get used to it, too," I say.

"Yeah," she mumbles, avoiding my gaze.

Damn. Was I wrong? Are they still fighting?

"Now, you," Neil approaches us, pointing a finger at me. "You and Pete have the whole morning off."

"Okay," I nod.

"You can spend it however you want, but, I have a suggestion" he says, a funny look on his face. "I think you should do something special for the fans. I was thinking," he continues, sitting down beside me, "you could use the last gig as a type of homecoming thing, since it's near your hometown. So, my idea is that you and Pete come up with something fun for the fans to do and win tickets to Glasgow."

"We can do that?" I widen my eyes. "Give away tickets?"

"If you agree, I'll make sure to secure a few," he says.

"Of course, sure, it's a great idea," I say with no hesitation. I'm not sure we'll have many people interested in tickets to see us, but surely The Hacks will make for a good lure. "What should we do, though?"

"I'm sure you can think of something," he grins. *I'm sure you have a lot of ideas and this is a test.* Before I can say it, though, he asks, "Are you okay?"

"Yeah," I say, a bit surprised. "Yeah, I'm fine. Why?"

"Nothing, it's just we haven't had a chance to catch up yet," he says, looking at me intently. "You look different."

I freeze. I don't know why it bothers me, but it does.

"It's because I have no make-up on," I try to joke.

"It's not that," Lindsey chimes in. "You do look different. You have this kind of..." she trails off, waving her hand around my face.

"Glow," Neil says.

"What?" I gasp. What the fuck are they talking about?

"Yeah," Lindsey nods, pensive.

"It's almost like you look younger," Neil says.

"Great," I scoff. As if I could look any more like a baby. "It's the make-up, guys. Trust me."

They don't answer, just keep staring with curious faces. I start to feel uneasy. Exposed. I don't like it.

"Can you stop?" I say, hiding behind my coffee mug.

"Sorry," Neil chuckles and then leaves us.

The rest of the journey is pretty silent. Lindsey and I stay where we are, scrolling through our phones, pretending we don't have a million questions to ask each other. The boys are milling about, gathering their things since these are our last hours on the bus. And Pete is still on his bed when we arrive at the hotel.

I stall as I gather my stuff, trying not to bump into Tyler—which is surprisingly easy—and waiting for everyone to get out. There are some fans at the door, waiting for The Hacks, so they go first. Neil goes through our schedule for the day once more before he follows them.

When it's just me and Lindsey on the bus, I ask her if she minds giving me some time in private with Pete. I know I might be overstepping it but, because it's Lindsey, she agrees. Finally, it's just me and him.

I walk up to his bunk and yank his curtain open. He yelps—already wide awake, as I suspected.

"Good, you're awake," I say, frowning as I notice he's hugging a pillow.

Without a word, he hops down, rushing to put on his pants and shoes. He stumbles around, leaning over the walls so he doesn't fall. If I thought I looked like hell earlier when I saw myself in the mirror, it's nothing compared to what he looks like. My heart tightens in my chest.

"Did you sleep at all?" I ask, trying to make him talk.

"Roughly," he answers. His voice is hoarse. "Did you?"

"Not really," I say. He finally stops fumbling around and looks at me. I'm startled to see his eyes are all swollen and a bit red. Like he's been crying.

"Yeah, I heard you and Tyler whispering in the kitchen last night," he says. My heart races. Does he know already?

"Yeah..." I hesitate. I'm not sure this is a good moment to tell him what happened. He's clearly going through something.

"Aren't you tired of him yet?" he asks, his voice full of accusation. I don't really understand why.

"Wasn't it you who asked me to be more friendly?" I try to joke.

"Don't put this on me. At least for once take responsibility for your actions."

I'm taken aback. What the hell is he talking about? Why is he being so aggressive? What did I do?

"What actions? What are you talking about?"

"Nothing. Just..." he sighs, closing his eyes and pinching the bridge of his nose. I suddenly want to hug him. But also punch him. He takes a long time to speak again but, when he does, he just says, "Never mind."

As he goes back to gathering his stuff, I try to make him look at me. He pulls away.

"I'm just cranky, I haven't slept, you know how I get."

I try touching his arm but he dodges my hand. In a swift motion, he walks past me and races out of the bus.

"Pete!" I shout after him.

"It's not about you, okay?" He barely turns around to look at me. "Forget what I said."

"Uh, no?" I race to keep up with his step.

"Becky, please..." he sighs again, running both hands through his hair.

"No. What is it?" I insist, finally blocking his way to make him face me.

"Leave me alone," he says, low and menacing. I feel sick.

"Tell me what's wrong," I match his tone, trying to keep the tears that are already burning my eyelids from falling.

"No!" he yells, making me jump.

I can tell he didn't mean it by how his face contorts when he sees my reaction. He doesn't take it back, though. He doesn't apologize. He doesn't throw his arms around me as he usually does in these situations. I don't know what to think. I don't know what to feel.

"Are you two fighting?" Lindsey approaches us, speaking softly.

"No," we lie at the same time.

"Thanks for leaving me behind, by the way," Pete says to her. I gasp. "I need a shower," he adds and walks away.

"What happened?" Lindsey asks, startled.

"I have no idea," I shake my head, trying to remember what did I do or say that might have put him in such a mood.

"I'll find out," she answers, running to catch up with him.

I take several deep breaths, walking around in a circle, trying to calm my nerves. Pete is prone to be dramatic sometimes, but I don't think I've ever seen him so distressed. So closed off. Whatever could possibly have happened?

"Hey," Neil stops me, a key card in hand. "Room 501."

"Thanks," I manage a weak smile. "What's Pete's room?"

"The 505," he says.

I don't even answer and run to the lift. So much for being okay.

When I reach our floor, I go straight to his door. I can hear voices inside. I can't tell if they're fighting or making up or just talking. I debate whether I should knock. I don't like to leave things upended like this. But I also think I already get in the way of their relationship too much.

"Hey," a voice startles me, making me jump around.

Crap. He's already clean and dressed up, his hair falling perfectly around his angelic face. He's *smiling.* Crap.

"Hey," I say back, except no voice leaves my mouth.

We stare at each other for endless seconds. We should talk, right? I should tell him we need to talk. We should talk about what happened. We should tell each other it wasn't supposed to happen and that it can't happen again.

Instead, what we do is kiss again. It's quick and uncertain this time. I'm not sure I'm the only one having second thoughts about this.

"I have to..." Tyler mumbles, pointing to the lift.

"Yeah, me too," I say, pointing in the opposite direction.

We take a few steps, widening the gap between us. I already miss his presence in my space. Then I curse myself for being so cheesy.

"Are you watching the interview?" he asks as we slowly part. "It's on channel 4, I think."

"I wasn't planning to, no," I say, making him smile.

"I think you should," he insists.

"Why?" I ask, already suspicious.

"I look really good on TV," he says, and now I'm the one smiling.

I roll my eyes and turn around, getting to my room before my feet lead me elsewhere. The first thing I do is turn on the TV and find out how the remote works.

***

I take a shower, get into my comfies and order room service. As I get in bed, I notice how soft it is and how tired I am. It's been such an eventful few days. I'm so, so tired. I'm sure I could just sleep until soundcheck. I don't really *have* to do anything. I'll close my eyes just for a bit...

I'm startled awake by the insistent knock on the door. I panic, immediately thinking I overslept, but my phone clock says it's been less than 20 minutes. I open the door to take my breakfast and promptly snuggle back into bed. I'm still tired. And I still have 30 minutes before the interview starts and I can't go pester Pete. So, as I eat, I call grandma.

"Petal, is everything okay?" That's how she answers. It makes me smile, but it also hurts.

"Yeah, everything is fine. Just checking in." There's a long moment of silence after that. "How are you doing?"

"Good, good," she says vaguely.

"Did I wake you up?"

"No, I've been up since five," she chuckles. "All this lying around is making me bored."

"But you must rest, doctor's orders," I say. She chuckles again.

"I know, I know."

And there's another long silence. I'm so bad at this.

"How was... uh... how was the rest of your day yesterday?" I ask. "Is Jo coming over again today?"

"Yes. She'll bring me lunch for a few days to spy on me, remember?" she says. I don't have the heart to scold her. "How was your day? Was the trip alright?"

"Yeah, I ended up sleeping, so I didn't even see the time pass," I say.

And, then, for some reason I can't quite explain, I give her a detailed report of everything that happened since I left—including kissing Tyler and fighting with Pete. I don't know what comes over me to do that. Maybe because I don't have my usual trusted confidant at the moment. Maybe because I'm not looking forward to uncomfortable silences again.

I wonder if this is why Pete does it—say everything that's on his mind unfiltered because he dreads the next silence as much as I do right now.

Grandma listens to me patiently, punctuating my pauses for air with a 'oh, really?' when I talk about Lindsey staying, a 'hadn't you already?' when I tell her about the kiss, and a 'oh, no, dearie, that's bad' when I recount my earlier interaction with Pete.

"You were right to give them space," she says when I finish my tale, "but you shouldn't wait too long to make things right with Peter."

"I know," I sigh. "I just don't know why he's so mad at me."

"Then ask him," she says simply.

"Okay," I sigh again.

"Do you like this boy?" she asks next, making me confused.

"Pete?" I frown.

"No, silly, Tyler," she explains. My heartbeat speeds up.

"Uh... I... I don't really know him all that well," I say, regretting having told her anything. What was I thinking to talk about kissing a strange boy with my *grandmother*?

"Oh, goodness, do you need to know his whole background story to decide whether you like him?" she says. "I don't know him and I like him."

I don't know what to say to that. I don't know how to tell whether I like someone. Because I usually don't. I don't like anyone.

"And I think he likes you, too," she continues in face of my silence. "Just the fact that he's come with you so you wouldn't be alone to deal with your old stubborn granny speaks volumes."

I remain silent. I hadn't thought of it through that lens. I thought he wanted to just... you know...

"People don't do that," she adds, for good measure.

"Okay," is all I'm able to say.

"Alright, dearie, I have to go now," she says in a chipper tone than the one she had when she answered the phone. "Time for my medicine and breakfast. Would you let me know how things go with Peter? I'm really worried about him now."

"Sure, will do," I say airily. "And could you not tell Jo? I'm not sure if he's told her anything or not."

"If he did, that's the first thing she'll mention today," she laughs.

"I guess," I smile. "I'll call you later when I have a minute."

"You can just text me," she says. "I know how to text, you know?"

"I'll call you," I insist. I liked talking to her.

"Okay, petal, I'll be happy to hear from you regardless."

My heart aches once again. We say our goodbyes and I immediately put a reminder on my phone to call her later. Whatever truce we've found now, I don't want to screw it up. Again.

I unmute the TV as I eat my breakfast, waiting for the damn show to start. My stomach flutters when the opening theme song starts to play and I curse myself. He's already ruined me.

The Hacks are announced as the morning guests and the camera closes in their fresh and sleepy faces. All three look too handsome for such an early hour. Bloody genes.

The presenter opens with a few 'news'—which turns out to be only celebrity gossip. I roll my eyes to most of the things she says. She calls a break and when the show returns, it's time for the band to play their first song. They play their most recent single, which I still don't understand why was chosen as a single, since it's by far the most annoying song on their set.

They get through it seamlessly and go ahead to sit on the couch for the interview part. The presenter is giddy as she makes those cardboard cutout questions everyone asks. A big screen behind them shows pictures that span their whole career. I laugh at their teenage ones—what a weird phase. It's good to see that even they had a gawky stage with questionable fashion choices.

As the interview advances, I notice Todd is the one to take over most of the questions, even though the presenter talks exclusively to Tyler most of the time. I'm impressed by his public persona—charismatic, sympathetic, warm. Not even close to the control-freak jerk I came to know.

"And you're touring with a local independent band, is that right?" the woman asks, sending a jolt of energy down my spine. "How did it happen?"

"Well, we try to choose local bands wherever we go," Todd says. "I think it's important to help up-and-coming artists. We've been there, we know what it's like."

What the heck?

"That's such a nice thing to do," the woman answers, as if they're single-handedly ending world poverty. "How did you come across this particular band?"

"That was Tyler's find," Todd says, handing it over to him.

'Are you watching this?' I quickly text Pete. This is more important than whatever our problem is.

"... you know, how sometimes you fall down a rabbit hole on YouTube..." Tyler is droning on, in a way-too-specific explanation, if you ask me.

'Watching what?' my phone buzzes with Pete's reply.

'The interview,' I text back. *'They're talking about us.'*

I have the urge to run to his room—we should be watching this together. This is great! Right? They're talking about us on national television. Of course, most of our audience must be asleep right now, but still...

"... and they're really good," Tristan is talking now. "I think it's safe to say they're some of the best musicians we ever got to share the stage with."

"Yes, speaking of sharing," the interviewer says, "you've been literally sharing the stage, right? We've been seeing videos of you playing each others' songs, and I have to say, what a brilliant idea! Who came up with it?"

"It was actually Becky," Tyler says. My heart pounds heavily at the sound of my own nickname on his voice. I think it's the first time I hear him say it. "She noticed we have some overlapping in our audiences and had this idea. We all loved it, right? Honestly, I was just looking for an opportunity to steal *She's Not Mine* to myself, it's such a great song."

I smile with that.

"And might I add, it sounds *a lot* better in your voice," the interviewer chuckles, touching his arm. My smile is gone.

'How DARE she???' I text Pete.

"You shouldn't have said that. She's watching us right now," Tyler jokes. Damn him. How does he know I'm watching? I could be sleeping. Actually, I'll tell him I was sleeping and didn't watch a thing.

"Oops," the woman laughs again and I roll my eyes.

'What part?' Pete asks.

What does he mean, what part? *'The part where she said our song sounds better in Tyler's voice???'*

"Thank you so much for coming here today and chatting with me. Best of luck with the rest of the tour."

"Thank you, it was our pleasure," Todd smiles.

"Would you sing one more song for us?" she asks and they all get up and walk back to their instruments.

Tristan makes the countdown and Todd starts to play a very familiar riff on his guitar. I get dizzy, my sight slightly blurry. My heart is beating so fast I'm certain I'm having a heart attack.

'PETE??????' I text him. I need to know I'm not hallucinating.

When the first verse of my song—the song I wrote years ago, alone, in my bedroom—leaves Tyler's mouth, I fly out of my room. This is too much to take on my own.

"PETE!!!" I screech as I burst his unlocked door open.

He doesn't even move. His eyes are glued to the TV, his mouth slightly agape. I run and throw myself down beside him. I reach for his hand, holding it tight as we watch our song being played live on national television.

***

It's a slightly different version than the one we've been playing on the concerts, yet it sounds amazing. They sound amazing. Tyler sounds amazing. The song fits his crying voice perfectly, almost as if it was written for him all along.

They finish it up and for the longest time Pete and I just stare at the TV. I turn to him slowly, a shocked expression on my face.

"What was that?" he asks, his voice barely over a whisper.

"I have no idea." I shake my head.

"What a trip," Pete says, blinking hard.

"I know."

"It was our song!" He widens his eyes, finally looking at me.

"I know!"

"And, I have to admit..." he sighs. "It does sound better in his voice."

"I know," I admit. And now I'll have a decent recording of it to listen to whenever I want.

"I think so, too," Lindsey says somewhere behind us, startling Pete. He jumps up, turning around to face her. Oh, God... maybe his weirdness isn't because of me, after all. "Although I like your arrangement better," she adds.

"Thanks," I say, glancing back and forth between the two of them. So much for giving them time, right? I sigh, feeling guilty for barging in. "Sorry to burst in, it's just that... you know..."

"Sure, no problem," Lindsey smiles. It's so... cold. Empty. Sad. My heart starts to break.

"Neil said... he kind of..." I turn to Pete, but he's not even looking at me. "I need to talk to you. Later. Business stuff."

"Okay," Pete nods. I'm not entirely sure he heard me.

I glance once more at Linds, who is now staring at the floor, and decide to leave. I carefully close the door behind me and lean over, trying to hear something. Awful, I know. Anyway, I don't succeed. I can hear that they're talking, but the TV is still on and I can't make out any words.

I walk back to my room—or, should I say, I glide back to my room—with a weird feeling weighing me down and lifting me up at the same time.

I'm worried about Pete and Lindsey, the way they looked at each other just now... I really hope they can work things out. Mainly because I really like Lindsey. I know it sounds selfish, but she's the first of Pete's 'significant others' that likes me. The first to actually want to hang out with me. The first with whom I don't feel pressured to explain our relationship. The first that actually deserves him.

On the other hand, I'm so... so... Christ... I'm so *happy*! Hearing a band like The Hacks praise us as they did and then play our song live—all things they didn't need to do—was such a thrill. Grandma was right, people don't do that. Maybe I do like them. Maybe I do like *him*.

***

I'm in front of the mirror, fixing my make-up. For the first time in days it looks flawless, exactly the way I want it to be. The foundation and concealer completely covered the pesky spots I have, and also the dark circles under my eyes. The wings of my eye-liner are perfectly symmetrical. My purplish shadow brings out the dark brown of my eyes. I pause to take a look at my creation before drawing my lips—it will be a darker purple today.

That's when an alarm starts to blare and fire sprinklers go off. I hadn't even noticed there were fire sprinklers in the room. I rush to the door, but fail to open it. It seems locked, which is so strange—I rarely lock my doors. There's no key in sight, so I start to bang on it, screaming for help, hoping someone will hear me.

I turn back around and gasp at my reflection in the mirror when I see my make-up is melting. Like wet paint, big drops of blacks and purples turn the edges my eyes and mouth down. They drip from my chin in heavy blobs, hitting the floor with an unnerving sound. I walk closer and notice it's not only my make-up—my whole face is melting. Whole chunks of painted skin fall off, hitting the ground with a loud thump. I scream again, but this time no sound comes out of my mouth—I have no mouth anymore. I want to close my eyes, I want to look away, but I can't. I'm stuck, frozen in place, just watching as I slowly become a disfigured mass.

I jolt awake and almost fall off bed. I sit up fast, reaching up, glad to feel the skin on my face is still whole and imperfect. My heart beats in my ears. This is my most recurring nightmare. It's so stupid. Yet, it always manages to scare the shit out of me.

"Becky?" I hear a voice on the other side of the door at the same time there's a knock. "Are you there?"

It's Pete. So, I yell back, "Yes, it's open."

And it is. I always forget to lock my doors.

I watch as he steps inside—his hair damp from a recent shower, his clothes immaculate and snuggly fitting his tiny body. He stares back, his hands in his pockets.

"What did Neil say?" he asks, at the same time I ask, "What is going on?"

He sighs, looking down. He's standing next to the door and part of me fears he'll just walk out.

"Have you eaten yet?" I ask, an idea forming in my head.

"Uh... no..." he mumbles.

"Let's go down and have breakfast," I say.

"It's almost noon," he scoffs.

"Lunch, then," I say, cursing myself for having slept for so long. "Even better."

"Okay," he says.

"I just need a wee," I say, jumping off the bed.

"And change," he adds, looking down at my pajamas.

"I'll just throw something over this," I say. He frowns, but says nothing.

I'm relieved to find him still by the door when I come out of the bathroom. I find my navy sweater, the one I brought back from home, and put it on. Then, I hold Pete's hand as we walk together to the hotel restaurant. I figured he'd be less likely to make a dramatic exit in a public place.

We walk around, silently picking up what we want to eat, and find a table at the back. The room is pretty much empty, since it's too early for lunch yet, but it's a good thing. The emptier, the fewer people will see me in my current state.

"So?" I ask after we've had time to eat half of our food.

He looks up to me, startled. Then, he takes a deep breath.

"I owe you an apology," he says. It sounds so formal, but at the same time it sounds so Pete. "I didn't mean to lash out this morning."

"Why did you?" I ask.

"I was... I was angry. At myself," he says, looking away.

"Why?" I insist.

"I'm..." He closes his eyes for a moment. "I don't even know where to start."

"Start from the beginning," I lean over, catching his hand and squeezing it. He stares at our hands for a while.

"Okay, so, remember you guessed Lindsey and I had a fight?" he says.

"Yes," I nod. It's pretty obvious they're *still* in a fight.

"It was because I told her we should move in together," he blurts out.

"Wow, that's, um... that's big," I stutter. I don't know what to say.

"Yeah," he nods.

"She doesn't want to."

"No."

"Because... because of me?" I ask.

He looks startled for a moment. And it hurts me. It hurts because I can tell he didn't think about me when he made that proposition. And he shouldn't, I know that. I know we can't be roommates forever. I know he can't take care of me forever. As much as we love each other, at some point, our personal lives will take different directions. That's just how life goes.

Yet, the fact I can be rational about it doesn't mean I don't feel slightly betrayed.

"No!" he exclaims, squeezing my hand tighter. "No, it's not you, it's just timing. She thinks it's too soon."

"Well, it is too soon," I blurt out. He flinches with my bluntness, so I say, "Sorry."

"No, you're right. You're right," he says, shaking his head.

"Am I?" I frown.

"Yeah, I mean... we've been together for less than a year. Fuck, we've known each other for less than a year. I don't know what I was thinking."

"You're in love, you were *not* thinking," I try to joke.

"I guess," he answers, looking away. I immediately know there's more to it.

"What is the problem, then?" I ask.

"Huh?" he mumbles, as if he didn't hear me.

"Well, it seems to me you're both on the same page. So, there's no reason for a fight. Am I right?" I insist. He only stares, his eyes widening as the seconds tick away. "What is the problem?"

"The problem is..." he trails off, studying my face. I'm sitting at the edge of my chair. He sighs. "It's not that simple. Something... something broke, you know? It's not the same anymore."

I don't know what to say because I *don't* know. I've never had a real relationship. The only time I thought I had one, it broke me—both literally and figuratively. And Pete was the one who had the right words to pull me through. I don't have any words. And I hate myself for that.

"Anyway, do you forgive me?" he asks, looking me back in the eyes.

"Oh, hun, you don't even have to ask," I try to smile. "And you know you can tell me anything, right? Even if I can't give you any advice, I can listen. I want to listen."

"I know," he says. And the look on his face—a mix of sad and lost and confused that I've only ever seen on my reflection in the mirror—breaks my heart.

Also, the fact that I know he's still not telling me everything breaks my heart. He's still hiding something, and I don't know how else to make him open up. I wonder if he feels *this* frustrated when I don't tell him things. Which reminds me I'm also not telling him everything.

"What did you want to talk to me about?" he breaks the silence, as if he can read my mind. It's on the tip of my tongue. But then, he adds, "What business stuff?"

My heart sinks. I can't tell him. I can't throw my mistakes and doubts on him this time. I have to stop being so selfish.

So, I just tell him about Neil's idea and we spend the rest of our lunch trying to come up with some type of challenge for the fans. Strictly business stuff.

***

We head to the venue not too long after that. Unfortunately, I can't replicate my dream make-up skills and end up with my average coverage. Still, it looks better than my bare babyface. It makes me feel better. I've been make-up-free for days, it's good to look nice and professional once again.

The journey over is rather awkward, although Lindsey chats with the driver as if everything is normal. It's only when we arrive and are left alone that I see she looks as sad and lost as my best friend.

"Hey, guys," Neil meets us in the dressing room. "Did you do your homework?"

"Ah, we've come up with a few options, but we want to run them by you first," Pete answers. Neil seems satisfied with that.

"Great, I'll be happy to discuss them with you," he grins. Wide. I start to get suspicious. "I have something to show you first," he says as he starts scrolling through his phone. "I think you're gonna like it. It's not out yet, but they had the courtesy to send me a copy of the finished text before-hand. It will be up on the website on Sunday."

I exchange wide-eyed glances with Pete. I start to bite the tip of my thumb. I'm already anxious.

Neil turns his phone screen to us. It shows an article. A *Peroxide* article. Our interview.

"Oh my God!" I snatch the phone from him and huddle up with Pete as we read through.

'Like it' is an understatement. I love it. With every line, I get more excited. The interview is everything we dreamed of and more—Graham didn't measure his words to commend us. He starts by mentioning the show he told us he attended all those years ago. He says how the precarious gig stuck with him and how he thought we had potential then, and goes on to tell the readers how we surpassed his expectations.

He describes our first opening show in vivid detail, and it's like I'm reliving it—starting off doubtful, winning the crowd, ending with half of the place singing along. He praises our interaction with the one fan that requested a song and our ability to improvise. He even mentions how we now have merged our sets and exchanged songs with The Hacks—something he didn't even witness.

The interview bit is funny and insightful, and although Pete's name is the one that appears the most, I never end up seeming distant or uninterested. He mentions more than once my passion for music and talent with the guitar, and every time I read it, my heart leaps in my chest. He finishes the article saying:

'In my profession, there's a myth that you only find true talent once in a lifetime. Throughout my career, every so often, I came across diamonds in the rough that left me wondering long after the last guitar chord was played. For the few with whom I got to cross paths again, one of two things happened: they were either not slightly as good as their first impression or just completely changed direction. That's not Becky and Pete's case. They're the real deal. They're my once in a lifetime. They're legends in the making.'

At the bottom of the page, there are links to our official website, social media pages, and Spotify channel.

I look to Pete and don't even have time to gauge his expression, as he engulfs me in a hug, almost breaking my bones. But, for once, I don't care. This article is worth breaking every single bone to.

"Congratulations!" Neil says excitedly and I feel his hand on my shoulder.

"Oh my God, mate, thank you so much!" Pete releases me to hug him.

"Oh, please," Neil chuckles, patting his back. "I did nothing."

When he releases him, he turns to Lindsey. She didn't read the article so she doesn't really know what we're celebrating. She walks up to Pete and hugs him, anyway. She loves him. I think she loves him more than he loves her.

"There's something else," Neil breaks the silence. We all look back at him. "The label wants to talk to you."

"What?" Pete and I gasp at the same time.

"Yep. They asked me to schedule a conference meeting as soon as you guys have a minute. I was thinking maybe Monday? I think that would give you time to come down from all this excitement," he says.

"Mate... does it... does it mean..." Pete stutters, putting a hand over his chest. I think he might burst into tears. Fuck, I think *I* might burst into tears.

"They didn't tell me anything else, just that they wanted to talk," Neil rushes to explain. "But, you know... when a label wants to talk to the artist..."

That earns him another hug from Pete. He laughs.

"Okay, I'll give you a moment," Neil says. "Don't be long, though, you need to rehearse today. Like, seriously."

"Of course, we'll be right out," Pete says.

Neil glances at me—I haven't said a single word to him. I still can't, though. So, I smile. I smile and I hope he knows everything I mean by it. He smiles back and winks—I think he does.

"So," Lindsey clears her throat when we're alone again. "What was that about?"

"The interview," I seem to find my voice. "We did an interview for *Peroxide* when the tour started, it was the text they're going to publish."

"Oh, right," she nods.

"We should have asked Neil to send it to us," I turn to Pete, "so Linds could read it, too."

"Don't worry, I'll read it when it comes out," she says. "I'm sure you deserve everything they wrote about you, though."

"Thanks," I mumble.

Then, completely out of character for me, I walk up to her and hug her. As I did with Neil, I hope she understands everything I mean by it.

I try to look her in the eyes when we let go, but she stares at the floor. I think she *did* understand.

"So," Pete interrupts our moment. "Let's... let's get going?"

I nod, taking his hand, and we walk to the stage. And my heart starts to beat even faster, if that's even possible.

***

"Okay, let's take five," Neil suggests. "Todd, Pete, come over here for a second, please."

We're on our second hour of soundcheck. We suck. Honestly, I have no idea what's happening. Well, to be honest, I have *some* idea.

Every time Tyler comes close to me, I get so nervous that I hit the wrong notes or sing the wrong words. It's ridiculous. It gets even more ridiculous when he notices what's happening and starts doing it on purpose—looking at me while he sings, or lightly touching my waist, or staring at my lips. He's having way too much fun with it. I hate him. Especially because I don't seem to have the same effect on him. *Well, you're not his type, after all.*

"Did you watch it?" He walks closer, taking the five-minute opportunity to harass me. We haven't properly talked all day.

"Watch what?" I ask back, even though I know what he's talking about.

"The interview," he says, raising his eyebrows.

"Oh, that," I say, smiling evilly. "No, I ended up falling asleep."

"Really?" He frowns.

"Yeah," I shrug.

"Well," he sighs, clearly disappointed, "you can always catch it online, I guess."

"Uhum," I mumble, trying my hardest not to let him find out I'm lying. He just stares—at my whole face. I start to get hot. "What?"

"I had forgotten how good you look in full-on make-up," he says. I thank the gods that I actually went for full coverage, so he won't see me blush.

"Were you tired of looking at my everyday face?" I ask.

"Not at all!" he frowns. "That's not what I meant."

"Right," I scoff.

He just keeps looking at me, trying to say something, but saying nothing. It kind of gives me a bit of satisfaction. A sort of payback for how jumpy he still makes me.

Then, suddenly, he asks, "Does your lipstick smear?"

"Tyler!" I gasp, looking around to make sure no one is within listening range.

"What?" he mocks my tone.

"Don't... do that," I say in a low tone.

"Do what?"

"What you're doing."

"Why not?"

"Because!"

"I can't help myself," he smirks.

"Well, get a grip!" I raise my eyebrows.

"Fine," he sighs, apparently giving up. "Sorry."

He walks back to the piano and sits down. I follow him, still making sure nobody is paying too much attention.

"If you behave," I lean over, whispering in his ear, making him jump, "I'll show you if my lipstick smears or not."

He turns to look at me, a bewildered expression on his face. And he *blushes*. Hard. Now I know why he keeps doing it—it's just too good to cause this reaction on the other person.

"You were right, by the way," I say as I walk back to my guitar. "You do look good on TV."

Then he smiles. The honest smile. *My* smile.

***

Do you know what's something I hadn't noticed before? How difficult it is to get a moment alone. We're constantly surrounded by people everywhere we go—the roadies, the band members, Neil and Seth, the venue's staff. Suddenly, there are people everywhere, all the time.

'Was my behavior in accordance with your standards?' Tyler texts me.

'A+' I text back, already smiling.

'So, where's my demonstration?'

I swear, I try to reward him. We meet up backstage, first checking our dressing rooms, which are populated, then trying to find an empty room—there's none. All the rooms that aren't locked have people inside. We try the bathroom, but decide against it since it would be an easy place for the others to find us. We walk up to the balcony and find Neil there, on a call meeting. He casts suspicious glances at us as we walk back down.

"Let's just do it here," Tyler says, stopping in the middle of the corridor.

And I'm tempted. It's dark, and there's no one around, and he smells so good.

"There you are!" Jake comes out from one of the doors. "Your presence is being requested over here."

Tyler hesitates for a second before sighing and following him. I grunt in frustration. I'm walking back to my dressing room when he texts me.

'Meet me under the stage in five.'

'Gross,' I reply. Yet, I find myself walking to the stage to find a way under it. I'll decide if Tyler is worth the effort after I see how filthy the floor is.

I'm distracted with those thoughts, so I only spot Tristan and Paul when they've already seen me. Tristan is sitting behind his drums while Paul is kneeling beside him. Both of them turn to me wide-eyed. Paul immediately starts to fumble with the plates, but I have the impression he wasn't adjusting the instrument before I made an appearance.

"There," Paul says after half a second. He stands up and starts to leave, but then turns around and points to Tristan. "Remember what I said."

He waits until Tristan nods and then rushes past me, without even glancing up.

"What did he say?" I ask.

"Just the usual," he shrugs. I don't know what the usual is, and I actually couldn't care less about anything Paul says, so I don't insist. When the silence starts to drag on, Tristan asks, "What are you doing here?"

I hesitate. I can't say why I came back to the stage, but I also can't leave without a word.

"Well..." I look around. An idea forms when I spot one of the acoustic guitars. "I was thinking about practicing a little more."

He frowns. He doesn't believe me. "Did you seriously forget the lyrics?"

"No," I lie. "I'm just trying to annoy your brother."

"Now I believe you," he smiles, looking at me with a funny expression. "Did he give you a hard time during your trip?"

"When does he not?" I joke and he chuckles again. "He didn't, though, actually. In fact, he was quite... helpful," I feel the urge to clarify. I owe him that.

"He can be." Tristan's eyebrows rise an inch and he nods slowly.

I feel things quickly escalate to awkwardness. So, I walk to the guitar and pick it up. When I start to play, Tristan follows, reciting the lyrics with me. Only then I realize he has a beautiful singing voice. I play it a second time, trying to harmonize with him. He laughs, but we manage.

"Don't you want to join my band?" I ask, making him laugh again. "I bet Pete would approve."

He stops laughing a little too suddenly, looking back at me with wide eyes.

"Did he... did he tell you?" he asks.

My heart starts to race. I obviously don't know what he's talking about, but I want to know. So, I use the strategy I use on Pete—say nothing until he assumes things and starts blabbering. It works. I shouldn't be surprised.

"God, of course he told you, you're his best friend," he sighs, burying his face on his hands. "Is he mad? I bet he's mad, isn't he? He hasn't talked to me the whole day."

"He isn't mad. Not at you, anyway," I say. It's not a lie. And I still have no idea what we're talking about, so I continue, "He's more mad at himself."

"But it's not his fault," he argues. "I kissed him first."

I sit very still. Things start to connect together in my head. Pete acting strange, Lindsey being so sad. They fucking kissed! And my best friend didn't tell me about it. How could he look me in the eye and not even hint at it? I was right to be concerned.

"Y-you—" Tristan stutters, bringing me back to attention. "You *didn't* know?!"

I don't know what to say. I don't want to admit it, but I'm also failing to conceal my absolute shock.

"Fuck!" he yells, standing up and starting to pace back and forth. "Fuck, why do I have to fuck everything up?"

"Tris," I get up, too, following him. "Calm down."

"Calm down?!" he yells again. I don't blame him—telling a person to calm down is really dumb. "How can I calm down? I just potentially ruined his relationship and my chances of being friends with him!"

"I don't think... I don't think that's accurate," I say. Now, Pete's recent behavior makes total sense.

"He won't even look at me!"

"Well, what did you expect?" I blurt out, making him stop. He looks... hurt. Damn. "Look, he's really... he's in a very delicate situation right now."

"I know," he sighs, defeated. "I knew it and I did it anyway."

That doesn't sound good. It sounds like he took advantage of the situation. Did he?

"Do you like him?" I ask.

He seems surprised by the question. He looks at me, frowning at first, but then kind of smiling.

"Yeah," he says with another sigh. "Yeah, I like him a lot."

"You should talk to him, then," I find myself saying.

"And say what?" he scoffs. "Apologize? I'd be lying because I'm not really sorry for what I did. But I also didn't want to hurt him. Or Lindsey. I really like Lindsey, too."

"Tell him... tell him exactly that," I suggest.

I'm not sure it will do any good. I probably would just stay away if I was him. Hide until the tour is over and then run home and forget anything happened. I might still do it, actually.

"Okay," he sighs. I smile, trying to be reassuring. "Can we... can we keep this between us?"

"Of course!" I tell him and the next thing I know he's hugging me. It feels a lot like Pete's hugs—full-body, bone-crushing. I hug him back.

When he lets me go, he looks at me with a funny face. "Do you like him?"

"Pete?" I ask.

"No," he smiles, "my brother."

I widen my eyes again. I feel my cheeks flush. My stomach somersaults inside my body. I can't answer.

***

I burst back into my dressing room fully intending to confront Pete and his secret-keeping ass. He's not alone, though. He, Lindsey and Seth are sorting through our new batch of merch.

"Right on time!" Seth beams. "Come have a look, we have a few different items."

I walk over to them, still casting a betrayed glance at Pete. He notices it. He notices my stare has meaning. Which unfortunately means he starts to actively avoid me.

I follow him around—both physically and with my eyes—but I only have a chance to tell him we need to talk when we're getting mic'ed up for the show.

After it—which was remarkably better than yesterday—he engages in conversation with Neil and Jake. I try to drag him to the merch booth, but he manages to make Neil intercede and stop us.

When The Hacks finishes their set and we all gather together backstage, I decide I've had enough. I storm into the dressing room, fully intending to confront him. but, when I see the look in his eyes, I stop.

"Let's go out," Pete suggests loudly before I have the chance to say a word. "Let's go dancing."

I observe his frightened expression, ready to refuse it and make him talk. But something in his eyes remind me I've been such an awful friend lately. There's a reason he didn't tell me about the kiss. There's a reason he still doesn't want to talk about it.

"Okay," I end up saying. Let him have it his way.

The decision quickly turns into a celebration for us and our upcoming article, so everyone decides to join in. This time, we decide to run back to the hotel and get properly ready. That is, as properly ready as a bunch of tired musicians on tour can.

I shower and change as fast as I can. I still have ten minutes to spare when I'm ready, which I vainly decide to spend doing my make-up. I know, I know. Priorities.

I'm the last one to get to the lobby, which yields me a round of applause.

"Thank you, thank you, I try," I roll my eyes.

"Definitely worth the wait," Tristan smiles, offering me his arm.

"Why, thank you," I lace my arm with his, purposefully avoiding Tyler's eyes. The whole turn of events with Pete meant I stood him up earlier. I'm not ready to find out how mad he is. "Is it possible that I am your type?"

"Maybe for tonight," he grins, lighting up the whole place.

"Okay, guys," Tyler clears his throat. "The cars are waiting outside."

This time we pick a less popular and more secluded place, trying to follow Neil's recommendation to behave. It's still a club—dark, loud music, drunk people dancing—but it feels a lot more tasteful. Once inside, we immediately split into smaller groups, which I'm grateful for, since I'm not looking forward to spending the whole evening with Todd and his sidekick Paul.

I follow Lindsey to a table on the back, while Tyler and Pete head over to the bar to order us drinks.

"This is nice," she comments when we sit down. "And you look amazing."

"Well, you're one to talk," I say, raising my eyebrows at her little black dress.

"Date night and all," she blushes.

"Is it?" I blurt out, unable to stop myself.

"Isn't it?" She gives me the same look, and then I blush.

The boys come back with the drinks and Tristan. I get anxious because I don't know if they talked, but when the conversation starts to flow easily, I relax. Apparently, everyone is trying to behave. The chat gets louder and more animated as our blood levels of alcohol increase. The group splits again, as Pete, Lindsey and Tristan talk among themselves, excluding Tyler and me. I don't know if it's on purpose, but I can't stop watching them.

"What is going on between them?" Tyler whispers to me after a while.

"I think they might be planning a threesome," I joke, already maybe too drunk.

"I think they picked the wrong brother, then," he says and I turn my head to him. My heart jumps in my chest because he's closer than I expected.

"Would you be interested?" I ask.

"Not with Pete," he says, and does that thing where he stares into my eyes and then at my lips. It's becoming scarily familiar.

"Do you wanna dance?" I ask suddenly. I need to regain a bit of space.

"I thought you didn't dance?" he frowns.

"Maybe you can teach me."

His eyes widen the same way they did in rehearsal. I smile. I like it. He doesn't answer, but guides me to the dance floor anyway.

It starts off so awkwardly that I almost regret suggesting it. Our movements are slow and restrained. Our eyes wander over every part of each other, but never meet. An image of him humping and twerking forms on my mind, and I turn around. *You're not his type.*

I feel him getting closer. I glance back and sync my body with his. He's still not touching me, so I take one step back. We fit perfectly. He puts his hands on my waist, so lightly I can barely feel them. I put my hands over his, trying to show him it's okay, and he leans even closer. I can feel his breath on my neck and it starts getting hard to move.

I reach my hand back, grabbing his hair—his *smooth* hair. I remember touching it last night. I remember how his lips felt on mine, the taste of his tongue, the way he smelled. *Shit.* This is torture.

One of his hands travels to my stomach, pulling me tighter against him. I cock my head to the side, pulling my hair out of the way, and his mouth touches my skin. I can barely conceal the shiver, and that seems to give him confidence. The kissing becomes harder and moister. He works his way up my neck with patience I certainly can't match until he reaches my earlobe.

I turn around and his mouth finally meets mine.

It's the best kiss yet. His lips are soft and delicious, his tongue moves slowly against mine. I can taste the vodka and strawberries on it. His fingers gently caress the back of my neck. His other hand firmly holds me by the small of my back. There's no space between us and, somehow, I still want to get closer.

He breaks away, cupping my face with the hand that was on my waist. He looks at my lips intently.

"It doesn't smear," he whispers. I smile. Which makes him smile. We need to get out of here.

"Do you want to go somewhere else?" I ask.

His eyes travel up to meet mine. Again, he doesn't even answer—he just nods and, the next thing I know, he's leading me out the club by the hand.

He calls an Über before we even step outside. We're about to continue what we started while we wait when we notice a group of girls across the street staring at us. One of them waves and the other two giggle. They're drunk. They're fans. I'm mortified.

"Can we take a selfie?" They stumble in our direction.

"My God, you're *so* hot," one of them says while Tyler tries to be professional.

"This is really happening, then," another one points to me.

"Guys, come on," Tyler snorts, in an 'as if' tone.

You're not his type.

But he didn't mean it like that, right? He's just trying to divert them. Trying to play it cool. If he didn't want me, what just happened inside wouldn't have happened at all. He could just easily pick anyone else to bring back to his room. *As he must have done after every other concert.*

Shit. I try to shush my brain, but the spell is broken. The heat and dizziness from a minute ago is crispy clear air. I start to shiver.

The four minutes we have to wait for the car are excruciating. When it finally arrives, we drive off in awkward silence. We can't even look at each other. I don't understand. *He thinks this is a mistake, too.*

My head starts to hurt. I decide I'll blame it on the booze. I shouldn't have drunk so much on a work night. We have a show tomorrow, we're still sounding like crap, we should be already in bed—separately. I start to think of an excuse, of how to explain we shouldn't be doing this, why this isn't a good idea.

And then we reach the hotel. And our floor. And his door.

I don't have time to hesitate—he pulls me in and suddenly his tongue is inside my mouth again. I walk slowly backwards as he slams the door shut and lets his hands slide down my back. They travel a little further down my waist, as I tangle both of my hands into his long, slick hair.

He breaks the kiss to move to my neck and his hands go back to my waist. He's taking his time and I'm so aware of the way I'm breathing that I'm embarrassed.

Once again, I'm confused. This is not going how I thought it would in my head. Not that I ever thought it would go anywhere, it's just that having seen him with those girls before I expected a different thing. Something like a dog-in-heat approach. We would probably be over with all of this if he was a little less sexy. And I wouldn't be... feeling all these things.

Christ, why even casual sex has to be so complicated for me? Why can't we just do it? Why can't I stop him and just throw him on the bed?

We reach the dresser and he stops the kissing to breathe. I take the opportunity to slide my hands down over his chest. He leans his forehead against mine and closes his eyes. I reach the hem of his white t-shirt and start to run my fingers back up, underneath it. He holds his breath and I can't even start to explain what that does to me. I try to be as gentle as he's being, but my hands are clumsy and hasty, and his shirt is on the floor in two seconds.

I don't get much time to enjoy the view as his mouth almost instantly covers mine. His hands slide down my back to my bum, which, surprisingly, he doesn't squeeze. He just rests them there, lightly, barely touching. I discover I like it.

I run my hands up his back, using just my fingertips. His skin is tender and warm. He clutches the hem of my shirt when I make my way from his mouth to his neck, kissing and licking as slow as I can manage.

He starts to pull my shirt up, letting his fingers slide across the sides of my body. Suddenly I remember I'm not wearing a bra. Suddenly I remember he'll get to see my practically inexistent breasts. My slightly pouchy tummy. The ugly scar from the appendectomy I underwent when I was seven. *He told you you're not his type.*

"Is this okay?" he breathes in my ear, interrupting my thoughts.

His palms are pressed against my sides, just an inch away from reaching my boobs. His fingers are drawing circles on my back. I just... I just really want to know how it feels.

"Yeah," I whisper back and he lets his hands close around my small bosom.

Again, he doesn't grab, he doesn't press, he just touches. Lightly. Sweetly. Sexily. I let him pull the shirt from my body and look me down. I feel exposed, like I never did before, not even in my first time.

He just looks, from a distance, letting his eyes lay longer on some specific parts—my hips, my waist, my neck. I'm afraid of what might be going on in his head but, when his eyes meet mine, he smiles again. He looks flustered and that relaxes me a little bit, and only then I am reminded he's shirtless and I have yet to see what he looks like.

He's not as muscle-y as his clothes suggest. He's lean, and thin, and I can see the tip of his bones through the skin of his shoulders and hips. There's also a lot more hair than I expected to find.

"We're going somewhere," I say when I look at his face again. He laughs.

"I hope so," he replies in a hushed voice as he walks closer again.

He brushes my cheek with the back of his fingers and kisses me. With intent. I reach the hems of his shirt again for balance, but find bare skin. I let my hands travel down and unzip his tight pants—which feel particularly tighter now—and he moans, pressing his whole body against mine. The urge to get it over with returns, but, again, he's taking his time.

He slides his hands down my body, following them with his mouth. He kisses the base of my neck, then my collarbone, then my chest. When his tongue finally meets one of my nipples, I bite my lip hard so I don't gasp too loud. I know he can tell I'm barely hanging on—he can definitely feel my heart trying to escape my body, not to mention the way my skin crawls under his callused fingers and warm mouth.

He continues his way down, kissing my slightly apparent ribs, the side of my hip, then my legs as he slowly pushes my skirt, pantyhose and knickers down at once. When his mouth meets my inner thigh, I have to grab the nightstand behind me not to melt down into a puddle, right there. I don't remember being this intimate with anyone in my life. Ever.

When he finally gets rid of the last of my clothing, he kneels down and lets his eyes travel up my body again. He bites his lip as he studies my generous curves. I'd give anything to read his mind now. When our eyes meet this time, he doesn't smile. He doesn't move. But his stare is so flaring that if spontaneous human combustion was really a thing, now would have been my moment.

I picture a very sexy scene in my head, where I take two steps in his direction and descend graciously to meet him on the floor. But in reality I can barely move, my legs fail, my entire body trembles, so I just stumble down to the carpet. I half crawl towards him and we kiss again.

I pull him until he's seated and hop on his lap—just to be immediately startled. It isn't there anymore. What I had just felt pushing against the jeans fabric, what his eyes and his hands and his mouth led me to believe I would find. My mind races. Maybe I'm too much for him to take, after all. Maybe my inner voice was right all along. Maybe he's not that into me.

"What?" He stops. "What's wrong?"

"Well..." I hesitate. Shouldn't I be the one asking this question? I let my gaze fall down to his lap and the lack of proof of his desire.

That's when I spot a wet stain on his dark blue underwear. I try to get off him, but he pulls me back by my thighs, securing me in place.

"Did you..." I can't contain myself, and enjoy it a little too much when his face turns crimson red.

"Yes," he admits, closing his eyes. And goes silent. He's uncomfortable. He's embarrassed. He's never looked so hot.

I wait until he opens those beautiful blue eyes of his again to smile. He doesn't smile back. I kiss him lightly on the lips. He doesn't move, so I do it again. And again. And again. Until he grabs my hair and holds my head in place for a real kiss. He lets me move away just an inch as I slide my hands down his chest and finally get rid of the remainder of his clothes.

"Let me see if I can do it again," I tease.

"I trust your abil—" he sucks in the air when I touch him, making me grin wildly.

✳DAY TEN

I WAKE UP IN THE MIDDLE OF THE NIGHT WITH MY BLADDER EXPLODING. I try to roll out of bed just to find that I can't— there's something pinning me down. There's *someone* pinning me down. My heart races as I slowly remember where I am, and what happened. I look to my side, to the body attached to the heavy arm that is sprawled across my chest. It's dark, so I can't really see him, but I can hear him snoring. That makes me chuckle.

I disentangle myself from him slowly, trying not to wake him up. When I'm almost free, his head jerks up and he throws his arm over me again.

"Don't leave," he says. His voice is raspy and creaked.

"I'm... I need a wee," I say back, praying he can't feel my heart speeding up in my chest.

He mumbles, lying back down and letting me go. I run to the bathroom and do my business. I yawn and the smell of my breath makes me grimace. I'm also sticky and kind of sweaty—just gross all over. I turn on the lights to try to at least brush my teeth and groan when I see my reflection in the mirror—makeup smeared everywhere, curls pointing out in every direction and a huge bruise near my collarbone. Hickey. That idiot.

I wash my face, try to tame my hair and brush my teeth with my fingers. And I still feel disgusting. What am I doing, anyway? Am I actually planning to just crawl back in bed with him? I never do that. I'm sure he never does that. I should just leave.

Of course, I'll still have to see him in the morning. It's not just one of those situations where I won't even remember his name. Where we'll never see each other again. Where we'll never have to talk about this. What is the proper procedure now? Should I stay? What will it mean if I do? Would he stay if we were in my room?

Ugh. What have I done?

"Hey," I hear a rapid-fire knock on the door. "I need to go, too."

"Just a minute," I shout back to him. I take another look at myself in the mirror and sigh. There's nothing else I can do right now.

I turn the lights off before I open the door, suddenly very self-aware of my nakedness. I walk by him without looking up. He runs to the bathroom and closes the door without a word. My stomach sinks.

I walk to the bedside table and turn on the little lamp. My phone clock says it's nearly 5. Gee. I kind of did spend the night, didn't I?

I hear the toilet flush and start to panic. I look around the room, at our clothes scattered about—just the memory of how they got where they are makes me hot. I debate for a moment about putting on his shirt, but then decide it would imply things I don't mean. So I just grab my knickers and my own top. When I hear the bathroom door opening, I run back to the bed, as if I'm a small child caught doing something she shouldn't. I'm so embarrassed. But at least I'm dressed now. Half dressed, anyway.

He takes two steps back into the room and pauses, squinting in the faint light. I avert my eyes. I can't look. I sense him shuffling and picking up something on the floor. Then, he walks up to me and sits by my side. He's put on his underwear, but that's the only thing he's wearing. We sit there, at the edge of the bed, in silence.

"You're dressed," he says, finally.

"*You're* dressed," I retort.

"Because *you're* dressed," he says. I bite back a smile. "Do you... do you... want to go?" he stutters. It reassures me, somehow. He doesn't know what to do, as well.

"Uh... I was... well... I was thinking about it," I say, still not able to look at him.

"Okay," he says, and I can tell he's nodding. "Well, I... I... I don't want you to."

That's when I finally look at him. He's frowning, his cheeks a bit flushed. He holds my gaze for two seconds and then stares at the floor, letting his hair cover his eyes.

"This is awkward," I blurt out. I don't know why. It's pretty clear it is. "I should go."

"Wait," he says, grabbing my arm and pushing me back down. "Just... wait a second."

I sit back, turning to him. We manage to keep our eyes on each other's faces for a moment. Then I sigh.

"Tyler..." I mumble, covering my face with my hands.

"Just wait," he insists.

"Wait for what?"

"Until... until it dissipates," he says. His voice is so soft, it makes me smile.

"What if it doesn't?" I ask, my face still hidden behind my palms.

"Let's... let's just wait and see," he says.

I take a peek of him from between my fingers. He's looking at me. He smiles when he sees I'm looking. It just makes me more nervous.

"Is this part of your strategy?" I ask, letting my hands drop to my lap. I immediately start to fidget with the hem of my shirt.

"What strategy?" he frowns.

"Do you ask them all to wait?" I ask.

I can see shock light up his eyes when he understands what I'm talking about. Needles to say, I regret it.

He opens his mouth to answer, but then shuts it again, along with his eyes. He lets out a small sigh.

"No," he says, eyes still closed. "I'm usually out the door before they're even asleep."

"Me, too," I admit. He opens his eyes again, meeting mine. Then staring at my lips.

"Well, you're still here," he says. And then he smiles.

"You, too," I say.

"It's my room," he reminds me.

Silence takes over once again, but it's not so bad this time. Maybe waiting it out does work.

After a while, he scoots closer, pushing my hair back to reveal my neck. It's all it takes to set me on fire again. It's ridiculous, I know. It's also true.

"Do you still want to go?" he asks, his mouth just inches away from my ear.

"Kind of, yeah," I say.

It takes him a few seconds to notice I don't mean it. And, when he does, he kisses me. I notice he's brushed his teeth, too. We're both ridiculous, as it turns out.

"Do I still taste like death?" I ask when we pull apart, not sure I was successful in my attempt to freshen-up earlier.

"You taste like someone who's going to spend the night on my bed," he answers.

"Christ," I laugh. I can't help it.

"It was bad, wasn't it?" he scrunches up his nose, clearly embarrassed.

"Yep," I say, still laughing.

"Well, it's the middle of the night," he tries to justify himself. "I just woke up, I'm really tired, you wore me off—"

I interrupt him with another kiss. It's deeper and slower this time. I know where we're heading.

"And you taste like someone who's about to get lucky," I tell him when we pull apart.

"That's not any better than—"

I cut his sentence short by sneaking my hand inside his underwear. I feel his grip in my hair tighten. The intensity of his eyes is almost too much to bear. So, I kiss him again. He tries to kiss me back at first, but soon he loses control of his tongue. He buries his face in my neck, moaning softly. Whispering my name. My real name. Gosh. It *is* too much.

In a quick move, he stops me, yanking my hand off his little friend and pulling me to his lap. I don't even know how it happens, but suddenly I'm straddling him. He kisses me again as his hands travel up my body underneath my shirt. Within a second, it's back on the floor and he's covering my chest in kisses and soft bites.

Then, he stops. He stares into my eyes intently, watching—watching as he slides *his* hand inside *my* pants. If I thought it was too much before...

"Stay," he whispers into my ear as I grab at his hair, pulling him closer. "Please."

"Okay," I moan.

The next word to come out of my mouth is his name.

***

I wake up again with my alarm clock when it's almost noon. This time, though, we're not all tangled up like a pair of teenagers. I sit up and look at him—his back is turned to me, moving slowly at the pace of his breathing. Once I questioned whether it was worth it for his fans to try so hard to spend one night under his sheets. And I'll never admit it out loud, but, yes. Yes, it's worth it.

I get up as silently as I can and go to the bathroom, gathering my clothes on the way. Somehow, I look even worse than I did earlier. And that goddamn hickey, too—it's gonna be impossible to cover it up. I'll need to rethink my clothes for these last days.

Last days. This is it. We have a little over 48 hours and then... then... it's over. Everything will be over. The thought makes me sad, although it's not a big realization. It was always meant to be over. And now I'm left wondering if it should have even started in the first place.

He's still asleep when I come back to the room. I debate whether to wake him up, since we have to be in a van to Glasgow in under two hours, but then I decide against it. I don't want to deal with what comes next right now.

I fish for the hotel's notepad inside the drawer and write him a note. As soon as I'm finished, I want to tear it apart and throw it away. A note? Like, really? What am I doing?

I sigh, leaving it on the pillow that was mine for the night. I stand there, my boots, thighs, and purse in hand, just watching him for a while. Like a creep. *Fuck.* I should have kissed him earlier. At the club, that night on the rooftop, while lying on my garden back in Alnwick. Our trip would have been dramatically different. Then again, we would have to deal with it for a lot longer. And that's where I usually screw things up.

I tip-toe to the door, opening it really slowly, stepping outside, and closing it with the same care. And then I bump into Neil in the middle of the corridor.

I freeze in place, feeling my face violently burn, as he looks me up and down with one eyebrow raised.

"Morning, Becky," he says cheerfully.

"M-morning," I stutter.

He just smiles, like this isn't the worst thing to ever happen on this tour. He glances at his clock, resuming his walk towards the lift. He presses the button and then turns around again. He frowns when he sees me still standing at the same spot.

"We're leaving soon, you know," he says.

That seems to do the trick. I rediscover how to walk and stroll down the few steps to my own room. Although my legs are working, my brain is definitely not, so I can't think of anything to say. I don't even know what I should say. That is, if I should say anything at all.

I don't—better to play it safe. I slide my card to unlock my door and rush inside, closing it with a slightly forceful bang. *Crap.* Crap crap crap crap crap! Am I in trouble? Will this affect our chances with the label? Goddammit, the label! Pete will literally kill me if this has professional consequences whatsoever.

Speaking of him, I take my phone out again, checking my messages. I clear all my notifications—so many useless ones—and open the chat app. My stomach sinks when I find nothing from Pete. And then it reaches a little lower when I find one from grandma.

'Jo doesn't seem to know about anything unusual. Have you talked to Peter yet?'

I forgot to call her, even though I set up an alarm for it. So, I decide that's the first thing I'll do. After taking a shower, I mean. I've never needed a shower so bad before.

***

By the time I hang up the phone, my head is pounding. Not from talking to grandma—it was, again, nice enough. Too nice, even. Although I did manage to not tell her about spending the night with Tyler. At least *some* of my best judgment is still intact.

The headache is probably hangover mixed with not sleeping and hunger. I'm *so* hungry. I decide to have breakfast in the room, since I don't have much time until we leave to Glasgow. And because I'm a coward and I don't want to see Tyler just yet. Although I can't stop thinking about him. His eyes, and his hands, and his mouth. The way he made me hot by just looking at me, the way he touched me like I'm made of glass, the way my name sounded in his breathless voice. *Dammit.*

I try to clear my head by ordering my food and texting Pete to see if he has any medicine. I keep the chat window open, suddenly way too worried about him. I wonder how his night ended. Was it as good as mine? Was it bad? Something starts to bubble up in my stomach and I can't wait for his reply. So, I call him.

"Becky?" he answers startled. I never call.

"Hey, how are you?" I ask.

"Wh-what? Why? Why are you asking?" he stutters.

"Because I have a mean headache right now," I say, although his jittery response throws me off a little bit. He's probably not okay. "I just texted you asking for some aspirin."

"Oh," he sighs. "Right, aspirin. Well, I... I don't have any."

"Have you had breakfast yet?" I ask, starting to get anxious with his airy replies.

"Breakfast?" he repeats.

"I just ordered room service. Come over here, let's eat," I say, trying not to let it transpire I'm suspicious. If he notices, he'll probably avoid me.

"Um... I..." he hesitates, making my heart race.

"Please?" I try, and then I have an idea. "I have something to tell you."

I wait, almost able to hear the engines in his head turning. If I can't get him by anything else, I can certainly get him by his curiosity.

"Okay," he sighs, finally. I smile. "I'm coming."

I stand at my open door to wait for him and the food. When he starts to take too long, I debate whether I should go knock on his door. But, then, the elevator doors open and he walks outside. He pauses when he sees me staring, and then walks faster until he reaches me.

"Where were you?" I frown.

"Outside," it's all he says.

I make room for him to enter and notice a stain in the back of his shirt as he walks past me.

"What's that on your shirt?" I ask.

"What's what?" he jumps, turning around fast. His eyes are wide, like a deer caught in the headlights. *This can't be good...*

"That stain," I say, slowly closing the door and blocking his way out.

"Nothing," he says, shaking his head. "I must have leaned against a dirty wall or something."

"Let me see," I ask. He just stares with those crazy eyes. So, I walk up to him and grab his shoulders, forcefully turning him around.

"Why, no, wait!" He tries to resist, but I'm stronger than his thin arms.

I examine the spot and it looks like... it looks like...

"Pete!" I gasp as I yank his shirt up and have the confirmation to my suspicion. It's blood. He has a nasty cut on the right side of his back, under his shoulder blade.

"Is it bad?" he asks, apparently giving up the idea to hide it from me.

"What happened?" I ask, still examining it.

"Do you have a first aid kit or something?" he asks.

I let him go for a minute as I walk to the bathroom. There isn't a kit here, but I take a roll of toilet paper, a towel, and a bottle of water I had left there yesterday.

"I don't think it's that bad, but there's a lot of blood," I say as I come back. "Take off your shirt."

He turns around again and lifts just half of it up. I wait for a few seconds for him to do as I told, but apparently he's not willing to.

"For fuck's sake," I complain, yanking the shirt back up. He flinches as it rubs against the wound.

"Are you sure it's not bad?" he asks again, his tone flat and distant.

"I'll tell you in a second," I say as I wet the towel and try to clean the blood around the gash.

I keep my mouth shut, waiting for the silence to make him start explaining himself. He doesn't, though. And, then, on top of it, he starts to shake.

"Am I hurting you?" I ask, stopping my efforts. The wound is clean, anyway. I was just buying time.

"Yes," he answers sharply.

"It has stopped bleeding," I say, retreating from him, "but I think we should bandage it."

"Okay," he says, pulling his shirt down carefully.

He turns around and my heart cracks. He looks so... sad. I'm about to ask what happened when someone knocks on the door—our breakfast. I take the opportunity to ask the guy for a first-aid kit, which he promises to bring back in a minute.

I roll the cart over towards the bed and spread its contents over it. I sit down, resting my back against the headboard. Pete sits on the other side, since he can't lean over anything right now. He immediately starts to eat, not looking at me.

"What did you want to tell me?" he asks.

"No way," I scoff, which makes him look up. "There's no way we're talking about anything other than what the *fuck* happened to you!"

He averts his eyes, chewing slowly. When he swallows, he takes a sip of his coffee, and looks back at me.

"I..." he starts and pauses. My heart is halfway out of my body already. "I fell."

"You fell?" I scoff again, not believing him.

"Yes," he nods once.

"Where?"

"On my way up to the roof."

"The roof?"

"Yes."

"What were you doing on the roof?"

"Kind of... hiding."

"Why?"

"I..." he sighs, running a hand through his messy hair. "I had a really terrible night."

"Tell me," I demand, but in what I hope is a kind tone.

He sighs, opening his mouth to do just so, I guess, but then interrupting himself. His expression changes, softening a little.

"No, you tell me," he smiles faintly, giving me a pointed look. "How was *your* night?"

Now, I'm the one who averts my eyes. I feel guilty for feeling... I don't know... good, when my best friend is clearly going through hell. I don't want to tell him about how my night was amazing when he's sitting here so hurt—both physically and emotionally.

"Oh my God," he finally breaks the silence, making me look at him again. "You did it, didn't you? You totally did! Finally!"

He laughs, the first one I've seen in probably days. That's encouragement enough to make me change my mind.

"I thought you wouldn't approve of my unprofessional behavior," I joke.

"I don't, but I couldn't stand all that sexual tension anymore," he says.

"Pete!" I gasp, feeling my cheeks heat up.

"Honestly, I don't know how it didn't happen sooner," he continues. *I'm with you on that*, I think. "You two almost made me barf a number of times already."

I throw a pillow at him for that. It hits him right in the face, making him spill some of his coffee down his shirt. He gives me an annoyed look, but it's a Pete look. A normal Pete look. I'm a tiny bit relieved.

"So?" he continues, raising his eyebrows. "How was it?"

"Well... it was..." I hesitate, fully aware of how juvenile I must look. "It was nice."

"Nice?" he widens his eyes even more. "That's all I'm gonna get?"

"What do you want?" I frown.

"A detailed report," he answers as if that's a normal thing to ask.

"As if!" I say, giggling like a moron.

"Okay, I can settle for a score, then," he says. "For now."

"A score?" I repeat.

"Yes," he nods. "From 0 to 10?"

I bite my lip, thinking. I don't think I can rate it. I mean, it was pretty... different... than what I'm used to. It's been a while—a *long* while—since the last time I enjoyed myself as much. But I can't tell him that. I don't want him reading too much into it.

"A solid eight," I end up saying.

"Eight, huh?" he nods approvingly. "That's pretty high for your standards."

"I hate that you know that," I say, making him chuckle.

"Why are you alone, then?" he frowns. Then, he gets outraged. "Don't tell me he left you in the middle of the night like you were just a random woman he picked up at the bar."

"No, he actually..." I hesitate. "He actually asked me to stay."

I can't look at him anymore. Why is this so embarrassing?

"Beckyyyyy!" he coos and, in a second, he's sitting by my side. "Did you?"

I nod. He squeals again, pulling me into him.

"I don't see why me getting laid deserves *this* type of reaction," I complain. "It's not like it's been *that* long."

"Becky!" he gasps, letting me go and looking me in the eyes. "It's not about the sex part."

He gives me *a look*. I don't really know what he means, I just know it makes me uncomfortable. So, I look away and eat some more. He doesn't press me and restarts eating as well.

I really want to ask him about his night again. But he's smiling, bumping his shoulder against mine, discussing what mine and Tyler's ship name should be. So, I don't. It can wait a little longer.

***

"Good morning!" Jake cheers as I step into the hotel lobby, giving me a wide smile. *He knows.*

"Morning," I frown, walking towards the reception desk to drop my bag with all the others.

"Are you all packed?" Todd approaches us, and for the first time I'm glad he's ignoring me.

"There are still a few people missing," Jake replies as he counts the bags.

"For Christ's sake," Todd complains, like he is the manager or something. The *real* manager, though, is leisurely sitting on a couch, talking on the phone. "We're planning to leave within the hour."

I snort. It's stronger than me. But I only regret it because it makes both Jake and Todd turn to me.

I want to say it's a really short drive and he doesn't need to get all worked up about it, but what remains of my best judgment speaks louder again. So, I say nothing. And just smile. Which makes Todd's frown deepen.

"Someone is in a good mood this morning," Jake says in the same cheery tone of when he greeted me.

"Aren't I always?" I tilt my head to the side, giving him my best sarcastic smile.

"Where's Tyler?" Todd apparently is having way less fun with the situation than his guitar tech.

I shoot him a surprised look, as if asking if he's really talking to me. He raises his eyebrows, so I decide to reply.

"How would I know?" I ask, without losing the light, ironic tone.

"Because you spent the night together?" he mimics me.

"Todd, come on," Jake tugs on his sleeve.

"What? You've seen the photos," Todd frowns.

Wait, what? Photos? What photos?

"What photos?" I ask, now completely losing composure.

"You haven't seen them yet?" he continues with the mocking sweet tone. "They're all over the Internet."

"What photos?" I ask again, a bit more desperate now. My mind is already thinking the worst—Tyler took pics of naked me and posted them online. It was all just a joke. I'm just a joke.

"Someone took pics of you guys kissing at the club," Jake is the one to explain. He's not in bantering mood anymore. "They're really blurry, though, you can't tell it's you two."

"Of course, you can tell!" Todd argues. "You can clearly see it's a blond person and a purple-haired person."

He looks back at me with a triumphant look. And then it occurs to me this is nonsense. It's none of his business what happened and, really, is he trying to humiliate me because I had sex?

"So, what?" I say nonchalantly, crossing my arms.

"So... well..." Todd stutters, thrown off by my sudden change of attitude. "You spent the night together."

"What if we did?" I continue. Jake smiles behind him.

"I... you..." Todd stutters again, and then sighs in frustration. "I just want to know where Tyler is."

"I already told you I have no idea."

"Whatever," he rolls his eyes, turning away to leave.

"You're worse than your psycho fans," I add, because I have to have the last word. Jake covers his mouth with a hand. I don't have time to regret it, though, because someone interrupts our interaction.

"What about our psycho fans?" Tyler's morning voice thunders behind me, making my stomach flutter.

"Oh, Todd, Todd!" I call, smiling brightly. "I know where he is! Behind me."

"Where were you?" Todd decides to ignore me, which is a good decision.

"Sleeping." I can hear Tyler's frown without even looking at him.

"We're leaving in less than an hour," Todd informs.

Tyler doesn't reply and I hear his footsteps retreating. Todd lets his gaze fall on me again and frowns. I wink, crossing my arms over my chest. He rolls his eyes and turns his attention back to his phone, finally walking away.

I immediately pick up my own phone, eager to open Twitter and see the damn photos. I don't even have to look for them—Todd was right, they're all over my feed.

"Shit," I mutter.

"It's not that bad," Jake walks closer to me, looking down at the screen.

I read some of the comments, which is a huge mistake.

Wow, Tyler reached a new low.

*So is he REALLY going at the punk bitch? *sighs**

Is this a joke?

Ew, I bet she doesn't even shower!

Calm down, people, he must have lost a bet or something.

I give Jake an annoyed look. *All* the comments are talking shit about me.

"Okay, I take it back," he gives me a sheepish smile. "Close it, don't read. Out of sight, out of mind."

"I wish that was true," I sigh. But I do close the app.

I notice I have a few unread messages, too. From Patrick. Letting me know about the clothes, asking about grandma and also confessing to stalking me.

'I've found you online! You're really good. Can't wait to see you on stage.'

I swallow dry and decide not to reply. Out of sight, out of mind. I put the phone away and look up to see Tyler walking back in our direction, a cup of coffee in one hand and a croissant in the other. He smiles when he sees I'm looking. I smile back.

"Hey, Beth," he says when he's close enough. "Jake."

"Someone is in a good mood today," Jake jokes again.

"Aren't I always?" Tyler replies in the same sarcastic tone I used.

I glance up at Jake. He looks back, widening his eyes. And we start to laugh.

"I'm glad I'm providing such a good time to everyone," Tyler says, a suspicious frown on his face.

"Okay, I'm gonna go help load the vans," Jake announces, grabbing a few of the bags and announcing, "We leave within the hour!"

I chuckle again. It's nice to know I'm not being entirely unfair with Todd. He *is* a pain in the ass.

When I turn back to Tyler, he's still frowning. I reach up, touching a finger to his forehead, between his eyebrows, and his expression relaxes.

"That's better," I say. He rolls his eyes.

"So, I got your note," he says. I feel myself flush. I had forgotten about the note.

"Oh, yeah, *that*. I didn't want you to think that I walked out on you as if you were some random guy I picked up at the bar," I say, using Pete's dramatic words. I know he knows I'm not the one who came up with that thought by the puzzled expression he gives me back.

"You did walk out, though," he says, studying me.

"I had to gather my stuff," I justify myself. "We're leaving soon."

"You could have woken me up," he says.

"I wouldn't have left if I did," I blurt out.

A slow, bright grin spreads across his face. I roll my eyes but I can't deny that I like it. Now, seeing him smile instantly makes me smile, too.

"Hey," Neil joins us, a somber expression on his face. "Good to catch you two together. Can we talk for a moment?"

Shit. We're in trouble. I'm going to get fired. Pete is going to kill me!

We follow him to a corner. When he turns to us, he sighs "So, I just want to apologize to you two. I tried to make it go away but by the time I found out about it, it was all over social media."

"What are you talking about?" Tyler asks.

The pictures.

"The pictures," he says.

"What pictures?" Tyler asks, his voice matching my panicked tone from just minutes ago.

Neil widens his eyes, glancing at me. I shrug.

"I didn't know about them, either," I say. "Until Todd mentioned it."

"Todd?" Tyler gasps.

"Okay, keep calm," Neil says, raising his hands, and then dives into the explanation. "Someone took pictures of you and Becky at the club last night. It's all over social media today. I've been able to stop the press from publishing anything, but... it's out there."

Christ. This is so not the conversation I thought we would be having. Neil is... protecting us? And not firing me? I'm shocked.

"So what if there are pictures of us?" Tyler scoffs. "We went out as a group."

"We're kissing, Tyler," I clarify it for his slow brain. "It's pictures of us kissing."

He freezes, his eyes cold on my face. I'm not sure what to make of this reaction.

"Fuck..." Or of his cursing.

"It'll be fine, people will forget it," Neil says. "But I'd recommend you stay out of social media for a couple of days. Especially you, Becky."

I nod. I choose to not tell them I've read some of the comments already. I don't want to talk about it.

"Now, the vans are outside, we're splitting into two," Neil claps his hands together, kind of making Tyler wake up from his trance. "You go first with your brothers and Jake and Paul."

Tyler doesn't move.

"You go now," Neil says again. Tyler glances at me, so he adds, "You'll have time to talk it over later. Now, go!"

He hesitates a while, but ends up obliging. His furrowed brow doesn't help my nerves.

"Are you okay?" Neil turns to me now.

"Uh... yeah... I guess..." I mumble.

"I'm really sorry," he says, actually meaning it. I'm amazed.

"It's not your fault," I argue. Which is true. "It's *our* fault. My fault. Why aren't you mad?"

"What?" he frowns. "Why would I be mad?"

"Because..." I pause, trying to formulate a sentence that doesn't include the word *fucking* in it. "I've been kind of unprofessional."

He widens his eyes with that and laughs. Full-on, belly-grabbing and all.

"Becky!" he exclaims when he recovers. "This is not an office! Your profession *demands* you wear your feelings on your sleeve, at all times! It's not surprising that some of you would end up getting too close too quickly."

Some of you. Does he know about Pete, too? Has this happened before? I decide to go for the second question.

"How many times has this happened?" I ask. His amused expression vanishes, but he manages to keep the smile.

"You don't really expect me to discuss this topic with you, do you?" he says in a sympathetic-yet-serious voice. "*I'm a professional.*"

I feel myself blush. But then he chuckles. He's joking. I guess. But he's really not gonna tell me anything about The Hacks' mating habits.

"Come on, we should get going, too."

I follow him to the van and sit on the back with Lindsey. She immediately puts her headphones on—we're not going to talk, then. I'm actually not bothered. I have too much on my mind now to fill the silence with words.

**

The hour-long trip to Glasgow is terrible. The load-in is terrible. The soundcheck is terrible. Not that we make mistakes, we don't. But there's clearly something missing. None of the songs sound the same. It's all stiff, and tiring, and hard to watch. You can count on music to be transparent like that. Everyone has seen the pictures, everyone knows what happened last night, and everyone is wondering why Tyler and I are acting so strangely. Not that anyone voiced any opinions, but it's written all over their faces.

We didn't have time to 'talk it over' as Neil said we would. Once again, I'm stunned by how much we're constantly surrounded by people. And, for once, I actually want to talk it over. I mean, I want to hear it—I want to hear what Tyler has to say, what his cursing meant, what the worried expression he's wearing right now means. I want to know... I want to know what's happening between us.

"Come on, guys," Neil sighs from the floor. "It's the end of the tour. Let's go out with a bang, shall we?"

"I think the bang might be the problem here," Todd remarks, making my blood boil. But before I have a chance to say anything, Tyler snaps.

"Good Lord, shut the hell up! Why don't you mind your own business for a change?"

"This is my business! If we sound like shit, it is my business," Todd tries to justify himself.

"Right, as if *that's* what you care about," Tyler snorts.

"I'm just trying to be professional," he digs again, making Tyler widen his eyes.

"How is commenting on my sexual life professional, you asshole?"

"Okay, enough!" Neil interrupts the argument. "Let's call it. But you two better get it together before the show."

"Just don't talk to me and we'll be fine," Tyler continues.

"Very mature," Todd snorts. "One would think that getting laid would put you in a better mood. Then, he turns to me and adds, "Maybe you should do it again, but try to get it right this time."

The next thing I know Tyler is flying across the stage towards him. Luckily, Tristan is faster and leaps from behind his drums to stop his brother.

"What is your problem?" Tyler yells.

"Jealousy, I bet," I barge in, for their surprise.

"What?" Todd snorts. "Do you really think I'd want anything with you?"

"No, that didn't even cross my mind," I give him an 'ew' look and he blushes. "I was referring to everything else, actually."

"You don't know what you're talking about," he babbles.

"You know, Todd, if there's anyone in need to get laid here, it's you," I can't contain myself. "Although I'm really not surprised as to why you can't manage."

"What? You... you don't..." he stutters, his face flushing in several different shades of red.

"I could offer to introduce you to some friends, if you weren't such a prick," I say as I put my guitar down, walk towards Tyler with purpose and reach out a hand.

He looks at me startled for a moment, but then smirks and accepts my hand. With a pointed look at Todd, we leave the stage. His hand is cold and clammy and I wonder if his heart is beating as fast as mine right now.

We reach his dressing room and Tyler lets go of my hand once we're inside. It's obvious we're not doing it. Not that I wanted to, anyway. I didn't.

"That was pretty bad-ass," he comments, leaning against one of the counters and turning back to me.

"Whatever," I mumble.

And then we just stare at each other awkwardly. I have the feeling he's expecting me to say something. No, it seems like he's *afraid* I'll say something. I'm really out of my depth here.

"Tyler—"

"It shouldn't have happened," he blurts out suddenly.

"W-what?" I stutter, my mind running off with my paranoid thoughts once again.

"We shouldn't..." he trails off, studying my face. "Isn't that what you were going to say?"

"No," I answer firmly. Even though it has crossed my mind a million times since I woke up this morning. "Is that what you were going to say?"

"I wasn't going to say anything," he argues. I can see him fidgeting with the seams of his shirt under his arms as he crosses them. "What were you going to say?"

"I..." I pause. *I* wasn't going to say anything. "I was going to ask you if you're okay."

"Oh," he frowns.

"You seem... really..." What? Pissed? Afraid? Regretful? All at once? "Upset. Is it because of the photos?"

"Um... yeah..." he says, closing his eyes and pressing them with his palms. I don't believe him. "My fans can be nasty, you know."

"We can deny it," I offer.

"We should stay out of it, as Neil suggested," he sighs. "Believe me, it's better if we don't engage."

That turns the paranoid thoughts inside my head into paranoid questions. And, of course, I can't keep them only in my head.

"How many times has this happened?"

"Uh..." he frowns, giving me a puzzled look. "*This* what?"

I fight the urge to roll my eyes. He knows what I'm talking about, why is he torturing me like this?

"How many times have the fans seen pictures of you making out with random girls?" I clarify.

"You're not a random girl," he argues. I can't tell what those words make me feel.

"That doesn't answer my question," I say.

"What do you want me to say?" he snaps. "Countless times. More times than I can even remember. Yes, I can't keep it in my pants, everything people say about me is true."

His outburst takes me by surprise. I still can't tell why he's upset. If this has happened before, so many times as he claims, then... well...

"You should be used to it, then," I say.

He looks at me with wide eyes and a semi-open mouth, like I'm totally missing the point. Which, probably, I am.

"I don't get it," I say, at last. "If you haven't noticed by now, I'm pretty clueless and paranoid, so if there's some point you want me to see here, you'll have to draw it for me."

That makes him actually smile. Which, of course, makes me smile. This is my default now.

"I didn't want..." he starts and pauses. "I didn't want anyone to know."

I nod slowly. "Because I'm not your type."

"No!" he says, in a tone that indicates he was expecting me to say that. "I think we've already established that I'm really, *really* into you, Eliza."

Gosh. These nicknames will be the end of me.

"So—"

"So," he interrupts me, getting up and walking in my direction, "people are mean and nosy and I didn't want to invite their opinions on... us."

Us. I start to panic. He's already talking about an us. And don't tell me it doesn't mean what I think it means because there was a pause there. He paused before saying it. He *means it.*

"What are we doing?" I ask, the question that no one who just had the amazing night we did wants to hear.

He stops his slow approach, but his eyes never leave mine. He chews on his bottom lip, his head to the side—the stance I already recognize as his thinking face.

"Do I make you feel good?" he asks next. It takes me by surprise—again. He doesn't allow much time for me to answer, though, as he adds, "Because you make me feel fucking amazing."

I feel the warmth spread from the pit of my stomach to my chest, my arms, my face. It burns away all the other thoughts and feelings that had been nagging at the edges. I'm fully just...

"Yeah," I answer, but it's just a whisper. "You make me feel like a person."

I think I'm the one to take him by surprise, now. His eyes harden, but not in the same frightening way it happened in the hotel. It's different, like... like... I don't know. I don't have time to figure it out, as he closes the gap between us and kisses me. I kiss him back, feeling a bit more powerful now that I know he enjoys it.

***

Unfortunately, our make-out session doesn't go very far. We're interrupted by none other than Todd—walking in on us while I have my hands underneath Tyler's shirt. I curse his timing. I mean, it's still not his business, but I'd prefer he didn't have a real image to go with his assumptions.

"Can I..." he stutters, blushing again and staring solely at Tyler. "Can I talk to you?"

"S-sure," Tyler stutters, too. He keeps me in front of him until he manages to sit on the bench in front of the mirror—in an effort to hide the boner I was giving him, I presume.

"See you later," I say, giving him one last *obscene* kiss. In part to make Todd even more uncomfortable, in part because I just want to.

On my way to my own dressing room, I automatically take my phone out of my pocket and open Twitter. I'm greeted by the first tweet on a thread trying to prove Tyler and I were on a secret relationship way before the pictures in the club were leaked. I should really stay away from social media for a while. So, I close Twitter. And open Instagram.

"Hey," Lindsey's voice makes me look up from my phone screen.

"Hey," I say back.

She's alone, sitting on our small couch with her legs up, chin resting on her knees. She looks like a small child. Like a small, sad child. She has her phone in her hands, as well.

"I'm sorry about the pics," she scrunches her nose. "Are you okay?"

And this is reason number 43 why I think she and Pete are a perfect match. They're both able to worry about other people even when they're knee-deep into their own shit. It makes me feel guilty because neither of them has even crossed my mind in hours. But I'll make it up to them.

"I'm fine," I say, sitting sideways beside her, so I can watch her face. "How are *you*?"

She seems surprised that I asked. I don't blame her. I usually don't ask. But it's the least I can do, right? I mean, I'm one of the only two people here she can talk to. And the other one is clearly avoiding her.

"I'm... well..." she hesitates. Then I remember I'm best friends with her problematic boyfriend.

"I won't tell him, I promise," I say. She turns to me wide-eyed. "You can say whatever you want. That is, if you want to say anything at all."

She spends a long time just looking at me. I'm not sure she believes me, or even that she wants to talk about it. I just wait, though. And, of course, the silence makes her spill the beans.

"He kissed Tristan," she blurts out. I don't react. I don't know what to say, so she continues, "I was a bitch to him last night. I tried to... I don't know... I was so drunk."

She sighs, hiding her face in her thighs.

"You know, I was a fan," she says in a hushed voice.

"What?" I ask. I'm not sure I'm following her line of thought.

"I was a huge fan of The Hacks when I was younger," she says, resting her chin on her knees. "I had posters of them on my walls and everything."

"No fucking way," I gasp, gob-smacked. "Does Pete know about that?"

She shakes her head. "I thought he'd be embarrassed of having me around, or something. You know how nervous he was about this."

"Yeah," I nod slowly. Then, for some reason, I ask, "Who was your favorite?"

"Can't you tell?" she raises her eyebrows.

I can. Everyone can by now. Well, everyone except Pete.

"I told Pete I was going to try to be cool about it, and I thought I was trying. I *am* trying. But... but..."

"You're jealous," I say, making her grunt.

"It's stronger than me," she admits, looking up again, at some invisible spot on the far wall. "He tells me he loves me, and I know it's true, I can feel it's true. And it should be enough, right?" She looks at me now. "He loves me, and I love him, and it should be enough."

I think she expects me to say something. What do people say to their friends in these situations? What would Pete say if he was here?

"Sometimes it isn't," I say.

Once upon a time, when I was the one knee-deep into my own shit, a little before Pete managed to pull me out, I justified myself with love. Pete would go on long rants listing all the ways my relationship with... Alex... was wrong. Slowly and persistently he made me see he was right. I think I had known for a long time that it was an unhealthy relationship. A dysfunctional relationship. An abusive relationship. I knew, but I still defended him. Because the good parts were very good. And because I loved him. I would tell Pete, when he was finished with his eloquent speeches, *'but I love him'*. And, then, he would answer *'but sometimes, Becks, love isn't enough'*.

I don't know if he was right. I don't know if what I felt was actually love. I do remember his words, though. All of them. They made me cry a lot. Just like they make Lindsey cry now.

She buries her face on my chest and I hug her. I run my hand up and down her back, feeling my shirt get wet and my heart break. I really like her. I'm a bit mad at Pete for hurting her like this.

It takes her a while to calm down, and when she does, she just stays there in my arms, letting me stroke her hair. She sniffles every once in a while, jumping as if she has a hiccup. When I deem enough time has passed, I break our companionable silence.

"You should keep in mind I don't know how love works, though," I say.

She chuckles and it tickles my neck. She disentangles herself from me, pulling her shirt up to dry her face. When she's done, she turns to me again, looking at me with sweet, swollen eyes.

"You know better than you think you do," she says. I feel myself blush.

She gives me a kiss on the cheek and gets up, saying she needs to take a walk. When she's gone, I text Pete. I need to convince him to not let her go.

'Where the fuck are you?'

***

He steps in, walks to the couch, throws himself down—flinching, since he clearly forgot about his wound—and leans his head back, closing his eyes. He looks like a zombie. The part of me that is mad at him shrinks.

"Where were you?" I ask.

"Hiding," he answers unashamedly.

"Alone?"

"Please, not you, too," he pinches the bridge of his nose.

I debate what to say next. Should I tell him I know he kissed Tristan? Should I tell him I know that Lindsey knows that he kissed Tristan? Should I tell him she just left the room after crying her eyes out on me?

I bite my lip, watching him in silence. He doesn't show any signs that he knows I'm staring. He doesn't show any signs that my strategy is working. And then I suddenly realize I've never seen him like this before. I don't know how to deal with this version of him.

So, I decide to try *his* strategy.

"Are you going to tell me what's going on?" I ask, giving him one more chance to open up. That's what he always does, even when he already knows what it is that I'm keeping from him.

"Shouldn't you be out in a dark corner with a certain blond pop star?" he asks back.

I sigh, defeated. This isn't going anywhere.

I reach out, smoothing his hair, similar to what I did to Lindsey. After a few seconds, he rolls over, hugging my waist and burying his face in my neck—similar to what Lindsey did with me. He doesn't cry, though, for which I'm glad. I don't think I'd be able to keep my composure if the tears on my shirt were his.

"Pete," I say softly.

"Hmm," he mumbles.

"Can I ask you a question?"

"That's already a question," he says, making me roll my eyes. When I don't continue, he adds, "Ask away."

"How do you know you're in love?"

It's like I hit him with a taser gun. He jumps, sitting up straight, his head bumping into my jaw in the process. It hurts.

"Where did that come from?" he shouts, dark eyes so wide I can see the little red veins in the white part.

"Don't read too much into it," I say as I massage the spot where he hit me. "I was just thinking about it."

"About being in love?" he asks, still surprised.

"About how it feels," I continue. "How do you know it's love?"

My intention is to make him remember why he's in love with Lindsey. How they met, how he fell for her, what it is that makes her special in his eyes. But, I can't lie—I'm a bit... curious.

"I don't know Becks, I think it's different for everyone," he answers, after a while.

"How is it for you?" I insist.

He sighs. For a moment, I think he's not going to indulge me. But he does. He always does.

"It's like... It's like I want to be near the person at all times. Even when things are shitty. I want them around even when I can't stand looking at them. It's... wanting them even when you're not sure you want them. It's wanting to make sure they know you care about them. That they're safe with you."

I think for a minute. I've felt all of this before. In fact, I feel it right now.

"It sounds a lot like what we have," I say.

"It does," he laughs a little, but it has no humor. "It's what we have plus something more. Something inexplicable, unquantifiable, untouchable. Something that every time you think you're on the verge of grasping, it slips away."

Okay... so... you *can't* tell when you're in love. That's what he's saying, right? I mean, chasing after something you can never hold sounds exhausting to me. I don't think I want that.

"Can you... like... control it?" I go on. "Like, if you don't want to fall in love, can you prevent it?"

"I don't know," he chuckles again. "I can't."

That seems to be quite unfair. Then again, I can't recall one single moment in my life I was in control of any emotion. I don't know why I thought love would be different.

"Are you still in love with Linds?" I ask, suddenly. His surprised look comes back. He doesn't answer, so I ask, "Are you in love with Tris?"

He shakes his head. I'm not sure which question he's answering. I feel sad, anyway.

"Are you...?" he trails off. It takes me a moment to realize what he's implying. I shake my head. Even though I don't know if I'm being honest.

"Do you think that..." I hesitate. I'm not sure I want to voice my thoughts. "Like, if we had more time..."

"I don't know, hun," he answers, going back to his previous position. "I have no fucking idea."

***

The show ends up not being as terrible as it could be. The venue is packed full and hot, and the fans are loud and engaging. Midway through our set I've already forgotten all about their hostility and those pics. But then comes the joint part of the show and they all take their phones out and exchange glances with each other. That makes everyone uneasy. Even though we run through both songs seamlessly, it's pretty clear it's two different bands playing together.

Our part of the show ends, and, at some point, Pete leaves me alone at the side of the stage. I assume he's going to talk to Lindsey—whom I haven't seen since our little heart-to-heart—so I don't follow him. I also can't pay much attention to the concert. The fans spot me standing there, watching them, and keep taking pictures. I really want to retreat and vanish, but between my will to leave Pete and Lindsey alone and not let the fans know I'm bothered by their actions, I stay.

After a few songs, Neil appears and sends Paul and Jake back to the hotel earlier. I can't really hear his reasons, I just know what the order is.

"Are Pete and Lindsey going, too?" I ask Neil before he follows the boys. I'll jump at the opportunity of leaving early—even if it means getting in a car with Paul.

"Not yet," he says, "although Pete and I are stepping out for a moment."

"Where are you going?" I frown.

"Just…" he shrugs. And doesn't answer. And then starts to walk away.

Now, I follow him. He enters my dressing room, where Pete and Lindsey are indeed talking. But they stop when they see me.

"Where are you going?" I ask again.

Pete glances at Neil and something in his eyes makes me start to panic.

"Pete," I call him, making him look back at me.

"There's something we need to take care of," he says, slowly, which does not make me calmer.

"What is it?" I ask.

Pete sighs—that tired, frustrated sigh he's been giving me so often lately—and runs a hand through his head.

"I can't tell you what it is," he says. I widen my eyes in rage and surprise. "I'll meet you and Linds back at the hotel."

They move to leave the room, but I bang the door shut and stand in front of it. I cross my arms and glare at Pete. Somehow, he's not surprised by my reaction.

"Becky, please—"

"No!" I yell. It comes out louder than I intended. "Enough with all these secrets! I want to know exactly what's wrong, and I want to know it right now!"

He just stares for a long moment. It makes me uneasy. I can't read his face, I don't know what's going on, and I'm terrified.

"Becky," he reaches for my arms, squeezing them, "I'm not going to tell you."

"Why?" I yell again. My vision gets blurry with tears. "Why are you doing this?"

"Please," he repeats, and his voice cracks. It's all it takes to break me. "Please, just trust me, okay?"

"You're scaring me," I say.

"I know," he answers, drying my cheeks with his sleeve. It's useless, because I keep crying. And, now, he's crying, too. "But you'll have to trust me, okay? Please."

I don't know what to say. I don't know what else to do. I feel powerless and alone and scared.

I don't answer, but let him push me to the side and open the door. But he just leaves when Neil walks to him and puts a hand on his shoulder, leading him outside.

"What the fuck is going on?" I turn to Lindsey.

She doesn't answer, too. She walks to me and hugs me and I let her. I let her because if I'm left alone right now I think I might die.

***

"He's not picking up," Tyler says once again. He's been trying to reach Neil ever since he walked into my dressing room and caught me sobbing in Lindsey's arms. "Are you sure he didn't say where they were going?"

"Would I be in such a state if they did?" I bark.

He glances at Lindsey, but she's been tight-lipped all along, claiming they didn't tell her, either. I don't believe her. I don't believe her for a second and now I resent her. I resent her, and Tyler—who's been absolutely useless so far—and Tristan, who said he has no idea what might be going on.

"Hey, guys," Seth knocks on the open door. He's been left in charge since Neil is out on his secret mission. "Time to go. There are still some fans outside, though."

"I don't want to talk to anyone," I say, getting desperate again. "Send them away. Ask security to send them away."

They all look at me with pity in their eyes, which only makes me more enraged. Are they seriously not getting how fucking *serious* this is? Do they think this is an act? What will I have to do for someone to tell me the truth?

I give up and storm outside. Fuck them. Fuck the fans. Fuck Pete. I just want to get to the hotel, take a shower, and cry myself to sleep.

I'm the first out of the back door, and sure enough, the handful of fans still there call out my name. I ignore them, marching towards the van, which is too fucking far.

I enter it, throwing myself on the last seat, sulking and staring out the window. I hear the small group scream a bit when The Hacks step outside. I look towards them and see that as Todd and Tristan stop to take a few pictures, Tyler and Lindsey come straight to the van, as well. Lindsey steps in first and joins me in the backseat. Tyler kind of stands in the middle of the corridor, looking from Lindsey to me then back at her. Without a word, she moves places, sitting on the middle seat. Tyler then takes her place by my side, but I look away, out the window again.

A few seconds later, I jump, startled, when his hand touches mine. He doesn't pull it away after my reaction, and I turn my palm up so we can interlace our fingers together. He runs his thumb in a circling, soothing motion near my wrist. I feel tears threaten me again.

I close my eyes, tight, and touch my forehead against his shoulder. He takes the hint and lets go of my hand so he can put his arms around me. I hug his waist and bury my face into his lean, long neck. He continues to lightly stroke my arm with one hand while the other massages the back of my neck. Now I know why Pete and Lindsey spent so long letting me do this to them. It feels *heavenly*.

When we arrive at the hotel, everyone heads silently to their own rooms. I ask Lindsey if I can wait for Pete with her and she lets me. I take a shower in their bathroom and join her in bed to watch true crime shows while we wait. After a few minutes, my phone buzzes.

'*Can I come over?*' It's from Tyler.

Ugh. I really wish he did. I really wish I could go back to my room and just get to replay last night all over again. I can't, though. For the first time in the day, the idea of spending time with Tyler doesn't make me less worried about Pete.

'No,' I answer. Then I think of giving him an explanation. '*I'm with Lindsey. We're going to wait for my traitor friend together.*'

'Ok,' he answers. '*Will you let me know if everything is ok?*'

'*Sure,*' I answer, with a smile. Then I hesitate a little bit, not sure if I should say something more. I decide to end the conversation. '*Goodnight, Ty.*'

I stare at the blue tick of the message. His online status tells me he's staring at it, too. It's a long time before his status changes to 'typing'.

'*Goodnight, Becky.*'

✱DAY ELEVEN

Pete cries for almost an hour straight. Lindsey and I just let him, sitting there by him on the bed, touching him reassuringly as he hugs a pillow so tight that I think it might explode. When he starts to calm down, Lindsey produces a pack of tissues, a bottle of water, and saltines—out of nowhere. Pete and I both blink hard at her. She's such a caregiver. Much like him.

He takes the water and gulps down almost half of the bottle. Then he breaks a biscuit in half and munches on it, apparently not really willing to swallow it down. I really, really want him to talk. I have a million and one questions to ask, but I decide to follow Lindsey's lead on this one and stay quiet. Until he feels comfortable enough to open up.

"It was horrible," he says, closing his eyes and letting a new flow of silent tears roll down.

My heartbeat picks up. What the fuck *happened*?

"It's over now," Lindsey says softly, squeezing one of his knees, which are folded against his chest.

He nods slowly. When he opens his eyes, he looks at her. There's so much exchange in this simple gesture that it makes me sick. I want to scream at both of them, but I bite my tongue—literally. I need to be patient.

He slowly turns his head to me, making my hands start to shake. He manages to give me a weak smile, which I can't reciprocate. *Please,* I beg silently. *Please, tell me what happened.*

"Something happened," he says quietly.

"No shit, Sherlock," I answer. I'm not good at this. "Sorry. I'm just really nervous."

"I know, I'm sorry, it's just..." he sighs, closing his eyes for a moment again. "I don't know how to tell you."

"Just tell me," I say, holding his free hand with both of mine. "Go straight to the point, like ripping off a band-aid."

He studies my face for long seconds. I squeeze his hand in what I hope is reassurance and not pressure.

"Neil took me to the police station," he says calmly. I have to let go of his hand so I don't break his bones. "I was assaulted this morning. That's why my back is hurt. And I have a massive bruise on my stomach, from a punch."

My mind floods with involuntary memories. Me sitting in front of a stone-faced woman. The smell of bleach, that made my stomach churn. The cold air on my bare skin. Shaking violently. Throwing up as strangers touched me. Running away through the bathroom window.

I don't know what to say. I don't know if I can say anything. I just keep staring at his tired eyes.

"I saw..." he starts again, but pauses, looking for the words. "I saw someone leaving Tristan's bedroom. And this person didn't like that I saw them because they were kind of... hooking up in secret."

"Who?" I ask. A part of my sick brain instantly thinks of Tyler. *That's* why Pete didn't want to tell me. *That's* why he's been acting so strange lately.

"Paul."

It takes a moment for me to register that.

"Paul?" I repeat, my voice barely passing through the lump in my throat. "The guy that I could have had fired eons ago?"

"Don't do that," Pete rushes to say, changing position on the bed so he can face me.

"He could have been miles away from us right now!" I argue, fighting back my own tears. "This would have never happened if—"

"If he wasn't such a vile person!" he interrupts me, reaching for my hands. "It's *not* your fault," he says, pausing in between words.

I take a deep breath, trying to think of the signs I should have noticed indicating something like this might happen. As if I'm any good at reading any signs.

"Did he hit you before today?" I ask, remembering I was away for three whole days.

"No," he says firmly.

"Did you know about him and Tristan already?" I continue.

"No," he shakes his head.

"What was Tristan even thinking?" I ask angrily. "Why would he be all over you if he's dating someone else?"

I see Lindsey avert her eyes when I say that, but I don't regret the question. I want to know.

"They're not dating," Pete argues.

"Right," I snort. "What was he doing in his bedroom, then?"

"It's not exclusive," Pete continues defending him.

"That's what *he* told you, right?" I ask. He doesn't have to answer. It's written all over his face. "I bet he knew this was going to happen. I bet he gets off on playing games like this."

"You're wrong," Pete sighs, closing his eyes again.

"Stop excusing him!" I get up from the bed, too worked up to be close to him. "He should at least have warned you that he was involved with someone else!"

"It's not his fault," he continues, apparently surprised with my reaction, which makes me even more enraged.

"Don't be stupid!" I yell again. "You told him about Lindsey, didn't you? For fuck's sake, she's here! She's here and he doesn't give a shit! He's manipulating you, using you, and you're letting him!"

"It's not like that," Pete says, exasperated.

"Why are you defending him?"

"Because he's a victim, too!"

Victim. That's the word they used in my report. I remember seeing it and the feeling of outrage it caused. I wanted to yell at the police officer I was no victim! I wasn't the weak, helpless person they were making me out to be. Even though I was sitting there with a swollen eye and a broken wrist. It took me so long to reconcile with that word. To accept it. To embrace it. Victim. That's what I am. That's what Tristan is.

The impact of what that means makes me stagger backwards until I reach the wall, and the next thing I know Pete is in front of me, holding me by the shoulders. Once again, I try to think, searching for the signs I missed. Searching for the things I should have noticed because they were familiar to me. Because they should have raised red flags to me. Because they should have made me remember.

I feel sick. I didn't see anything. I didn't notice anything. He was here, right in front of me, in close proximity, needing help. And I. Did. Nothing.

"I'm sorry," I say. It's just when I look at Pete's face that I notice I'm already crying. "I'm sorry, I'm sorry, I'm so sorry."

"Becky, no," he hugs me, letting me cry on his shirt.

He flinches when I hug his waist. I let go and pull his shirt up, taking him by surprise. He pulls it back down fast, but not fast enough that I don't see the dark bruise spreading under his ribs on his left side. I cry harder.

"I should have known," I mumble as I sob. "I should have done something."

"No, sweetie," he says, walking closer and hugging me again.

And then it occurs to me—*this* is why he didn't tell me. Because he knew he couldn't count on me. He knew I'd be weak and freak out and make it all about me. He knew I'm a terrible friend.

I scream. I scream into his chest until my limbs lose all strength and slide to the floor.

"I'm sorry," I repeat. "I'm sorry, I'm sorry, I'm sorry."

"It's okay, it's okay," he chants as he holds me so tight I can barely breathe. "It's okay now, it's over, it's going to be okay."

***

I wake up a bit panicked, breathless and hot, like there's no air in the room. When I open my eyes, I see there really isn't—Pete and Lindsey are kind of hugging each other over me, his arm over my face, her knee in between my legs. I'm lying in the middle of them. On their bed. In their room. I don't remember getting here. I don't remember falling asleep.

I try to move but find I'm trapped in from every direction. I won't be able to get out without waking someone up. I decide to go for Lindsey.

"Hmm... what..." she mumbles.

"I need to get up," I whisper.

She rolls over, lying on her back. And stays there. I don't think I succeeded in waking her up.

I carefully remove Pete's arm from over my head and feel my way out of bed over Lindsey. Once I'm up and standing, the claustrophobic feeling dissipates. That is, until I remember why I spent the night here.

My heart jumps in my chest and my head feels heavy, but I decide to not fight it. I let my mind run with everything—Pete and Lindsey, Pete and Tristan, Paul. Alex and all the memories I lost with him. Tyler and all the memories I already have with him. Alnwick, grandma, my parents, the piano, the stars... all the beginnings and all the endings. All the times life has crushed me under her thumb, and how many more times she will do that.

I brace myself for the pain, hugging my chest and closing my eyes tightly. I feel like standing in the middle of the road, waiting for a truck to wreck my bones. But, when I open my eyes, there's no road. There's no truck. I can breathe.

The pain *is* there, but it's not nearly as overwhelming as it was last night. It's faint. Just throbbing, like an old bruise that when you press, elicits only an echo of the ache deep inside the flesh. Like it's almost healed.

I'm not sure what to make of it. I'm suspicious—maybe my mind is playing a trick on me. Maybe I'll take one step and set off an avalanche. I do it, just to test it out. I take one step towards the bathroom. And then another. And another. I pause beside Pete on the bed, removing his sweaty hair from his face. I enter the bathroom, close the door, and turn on the lights, staring at my swollen eyes in the mirror. Yeah, it's there, I can see it. I can feel it. Pulsating, constant but not unbearable.

I think that... maybe... I'm going to be okay.

I wash my face and take a wee, walking back to the room to check the time. My phone says it's already morning. It also says Tyler texted me three times during the night.

'*News from Pete?*'

'*Is everything okay?*'

'*I'm outside your door.*'

They all make me smile for different reasons. I tuck the phone in the waistband of my comfies and decide to step out.

I take one last look at Pete and Lindsey, now turned away from each other on the bed. I hope their pain is tolerable when they wake up, too.

As soon as I'm out in the corridor, Tyler stands up. He was actually sitting in front of my door. He's still in his night clothes, as well, but his hair is wet from a recent shower. My stomach churns.

"Hey," he says softly as I walk over.

"Hey," I say back. My voice is hoarse from all the screaming.

"I knocked, but you didn't answer," he says, pointing to my door.

"I wasn't there," I say dumbly.

"I know that now," he smiles. We stare at each other awkwardly, not really knowing what to do. "Are you okay?"

I open my mouth to say I am, but can't. Because I'm not. Not yet. And, for some reason, I don't want to lie to him.

"Not really," I confess.

"Is there anything I can do?" he asks without hesitation, his worried eyes glued on mine.

It makes my heart ache with a different emotion. A good one, for a change. I don't know how to answer, because he's already doing something, so I kiss him. I can tell it takes him by surprise, but he kisses me back. He holds my face with both hands while we do it. When we break it, he rests his forehead against mine, and I pull him closer by the waist.

"This helps," I whisper.

"Really?" he asks. I pull away to look at him and smile when I see true disbelief on his face.

"Really," I answer. He smiles back, although the frown doesn't go away. And then kisses me again.

"Are you okay now?" he asks when we break away, a playful look on his eyes.

"Not yet," I answer, so he kisses me again. God. I could do this forever.

"We should get out of the corridor," he says after that one. The implication in his voice makes me uneasy. I'm not really in the mood.

"Uh..." I hesitate, unsure of how to tell him he's not getting what he wants.

"Are you hungry?" he asks suddenly.

"Uh..." I frown. "Kinda."

"Let's go grab breakfast," he suggests.

"Downstairs? Or room service?" I watch his face as I ask, trying to read his thoughts.

"Whatever you want," he says.

"Room service," I choose, not ready to deal with anyone else yet. But, when his eyes start to glisten, I add, "But we're just going to eat."

"That's usually what people do at breakfast, isn't it?" he jokes.

"Tyler—"

"I got it," he interrupts me, brushing a few curls away from my eyes. "We'll just eat."

I observe him suspiciously for a few seconds, but decide to trust him. So, we let go of each other and I open my door. He throws himself on my bed and as I call reception, he massages the back of my neck. I stay in that same position after I hang up until he removes his hand.

I turn to him, biting my lip. He looks so cozy. He looks like he smells so good. So I scoot over and sit on his lap, sideways. He stiffens. I throw my hands around his skinny waist and bury my face on his neck, kissing it softly. Then I find out he does smell amazing.

"Is this too much?" I ask when he doesn't hug me back.

"No. This is nice," he says, kissing my forehead and adjusting his arms around me. "But if I get a boner, I can't answer for it."

I laugh and pinch his side, making him yelp. And then we stay there, in silence, stroking each other lightly, until the food arrives.

God. I could do *this* forever.

***

We eat, then we risk checking our social media, he gets mad with the comments, we get out of the Internet, we talk about fanfiction—because I have a big mouth—, he watches me as I talk to grandma, avoiding any mention to Pete, he asks me how she's doing when I hang up, then he tells me stories about spending his summers at his grandparents' farm somewhere in Kentucky, hating horses, building tree-houses, learning how to cook.

I'm not sure when it became so easy, but it is. Hanging out, talking, not talking, kissing, not kissing. I can't even remember why I was so afraid of screwing up in the first place because, now, it seems impossible. Even when I'm blunt or accidentally say something potentially mean, he gets over it quickly. Even when *he* does that, I don't really mind. I don't understand. But I also decide to not try to, since we don't have time. Maybe this is the reason—we don't have time. We both know it'll be over soon, so we're both making an effort to not ruin it before our validity period.

We're comparing early song lyrics when the door flies open, startling both of us. Pete freezes in place when he sees I'm not alone, his mouth hanging open, staring at Tyler.

"S-sorry," he stutters. "I didn't know you weren't alone."

"It's fine!" Tyler jumps from the bed, clearly embarrassed. "I'm just... I should go." He checks his phone and his eyebrows shoot up. "I should actually go."

"Okay," I smile. He smiles back. I wonder if he likes making me smile as much as I like making him smile.

He leans in, probably for a goodbye kiss, but then stops mid-motion when he remembers Pete is at the door. His face turns crimson red as he turns to him.

"Okay," he says instead, glancing from Pete to me and back at Pete. "Okay. I guess we'll talk later."

"Maybe, maybe not," I answer, making him frown. "Anything could happen."

He rolls his eyes, trying to hide a smile. Then he nods at Pete as he walks past him. He stops before leaving, kind of wanting to tell him something, but nothing comes out. So, he nods again, squeezing the back of his own neck, and runs away.

Pete turns back to me slowly, his eyebrows raised high.

"Match made in heaven," he says as he closes the door. Now, *I'm* the one blushing hard.

"How are you?" I ask, eager to change the subject.

"Better," he sighs, collapsing on the mattress beside me. "You?"

I only nod, finding out I'm too embarrassed by my meltdown the night before.

"I'm sorry," I say again.

"Honey," Pete tries to comfort me, reaching for my hand.

"No, let me say it," I ask. He sighs, but lets me speak. "I called you stupid, but *I'm* the stupid one. I'm so blind and selfish. You're so hurt and going through so much and all I could think about was my own little fling. And even when you did open up and tell me things, I still managed to be absolutely useless and make everything about me. I understand why you didn't want to tell me, and I don't blame you."

Pete stares at me with a blank face, blinking hard. After a few moments he lets out a long, tired sigh, pinching the bridge of his nose with two fingers.

"Rebecca," he says, "the only accurate statement in that whole rant is that you're stupid. We're both stupid, to be honest. I didn't want to tell you because I thought I was protecting you. I was afraid of what... knowing was going to do to you."

"You were right," I tell him.

"No, I was not!" he argues. "I should have told you, I should have trusted you."

"You saw how I reacted," I say, a shiver running down my spine.

"Yes, and I'm seeing you now," he says. I don't really know what he means. "Becky, you... you're the strongest person I know. I don't know why I keep forgetting that. I'm sorry."

I want to argue, I want to say he's wrong, I want to say that *he's* the strong one. I can't, though. If I open my mouth, I'll start to cry.

"So," he clears his throat, "we need to talk about tonight."

I nod, indicating he can continue.

"Neil said that if we're not up to it, we can cancel the show. No harm done," he snorts after he realizes the irony of his last sentence.

"Do you want to?" I find my voice again. I watch as he debates for a minute.

"No," he sighs. "I know it's silly, but I feel that if we give up now, it was all worthless. I feel like Paul will have won."

"It's not silly," I say quickly. Then, when he looks at me, I add, "But that's not the reason why we should go on."

He frowns and nods. I'm not telling him anything he doesn't already know.

"What's gonna happen to Paul?" I ask, realizing he never told me how the situation was handled.

"Neil fired him. He must be on a plane back home as we speak. Out of our lives," he smiles sadly.

"And Tris?" I ask. His smile disappears and he looks away.

"I don't know what happens to Tris."

I watch him, his eyes full of concern and sadness, his slumped down stance. I think of the cut on his back and the bruise in his stomach. I think of Tris and what he must have been through already, and what he'll still go through. I think of myself.

And I'm so angry. I'm so, so angry.

"How did you manage?" I ask suddenly. He looks back at me, puzzled. "With me? How were you so patient? Yesterday, I was ready to storm out of your room and kill someone."

He studies me for a bit, frowning. Then he snorts, giving me a weak smile. "It crossed my mind, I'm not gonna lie."

I scoot closer, running a hand up and down his back, over the unbruised side.

"We're going to be okay," I tell him. The puzzled look comes back. "*He's* going to be okay. He really likes you, you know?"

I don't know why I say that. I don't know what difference it will make. Maybe I'm just complicating things for him. I can't tell, though, as he just keeps staring with that expression of someone who's never seen me before.

"I want to do it," he says, at last. "The concert. I want to play our last concert on this tour."

"Okay," I nod, wondering how much of his decision has to do with my big mouth. "Let's do it."

***

He waits on my bed while I shower and get ready. When I ask about Lindsey, he only says she's getting ready, too. Once again, I have a million and one questions I want to ask but, once again, I keep my mouth shut. It's not like I can offer any help, anyway.

Neil instructs us to meet him at the restaurant so we can talk, but I freeze as soon as we step outside the lift in the lobby. Tristan is there, leaning against a wall, his phone in his hands. Gosh. He didn't even hear me going at him and I feel guilty. I feel sorry for him, even though I hate it when people feel sorry for me. I feel responsible. I feel like I'm connected to him somehow. I wonder if this is what normal people feel like when they find out they like the same band or movie.

As if he can sense my stare, he looks up, directly in our direction. He visibly stiffens. He knows I know. I know he knows. It's all so very sad but, also, comforting in a twisted way.

Without thinking twice, I make my way to him and throw my arms around his neck. I hug him tight, like you hug someone you love who you haven't seen for a while. For a moment, he doesn't really know how to react. But, then, he understands why I'm holding him and hugs me back. He buries his face in my shoulder and clings to my waist, almost lifting me off the floor. I'm not sure how long we stay like that, but I only let go when he lets go.

We stare into each other's eyes, not saying a word. There's nothing to say, anyway. Words rarely help, I know that. But he manages to give me a sad smile and a small nod. I take his hand and squeeze it twice. I don't know what I mean by that, but I hope it means something to him.

When I turn around, there are several people watching us—Todd and Jake included. They glance from me to Tris, apparently surprised by our explicit and silent exchange. They don't know. I wonder if Tyler knows. Probably not.

The same way I approached him, I walk away. Pete puts a hand over my shoulder when I walk past him. Squeezing twice.

We find Neil and Seth sitting alone at a table in the far back. When we join them, they both turn to us with careful smiles.

"How are you feeling?" Neil asks, addressing Pete.

"Better," he says.

"You?" Neil turns to me now.

"I'm fine," I say. It's easier to lie to him.

He nods and then updates us on how things went—he fired Paul, who threatened to throw a fit but quietened down when Neil showed him the police report. He went away without talking to anyone. Neil called The Hacks' manager and explained everything that happened, and he will take the necessary measures on his side. Then he told the band and Jake that Paul was fired due to extreme and serious circumstances. He didn't give them any explanations and instructed them to not bother anyone with questions.

"I don't know if that will be effective, though," he says, shrugging. "Paul might text or call them, or Tristan might talk, or even you. But that's entirely up to you, if you want them to know or not."

"Thank you," is all that Pete says.

The three of us stare at him for a moment, full of concern. He doesn't move.

"Okay, so," Neil breaks the awkward silence. "You said you've come to a decision about the concert tonight?"

"Yes," Pete nods, "we're doing it."

"Are you su—"

"Yes," Pete interrupts him. "We're doing it."

Neil leans over the table and stares at Pete in silence for a moment.

"Are you positively sure," he starts again, talking slower, "that you want to do it?"

"Yes," Pete nods once.

"Pete," Neil sighs, "I'm worried about you."

"Me, too," I say.

That seems to make him snap out of it, whatever *it* was.

"I'm sorry," he says, sounding a bit more like himself. "I'm just... a bit overwhelmed, I guess."

"Which is understandable," Neil says.

"But I really want to do it," he argues. "It's the last concert of our first tour. And if there's one thing I know will make me feel better, it's being on stage."

Now, that I can believe. Music was the one thing that got me through, too. Through everything.

"Okay," Neil nods, apparently convinced.

"Can we still do the promo thing for the fans?" Pete asks.

"Oh," Neil seems surprised. "Do you still wanna do that?"

"Yeah, although the original idea won't work anymore," Pete answers.

"Okay," Neil nods, pondering, apparently trying to decide whether he trusts Pete's mental state enough to do that. "I can suggest something different."

"We're all ears," Pete says.

Neil glances at me. I'm surprised. I'm usually not on this side of these situations—the side of reassuring. Still, I find myself nodding. *I'll take care of him.*

"Okay, well, what about a treasure hunt?" he says. "You could go out, hide the tickets at a few different locations, and post pictures on social media. Let the fans guess where they are."

"That sounds fun!" I say. Pete frowns, giving me a dubious look.

"Yeah," he says, "fun."

"Okay, I actually have the tickets in my room," Neil says. "Let's go grab it."

We follow him out to the lobby. I watch Pete, still worried, but at the same time glad we'll have a few hours together, just the two of us. Maybe he'll relax and we can talk.

"Guys, I'll wait here." I stop before we reach the lifts.

Pete frowns, then looks around. When he spots the blond bob of Tyler's head, he gives me an annoyed look. And then fakes barf. I punch his arm.

I wait until he's out of sight to walk over to where Tyler is. He's leaned against an armchair, alone, narrowing his eyes at his phone. I think of scaring him, but as soon as I'm on his line of sight, he looks up. And his frown vanishes.

"Hey," I say, stopping in front of him.

"Hey," he answers, pulling me closer and kissing me.

I break away quickly, looking around. The lobby is not crowded, but the few people in here are looking at us. I give him a wide-eyed look.

"They already know," he shrugs.

"We don't need to show-off, though," I argue.

"That's not what I'm doing," he frowns.

"What *are* you doing?"

"Kissing you," he says, pulling me closer again, "because I want to."

This time I let it last for as long as he wants. Because I want to kiss him, too.

When we break apart, he doesn't remove his hands from my waist, so I don't remove my hands from his hair. I start to play with it, swooshing it from side to side, giving him an emo fringe, a side part, a messy bun. It doesn't matter what I do, it falls back exactly where it was before—perfectly neat.

"It's infuriating," I complain.

"What?" he frowns, closing his eyes as I pull his hair in front of his face.

"How perfect your hair is," I say. I regret it when I see the smug look on his face.

"Jealous much?"

"I am, actually," I admit. "If I had blond hair, it would be so much easier to dye it."

"I like your hair," he says as one hand travels to my tangled, frizzy mop. "I like the purple."

It's silly. I know he's just saying that because I complimented his hair. Still, it makes me at least two degrees warmer.

"You should try it," I say. "Maybe not purple. I think blue would suit you better."

"Dye my hair?" he laughs.

"Why not?" I ask, offended.

"I don't want to end up bald by thirty," he says, and I pull his hair slightly. He smirks and adds, "I kinda like that."

"Shut up," I tell him, removing my hands from his scalp.

He pulls me closer and kisses me again. It's different now, full of the energy we've been bottling up since yesterday.

It takes me a huge amount of strength, but I manage to disentangle myself from him and take two steps back. I feel dizzy and breathless.

"Where are you going?" he frowns, trying to stop me.

"Nowhere," I fight his hands.

"Come back here," he complains, reaching out.

"Just... calm down," I give him *a look*. He raises his eyebrows and laugh.

"I'll behave, I promise," he says.

I narrow my eyes and slowly take back my previous position—in his arms. He keeps his word and doesn't do anything, he just looks at me. It's really not his fault that it's more than I can take.

Someone clears their throat beside us, breaking our intense eye contact. It's Pete. Looking annoyed, again. He glances at Tyler, then at his hands on my waist, then at me again.

"Let's go," I say, stepping out of Tyler's embrace.

"Where are you going?" Tyler asks.

"To do that fan promo thing Neil told us to," Pete explains.

"Oh," he nods, turning to me, "okay. Just don't take too long."

"Why? Will you miss me?" I tease. He flushes, casting a sideways glance at Pete.

"Will you not?" he manages to ask back.

"I'll tell you when I'm back," I say, winking. He rolls his eyes but it doesn't conceal his grin.

I follow Pete outside in silence. It's only when we fall into step side by side and he looks at me that I notice I'm still smiling. So, I stop. He keeps staring, though.

"What?" I ask, anticipating a joke or snarky remark.

"Nothing."

***

We get on the train and start to look at places where we can leave the tickets. We look through lists of tourist spots and easily choose three.

First, we head to the Crookston castle. We choose it because 1) it's a castle and 2) it's called Crookston. It's just too good to be true. We walk around for a bit, trying to decide where a good spot would be, until Pete finds a loose stone on one of the walls. He removes it, places a pair of tickets in the hollow space, and slides the rock back. He leaves a bit of the stubs appearing. Then, he takes a photo of me in front of the wall and posts to Twitter and Instagram.

We sit on the grass, waiting a few minutes to see if we'll get any reaction. We do. The fans go crazy—local ones arguing to try to guess what the place is, fans from other parts complaining we didn't do something similar for them. Either way, it seems to lift Pete's spirits. It's only when we see the fans' reactions that he actually starts to have fun.

The second place we pick is The Lighthouse. I regret it the moment I see how many steps we have to climb to reach the top. I argue with Pete that only one of us should go and we play rock-paper-scissors to decide. He loses, but doesn't complain. I take it as a good sign. I take a picture of his smiley face popping in the middle of the stairs from the ground floor. People immediately know where we are. Someone says they're five minutes away, so Pete and I run outside and hide to see if they're really coming. In less than five minutes, two girls in long coats and scarves run inside.

The third and last one is the Necropolis, a Victorian Gothic garden cemetery outside the Glasgow cathedral. We walk around, trying to locate the most outrageous tomb or statue. Then we decide that will be too easy, so we try to find something that will not give away immediately where we are. We find a stone cross in front of a tombstone and decide to go for it. We lie down at each side of the cross, put the tickets on our mouths and close our eyes. It takes a few tries to get the picture right, but Pete manages. He posts online and we wait for the reactions. Fans immediately guess we're in a cemetery, but they take a while to bet on the Necropolis. That is, until someone looks up on Google the time we would take from our last spot to this one and do the math.

"These girls are too smart," Pete remarks.

We stop by a small store to buy sandwiches and Coke to eat in the train—which we almost miss. We eat in companiable silence and, when we finish, Pete curls up to me, resting his head on my shoulder. I chuckle at the way his long legs take half the space in the corridor. Luckily, the train is not crowded.

"Did you tell your parents?" I blurt out. I don't know how to approach a subject slowly.

"No," he sighs.

"Are you going to?" I insist.

"I don't know, Becks." He buries his face further into me, probably indicating he doesn't want to talk about it.

"I think you should," I continue. He grunts a little. "It helps. It helped *me*."

He stiffens when I say that, removing his face from my shoulder to look at me. I can't look back. I still have more to say.

"I don't think... I don't think I ever got to thank you and them for..." I stutter, feeling my face heat up. "... well, for everything."

"You don't need to," he says, sitting back up and squeezing my hand. "We're family. Family takes care of each other."

"Yeah, when they don't run away and leave you behind," I blurt out. I don't know where this comes from. Maybe because it's all back on the surface again. Maybe because it's all *always* on the surface.

"You don't really think that," he says after a while, his tone quiet and cautious.

"I don't know what I think anymore," I sigh. Not sad, or angry. Just... done. "It doesn't matter, anyway. They're gone."

We stay silent for a long time, but I can feel his eyes on me. So, I take a deep breath and turn to him.

"What?" I ask.

"Nothing," he frowns, but his eyes are wide. He debates whether to complement his answer and I wait until he makes up his mind. "It's just... it's just you never talked about it before. You never talked about *any* of it before."

It's not an accusation, it's just a remark—an accurate one—, but it hurts, anyway. I should have. I should have talked to him. I should have talked to *someone*. I shouldn't have carried it around with me for so long.

"I know," I say, squeezing his hand back. I smile, but he keeps frowning.

"What happened on that trip?" he asks after a while.

And it's just when he asks that it dawns on me—yes, it was the trip. It was coming home, and making peace with grandma, and seeing his parents, and...

"Nothing," I say. He sighs, frustrated, but I have an explanation. "Literally nothing. I thought... I thought it would be so hard, you know? The house, grandma, the memories... But it wasn't. It was painful, yes, but not overwhelming like I thought it would be. Like last night. It was horrible, but this morning, it was over. I don't know. I thought that I had to push everything away to stop feeling these things, but I realized it's impossible. I'll never stop feeling these things."

I stop for breath, trying to gauge his reaction. But he has that expression of someone who's never seen me before. It makes my heart ache because, maybe, he hasn't. Maybe he doesn't know me all that well. And maybe it's all my fault.

"Not talking about Alex doesn't mean I'm not constantly thinking about him," I continue. He flinches at the sound of his name the same way I think I do. Or did. I don't know, it's just a name now. "Staying away from Alnwick doesn't mean I'm not constantly thinking about my parents. And I miss things, you know? I miss grandma, I miss your parents and your sisters and how chaotic it is being around them. And I only realized I missed them when I was there. I miss..."

I hesitate, afraid of what I'm going to say next. But I say it, anyway. It's true.

"I miss Alex. I miss what I thought I had with him, you know? I miss the good parts, the laughter, the quiet nights, the... the intimacy," I feel myself blush with that and have to look away. "Not only the sex, but other things, silly things, like holding hands, you know? Playing with each other's hair, talking over movies, watching the rain. I've never had that before him. I never had that *after* him."

I sigh, the anxiety of saying all of it out loud slowly dissipating.

"I thought I didn't need it," I continue, looking back at Pete. "I thought I didn't want it, any of it. But... but I do. I want grandma, I want your family, I want..." *Tyler.* I stop myself. It's not *him* that I want, specifically. It's just what we're doing. It's just the fun. Right? "I want it all," I complete, "pain included."

He just looks at me in silence, nodding slowly, kind of smiling, kind of not. And then it occurs to me that, again, I made it all about myself. I must be the most selfish person he knows.

"What happened while I was gone?" I ask, then, hoping my impromptu monologue will encourage him to do the same.

His expression softens and he smiles—for real. I think it's the first one I've seen in days.

"I realized..." he starts and trails off. He sighs and looks away, as if resisting to admit what he has to admit. "I realized I don't know myself at all. I'm only the person other people need me to be. I'm a big brother to you, I'm a cheating boyfriend to Lindsey, I'm a knight in shining armor to Tris. I just adapt. Like that song says, *be that girl for a month*, except that in my case, I manage to play the role a little longer."

I feel my heart shrink in my chest. I want to tell him that's not true, but I can't. Because it is. In my case, anyway. I needed someone to take care of me, I needed someone to be strong for me, and he was that person. He was that person even when *he* needed someone to take care of him and be strong for him. I wonder how many times it happened. How many times I was so blinded by my own woes that I didn't see his?

"I never know what I want," he continues. "I can't make choices. When things get a little bit harder, I give up. Move on. Move away. To the next role, to the next version of myself. I just throw myself wholeheartedly at everything and everyone and then resent them when they don't do the same. And I don't even know if my heart is ever really with the people I love. I don't even know if I know what love is."

He pauses and I have to bite my tongue again. Did he feel the need to interrupt me as I was talking, too? Did he disagree with me the way I'm disagreeing with him now?

"I love Lindsey," he says, almost in a whisper. Then, he corrects himself, "I *thought* I loved Lindsey. I thought I was ready to commit the rest of my life to her. I thought I'd found my happily ever after. But I never for once thought about her end of this fantasy, you know? It never occurred to me that she might feel differently. It never occurred to me..." he trails off again, lost in his head. "I always want more. It's like I keep testing everyone, always asking for more, always pushing their boundaries. Until it breaks and there's no way to fix it."

Now it's my turn to watch him in silence. I feel like I'm hearing myself talk. I've never witnessed him being so hard on himself. Pete! The most giving person to ever live! But that's the problem, right? He's always so ready to give his all that he loses himself into the others. I chuckle with the realization of how much of polar opposites we are.

"What?" he frowns at my reaction.

"We're quite a pair," I say. He smiles.

"We are," he says, squeezing my hand again. "Opposites attract."

Indeed.

"Just for the record," I say, making him look at me again, "I love you exactly the way you are."

He smiles—a certified Pete smile now—and throws his arms around me.

"Just for the record," he repeats, "same."

We laugh. And spend the rest of the journey in silence.

***

We're late to the venue. Neil doesn't seem surprised, though. I think he said four-ish actually meaning five-ish, which is the time we arrive.

We go to our dressing room, finding Lindsey sitting alone once again. She asks how our little adventure was and when Pete starts to chatter about it, I decide to leave them be. Maybe a little time alone with him will help her, too.

I wander around the venue until I find the way to the stage. I sit at the piano, running my fingers along the keys. I automatically start to play *Clair de Lune*. I remember the start of the tour and how nervous I was to play it. How resistant. How scared. I know past Becky had good reasons. I just wish I had realized sooner that avoiding the memories is still a way of keeping them. They're always with me. I can't hide inside my own head.

The last time my father ever asked me to play the piano, I didn't.

It was November and I was 13 years old. There was going to be a school trip—we'd spend a whole day in London to visit the Natural History Museum. Pete's parents had authorized him to go, and I spent the entire month talking about it to my parents. They still didn't sign the consent form. They gave me reasons, none of which I remember, because I was so mad I wasn't even listening.

The Friday the trip happened, I didn't say a word to either of them. The next day, my father invited me to go for ice cream. I declined. On Sunday, they went out to buy Christmas decorations and I refused to participate. When they came back, with bags full of holiday-themed ornaments and cookies, dad asked me to play some festive tunes. And I said no.

I continued taking classes until I left Alnwick for good. It was a way of keeping him close, but also a way of punishing myself. Because every time I played, I remembered that Sunday in November and how I denied him the last thing he ever asked of me. I still do. It's still equal parts comforting and painful. But I'm starting to think that everything in life is.

When I'm done warming up with classical music, I try to put an insistent melody that has been playing non-stop on my mind into chords. It's a simple melody, so I don't take long to find it on the keys. I play it a few times, trying to build around it, but it still sounds bare. It's been a while since I composed anything on a piano.

Then something else pops up on my mind—Tyler, standing in the kitchen, under the morning light, singing. I'm slightly embarrassed by the fact that I can still remember the song, but also proud when I manage to find the right chords for it. I play it a few times. Then I play mine. Then I try to merge them together. They fit.

With every run, the song becomes stronger, more fleshed out, and less punk. It's too flowery, too pretty, too sweet. Some other day, it would give me nausea. Today, it makes me warm.

I play it one last time, hitting the endnotes hard to enjoy the effect of the sound fading slowly in the air.

"That sounds familiar," he says from somewhere behind me. I smile. Perfect timing.

I don't turn around, but make space for him on the stool. He walks over and sits beside me, playing the song I've just written, but with much more elegance. His long fingers run flawlessly over the keys, his turns are seamless, his tempo is perfect. He's such a good musician.

"I like it," Tyler says when he finishes.

"You can have it," I say, since I already know I'm not going to use it.

"Are you okay?" he asks, looking at me intently.

"Almost."

He stares at me for a while with that curious expression he wears sometimes—a frown, biting his lip, head tilted. I wait. I already know it means he has something on his mind.

"Paul is gone," he says carefully. "Was it you or was it Pete?"

"It was *himself*," I say angrily.

"I know," he says, unaltered. "I was just wondering who he..."

He trails off. He clearly doesn't know, not about Paul, not about Tristan. Not about me.

"Pete," I say simply. He nods, as if he was expecting that answer.

"What happened?" he asks quietly.

"Weren't you instructed to not ask questions?" I joke. He blushes.

"Sorry, I just..." he stutters, looking away and restarting to play.

"It's not my place to tell," I find myself explaining. He just nods again. He seems weird. "Are *you* okay?"

"Yeah," he frowns, staring at his own hands while he plays.

"I want the honest answer," I say.

He stops playing, sighing and running a hand through his hair.

"I'm..." he hesitates. "I'm worried."

"About what?"

"About..." he looks at me, frowning as if deciding whether to tell me or not. "Neil said he was fired under *extreme* circumstances."

He pauses, watching me. I don't move.

"I'm worried about..." he hesitates again. "We've been working together for many years. I never liked him very much, but I never like *anyone* very much, so I just never said anything. And he seemed to be pretty close to Todd and... and even Tris."

Okay. He's not as dumb as I initially thought. I still say nothing.

"I don't know, I just..." he trails off again, looking down at the piano keys. He doesn't play, though.

"You should ask them," I blurt out.

"I did," he says. "Both of them claim they don't know what happened."

"Well..."

"I don't believe them!" he exclaims, getting angry. "I know they're lying! At least one of them is."

"Then ask again," I say.

"He never tells me anything!" he complains. I know who he's talking about.

"He will," I say. He gives me a suspicious look because now *he* knows I know who he's talking about. "Eventually."

We stare at each other in silence for a while—he with that suspicious frown, me in what I hope is a blank expression. He's the one to look away first, sighing and pressing his palms against his eyes. I reach a hand up, brushing his hair away from his face. It's useless but I keep doing it until he opens his eyes again.

"This helps," he says, smiling.

"Really?" I gasp, mocking him.

And then he kisses me.

***

"Ouch!" he yelps as I pull his head down.

"Shhh!" I cover his mouth with my hand.

He gives me an outraged look. I motion to the stage with my head. We both raise our heads just enough so we can see past the balcony rail. The boys are entering the stage and taking places at the instruments. Jake is with them, apparently filling in for the missing members. Us.

"Should we join them?" Tyler whisper. I bite my lip.

"They can manage," I whisper back. His eyes glisten.

We do have to move to another place, though. We've spent the last few minutes—or could be hours, for all I know—hiding behind the first row in the balcony. Doing what, you ask? Use your imagination.

We crawl around, trying not to laugh too loud, until we reach the last row in the balcony. Tyler sits with his back against the seat and I immediately leap on him, restarting from where we left it. But when I reach the hem of his shirt, ready to run my hands underneath it, he stops me.

I give him a *what* look. His face flushes in a deep red.

"Just... *calm down*," he says. I roll my eyes. "There are people just a few feet away."

"They don't know we're here," I argue.

"They will if we keep this going," he raises his eyebrows.

"They won't if you keep quiet," I mock his stare.

"Me?" he scoffs. "I'm *not* the loud one!"

And now I'm the one blushing. I dig my fingers at his sides, making him yelp again. He grabs my wrists, pinning my hands behind my back. I fight him, but he's stronger than his lean arms suggest. He grins evilly. So, I stop, and instead of fighting, I thrust my hips against him. His eyes widen again.

"Stop!" he lets go of my hands to hold my waist and keep me away. But it's too late. He's already *on*.

"Your mouth says one thing, your body says another," I tease, running my fingertips up his arms.

"My body says nothing," he argues, grabbing my hands again and pulling them away from him. "My body can't talk."

I dive in, kissing his neck—slowly. He sucks in his breath. It's glorious.

"Dammit, woman," he complains, managing to stop me once again.

Without much effort, he turns me around, so I'm sitting in between his legs, my back crushed against his chest. I reach my hands up, squirming around to try to grab his hair, but he locks my hands over my stretched legs.

I sigh, about to complain, but then I have an idea. I sit still, catching my breath, and wait until he rests his chin on my shoulder. I glance at him sideways, making sure he's looking down at me. Then I start to pull my skirt up with the tip of my fingers. He starts to laugh.

"You're impossible," he whispers into my ear, kissing his way down my neck.

I tilt my head to the side, giving him full access. And when I try to turn around to my previous position, he holds me down again.

"*You're* impossible," I complain. He laughs again, giving me a hard peck on the cheek. "Why are you being such a spoil-sport? We could be having fun!"

"Oh, I'm having fun," he says and I can hear the smirk without even looking at him.

"I'm *not*," I complain again. It's ineffective.

We sit there in silence, catching our breath until the music starts to fill the room. They've started soundcheck.

"They won't hear us now," I try again.

"Shut up," he says, with a gentle kiss near my ear.

Then, Pete starts to sing. His voice sounds loud and clear as he goes through The Hacks song.

"Wow, is that Pete?" Tyler asks. I nod. "He sounds great! I didn't know he could sing."

"He can, but he doesn't like it."

Tyler uses my hands to play an air-guitar as he softly sings in my ear. He covers my mouth with his when I start to laugh too loudly.

Next, Tristan starts to sing my song. His voice is much too sweet for the lyrics, but he's a great singer, too.

"Tris is a great singer, too," I say.

"Yeah, he doesn't really think so," Tyler answers airily.

I take the opportunity to turn sideways and look at him. He's frowning, his thoughts distant. He's thinking about what happened again.

I press my index finger in between his eyebrows until the frown dissolves.

"Better," I say. He chuckles. And then he watches me.

It's kind of like the way he was looking at me before I ditched him to go out with Pete. Now, though, since there's no one to interrupt us, I start to get uneasy.

He reaches one hand up, brushing his fingers down my cheek, running his thumb over my mouth—his eyes following his movements. I get embarrassed. I think he can tell. When his eyes meet mine again, he opens his mouth to say something, but closes it again. I keep staring, getting lost into the deep blue, until he decides to break the silence, after all.

"You're so pretty," he says softly.

I frown. I remember the first time he mentioned he thought I was pretty and how embarrassed he got. He's not embarrassed now.

"You are," he insists.

"Okay," I roll my eyes.

"Why don't you like it when I say that?" he asks, still watching me intently.

"Because it's dumb," I blurt out. I look away so I don't see his reaction while I explain it. "Beauty is subjective. What is pretty to one person, can be disgusting to others," I pause, looking down at my own hands. And, then, because I can't help myself, I add, "Like your fans."

I don't have the guts to look at him. After a few seconds, he hooks his fingers under my chin and gently turns my head around. I close my eyes, stubbornly, but open them again when he takes too long to say or do anything.

"In *my* subjective opinion," he says, without any hint of sarcasm, "you are absolutely beautiful."

I don't know what to say to that. I could say I think he's beautiful, too. I do. He is. He *knows* he is, and that's the difference between the two of us.

I remove his hand from my face, holding it in mine, and kiss him. If anything, just to break the intensity of his eyes on me. He lets me, and it's already different than five minutes ago. All the heat and hurry are gone. It's soft, slow, calm. It's... familiar.

He rests his forehead against mine when we break apart—another thing that's becoming familiar. I open my eyes, but his remain closed. I just watch him.

"Becky," he whispers, making my heart leap inside my chest. That's the only way he's ever said my real name—whispering. "Will I ever see you again?"

The question takes me by surprise. I don't move, though. I don't want him to open his eyes, I don't want him looking at me while I hesitate. I think *he* doesn't want to look at me while I hesitate. I haven't thought about this. I mean, I thought about this—whatever it is—ending. But I didn't think about it *not* ending. Will he ever see me again?

I hope so.

I do want to see him again. But wanting and doing are two very different things. We lead such crazy lives. The same life choices that made us find each other might be the ones that prevent us to ever meet again. And even if we do meet, it will never be the same. We'll never be the same people we are now, the same people we were when we met. We will never be able to replicate whatever spell fell over us during this tour. Still... will he ever see me again?

I hope so. I hope so. Oh, God, I hope so.

"I hope so," I say it out loud.

He smiles, small and shy at first, then bright and wide. He opens his eyes, his forehead still against mine. He's surprised to see I'm watching him. I smile. And we kiss.

***

"Okay, guys," I shout in the mic, drying my face with the sleeve of my shirt. "I wanna thank every single one of you for being such a fantastic crowd!" They cheer loudly. "This has been an incredible tour. Thanks for learning the lyrics, for singing your hearts out and for letting us entertain you. I hope to see some of your faces at our next concert," I point to a few random people and they scream. "But this is not the end yet! You know what's coming next, don't you?" I ask and the place explodes.

I sit at the piano and start the intro of *She's Not Mine* while The Hacks walk on stage. I look up and kind of stop playing, staring in shock. And then I laugh—they're all wearing purple wigs, in different lengths and styles. They look ridiculous! It's so cool! I've never been more flattered. We start to play but I can't concentrate, I can't stop turning around and looking at them and laughing. Halfway through the song I abandon my position to take selfies with them. I know I won't have another chance—Todd will never put on the wig again to let me take a stupid photo with him, so I take advantage while I can.

The song ends and I ask them to keep the wigs for our last one. The crowd supports me, so they oblige. I can't wait to see the videos of this night.

Our second song ends, we take a bow and walk off stage. That's it. It's over. Twelve days, eight shows, six cities. We're done.

Tyler says something about us to the crowd, but I can't hear it—I'm too busy screaming and hugging Pete.

"We've made it!" he shouts in my ear.

"We've made it!" I shout back.

Lindsey hugs us, too, and then we all hug Neil when he comes over with a few bottles of beer.

"Congratulations, guys!" He raises his bottle and we cheer. "You've been great."

"Thank you so much for the opportunity, mate! We'll never forget it." Pete pats his shoulder.

"Well, it's not really me you have to thank," Neil remarks, looking out to the stage.

I follow his gaze and let my eyes rest on Tyler. I watch as he prances around, jumps, whips his hair, bangs the keys of the piano—he still very much looks like an inflatable tube man, yet I still very much can't look at anyone else. It's so weird. How, among millions of similar videos and bands on the Internet, did he find me? How, when being in such separate genres, did this gig work out? How, after years of scaring people away, did I let him in?

Tyler sits on the piano, preparing for one of their slower and cheesier songs. He looks up and when he sees I'm watching, he starts to sing directly to me. I smile. I hate this song. Yet, by now, I know the lyrics by heart, so I start to sing along. His eyebrows shoot up in surprise, and I get more confident. I sing louder. I start to perform. I use my bottle as a microphone and really go for it, feeling the pain of the mellow chords and depressive lyrics. Then, he starts to laugh. He looks down, at his own hands, never stopping playing, but he's out of it. He can't sing it anymore. I ruined it. Victory.

"Nice job," Pete says from behind me.

"Thanks." I turn around and we click our glass bottles together.

"So..." he raises his eyebrows slightly, glancing at the stage and then back at me.

"So?" I ask innocently.

"Come on!" he insists, tugging at my sleeve. "Give me *something*!"

I try my best not to smile, but seeing him show his nosy side again makes me happy. Yeah, yeah, I said it. I'm happy.

"You already know all there is to know," I roll my eyes.

"The only thing I know is a stupid score," he complains. "I want details!"

"Gross!" I frown.

"Pleeeaaase!" he chants, making me laugh.

I look around to make sure everyone else is out of earshot. It's not like I'm going to give him an R-rated report. I still don't want anyone listening to me talk about Tyler, though.

"He is... like..." I stutter, already feeling my face hot. Pete's grin encourages me to continue, though. "He's a lot more gentle than I thought he'd be."

"In bed?" he asks, making me give him an exasperated look.

"In everything," I answer. The way he kisses me, the way he touches me, even the way he talks to me. It's all so... I don't know... sweet. Sickening, at times. I still like it, though, although I'll never admit it out loud.

Pete stares at me, waiting for more information, but I suddenly don't want to give him any. I shrug, making him roll his eyes.

"So, where do you stand now?" he asks. I'm not sure what he means by it.

"I don't know," I say, looking back out to the stage.

"I think he likes you," he says after a while, close to my ear. I can't help but smile. Because I *know* he likes me.

That reminds me of a conversation I had with a different Hackley brother. My eyes dart to him, behind his drums, lost in the song, eyes closed, hair wet. I look around again, searching for Lindsey. She's standing next to Jake and they're talking—this is my chance.

"Your turn," I turn to Pete.

"My turn?" he frowns.

"Yes," I nod. "I want details."

He keeps frowning, like he doesn't know what I'm talking about. I raise my eyebrows, giving him the same suggestive look he gave me.

"What are you talking about?" he asks.

"For fuck's sake!" I say, looking around once again. "I know that you kissed Tristan, okay?"

"Well, I told you," he argues. I can't believe him.

"No, you didn't!"

"I did! Didn't I?" he pauses, thinking for a second. "Gee... it must have slipped my mind."

"Was it *that* bad?" I joke. Now, he's the one getting flustered.

"How did you find out, then?" he tries to dodge my question.

"He told me," I say, to his absolute surprise. "Lindsey mentioned it, too."

He glances at her, then, that deeply sad look back to his eyes. I regret mentioning it. His thing with Tris is not the same as my thing with Tyler. I should have known.

I poke his side—the unbruised one—making him look back at me. He sighs.

"Where do you stand now?" I reciprocate the question.

"I don't know," he shrugs, looking at the stage behind me. "I think I like him."

I bite my tongue not to give him a snarky answer. Because I *know* he likes him. It's pretty obvious. But, then...

"And Linds?" I ask. He looks back at me.

"I like her, too," he says.

"What about love?"

"Here you come with this love stuff again," he frowns.

"I just want to know!" I argue. Although, now, by his answer, I already do.

"Well, I want to know, too," he complains. "I'd *love* to know."

I sigh. I hate seeing him like this. I wish there was something I could do, for both of them. For the three of them.

"Pete?"

"What now?" he widens his eyes, already irritated.

"I love you," I say. It melts all his annoyance. He pulls me closer, hugging me tightly.

"I know."

***

Tyler manages to avoid my teasing gaze for the rest of his concert. But when it ends, after they take their bows and thank the crowd, he runs towards me, holds my face with both hands and kisses me. In front of everyone. It's salty, and hot, and I get a little grossed out when I touch his wet t-shirt. Still, I kiss him back. I can't not do it.

"Come on, guys!" I hear Tristan complaining. "Just because we know it's happening, doesn't mean we need to watch it."

"Speak for yourself, I'm quite enjoying it," Pete says, making us both laugh and break the kiss.

"This is a weird friendship," Tyler jokes.

"Oh, you haven't seen anything yet. You better get used to it." Pete winks at Tyler as he walks past us, and his choice of words doesn't go unnoticed.

Tyler looks back at me with a funny expression. Then he takes my hand and we follow the others to the dressing room to have a commemorative round of beers and hang out for a few minutes.

Backstage is crowded, more than any other day. There are Hacks fans, some celebrities—both that I have and haven't seen before—, label people, some members of the press. It's hard to navigate our way around, but Neil manages to cram us all inside a room. And Tyler's hand never leaves mine.

"Okay, now that I have you all here," Neil says over everyone else's chatter, making us shut up, "I have a few words to say."

"Speech, speech, speech," people start to chant.

"I just want to thank you all for what has been an incredible tour. To Jake and Seth, who have worked harder than any of us combined," he points to them and there's a round of applause. "To the Hackley boys, it's always a delight to spend so much time staring at your handsome faces."

"I'm so glad *that's* your highlight for us," Tyler complains jokingly.

"And to Becky and Pete," Neil continues, ignoring him, "who for some nonsensical reason haven't yet named their stellar act, you've really brought it. I can't wait to see what the future holds for you in the music business."

People cheer again, making me uncomfortable.

"Hopefully, a lot of money," Tristan leans in, whispering in my ear. I laugh.

"Let me take the opportunity to thank you all, too, on behalf of the whole band," Todd interrupts and I have to make an effort not to roll my eyes.

"Yes, Neil, you're the real MVP," Tristan says, making Neil wave a hand in the air.

"I also want to take the opportunity to address you, Becky," I jump at the sound of my own name coming from Todd's mouth. "I owe you an apology. I crossed a line yesterday, I shouldn't have meddled in your personal life like that. It was really inappropriate."

I just stare, paralyzed. I can hear people start to murmur, asking themselves what he's talking about. Why the hell did he choose this moment to apologize? I glance at Neil, but he doesn't meet my eyes.

"Well, we have to thank you, too," Pete breaks the awkward silence. "I guess," he adds, making people laugh. "Thanks to the band for fighting for us," he says, looking solely at Tyler, "thanks to the label for believing we could pull it off, and thank you, Neil. For everything else."

There's a second of heavy silence after that. Neil nods, raising his bottle. Everyone in the room follows suit.

"To unforgettable memories and new friendships!" he toasts and we all drink.

Since it's our last show, Neil suggests it's a good idea for us to go out and talk to the fans, take pics and autograph stuff. The Hacks go first, so their psychos can go away and we'll have just our few lovely fans to meet afterwards.

Neil makes us wait a few minutes after the Hackley boys and their fans leave before we go. I think he's aware there's a part of their fandom that already hates me with a passion, so he wants to make sure they're not the ones to greet us when we step outside.

As expected, the group waiting for us is small and lovely. We start to go around, chatting easily and taking photos. And then someone catches my attention.

"Hey, just Becky," he says, a large grin on his face.

My heart beats faster. I can barely conceal my astonishment to see him here—it's really him. Patrick. The nurse. He reaches out a hand to greet me and smiles and—oh, Gosh—I had forgotten how handsome he is. He's even more handsome *without* his scrubs and in his everyday clothes.

"You're here," I say dumbly.

"I am," he chuckles. "I told you I'd come."

He did. I didn't think he would, though. I thought it was just pointless flirting. Well, to me, it was pointless. I'm not sure what it was for him.

We stare at each other in silence for a while until Pete catches up with us and Patrick introduces himself. They start to chat, as Pete asks him how do we know each other and Patrick explains how we met. I can feel Pete's change of stance upon the knowledge that this is the nurse. The cute nurse I told him all about on the phone. *Oh, God.*

"You're great, by the way," Patrick says, turning to me again. "If I'm being honest, when you said you were in a band, I did *not* expect you to be *this* good."

Oh, God. Oh, God.

"She's a rockstar," Pete chimes in when it becomes clear I can't find my voice.

"Indeed," he says, smiling again. *Oh, God.*

"Sorry, guys, we need to go," Neil interrupts our chat.

"Well, Patrick, it was nice meeting you," Pete reaches out a hand.

"You, too," he says politely, taking it.

And, then, we're alone for a second. He's staring at me, with that smile, that hopeful smile, and I feel terrible because he's most definitely not gonna get what he came here for. I never feel bad for turning guys down. Granted, they're rarely as nice as he is.

"Guess I'll see you around, just Becky," he reaches out a hand to me.

"Thanks for coming," I say idiotically. He laughs a little.

"No problem," he says. "You've just gained a new fan."

I can't help but smile with that. I watch for a few seconds as he walks away. Then I wave when he looks over his shoulders.

When I finally get to the van, both Pete and Lindsey look at me wide-eyed.

"Oh my God!" he's the first one to say something.

"Stop!" I warn him immediately.

"Was that a friend of yours?" Neil asks, curious about the exchange.

"No," I say. Then, since I remain silent, Pete fills him in.

"Oh," Neil nods. "It's nice of him to come all the way from Alnwick."

"It's not that far," I argue.

"And completely worth it," Lindsey contributes. "I'd come all the way from *anywhere* to see Becky on stage."

She winks, making me smile.

"Okay, so, tomorrow," Neil changes the subject, for my relief, "the conference meeting is scheduled for noon. I reserved the conference room at the hotel."

I widen my eyes with this news. Then I look at Pete, who has the exact same expression on his face. Neil glances worriedly at both of us.

"It's just gonna be a call," he continues. "And it won't be long, as well. Like, fifteen minutes, tops. We'll get right to the airport afterwards."

We both nod in agreement. Then we nod at each other. I had *completely* forgotten about this 'meeting'. The meeting with the label. The one where they'll probably offer us a record deal.

Oh, God.

***

We get to our floor at the hotel to be received with a racket. It comes from the last door in the corridor, which Neil opens to find a full-on party inside.

"What the hell?" He stops at the sill and stares inside wide-eyed.

"It's a wrap!" Todd shouts. "Come on in, join us!"

Neil sighs and steps inside a little hesitant. Pete and I follow him, and I'm impressed to find out that so many people fit inside one single room. It's quite dark, but I recognize a few faces from backstage earlier. Mostly women.

I'm also impressed to see how organized it is—clearly a Todd project. They somehow managed to disassemble the bed, putting the mattress over the window to possibly muff the noise. The nightstand is a snack table, with all sorts of chips and candy spread. The TV is the sound system, playing music videos from some random playlist online. The bathroom is transformed into a big refrigerator—the bathtub is filled with ice and multi-colored bottles.

"Help yourself!" Todd grins when he walks past to close the door.

I enter the bathroom, followed by Pete and Lindsey, and start to rummage through the colorful cans and bottles.

"Wow, they have quite the selection," I say. When did they have the time to get all this? *Who* had the time to get all this? I have to give it to Todd—I'm impressed. "What are you having?" I ask my friends.

"Nothing for me," Lindsey says. "Actually, I think I'm going to bed."

"Me, too," Pete says eagerly.

"No, you stay. You guys deserve to celebrate," she smiles over his shoulder. I try to smile back. She still looks so sad.

"How am I supposed to celebrate anything when you're breaking up with me?" Pete blurts out and I drop the bottles that I was holding. I can't even look down to see if they broke. *What* is happening?

"I didn't... I wasn't..." Lindsey stutters, apparently as shocked as I am.

Pete fully pulls her into the bathroom and closes the door, locking us inside. The three of us. *I shouldn't be here.*

"What were you going to say, then?" he asks. "How was that conversation going to end?"

What conversation?

Lindsey bites her lip and even from a distance I can see her eyes well up. Oh, God. She's actually gonna do it.

"I just said I still love you," Pete says, which almost makes me frown. If he did say it, he was lying. And that's not cool. "We were gonna live together."

My heart breaks. Why is he doing this?

"No, we weren't." Lindsey shakes her head, her voice wavering. "You asked and I said no, remember?"

"Linds—"

"Pete, please," she interrupts him, holding his hand. "It was over before I came after you."

He shakes his head. In denial. It's so hard to watch.

"I know we have a lot more to say to each other, but let's not do this tonight, okay?" she asks quietly.

"I'm sorry," he whispers.

"I know," she sighs, as if tired of hearing it. She hugs him by the waist. When she lets go, she says, "He leaves tomorrow. You should make tonight count."

Oh, God. I don't... I can't... I don't know what to think. I watch as Pete stares at the open door, after she leaves. I take a few tentative steps towards him. He jumps when I touch his arm. He turns to me, his eyes filling with horror when he realizes I'm still here. Then, he covers his face and lets himself slide down the wall to the floor.

"Is everything okay?" someone asks. I turn around to find a girl I've never seen before staring at us.

"Could you give us a moment?" I ask, already closing the door again on her frowning face.

"I'm fine," Pete mumbles from behind his hands. "I'll be fine. You should be out there, with your pop star, making the most out of your last hours together."

His words tug at my chest, but I push my own feelings away.

"You make it sound like he's going to war or something," I try to joke. "Plus, the booze is on this side of the door."

He removes his hands from his face, looking wistfully at the bathtub. I regret mentioning the alcohol. Getting wasted now isn't a good idea.

"I should have known this would happen, right?" he asks, more to himself than to me. "I should have seen it coming."

"Well, you did kiss someone else," I say. He looks at me, offended at first, but then just defeated.

"Jesus, I'm an asshole," he sighs, covering his face again. I just sit there, unsure of what to do or say. "This is the part where you're supposed to say I'm not."

"Sorry, I'm a terrible liar," I joke. He kicks me. I wait until he looks at me again to continue. "What can I do?"

He sighs, taking my hand in his. "You can go out, get that blond fellow of yours, and spend the rest of the night wide awake with his gentleness somewhere I can't hear you."

"Why are you so gross?" I frown.

"I can't help it," he shrugs.

"What about you?" I insist.

"I think I'm just gonna pass out," he says. Then he widens his eyes. I bet he's remembering he's currently sharing a room with his girlfriend. Ex-girlfriend.

"You can sleep in my room," I offer.

"I just said I want no part in your business with the blond one," he argues, making me roll my eyes.

"Come on," I pull him off the floor.

"Wait, I'm gonna grab something to drink," he says before I can push him out of the bathroom. I watch as he picks up several random bottles and cans. "Dumped and drunk, that's not how I pictured this tour ending."

"Shagging the lead singer, that's not how I pictured it, either," I joke.

He looks up, that unreadable expression on his face. Then he follows me outside and into my room, silently.

"Do you want me to stay with you?" I ask.

"Absolutely not!" he exclaims. "Go find your prince charming."

"Pete—"

"I'm serious," he cuts me off, holding me by the shoulder after he drops all the booze on the bed. "I'll be fine."

"You don't have to be in a relationship to be happy, you know?" I say suddenly. I don't know exactly why. Maybe because I've never seen him happy outside of one. "You can be happy on your own. You *should* be happy on your own."

He blinks, studying me. I know what he's thinking. This is so *not* me to say.

"Are you happy?" he asks after a while.

I shrug. I don't know. I'm just not sad anymore. "Something like it."

"Aren't you afraid, though?" he goes on. "Of ending up alone?"

Oh, Pete.

"Of course not!" I answer. "I have you."

***

I decide to follow his advice and get back to the party. As soon as I step inside, I spot Tristan hanging out alone by the snacks. He's just watching people as they dance and chat, absentmindedly munching on some peanuts. Once again, as if he can sense my stare, he finds my eyes. He stands up straighter, waving a hand awkwardly in the air. I walk over to join him.

I grab a handful of the same things he's eating and stand there, watching people with him. It seems there are more now than when I first got here.

"I'm sorry," he says suddenly, near my ear. I turn around, curious.

"For what?" I ask. He shrugs.

My mind races in search of something to say. Anything. I have a list of all the speeches Pete used on me, all of them memorized, because he repeated himself so much. I could easily recite them to Tris now, word by word. But I don't. I know it won't help. At least, not right now.

"I'm gonna miss you," I say instead. I watch as that megawatt smile spreads across his face, lighting up his dark eyes.

"I'm gonna miss you, too," he answers. Then, he adds, "I'm gonna miss you the most."

I smile back. "The invitation to join our band is still open," I joke, half-wishing it was a real possibility.

"Good," he chuckles, "I might accept it."

We stare into each other's eyes for another moment, and then he hugs me. It's not so desperate as it was this morning, but it's still tight. And then I realize what I said is true—I'm *really* gonna miss him.

"He's in my room," I whisper into his ear. I don't know why. He tenses up in my arms. "Alone."

He lets me go, looking at me with a frown and head tilted to the side. A genetic trait, it seems.

I'm about to ask if he's seen his brother—the blond one—when a voice interrupts us. A voice *too* close to my ear.

"Hey, just Becky!"

I turn around, suddenly dizzy. If I wasn't sober, I'd think I might be hallucinating.

"We meet again," he grins.

Oh, God.

✱DAY TWELVE

Patrick Donegan Crowley was originally born in South Shields three years before me and moved to Alnwick when he was five. He was a rugby player growing up, but always wanted to be a doctor. That is, until he found out what he really liked was taking care of people and not opening them up. So, he went to nursing school in Birmingham. He never planned to move out of Alnwick, though. He likes it there.

He knows Evelyn—of course he does, everyone knows her—and is a bit too surprised upon learning she's Pete's sister. They're not friends, he says, but he always passes on confidential information to her. He probably shouldn't tell that to people, but alas.

He lives alone in a flat near the hospital. Well, not totally alone—he has a dog named Bark Ruffalo and a goldfish named Thor. He comes to Glasgow on the regular, to watch rugby matches, go to concerts, meet with mates.

"Where do you live?" he asks me.

"London," I say.

"No, I know, I mean what part," he explains, smiling.

"North," I say. And before he can make any more questions, I ask, "Have you ever been to London?"

He has. He embarks on yet another long tale about whens and wheres that I only half-listen. I'm trapped. He's been talking my ear off for what feels like hours. My lack of engagement doesn't seem to turn him off, so I don't really know how to get out of it. I mean, I *could* just let my bitch side take care of it, but he's being so nice. So polite. So smiley. I can't do that.

"Where is your phone?" Someone rudely interrupts Patrick's monologue.

"What?" I turn to him. His hair is wet and he's wearing his comfies. It causes my stomach to churn.

"I've sent you a million texts," Tyler continues.

"I think my phone is dead," I say, taking it out of my pocket. It isn't. I just didn't check it.

"Tyler, right?" Patrick says and only then Tyler turns to him. His eyes widen. "Patrick, remember?"

Tyler stares at him, mouth half-open. Patrick holds out a hand and then he stares at the hand, not taking it. *Oh, God.*

"What are you doing here?" he asks. I don't like his tone.

"Erm..." Patrick recoils his hand. "I was at the concert."

Tyler narrows his eyes. Then turns to me. I don't know what he's thinking but I know I don't like it.

"This is why you've been ignoring me?" he asks me. I don't even know how to answer.

"Are you two together?" Patrick asks suddenly.

"No," I say, at the same time Tyler says, "Yes."

This can't be good, right? No. No, it can't.

"Okaaaay..." Patrick says awkwardly. "I'm gonna... go grab a drink."

"No?" Tyler immediately turns to me, irritated.

"Yes?" I match his tone.

"I thought it was pretty obvious from the last few days that we *are* together," he argues, talking loudly. I notice people around us start to pay attention.

"Yeah, for now," I say. His eyebrows shoot up. "I mean, it's not like an official thing."

"What does that even mean?" he asks exasperated.

"I don't know!" I exclaim. A lot of people are looking at us now.

"You're unbelievable!" he says, running both hands through his damp hair. "I thought... I thought..."

"What?" I demand. He looks at me, frowning, angry, frustrated.

"Never mind," he ends up saying, turning away.

"No, don't do that," I ask, grabbing his wrist.

"What do you want?" he snaps. "Huh? What were you trying to prove by inviting him here?"

What is he talking about? Does he think I told Patrick about the concerts to get to him somehow? How would I even know he'd turn into such a jealous bitch? We weren't even *together* when it happened.

"It was before you and me..." I say and stop myself. "And it was barely an invitation, you were there, you saw it."

"Don't play dumb," he scoffs, which leaves me *livid*. "I mean *here* here, to the party."

"First of all, if you ever call me dumb again, I'll give you a black eye," I say between gritted teeth. "Second of all, I didn't invite him *here* here. I don't even know how he knew about the party."

"Uh..." Patrick chimes in, then. I didn't even notice he was back. "The other guy invited me."

"What other guy?" Tyler and I ask in unison.

"Um..." He looks around, until he finds him and points. "That one."

Todd.

"Todd?" Tyler snorts.

"I didn't know you knew each other," Todd defends himself. He, too, had been watching our row.

"Actually, you did," Patrick busts him, turning to us. "We chatted briefly and I told him I was here for Becky."

For a second, I think Tyler is going to fly at his brother the same way he did when he commented on us sleeping together. He doesn't, though. He laughs. It's a bitter, evil laugh. I don't like this one.

"I'm sorry, Patrick," Tyler turns to him then, a totally different look on his face. "I guess it was all a misunderstanding."

"Erm... no... no problem," Patrick stutters.

"What did you think of the concert?" Tyler continues, as people resume what they were doing before.

Patrick glances at me nervously, but answers the question. They keep chatting for a few minutes while I glance back and forth between them, having absolutely no idea of what's going on or what I should do.

"Well, Patrick, thank you for coming," Tyler ends the interaction. "Enjoy the rest of the party."

With that, he turns around and leaves the room. Patrick and I stand there, staring at the door, for several moments.

"I'm sorry," Patrick says.

"Don't be," I find myself replying. "You did nothing wrong."

"I *did* have ulterior motives to come here, though," he says. And that gorgeous smile is back on his face.

"I-I noticed," I stutter. "But it's not gonna happen."

"I noticed, too," he says, not even slightly disappointed. "It was nice getting to know you, anyway."

Know what? You didn't even let me talk.

"You, too," I say. Then we stand there, staring at each other.

"This is the part where you go after your boyfriend," he jokes.

"He's not my boyfriend," I blurt out.

"Good to know," he says. I feel myself blush.

"I will go after him, though," I say.

"Okay," he nods. "Guess I'll see you around."

I don't know how to respond to that, so I don't. I turn on my heels, leaving the room after Tyler. Before I knock on his door, though, I wonder if I'm doing the right thing. I really, really disliked his attitude. But I don't think that's enough reason to ditch him for the next pretty face I see, right? I mean... we kind of *are* together.

"May I help you?" he says when he opens the door and finds me there.

"Maybe," I say, faking a thoughtful expression. "There's this guy I've been hooking up with for the past few days. Really handsome, tall, dyed blond hair, have you seen him?"

"It's *natural*," he argues, an annoyed look on his face.

"Guess you haven't seen him, then," I sigh, turning around to leave. "Well, in case you do, tell him I'm looking for him."

I don't make two steps away before he grabs me by the waist. I squeal as he pulls me inside his room, kissing the back of my neck. When he closes the door, he pins me against it and stares into my eyes.

"Guy you've been hooking up with?" he raises his eyebrows.

"Do you know a shorter term for it?" I joke, but his face gets serious. His eyes fall to my mouth and he takes a few steps back.

"What did you mean with official?" he asks.

I sigh. I don't really know what I meant. I don't want to make him think I want more than what we have. Especially because we can't—he's leaving tomorrow and I'm staying. That's the end of it.

"When he asked if we're together, I assumed he was asking if we're in a serious relationship," I try to explain. He nods slowly, biting his lip. Then he walks to his bed and sits down, staring at the floor.

"Do you want to be with him?" he asks suddenly.

"What?" I gasp.

"I would understand," he continues, looking up to me. I'm shocked to see he actually means it. "I mean, I would *try* to."

"Why would I be *here* if I wanted to be with *him*?" I ask, walking towards him with wide eyes.

"That's my point," he says. "I don't want you to feel pressured to be here just because—"

I interrupt him with a kiss. He clearly wasn't expecting it, which makes my heart break a little.

"You have a better shot with him," he continues when we break apart. "I'll be gone in a few hours. He'll still be here. If you want—"

I kiss him again. This time he reciprocates a bit better. I make it last as I straddle him and guide his hands to my waist. He still has an uncertain look on his face when we break apart. It's quite cute, to be honest. Who would have thought Tyler Hackley could be so insecure?

"You know what I want?" I whisper. He shakes his head. "I want you. You idiot."

He finally smiles, blushing slightly.

"You know what I want?" he asks back.

"Yeah," I say. "I'm not as dumb as you are."

He tickles my ribs, making me giggle manically. Then he throws me on the bed. And we both get what we want.

***

The sun is in my eyes. They're still closed, but I can feel the brightness behind my eyelids. I was having a nice dream—that already evaporated from my mind—and the sun woke me up. I guess someone forgot to shut the blinds last night. We were distracted by something else.

I carefully stretch my arm in his general direction. My stomach drops and, for a split second, I think he's gone—he left in the middle of the night. He's bitter because of the nurse. But, then, the tip of my fingers brush against his soft, bare skin. He's here.

"Good morning," he says, his voice cracking at the edges.

I open my eyes to find his sleepy face staring at me. There's something about him and the morning light that makes me warm inside.

"Morning," I smile. "What are you doing up?"

"Just watching you," he smirks.

"Creep," I try to frown, but can't. He chuckles, running a single finger through my tight curls. I close my eyes again. "How much time do we have?"

"The rest of our lives," he says, making my eyes shoot open again. He doesn't wait for a reply and sighs, "A couple of hours."

I nod, taking him in. The way his naked chest rises and falls in the rhythm of his breathing. The way his arm muscles tense up as he reaches out to caress my scalp. The protuberant bones of his shoulders, his golden hair falling to one side, his ocean blue eyes glued on mine.

"We should make the most of it," I suggest.

"Aren't we already?" he raises his eyebrows, making me melt.

"Ty..." I whisper, trying it out. His eyes shrink with a smile. I think he likes it.

"Yeah?" he whispers back.

"Would you hold me?" I ask.

Without a word, he pulls me closer and I rest my head on his hairy chest. I listen to his heartbeat intently, running a lazy finger over his collarbone. He does the same down my spine. It's pure bliss.

"I'm gonna miss you, Ella," he says quietly, and it pains me to realize I'm gonna miss him, too.

"How many different nicknames can you come up with?" I ask. I don't think he repeated a single one.

"I'm just trying to give you options, so you can decide which one you like the most," he says.

"I already have a favorite," I say, grinning.

"Oh, yeah?" he asks. "Which one?"

I lift my head from him so I can look him in the eyes and then I say, "Becky."

He smiles, rolling his eyes.

"I knew you'd say that," he says. I don't believe him.

I lie back down and we stay silent for a while. I could easily go back to sleep.

"Will you go out with him?" Tyler breaks the silence.

"With who?" I frown.

"Patrick."

I don't answer. Mainly because I don't know how to answer. I don't want to say no and give him some kind of hope or make it sound like a promise. I also don't want to say yes because I don't want to hurt him. And probably because I *won't* go out with him, anyway.

"He seems like a nice guy," he continues before my silence.

"I guess," I shrug.

"So?" he asks.

"So what?"

"Will you go out with him?"

"Why are you insisting on this?" I ask, lifting my head once again.

"Morbid curiosity," he says.

"I don't know, Tyler," I sigh. "I don't know what my life will be like tomorrow, let alone if I'll eventually go out with a guy that lives six hours away from me."

"Would you tell me if you did?" he asks, making me widen my eyes.

"Will you tell me when you do?" I ask back. "When you hook up with fans or go on wild nights with crazy beautiful supermodels?"

"Oh, yes, I'll tell you all about them," he says, smirking.

I roll my eyes, lying back down. I can't take the image of what I just described out of my mind. Maybe that's how he's feeling, too. I just can't tell if it's a good or bad thing.

"Are you upset?" he asks softly, squeezing the back of my neck. "I don't want to upset you."

"I'm not upset," I say.

"But we will talk, right?" he asks and something in his voice makes me look at him again. "Maybe not about that stuff, but other things."

"Like what?" I ask, resting my chin on my hand.

"Like your grandma," he says, making me smile. "I would like to know how she's doing."

"Okay," I nod.

"And your career," he continues. "I want to know when you get your record deal, if the label is nice to you."

"Okay," I nod again, smiling wider.

"Pete," he says. "I want to know if... he's alright."

I don't nod at that. He notices and watches me closely. I wonder if he knows already. I wish Tristan would talk to him.

"I wanna ask for something," I say, making him frown. "Be nicer to Tris."

"What?" he gasps. "I am nice!"

"Be nicer," I insist. "I think you could be his Pete."

"What?" he chuckles.

"I'm just saying you could be friends," I try to explain, not sure where I'm going with this.

"We are!" he argues. "I think it goes without saying that he's my favorite brother."

"Maybe you should say it," I suggest. "He needs to hear it, every once in a while."

"Okay..." He narrows his eyes, considering it.

"It's nice to have someone on your side, no matter what," I say. Now, *this* is something I can vouch for.

He nods, studying my face. I have the feeling he'll ask questions about it, but he says nothing. He reaches up, touching my face, and I rest my cheek against his palm.

"Now it's my turn to ask for something," he says softly.

"Choose wisely," I warn. He holds my gaze for a moment.

"Don't forget me," he says rashly, catching me by surprise. "I know this sounds corny, and I'm not asking it in hopes that this can be anything more than it already was—"

"I won't," I interrupt him. His relief is so intense that it makes me chuckle. "You didn't really need to ask, though."

"I wanted to make sure," he smiles.

"Will you write songs about me?" I ask jokingly.

"You'll have to keep track of our records to know," he smirks, making me roll my eyes.

"I probably will. I like to torture myself," I say, and he tickles my ribs.

"Will you write songs about me?" he returns the question.

"You wish," I scoff and he laughs.

We stay like this, in silence, for what feels like an eternity. He holds my face, running his thumb over my mouth, while I trace his jawline with my fingers. It's almost like time stopped.

"I won't, either," he says quietly.

"Won't what?" I gaze into the calm waters of his eyes.

"I won't ever forget you, Becky."

***

We decide to have breakfast in bed so we can stretch the moment as much as possible. Then we have a shower—together, finally—and then we have to part ways to pack our bags. That's our couple of hours over. Actually, that's our twelve days over. How is it possible? Twelve days seemed like a lifetime before we started. And, now, it feels they were gone in the blink of an eye. Yet, so much has changed. A professional direction, some personal closure, and even the possible rediscovery of my heart. Indeed, a lifetime. In two weeks. How is it possible?

I decide to ask for a second breakfast before I go to my room, for Pete. I call reception from Tyler's phone and ask for a simple coffee, a chocolate croissant and some aspirins. If he drank everything he took to the room yesterday, he's gonna need it. I wait in the corridor until the order arrives, and then I enter the dark room.

I wait until my eyes adjust to the lack of light, then approach the bed. He's curled to one side, taking less than 10% of the space. I trip on something on the floor, almost spilling the coffee. I look down to find the bottles and cans from last night, unopened. So he didn't get drunk. Hmm.

I rest the mug on the nightstand and hide the croissant behind me as I jump on the mattress, bouncing slightly. It takes a few seconds, but he finally reacts—pulling the covers over his head and muttering unintelligible things.

"Good morning, sunshine!" I chant, trying to impersonate his morning mood. Well, his *usual* morning mood. "I brought you coffee and drugs."

"Coffee *is* drugs," he argues.

I pick up the mug from the table and wait for him to uncover his head with a manic smile on my face. When he does, he frowns. He sits up with difficulty and I hand him the coffee and the blister of aspirins.

"Chocolate is also drugs," he says. Then I take the plate I'd hidden and give it to him. He smiles.

"How was your night?" I ask, sitting beside him.

"Lonely," he says, taking a sip of coffee. "Despite your efforts."

"I have no idea what you're talking about," I say nonchalantly. He glares.

"How was *your* night?" he asks.

"Good," I answer, trying not to look as giddy as I'm feeling. Of course, I fail.

"Jesus," he narrows his eyes. "You're fucking glowing! I hate you and your skin and that subtle smile and those tired eyes of who spent the whole night gently doing it with a famous pop star."

"I should have never mentioned that to you," I frown in disgust.

"Too late now," he mumbles.

I watch as he cradles his mug and pretends he's eating but is just picking the croissant apart. So I grab his face, making him look at me. He's startled at first, but then he sighs, defeated.

"How was your night?" I ask again.

"Lonely," he repeats, in a different tone. "I'm sad, Becks. I'm so fucking sad. And guilty, even though I don't regret it. I can't regret it, you know? I do like him, I like him a lot, and I think I was able to help him in some way—and I'm fully aware of how self-indulgent this sounds. But at what cost? Not only losing Lindsey, but hurting her, repeatedly. Making her watch as I slowly burned our bridges down."

"You're not the only one to blame for it, you know that, right?" I say, still holding his long face. "The three of you had a part in this mess."

"I know," he sighs, closing his eyes. "I still wish I had handled it better."

"We all wish we had handled things better," I tell him, letting go of his face to hold his chocolate-smudged hand. "It's easy to look back and see where we went wrong, but no one has that clarity when the thing is still happening."

I know that now. I think I've known for a while. And it's knowing exactly where things could have gone differently that makes it all so hard, so painful. The hard thing is accepting there's nothing you can do now and move on.

"Where did this wisdom come from?" he asks suspiciously. It makes me laugh. How can he be so blind?

"You, silly," I say, bopping the tip of his nose. "You've been telling me different versions of it for years. I guess I was listening."

It's true. He was always the one to make me see the bright side, to make me try, to make me not so fucking depressed all the time. I guess it's my turn to try to do the same for him.

"I sound really smart," he says after a while, almost himself again. I roll my eyes but smile. He rests his head on my shoulder. "How do I stop being sad?"

Oh, Pete.

"You don't," I answer honestly. "You have to ride it."

"Are you sad?" he asks, looking up. "That he's leaving?"

I feel a tug in my stomach that indicates that yes, I am.

"A little, yeah," I admit.

"Will you see each other again?" he asks. The million-dollar question, I guess.

"Who knows?" I shrug. I'm trying not to get my hopes up.

"I don't like those odds," he says, clicking his tongue.

"Please, it's not like we'll be out of reach," I argue, remembering how Tyler said he'd like to stay in touch. "We have each other's number, we know where each other lives."

"He'll be stupid if he doesn't come running back to you the first chance he gets," he says, making me chuckle.

"I don't think he's stupid," I say. Then I feel myself blush. When did I become so ridiculous?

"My God," he sits up straight, staring at my face. "That's high praise coming from you."

I roll my eyes, punching his shoulder lightly. I want to ask him the same question—will he and Tris ever see each other again? Stay in touch? Will he and Lindsey do that? I don't have the courage, though. He's smiling and making fun of me and I don't want to make him think of those things right now. He doesn't need to have answers right now.

"Finish up your breakfast," I say, getting up from the bed. "We have a meeting soon."

His eyes widen. He's probably forgotten about it again. I didn't. That's a first.

"I need a shower," he says suddenly. Then his face darkens—the thing I wanted to avoid. "Have you seen Lindsey today?"

I sigh. I'm so sorry for him. I'm so sorry for *her*.

"No, I think she's still in her room," I say. "Do you want me to go over there? Get your stuff?"

"No, I'll go. I don't want to avoid her," he says.

"Okay," I say, kissing the top of his head. Just by this attitude, he shows that he's a better person than I am. I think he'll be fine.

***

I call grandma before heading out. She sounds a lot better, with more energy, less grumpy. She asks me about Pete, saying Jo is worried that he's been ignoring her calls. I don't know what to say to that. I try to lie, say there's nothing to worry about, that we've been busy and tired. Of course, she doesn't believe me. But also doesn't push me. I think she's not willing to strain our renewed, yet frail, bond. I end up promising her I'll bring him with me when I go to see her again, which actually sounds like a good idea. We should both go home for a few days. *Home* home. I'll talk to him about it.

When I'm ready, I head to the lobby where Pete is already waiting for me. As I walk towards the desk to leave my suitcase, I see Todd hanging around, worriedly glancing at his watch. He approaches me when he sees me.

"We leave—"

"—within the hour," I don't give him a chance to say it. He stares at me blankly. "I know."

"Then why didn't you come down earlier?" he complains.

"Todd," I sigh, turning to him, "fuck off."

He widens his eyes in shock. As if he didn't deserve it.

"I just left Tyler packing his things, by the way," I say as I walk towards Pete. "He'll be down in a second."

I don't look at him long enough to appreciate the rage on his red face. I still enjoy it, anyway.

"Ready?" I ask Pete, who's sitting alone, his leg bouncing up and down.

"As ready as I'll ever be," he says.

We text Neil, who tells us to wait for him in the conference room. We have to ask the hotel clerk where it is. It ends up being just a sort of office room near the back exit—a small, stuffy room, with a round table and four chairs around it.

"Fancy," Pete scoffs.

We wait three hundred hours for Neil to show up.

"Hey, guys!" He greets us excitedly when he enters. "We're still a bit early, but I'll see if they can move the meeting up."

We watch in silence as he sits in front of us and texts someone. Another one hundred and ninety-eight hours go by before he speaks again.

"Great!" He claps his hands, looking up. "Ready?"

We only nod and watch as he makes the call. I'm not sure how I'll be able to participate in a call meeting when I can't talk.

"Neil, good to hear your voice," the guy on the other side of the call says.

"You, too, Glen," Neil says, placing his phone in the middle of the table. "I'm here with Pete and Becky."

We say our hellos to this Glen guy. Then I realize I have no idea who he is.

"Okay, I'm here with Jeff and Chris," Glen says. I also don't know who they are, but Neil wiggles his eyebrows. "And let me start by saying what a fantastic run you two had!"

"Thank you, mister Reynolds," Pete says. Of course, he would know who the guy is.

"Please, call me Glen. This is an informal conversation," the man replies. We glance at each other. "We've been hearing a lot of good things about you two, you've created quite the buzz! That article on *Peroxide* caught a lot of people's attention, we think an offer might be popping up on your emails very soon."

Pete and I glance at each other again. Something sounds off. Then we look at Neil, who is now significantly less confident than when he entered.

"Erm..." Pete hesitates, looking at Neil for guidance, but he's staring at the phone with a deep frown. "Offer? For a record deal, you mean?"

"Oh, yes, yes!" Glen continues. "I'm certain you'll have plenty to choose from. Isn't that exciting?"

"Sure," Pete answer flatly.

"I just wanted to let you guys know that you'll have our full support. We're making ourselves available in case you need help with anything," he says.

Wait, so... no deal? Is that what he's saying?

Pete looks at me, deflated. I feel exactly the same way.

"Thank you, mister Reynolds," Pete says. "This means a lot."

"We here at Blast Records are very excited to see you guys blossom and take the industry by storm."

There's a long pause after that, in which neither of us knows what to say. Luckily, Neil takes the lead.

"Glen," he clears his throat, pulling the phone a little closer to him. "Let me see if I'm understanding this correctly—you're *not* offering them a deal?"

"Oh, Neil!" Glen gasps, as if that was such an outrageous notion. "No, we're not. Not at this time, anyway."

"When, then?" Neil asks, getting irritated.

"Neil—"

"I'm sorry, Glen, but I think there must have been some kind of miscommunication between us," Neil cuts him off, now fully grabbing the phone. "I was under the impression—and, see, I may have passed the same impression onto Pete and Becky—that Blast was interested in adding them to their roster."

"I'm really sorry to hear that, Neil," Glen says, in such a condescending tone that even if they do offer us a deal now, I'm inclined to refuse. "Unfortunately, I'm not in a position to do that right now."

"You're the fucking CEO!" Neil snaps.

I can feel Pete's hand find mine under the table, but I can't take my eyes off Neil—I think this is the first time I hear him curse.

"As I said," Glen speaks up, after a moment, "at this time, there's no deal on the table. But I would like to reinforce our interest in being useful, in however way we can, to Pete and Becky in the future."

"Thank you, mister Reynolds," Pete kind of shouts, making Neil jump. He puts the phone back on the table. "We really appreciate it."

He squeezes my hand, maybe wanting me to say something, since I've been mute the whole time. I refuse, though. I don't appreciate anything.

"I'm really looking forward to building a strong relationship with you two," Glen says, his fake cheery tone back. "Thank you for your time and I hope to talk to you soon."

"Thank you," Pete says.

"Okay, Glen, we should go," Neil says, grabbing the phone again. "We have a plane to catch."

"Yes, call me as soon as you land in Paris, will you?" Glen asks, the playfulness completely gone.

"Sure thing, boss," Neil says. And then hangs up.

Pete's grip tightens around my hand as we observe Neil, who's still observing the phone. This is clearly not the meeting he was expecting to have and, somehow, it soothes a bit of my frustration.

The silence drags on. Pete opens his mouth to say something, but I squeeze his hand, shaking my head. We wait, until Neil takes a deep breath and shouts.

"Those fucking bastards!"

We both jump in our seats. I have to bite my lip not to laugh.

"I'm so sorry, guys," he looks at us, true regret in his eyes. "I had no idea this would be the outcome of this meeting. I should have never hinted at anything."

"It's clearly not your fault," I say.

"It was because of... me, right?" Pete blurts out. Both Neil and I look at him wide-eyed. "Because of what happened with Paul?"

"No, Pete, it wasn't," Neil argues. "It definitely wasn't."

"How can you be so sure?"

"Because I haven't told them!" he kind of shouts again. He's so worked up. It's funny because he's always so calm and laid back. "I didn't tell anyone, except Mike. You know, The Hacks manager."

"Maybe he—"

"No, Pete, he didn't," Neil cuts him off. "This is just them being the assholes they usually are."

"Well..." I sigh. "What now?"

I ask it to Pete, but it's Neil who answers.

"One thing he was right about is that a lot of people are interested," he says. Which kind of gives me a little hope again. "I know for a fact there were industry people at some of the concerts. They're holding back because everyone was *sure* Blast would make an offer first, and you guys would accept it, seeing as we've been working together throughout the tour."

"I'm not accepting anything from any of them," I say bitterly. It actually makes Neil smile.

"That would be my advice," he says. "Even if Blast does come up with an offer in the next days or weeks—don't take it. You can definitely do better."

"How will we know which one to take, though?" Pete asks. "How will we know we're not getting someone like Glen? That is, if we even get an offer at all."

"You will, I promise," Neil continues. "I can help, if you want. I can look through it, talk to people. Not everyone in this business is a dickhead like Glen."

"Okay," I nod. An idea starts to form in my head. "Should we just wait, then?"

"Yes," he says. "I mean, you're just coming off a tour, and an exhausting one at that. I suggest you take a few days or even weeks off. But also..." he stops himself, kind of unsure whether to continue.

"Also?" I encourage him.

"I'd suggest you compile a few demos together," he says, and then the rhythm of his speech picks up. "Make sure you include a good version of *She's Not Mine*, that's the one everyone will want to hear. But if you could write a couple of new songs over the next weeks, that would be great. It will sit really well with any label if they get the impression that you're not willing to wait around for a deal. When they see you're already working towards the next project, they'll get anxious to snatch you."

I nod, looking at Pete. He nods, too. I have the impression he's thinking the same thing I am.

"I could get the word out that Blast is out of the battle," Neil continues, "but I think that would speed up the process, and I really think you guys should rest for a bit."

We look back at him.

"And you have to take care of that restraining order," he points a finger at Pete. "Don't forget, please. It's important."

"Okay," Pete nods.

We glance at each other for a few more moments.

"I'm really sorry, guys," Neil repeats.

"Please," I say, waving a hand in the air. "This was actually a really helpful meeting."

"Indeed. You could actually be our manager, mate," Pete says, confirming my suspicion that we were thinking the same thing.

Neil laughs, but we don't. When he notices Pete is not joking, he stops. His eyes widen in surprise.

"You should be our manager," I say bluntly. He scoffs, shaking his head, but saying nothing.

"Yeah, mate," Pete speaks again, "we'll be rich! We can pay you a lot more than this pop label of yours."

"I'll really miss working with you guys," he sighs, giving us a warm smile.

"You won't need to if you are our manager," I insist.

He glances from me to Pete several times, scratching his beard. He's going to accept it, I know he will.

"I'd love to give Glen the middle finger, if I'm being honest," he admits. "But I can't abandon The Hacks in the middle of the tour."

"You don't need to," I argue. "Finish the tour. We'll be waiting."

"Yeah," Pete nods slowly. "It's not like we're in a hurry or anything."

Neil nods, staring at us. He's accepting it. We have a manager.

"How about this," he says, leaning over the table, "Go home, get that restraining order, write and record two new demos, don't schedule any gigs or reply to any emails. And we'll talk in two weeks."

"Is this a yes?" I grin.

"No," he says, but smiles, too. It *is* a yes. "It is a 'we'll talk in two weeks'."

"Deal," Pete says. He's grinning, too. "We'll talk in two weeks."

***

When we get back to the lobby, everyone is already waiting. My eyes immediately lock on Tyler. As if he knows I'm looking, he turns to me. His permanent frown immediately dissolves into a smile. Which makes me smile. Default.

I make a beeline to him and when he hugs my waist, leaning down to kiss me, I let him.

"Ew," I hear Tristan complaining. So I make the whole thing a little hotter.

"Okay," Tyler breaks the kiss, pulling me away a little bit and mouthing *calm down*. I giggle. I don't even care.

I throw my arms down, hugging his waist and resting my head on his chest. When I turn around, I see Tristan with his phone on his hands, pointing towards us.

"What are you doing?" I frown.

"Just a little souvenir," he says.

"Perv," I scoff, making him laugh.

Our brief moment is interrupted by Neil and instructions to get to the airport. Apparently, there are fans outside—a lot of them. Upon hearing this news, I automatically let go of Tyler and glance around the lobby. What if one of them is here?

We change exit routes four times before Neil is convinced it's safe, and then he separates us into the two usual groups. He sends The Hacks off first, in hopes they'll drive the crowd out with them, but it turns out to be a bad idea. A lot of the people waiting outside decide to follow their van, which only slows things down for us.

We sit around, waiting in silence. I watch Pete and Lindsey ignoring each other as they go through their phones. I suddenly have the urge to talk to her—we haven't properly talked in days. I've been so busy, so *distracted*, that I completely neglected her presence, when she probably needed it the most. *Ugh*. If there was an award for terrible friends, I'd have no competition.

Before I have the time to come up with something, though, Neil beckons for us to leave. I'm surprised to see there are still people waiting outside for us.

"Sorry guys, we can't stop," Pete waves at them as we head to the van.

"Can we just take a group photo?" one of the girls shouts eagerly. "Just look our way, we're already organized!"

We both stop and look at them—turned around, crowding together, kneeling on the ground, just waiting for a quick pic. We exchange a knowing glance and run up to the small group.

"Guys!" Neil calls after us, but we don't stop.

"Quick!" I say as we huddle together and half a dozen cell phones take pics.

"Thank you!"

"You're the best!"

"Marry me, Pete!"

They yell as we run back to the van.

"Sorry," I say when we head off, "but we're already late, anyway."

"This is my fault, guys," Neil sighs. "We spent three days in the same place, of course fans would show up."

"It's okay," Pete replies, "we have the best fans."

"You really do," Lindsey chimes in. "They're so polite, I can't get over it. Especially after seeing The Hacks' ones."

"I just hope you'll do a better job in the future, Neil" I joke, but he looks at me in panic. "I'm joking!"

We take our seats—me and Lindsey in the back, Pete and Neil in the front.

Lindsey puts on her headphones and stares out of the window. I don't have much time to show her my support and actually tell her I want to stay friends, and it's not like I can say it out loud now, anyway. So I text her.

'*Are you okay?*'

It takes her a few minutes to notice her phone buzzing. When she sees the text, she turns to me with a frown. I smile.

'I'm hanging. You?' she replies.

'I'm fine,' I say.

She replies with a smiley emoji, flashing a real smile my way, too. And then looks out of the window.

It's not good enough. Christ, why am I so bad at this? But if I have any chance to tell her what I want to tell her, it's gonna be through text—with time to think about it and delete and rewrite the same thing a dozen times. So, it's what I do. I spend long minutes compiling a long, long text. If Pete saw it, he'd be *dead* jealous—I usually just reply to him with emojis.

'I'm really sorry about what happened. I'm sorry I've been kind of distant these past few days, but I don't want you to think it's because I'm picking sides. I'm not. I've been meaning to tell you that I'm here if you want to talk about it. About anything, really. I know I have this thing with Pete, but I'm your friend, too. And I'd like to keep being your friend, if you think it's possible. You're an amazing person and you deserve to be happy.'

I watch her in silence as she reads it. She takes longer than necessary, which means she's reading it more than once. I can't tell what she's making of it because she's frowning. *Oh, God.* Maybe this wasn't the best moment to talk about it.

After a while, she locks her screen and looks up—at Pete. She's still frowning. Then, she takes her headphones off and hugs me. It takes me by surprise, but I hug her back. I hope this is a good sign.

"I would *love* to keep being your friend, Becky," she whispers into my ear.

"Okay," I say, because I don't know what else to say.

"And the same goes to you," she says when she lets me go, staring into my eyes. "I'm here if you want to talk about anything."

"Thank you," I say.

After that, she puts her headphones back on, but keeps holding my hand. It makes me all warm inside. I like it.

***

We make it to departure and locate the rest of our group scattered around. As it's become usual, my eyes immediately find Tyler—sitting alone, headphones on, squinting at his phone. I wonder if he needs glasses. Then I picture him wearing glasses. *Oh, boy.*

"Do you mind if I talk to him first?" Lindsey's voice pulls me out of my fantasy.

I look at her, who's looking at Pete. He nods. Then we both watch her walk towards Tristan—who's also sitting alone, on the floor—and sit down beside him.

"What is she doing?" I ask. Pete jumps, apparently not seeing I was still here.

"I have no idea," he says faintly.

We keep watching. They're talking and smiling a little. Are they making up? Are any of them apologizing? Then, they hug. It takes me by surprise.

She stands up and instead of walking back to us, she joins Neil and Seth in a corner. When I look back at Tristan, he's looking at us.

"He's all yours," I joke. Pete doesn't smile.

"I have to talk to someone else first," he says. I watch as he walks towards Tyler and sits beside him.

I frown, not really liking this turn of events. Then, I glance at Tristan, who's back to his phone. I walk over and join him.

"Lunch in Paris, eh?" I elbow his ribs and he glances up from his phone for just a second before burying his face back on it. So I continue, "I've never been to Paris."

"It's not that special," he says in a boring tone.

"What's your favorite place you've ever been to?" I ask.

"Probably Japan, it's the most different," he continues without looking at me.

"And your least favorite? Please, don't say here," I joke, making him finally smile.

"I don't think I have one," he says to his phone. "I like traveling to different places."

"And meeting different people?" I ask.

"Sometimes," he shrugs.

"Did you like meeting me?" I blurt out. He immediately stops scrolling and turns to me.

"Of *course*," he says, frowning. "You're currently my favorite person ever."

"*That*," I say, pointing to his face, "is a lie."

He blushes slightly, looking away. Not to his phone, but not to anyone in particular.

"Do you regret it?" I ask. He takes a long time to answer, which makes me think he doesn't know what I'm referring to. He does, though.

"I don't know," he says sadly. "I'll tell you in a few days."

We stare at each other in silence and, for the first time, I'm overwhelmed by the feeling of not wanting to say goodbye. I don't want him out of my life. I don't want him to feel alone.

"I don't have your phone number," I say suddenly.

He reaches out his hand and I give him my phone. He punches his number in and then texts himself.

"Now you have, and I have yours."

I open the messaging app to see what he wrote. *You're my favorite brother.* And he saved his name as 'Best Hackley'. I chuckle.

"True," I confess, making him laugh. "You can call me, you know?" I continue, desperately wanting to let him know he can. "Or text me. Anytime. For any reason. I'll always pick up."

He nods, smiling sadly again. He looks down, biting his lip, and when he speaks again, his voice is just a whisper.

"Do you think we can be friends?"

I glance at Pete, who is still talking to Tyler. My heart breaks a little.

"Well, I'm sure you can call and text him, too," I say.

He looks up, frowning. Then he does the same thing I did and glances at Pete. When he looks back at me, he's wearing his trademark smile.

"I was talking about *you* and me, Becks," he says.

"Oh!" My eyes widen and my skin heats up. Two friends on the same day? "I thought we already were."

His smile broadens, as if it's even possible, and then he hugs me. I let him, even though I feel awkward and embarrassed.

"What's up?" Tyler interrupts us, sitting beside me. And startling me. "Ah, I see you're back to your jumpy state."

I don't even have time to answer, as he kisses my lips and sneaks a hand around my waist. I look around and notice some people watching. People that look like fans. I get restless.

"What?" he asks when I try to break away from his embrace. "Are you embarrassed to be seen with me?"

I look at him and smirk, because I want to say I am. Then he narrows his eyes and pulls me closer. He buries his face in my neck and snaps a picture with his phone.

"You're not posting that online, are you?" I ask a little too panicked.

"No," he smiles. And then looks at the pic.

We look... adorable. I mean, we look like we've come from different planets—his cut-clean, pretty features are such a contrast against my heavy make-up and poorly dyed hair. Still...

"Hey, look at this place I've found." He closes our photo before I can ask him to send it to me and opens a webpage. Then he shows it to Tristan. "It's near the venue we're playing tomorrow, we could go before soundcheck."

Tristan stares at him suspiciously for a few seconds before taking his phone and scrolling down the page.

"I don't know. I'm not really in the mood to go sightseeing," he sighs, handing back Tyler's phone.

"That's the best mood to go sightseeing," Tyler replies, earning yet another suspicious look.

Tristan mumbles a 'maybe' and then gets up and away from us.

"You get an 'E' for effort," I smile. He rolls his eyes. The he leans over and kisses me—a proper one, with tongue and everything. I look around when we break apart. I'm *certain* some of these people are fans.

"You know what I was thinking?" Tyler asks, making me look at him again. "We could be the opening act of your American tour."

"If we ever get one," I snort.

"When," he corrects me. He smiles. *My* smile. "I'd also love to give you a tour of Clivesdale like you gave me one of Alnwick. Although we have no castles."

"Bummer," I pout.

"We're going to see each other again," he says, staring at our hands together. It sounds like a promise. I want to ask him to not do that, but I can't. So, I kiss him. While I still can.

He's right, anyway. Eventually, he'll come back to England. Eventually, I'll go to America. Eventually... we'll meet again.

***

My flight is called in the sound system. I see Pete and Lindsey getting up and starting to say goodbye, so I do the same. I wave from a distance to Todd and Jake. I don't get away with it, though, as Jake makes his way to me and hugs me. I let him. He's a cool guy.

Next, I hug Tristan. I realize that in addition to the killer smile, he has a killer hug. He whispers a 'see you soon' in my ear, that I don't dare answer.

I then walk to Seth and Neil and hug them, too.

"Don't forget your homework," Neil says when he lets me go.

"See you in two weeks," I say back. He winks. He's my manager.

I turn around to find Tyler waiting for his turn. I walk into his arms, letting him hug me and hugging him back. Just then I realize we haven't shared that many hugs. What a shame. He also has a killer one.

We don't say anything to each other. We don't even kiss. We just hug, smile, and I walk away. And that's it. It's over. I'm going home.

Pete and Lindsey are already waiting when I turn around. Pete holds my hand as we walk.

"I want to go home," he says, for only me to hear. I look at him. "*Home* home."

"Okay," I squeeze his hand. "Me, too. We can write those new tunes in my living room piano."

He smiles, bright and wide. A Pete smile. "That sounds good."

We take our seats on the plane—Pete and me together. I reach out to squeeze Lindsey's shoulder in the front. She pats my hand. When I sit back, Pete is looking at me. I shrug. He throws his arm over my shoulder.

"You know, we really need a name now," he says.

"Oh, God," I complain, already anticipating the never-ending discussions we'll have about this in the next few weeks.

"I already have a few ideas," he grins.

"Of course you do," I roll my eyes.

"Don't be like that," he argues. "I'm not the one who comes up with crap suggestions."

"Hey!" I punch his shoulder. "My suggestions aren't crap!"

We banter back and forth for a while until the air hostess asks for everyone to put their mobiles in flight mode. I take out my phone and, instead of doing that, I text Tyler.

'When?'

I regret it as soon as I hit send. But I can't stop staring at the screen.

The tick turns blue and he starts to type. My heart races.

'We'll have a tour break in two weeks' time. Sounds good?'

I read it over a few times before I reply.

'Yep.'

He starts to type. Then pauses. Then types again. He can't decide what to say, and I get anxious.

'I can't believe you already miss me' it reads. There's also a smirk emoji, for good measure.

Idiot. I smile and reply with the emoji rolling its eyes. But, then, I answer.

'I do.'

Cheesy queen. But what is the point in hiding it? Something has happened over the last two weeks. Something that I can't yet explain, something really scary. Something that makes me miss him only five minutes after saying goodbye.

Right when I hit the flight mode button on my phone, it buzzes.

'I already miss you, too.'

READ, LOVE, SHARE, REPEAT

Enjoyed this book? You can make a big difference!

If you've enjoyed this book, I would be very grateful if you could spend five minutes leaving a review on the book's Amazon and/or Goodreads page. Honest reviews help bring the books to the attention of the readers, which is a powerful tool to an independent author, like me.

You can also join the conversation online! Post about the book on your social media! Tag me or use the hashtag #OiaL so I can get in touch. You can also follow me on Twitter and Instagram (both @lua__ferraz).

This book has a playlist! Search for the book's title on Spotify to find it and listen to the songs that inspired this story.

Now, if you'd like some exclusive content about this story and sneak peeks into the next ones, subscribe to my newsletter!

Just visit my website at www.luanaferraz.com.

I'm looking forward to hearing from you!

ACKNOWLEDGEMENTS

Once upon a time, a younger version of me stumbled across what they called "fanfiction". As someone who had always loved to write, but who also had always had a hard time creating believable characters, fanfiction was the answer to all of my writing hurdles. *Once in a Lifetime* started like that, sometime in the early 2000s. So, thank you to all those fanfic writers who opened the doors to a whole new world and somehow helped this story come to life almost two decades later.

I owe perhaps the biggest thank you to the friends I've made through the band that inspired the original idea for this story—we loved them, we cancelled them, and we remain together. Thanks to everyone at FDM Publishing Inc. for encouraging me, pushing me, reading all my raw first drafts, and pointing out where I can do better. They're the reason there's a whole other book from Pete's POV. It was their compensation for putting up with first-draft Tyler.

A very special thanks to my beautiful writer/editor friend Marina, who was my soundboard throughout this whole process. Thanks for the writing sessions, the late-night discussions, the guidance when I was lost, the last-minute read-through, and for showing me the trick to conquering writer's block. I'm honored to share one brain cell with you.

Thank you to the lovely Beatriz, president of Pete's fan club and curator of this book's playlist. Her pop-punk love was what inspired the unnamed duo (and Becky's purple hair). Thank you for your endless enthusiasm and for always having my back. I'm not sure I would have come this far if it wasn't for your faith in me.

A heartfelt thanks to my beta-reading team, who provided me with amazing feedback in record time! I'll never be able to express how grateful I am for your support. Working with you all was a dream, and I hope this is only the beginning of our partnership.

And lastly, as always, thank YOU! A writer is nothing without a reader, so thank you for allowing me to tell you my stories. Until the next time—be safe!

ABOUT THE AUTHOR

Luana Ferraz is a Brazilian writer and translator. She currently lives in São Paulo, but her mind wanders everywhere.

She's graduated in translation and interpretation and has been working in this area for years. She loves translation, as for her it's nothing more than reinterpreting stories, but her greatest passion is telling stories of her own.

Luana has been writing and creating stories for as long as she can remember. Her first creative work was a series of comics on a thief that wore a beanie and always ended up in jail. She was seven years old.

As a teenager, she started writing poems and even music–the quality of which was very questionable. She discovered fanfiction and ventured into that for a while, until she found out how to create her own characters.

She's usually found wearing headphones and typing–on her computer, phone or just writing down an idea on the Disney-themed notepad she keeps in her purse.

She's probably writing right now.

MORE FROM THIS AUTHOR

Welcome to New York
Once in a Lifetime (Pete)

CONTENT WARNINGS

This story deals with some issues that might be harmful to some readers. Those include:
- Mention and/or discussion of domestic violence—that took place before the events of this book;
- Mention and/or discussion of alcohol and substance abuse—that took place before the events of this book;
- Mention, discussion and/or depiction of violence—both that took place before the events of this book and during the story;
  - Trauma from those instances is discussed at several different points throughout the narrative. Also, there might be some flashbacks that depict some of those moments.
- Mention, discussion and/or depiction of alcohol consumption—during the story;
- Bad language—light swearing.

Printed in Great Britain
by Amazon